Praise for Previous Books in the Series:

'*Close to Midnight* illustrates what great shape the genre of horror is in… If you're a reader who enjoys quality fiction of the dark kind, this is a series to be cherished. There isn't a bad story in the entire book.'
Stephen Bacon

'*Close to Midnight* is a very solid collection of horror featuring stories of varied themes and content, and yet they all feel very comfortable inside the spine of one book. Worth a look if you like chills down your spine late at night as you lie in bed reading.'
Horror DNA

'Morris has assembled an especially strong group of stories with dazzling, diverse approaches to horror. Highly recommended.'
Cemetery Dance on *Close to Midnight*

'If you love short and sometimes shocking horror stories, you can't go wrong with this collection!'
On The Shelf Reviews on *Close to Midnight*

'A fine anthology of creepy tales perfect for you to get comfortable with until you realise that your house is now very quiet, you appear to be all alone and yet you feel watched. Definitely recommended!'
Runalong The Shelves on *Close to Midnight*

'I'm impressed with the imagination and variety coming from the writers. *Beyond the Veil* is another happy clump of ickiness...and I mean that in a good way.'
The Happy Horror Writer

'There is no end to the talent Mark Morris has brought together here. Fans of the genre will be pleased to see new work from such favorites as Nathan Ballingrud and Gemma Files, among others. So if you're ready for a long fall night, pick up a copy of this massive anthology and fall into the mysterious worlds *Beyond the Veil*.'
Phantastiqa

'Beautifully written pieces that lean into the intuitive and fantastic.'
Publishers Weekly on *After Sundown*

'This rich and masterful collection of horror highlights both up-and-coming and established authors in an interesting twist on the standard anthology [...] Highly recommended for longstanding horror fans and those readers who may not think horror is for them. There is something for everyone in this one.'
Booklist on *After Sundown*

'This is a short story collection that does exactly what it sets out to, delight and scare. With stories from well-known authors in the genre as well as a few from emerging voices, *After Sundown* has something for everyone. Highly recommended.'
The British Fantasy Society on *After Sundown*

'An entertaining, slickly written, mainstream, fun, something-for-every-horror-fan anthology.'
HorrorTree on *After Sundown*

A FLAME TREE BOOK OF HORROR

DARKNESS BECKONS

An Anthology of New Short Stories

Edited by Mark Morris

This is a **FLAME TREE PRESS** book

FLAME TREE PRESS
6 Melbray Mews, London, SW6 3NS, UK
flametreepress.com

US sales, distribution and warehouse:
Simon & Schuster
simonandschuster.biz

UK distribution and warehouse:
Hachette UK Distribution
hukdcustomerservice@hachette.co.uk

Thanks to the Flame Tree Press team.

The cover is created by Flame Tree Studio
with thanks to Shutterstock.com/Arman Ogandzhanyan.
The font families used are Avenir and Bembo.

Flame Tree Press is an imprint of Flame Tree Publishing Ltd
flametreepublishing.com

A copy of the CIP data for this book is available from the British Library and the Library of Congress.

1 3 5 7 9 8 6 4 2

HB ISBN: 978-1-78758-730-4
US PB ISBN: 978-1-78758-728-1
UK PB ISBN: 978-1-78758-729-8
ebook ISBN:978-1-78758-732-8

Printed and bound in Great Britain by Clays Ltd, Elcograf S.p.A.

A FLAME TREE BOOK OF HORROR

DARKNESS BECKONS

An Anthology of New Short Stories

Edited by Mark Morris

FLAME TREE PRESS
London & New York

CONTENTS

INTRODUCTION

Mark Morris

As a reader of horror growing up in the 1970s, and as a young writer starting out in the genre back in the late '80s and early '90s, I have to admit that it never occurred to me at the time that the vast majority of books published and promoted for the mass market were being written or edited by white, male, middle-class writers, based in either the US or the UK.

But pick up any major horror anthology from that era – aside, of course, from those specifically themed to be more inclusive, such as Kathryn Ptacek's *Women of Darkness* series, or Lisa Tuttle's *Skin of the Soul*, both of which I highly recommend – and you'll find that around 90 per cent of the contributors fall into most, if not all, of those categories listed above.

The narrowness of this particular demographic does not detract from the innovative and inspirational work being produced back then, of course. The half-century between 1960 and 2010 saw the emergence of many great writers – Stephen King, Ramsey Campbell, Dennis Etchison, Karl Edward Wagner, Peter Straub, Clive Barker, Michael McDowell, Stephen Gallagher, Stephen Laws, James Herbert and more – and the appearance of a whole slew of seminal anthologies, among them Kirby McCauley's *Dark Forces*, Ramsey Campbell's two-volume *New Terrors*, Dennis Etchison's *Cutting Edge*, and Charles L. Grant's *Shadows* series.

Despite the high quality of much of the fiction available, however, it cannot be denied that not all horror readers and fans felt well-represented by what they were reading. It is often said that horror is a genre that appeals to 'outsiders', but whereas many horror writers of the latter part of the twentieth century will readily admit to writing fiction about, and for, the kind of kid they were at school – most commonly the 'geeky, sports-hating bookworm' – not many novels or stories from that era feature protagonists who identify as members of the LGBTQ+ community, or who hail from a different ethnic background to the one in which the story is set. Indeed, despite the sterling work of authors such as Anne Rice, Suzy McKee Charnas, Melanie Tem, Tanith Lee, and the aforementioned Lisa Tuttle and Kathryn Ptacek, even female horror readers of the time would have found books written by and about women a little thin on the ground.

I'm happy to say, however, that in recent years the number of voices rising to prominence in the field has shown a far greater diversity, and the genre is all the richer for it. There are more women writing in the field than ever before, there are more LGBTQ+ themed horror stories being told, and with the work of authors such as Silvia Moreno-Garcia, Usman Malik, Mariana Enríquez, Junji Ito, Ryū Murakami, Attila Veres, Anders Fager and Luigi Musolino being brought to the attention of English-speaking readers, the genre is enjoying a breath-taking, eye-opening, mind-expanding explosion of culturally diverse work that can only feed and enhance the imaginations of generations of readers and writers to come.

My particular reason for drawing attention to this new and refreshing diversity in horror – aside from the fact that it's both important and topical – is that, for the first time ever, I have more female than male contributors in one of my anthologies. As an editor, my story choices have always been based purely on the quality of the work submitted to me; anything less, and I feel I'm doing both the contributors and the readers a disservice. And although establishing gender parity within genre anthologies is clearly an important consideration nowadays, there's no getting away from the fact that, until recently, that has been something of a struggle, simply because around 75-80 per cent of non-commissioned stories submitted have come from the pens, or rather keyboards, of male writers.

I'm happy to say that there are so many excellent female writers making a real impact in the previously male-dominated horror genre now, though, that the commissioning process is no longer a struggle to achieve gender parity, but more a case of jotting down potential contributors for future volumes because the current volume is full. As for my non-commissioned stories, I choose them blind – which means I'm sent them without by-lines, so know nothing about their authors. In the past, this has resulted in a roughly 3:1 bias in favour of male authors, again reflecting the fact that an overwhelming percentage of stories were submitted by men. For this particular volume, however, it turned out that all four of the stories I selected as a result of the open subs process had been written by women, which I found a heartening, and extremely welcome, outcome.

Like many readers, I'm discovering newer, and more diverse, writers all the time, and my hope is that my discoveries will be further reflected in future volumes of this series. For now, I'm thrilled that this latest annual anthology of horror stories for Flame Tree Press – my fourth for them as editor – is the most far-reaching yet in terms of approaches, styles and story content. In *Darkness Beckons* you'll find stories of human evil, of folk magic, of shifting realities, of phantasmagorical horror, of ghostly wistfulness, and of dying worlds. You'll meet a multitude of characters *in extremis*, some of whom are seeking love, others peace, others redemption, others a way out, and yet others simply an opportunity to belong.

Diversity is the watchword in horror, and more so now than ever before.

Vive la difference!

Mark Morris

SAINT BARBARA

Nina Allan

Deb first encountered Barbara at the launch event for a collection of stories by a writer Deb admired, a native of Lviv and part of the loosely affiliated collective that had come to be known as Eastern Gothic. The audience were mainly turtleneck types: writers, film-makers and installation artists in the thirty-to-forty age range and mostly, Deb suspected, known to one another, though she was prepared to concede this was probably just her being paranoid.

She noticed Barbara immediately because of how out of place she seemed. She looked older than those around her, middle aged in the way of women from Deb's mother's generation or even her grandmother's. Her shoulder-length hair was grey and frizzy, the epitome of dowdy. She was wearing a suit in pink tweed – baby pink, or powder pink, an insipid shade made dull by the black thread of the dogtooth pattern woven through it, the kind of garment you might find at a jumble sale, or stuffed to the back of a wardrobe, reeking of mothballs.

A teacher from Surrey or Surbiton, sometime last century. The suit cost a lot of money and so she keeps on wearing it. Twenty years ago it might have looked smart. Thirty years ago, anyway. Who wears stuff like that now? Deb felt perturbed by the woman's presence, by the feeling she had that the two of them were alike: eternal, hopeless exiles from the tribe of turtleneck.

She pushed the thought away. She was here to see Pohorska, whose works she had read in their entirety, those in English translation anyway, which was probably more than you could say for most of the turtlenecks. Pohorska, in a charcoal-coloured skirt and baggy sweater, read a passage from her story 'The Wood Demon' and then went on to answer questions in her sweet-toned, hesitant voice, as if she were questioning the veracity of every word she uttered.

Most of the audience's questions circled around Pohorska's experience of living through a siege, facts that were already known from the multitude of profiles and interviews in the literary press. Deb wished someone would ask her about the stories instead, the uncut gems that made up *The Snow Maiden*, that sang and yelled their nightmares with hallucinatory brightness.

She held back from asking anything herself, afraid that she was prompted more by the desire to have her voice heard than to learn the answer. As the interview came to an end she hovered next to the wine table, tormented by her irrelevance yet unable to rid herself of the conviction that she needed to be here. She had forgotten all about the woman with the frizzy grey hair, the frumpy teacher in the pink suit. Catching sight of her again in the aftermath of the event was a shock, an affront almost, like coming suddenly face to face with someone she had made a deliberate decision to avoid.

Deb watched her approach with a feeling of dread. Cultural flotsam without social capital, the two people in the room none of the others wanted to talk to. Their drifting together seemed inevitable. The woman smiled. Deb clutched her beaker of chardonnay, appalled.

"Aren't you going to get your book signed?" the woman said. Her voice was low and strong, with a gravelly undertone so at odds with the weak soprano Deb had imagined for her that she found herself glancing over the woman's shoulder as if she suspected she had been the target of some sort of scam.

Embarrassed, she looked down at her feet, planted either side of her backpack. On top of the backpack lay her copy of *The Snow Maiden*.

"There's a queue," Deb said, which there had been, although it had mostly dispersed by this time, leaving Pohorska surrounded by turtlenecks, laughing together as turtlenecks do, each trying to achieve the perfect, performative blend of knowingness and humour.

"Don't worry about them. This is what you came for." The woman grabbed her copy of *The Snow Maiden* and barrelled towards the turtlenecks, as if their presence in her space was entirely incidental. Deb followed, as if compelled, and she found herself thinking of a toy she had owned, a plush little pony on castors she used to pull along behind her by its leather bridle.

She had been fond of that pony.

The woman in the pink suit was standing in front of Pohorska; the expression on the face of the whip-thin, copper-haired turtleneck who had been there previously flipping from surprised to contemptuous to outraged in under three seconds. Her thunder stolen, and by a nobody. What the actual fuck?

"My friend," said the woman in the pink suit, "has read everything you've written." She presented Pohorska with her own book as if it were a prize she had won, a gift she should be honoured to accept.

"Whose name should I write?" said Pohorska. She stared at the woman and then at Deb. She looked tired, Deb realised. Probably she was aching to be away from here, back in her hotel room or wherever. Not having to talk.

"Deborah," Deb said, "with an 'h'."

Pohorska made swift movements with her pen.

"I loved 'A Rose in Winter'," Deb said. She wanted to tell her how the story had kept her awake into the small hours, that it had reminded her how endless and how terrifying a single night could be, even when on the other side of the wall your neighbours were soundly sleeping in warm beds. The moment passed.

"Thank you," said Pohorska quietly. She handed Deb the book, closing the cover. The newspaper critic who had conducted the interview stepped in front of her, angling his body deliberately to block her from view.

He reminded Deb of Clive. Clive was ancient history but his presence lingered, a fact Deb found both curious and annoying.

"Do you have time for a drink?" said the woman in the pink suit.

Deb turned to brush her off – this had gone far enough – but when she met the woman's gaze she found herself saying yes. She had been mistaken about her, Deb realised. *She's younger than I thought, or maybe older. She looks like that drama teacher we had, the one who ended up in a mental hospital, that same blazing gaze.*

To Carthage then I came, burning.

"I didn't catch your name," Deb added. *Who the hell are you?*

"I'm Barbara," the woman said. "Let's go, shall we?"

* * *

"But how did you know," Deb asked her, later, "that I'd read her work?"

"It was written all over you. You're like the woman in that story of hers, the one who lives in a caravan and keeps the village where she spent her childhood inside a wooden box."

They were in The Plough, a pub just round the corner from the bookshop on Little Russell Street. The bar was so crowded they'd been forced to sit at the far end of someone else's table, side by side instead of opposite one another, two schoolgirls sharing a desk. Barbara was drinking Guinness. Her pink jacket looked different from how it had looked in the bookshop. Something to do with the way she was sitting, leaning forward over her glass, sleeves pushed up around her elbows.

Louche, Deb thought, and very nearly cool. She had no idea what she was doing here, or who this woman was. The lack of knowledge excited her. She knew this was out of character – spontaneous actions were not normally part of her repertoire. She was semi-convinced that her decision to leave with this woman was not in fact spontaneous, that she must have met Barbara before somewhere, that their presence here in the pub was the unexpected follow-up to an earlier encounter.

What else would account for it? What else could?

"You think you're like her, don't you? That writer," Barbara was saying.

Deb blushed.

"You won't admit it, but you do. You read those batshit stories of hers and for you they're like music, the *repeating leitmotifs* and *fragmented structures* and *disturbing imagery*, all those things you like to talk about, and you think that because you understand her work better than most people – because that at least is true, you do – you think you can be the same sort of writer. That – be honest with yourself – you already are the same sort of writer. You aren't, though."

Deb's lips felt numb. From the vodka, she told herself, though that was not it. The word 'batshit', fresh from Barbara's lips, was still flapping around inside her head like its own living avatar.

Barbara's lips were coated with rust-coloured lipstick, a shade that clashed with her suit in a way that seemed deliberately provocative.

How can she know this? How can she possibly know any of this?

"I'm not as good as her yet, I realise that," Deb said. The noise of the pub was so loud she was almost shouting.

"It's not a question of good. It's a question of risk. Olena Pohorska knows about risk. I'm not talking about coming under fire, or having to shelter in someone's basement for six weeks. I'm talking about being honest with your feelings. You curate everything within an inch of its life. You won't admit your fears because you believe fear is a weakness. You won't admit to love, either. Where's your sense of adventure?"

"Love is not an adventure, it's a disease. Something you catch, like a virus. I almost died of it."

"You won't write about it, though. Why not?" Barbara turned in her seat, then leaned forward to kiss Deb on the mouth, a kiss delivered with such heat and such force it was almost vengeful, more a bite than a kiss.

She drew back, her orange lips curled in a half-smile. "Will you write about that?"

* * *

Saint Barbara was the patron saint of miners, tunnellers, and artillerymen – of anyone who worked with munitions or with explosives. Her name day was December 4th, and her relics were kept in the Cathedral of St. Volodymyr, in Kyiv, the cathedral that appeared in Pohorska's story 'The Devil's Men'.

An interesting coincidence, though Deb had found that was often the way with stories: strands of narrative that seemed distinct from one another turned out to be connected. As if the writer was taking you into their confidence, encouraging you to look for clues to what was going on. Saint Barbara's story turned out to be yet another sordid tale of misogyny, a parable about the seemingly insuperable male need to control women's bodies and actions and lives. Of a father who loved his daughter so much he locked her up in a tower to protect her from, well, whatever, then when she had the gall to go against his wishes, arranged to have her tortured. When she still wouldn't agree to be his prisoner, this so-called father settled the argument by cutting off her head.

There was an altarpiece in the Church of Saint Barbara in Wrocław, painted by the fifteenth-century German artist Wilhelm Kalteysen, depicting various scenes from Barbara's life. One of them showed her tied up, bleeding from the head, surrounded by her male tormentors, one of whom was taking a knife to one of her breasts. The image was remarkable: robust and full of energy. Like so much mediaeval painting it looked strikingly modern. Deb also found it utterly enraging, the figure on the far left especially, a dumb-looking lout with a shaved head, one hand clamped across Barbara's mouth, the other raising a mallet, about to smash her skull.

Shut the fuck up, bitch. Deb could hear his words, quite clearly. It was the speaking your mind men hated – now, then, always. But Barbara's story had a payoff, at least. On his way home from committing murder, Barbara's father Dioscorus was struck by lightning and consumed by fire. Burned to a crisp, right there on the roadside. Hence Saint Barbara's affinity with dynamite.

Nice one, Babs.

The name Barbara, Deb read, comes from the Greek word barbaros, meaning foreigner, or stranger, and this too seemed like synchronicity, a way of making sense of what was happening: *a stranger comes to town*, the inciting moment of so many stories.

Deb had not spoken to or heard from Barbara since they had gone their separate ways outside The Plough, Deb to Tottenham Court Road tube and Barbara to who-knows-where. She had said nothing to Deb about where she lived. In fact she had let slip no personal details whatsoever, though she had promised to be in touch, snapping open her handbag and extracting her phone to record Deb's contact details.

Barbara's handbag was brown and shiny with a gold catch, the old-fashioned, rigid kind, like something the Queen might have carried, yet the phone she took out of it was new, one of the recently revamped flip phones. There was something shocking about the appearance of such a gadget from this throwback of a handbag, so much so that Deb had initially mistaken the phone for a powder compact, or a pocket mirror, something small and silvery and refined from the 1950s.

In the days since, she had asked herself repeatedly whether it was this moment of confusion that had made her forget to ask Barbara for her own number. *I've lost her,* she thought, without understanding why she would think such a thing, why she would care even, when Barbara's existence had been unknown to her before that day.

She's an old woman, she told herself. That coarse greying hair. The pink suit and Thatcher handbag. The only way Barbara made sense was as part of a story, and when she came in from work in the evenings, Deb took refuge in the labyrinth of hearsay and speculation around the hagiography of Saint Barbara, a woman whose identity had been questioned and brought into doubt more often and more vociferously, it seemed, than that of other saints. There were those within the Catholic hierarchy, both now and in the past, who insisted that Barbara of Antioch had never existed. In 'The Devil's Men', Olena Pohorska had repurposed an ancient tale of treachery to fit a modern context. Deb thought it might be interesting to try and do something similar with the legend of Saint Barbara.

So little was known of her, so much of what had been recorded cloaked in pious mysticism. What interested Deb about Saint Barbara was not the Christian symbolism that was used to whitewash the reality of her terrible death, but the woman herself, her capacity for rebellion. Should her Saint Barbara be an activist? A terrorist, even? The possibilities were interesting, especially when you took account of what happened to her father.

The thought of the young woman's physical suffering rendered her speechless. Not only the pain, but what it signified, the stripping of agency from the oppressed by those in power. How might such evil be conveyed in words? Saint Barbara had been robbed not only of her voice, but of her identity. No single act of revenge seemed adequate as compensation.

Deb went to bed thinking of Barbara, of the kiss she had bestowed – for there was no other word – with her hot orange mouth. *You won't admit your fear,* Barbara had said, and Deb knew she was right.

★ ★ ★

When she returned from work the following evening there was a parcel waiting. A label stuck to the back gave the sender's name, 'B. Burns', and an address in Queen's Park. Deb undid the package carefully, trying not to tear the paper. Already she knew more about Barbara than she had a moment ago: her surname, where she lived.

Inside the packaging was a lacquered box, its shiny black surface painted with an intricate gold overlay of pine cones and leaves. Inside the box were half a dozen photographs. All but one showed views of a street, a row of nondescript post-war houses with identical front gardens. In one photograph, a child wearing a grey school uniform could be seen, coming out of one of the houses. The final photograph appeared to be a close-up of the same child, a girl of eight or nine with fair hair and a serious expression.

On the back of the photograph, someone had written 'Chloe' with a blue Sharpie.

In Pohorska's story 'The Village Idiot', the one Barbara had mentioned on the night of the pub, the wooden box was a pocket universe. So was this one, in a way, if you accepted the photographs as stand-ins for actual houses, for an actual street. Who was Chloe? Deb examined the photograph carefully, trying and failing to find in the child's pinched features some echo of Barbara's. The child seemed pale and maybe scared, uncertain of itself. Deb wondered what might have happened, to make her look like that.

She was still wondering when her phone pinged. *Do you like Asian food?* read the text, together with a link to a Vietnamese restaurant on Kilburn High Street. *7:30 tomorrow eve if you are free?*

Deb felt her muscles relax, as if she had finally completed a task she had been dreading. It was only when she went to bed at around midnight that she remembered today was December 4th, Saint Barbara's Day, and why the Christmas lights that had begun to appear in the windows along her street always caused her such anguish. They reminded her of Clive, of course. Of the Christmas she had spent alone in a dingy hotel room in the far north of Scotland.

★ ★ ★

"I should be able to get away for at least a couple of hours on Boxing Day," Clive had said. "Perhaps all day on the 27th. Think about it. We can have our own Christmas."

The joy she had found in planning that trip, the underhum of excitement that transformed the whole of December from its customary troubled hiatus to a numinous shimmer. The endless journey north, the darkness hounding the daylight from the cobwebbed skies over Inverness. The arrival in Thurso, that bleak little garrison town that served as quarters for the technicians, contractors and army personnel who worked at the Dounreay nuclear facility ten miles to the west, its huddled streets and half-empty chain stores, like a glimpse of a desperate future many claimed would never happen but that now seemed inevitable.

Deb had imagined walking by the ocean in the silver northern light; the low, pewter-coloured cloud, the rain-soaked, gusting wind had made a nonsense of such an idea, and in any case, she had not wanted to look at that sea, battering the concrete harbourside, more than once. There was something uncanny about the place, a sense of abandonment and thwarted desires that assailed her almost from the moment she stepped out of the train. But still, she had made light of such feelings, texting Clive from her chilly little room at the Station Hotel to announce her safe arrival and her hope that they might meet, if only for an hour, the following day.

Clive was not staying in Thurso. He and his wife Clarissa and another couple were renting a luxuriously appointed barn conversion further up the coast. The house had won an architectural award, Deb had discovered when she looked it up online, and there was a celebrated gastro-pub within what was billed by the owner's website as easy walking distance. Deb's text received no answer, because Clive's phone was switched off. He swore to her later this had been an accident, though of course it was not.

Forty-five minutes in a gloomy tea shop, the day after Boxing Day. They held hands across the table, *Now That's What I Call Christmas* playing on an endless loop through the tinny speakers.

"I have to go," Clive said, brushing scone crumbs from his trousers and on to the floor. "I was lucky to get away at all, actually."

Deb walked back to the hotel through the gathering dusk. She gazed at the lights in the windows, wreaths and stars, fairies and Father Christmases and in one instance, unfathomably, a Japanese bullet train, and realised for the first time that they were there not only as a reminder of the coming spring but as a warding-off of the devil, who seemed to be everywhere in that landscape, and ever-vigilant.

"You're wondering why I put up with it," Deb said. Seeing Barbara again had made her realise how much she had dreaded not seeing her. Barbara was wearing a high-necked blouse in silk brocade, her head protruding from the stalk of the collar like a frost-tinged flower. She looked, Deb thought, like the secretary to an executioner. The idea made her shiver. Barbara had ordered the squid with shitake and chilli, red rounds scattered on white.

Barbara laughed. "I'm thinking how angry you must have felt, sitting in that hotel room, waiting for that man to call."

"The room was so ugly. Polyester sheets and flat-pack furniture, that Seventies varnished pine everyone had back then. And Clive really didn't care – that's what I realise now. If he thought about me at all it was just to feel guilty, or more likely worried, in case this turned out to be the time he was found out. I kept imagining how good it would feel, to switch off my phone and head back to London without telling him. I didn't, though. I stayed."

"Are you going to write about it?" Barbara said.

Deb shook her head. "I've been researching the life of Saint Barbara, actually. I thought I might try and write something about her." She attempted to smile and failed. On her way to the restaurant she had tried to imagine how the words might sound when spoken aloud. She had been going for clever, flirtatious even. In Barbara's presence they came out sounding hesitant, apologetic, the words of a nervous student agonising over her PhD proposal.

"Can you make your story count, do you think?"

"I hope so," Deb said, and then added, before her courage failed her, "Who is the child – the one in the photograph?"

"My goddaughter. She was eight when those pictures were taken. She's ten now. Her mother was a friend of mine, a very dear friend. She died quite suddenly. Her parents came and took Chloe away, to live with them." She named a street, a town. "They won't let me see her. They say I'm a negative influence. No doubt they blame me for Dody's death. You remind me of her. Dody. The same nervous, broken look. When I first saw you at the bookshop you quite undid me. And now we're even. In terms of personal confessions, I mean."

"Is that why you spoke to me? Because I reminded you of someone else?"

"Maybe. Partly. But we're beyond that now, don't you think?"

Which is why when they left the restaurant, Deb knew what would happen, the outline if not the detail. Barbara's flat was on the third floor of a tottering Victorian villa, a single L-shaped room, the tiny bathroom and kitchen tucked under the eaves.

Books, expensive art magazines, a silver candelabra, its branches mossy with tarnish. An ancient-looking corduroy sofa. Improbably, a harpsichord. Barbara poured her a drink – amaretto, Deb thought it was – pungent with the scent of almonds and a kick like bourbon. The glass it came in looked very old. Deb had a suspicion that it might be Roman. She didn't dare ask.

"So, tell me about Clive," Barbara said. "What happened next?"

"Nothing. We carried on seeing each other twice a week for another five years. Then Clive was offered a job in the States. He was supposed to be there for a year, it was part of an exchange programme with an American university. He didn't tell me a thing until the week he left. He said he would be in touch but that was the last I heard from him. I was ill for a while. I thought I could never recover. Then gradually I began to realise that I was glad. Glad not to have to think about him all the time, glad not to be in a constant state of panic and anticipation. I resisted those feelings at first. It was as if pain had become my comfort zone. But when I finally realised it was over, it was as if my life had been returned to me. Like being let out of prison."

"You must have been furious, though. With Clive."

"I wasn't. I never have been. If anything it's myself I feel angry with. For being such a fool."

"A man exploits you for seven years and you call yourself a fool?"

"For wasting all that time, then."

"Do you always have to see the other side? Sometimes, there is no other side. You have to take on the anger. You have to let your soul become compromised by it. To not do that is a form of cowardice. You think you're being strong, but in reality you're just lying to yourself."

"I do sometimes wish she knew," Deb said. "Clarissa, I mean. That Clive was messing around behind her back for all that time. I wish she knew that he was never who she thought he was, that her whole marriage was never what she thought it was. I hate the fact that Clive got away with it, that he slotted back into his normal life and no one knew a thing." She took a sip of her drink. "So far as Clive was concerned, I never existed."

"You can say the word hate, then. I suppose it's a start."

"There are things I still have. Letters, postcards, concert programmes. Photos." Deb spoke softly, as if to herself, raising the ancient goblet to catch the light. "Can you imagine if I boxed it all up and sent it to Clarissa? It would be like a bomb going off."

The thought of blowing up Clive's life. Especially now, years later, when he would believe he was in the clear. The idea was exhilarating, a hit of adrenaline so massive it made Deb want to laugh, to make a whooping noise, to roll naked in the snow. And it was not the picture of Clive's life coming apart she relished – the yelling and the screaming, the clothes thrown into suitcases, the poxy one-bedroom flat way out in South Norwood, which, by the time Clarissa had finished with his bank account, would be all he could afford. What set her heart racing with a sense of vindication so raw it might as well have been rage was the thought of two worlds becoming one – the world Clive strolled about in, unbothered, and the shitty little space he had been happy for her to live inside. With Clive's unmasking, the two would merge. Finally, Clive would be forced to admit to those snooty colleagues of his at the Courtauld that Deb was real.

She put down her glass on a nearby table. Glass-topped, etched with a design of frost flowers, and as she knelt on the rug in front of Barbara she was conscious once again of her delirium in being free.

This was who she was now.

Her world had been the real world, all along, and when she undid the buttons that fastened the back of Barbara's blouse she was not surprised by what she found nestled between her shoulder blades, the twin excrescences that many would have termed a disfigurement, a freak of nature, but that Deb regarded with wonder and a sense of awe.

Wings, no larger than a pigeon's wings, one more crumpled than the other and slightly askew, the few feathers clinging to the delicate, flesh-coloured radial bones soft and mottled as duck down.

"They never developed properly," Barbara said. "It happens."

One of her breasts was deeply scarred, the cleft flesh puckered and hardened as if from botched surgery years before. Her knees and elbows and collarbone were angular, pointed, vulnerable as a child's. *Are you an angel?* Deb wanted to ask, *a demon?* though such distinctions seemed meaningless. All she knew was that Barbara was glorious, and that her wounds and imperfections were like badges of power.

At one point she thought of Clive, and softly laughed.

"Do you hate them, then?" Deb said, afterwards. "Chloe's grandparents?"

Barbara pulled on a dressing gown, yellow and shapeless, like one Deb's mother used to have. Her hair was wild as a briar patch. She held her head on one side, like a crow: watchful and darkly intelligent and wryly amused.

"I hate all little people. People who never question why they're alive," she snapped. "Dody used to say her parents were good people, but what they are is small people. Trying to force Chloe into their way of thinking, into their pathetic, limited lives, like they tried to with Dody. I wish they were dead."

"You don't mean that."

Barbara glared, but said nothing. Her eyes were like flints. As Deb was putting on her coat, Barbara kissed her hard on the mouth, the way she had done in the pub the night they first met.

Deb retraced her steps to the tube. Automatically, as if the route was pre-programmed, as if she was drunk. Her strides seemed weightless, her feet barely making contact with the pavement. The stars shone down, points of diamond hardness against the filmy orange gauze of the London night. The air seemed to seethe with alien signals, the universe massively present and insistently alive. From somewhere beneath her came the rumble of trains, forcing their way through the bedrock like metal worms.

* * *

Do godparents have rights?

Deb typed the question into her search bar without knowing the answer and without a clear understanding of why she was asking it. She told herself she wanted to know more about Barbara's situation, though she suspected that what she really wanted to know more about was Dody.

It turned out that godparents had no rights, or at least not legally. All the family law sites concurred that if a parent or parents died, responsibility for the care of children would automatically pass to their legal guardian. The legal guardian might also be a godparent, but only if that had been specified in the parent's will.

Had Dody made a will? Deb's questions were endless, and seemingly unanswerable. She looked again at the photographs in the lacquered box, the row of suburban houses, the street with its concrete driveways and dismal-looking trees. She was afraid, she realised, afraid of setting off an alarm, of breaking something with her prurience, though in the end her greed for knowledge proved greater than her fear of being caught looking.

Did this exempt her from being a little person? She doubted it was that easy. She remembered how in Pohorska's story 'The Devil's Men', Nadiya finds herself caught between admitting the truth about who her husband is working for and understanding what has happened to her sister. For Nadiya, pursuing the facts about one part of her life would inevitably bring about the destruction of the other, and so she remains in limbo, watching the devil's men ride out from the city night after night, not daring to look in their faces in case she recognises one of them as Mikhail, refusing to believe the shoe she finds in the street is really Lena's.

When Deb Googled the name of the street Barbara had mentioned she found nothing but property listings. *Dody died quite suddenly*, Barbara had said, *her parents blame me.* Deb typed in the name of the town, then added 'Dody'. She told herself there was nothing to find, except that sometimes when you tempt fate, fate is tempted. Deb read through the linked articles, one at a time, searching for mentions of Barbara and finding none.

"How can they blame you?" she asked Barbara, later.

"By saying I broke up their marriage. By saying I drove him to it, that if Dody and I had never met, she would still be alive. Six bullets he put into her. The only thing that helps is imagining what ecstasy it would be, to fire them back at him. I think of the little park where it happened, and then I picture him rolling on the ground in agony, clutching his stomach. His blood blackening the tarmac. There's no sound, just the swings in the background, the witch's hat, the little roundabout. Do you know how many crimes take place in children's playgrounds? People think of them as safe spaces, but they're not. Why did you spend time looking up all this stuff, anyway? You only had to ask."

Deb found she could not answer. She remembered a terrible thing, a child from her primary school who had gone missing from the local recreation ground. Gavin Betts, his name was. She hadn't thought of him in years.

Dody Springer.

Local artist, Dody Springer.

Victim of playground shooting named by police.

Grainy photos of the taped-off park, the nondescript street, net curtains in all the windows, cars parked at the kerb.

"In a lot of countries, that man would be executed," Barbara continued. "In some places, they would let me watch him die. That's what love is – not only wanting him dead but watching it happen."

"I can't imagine it," Deb said. Her throat felt tight.

"Then you have never been in love. Not really. If you had then you would understand what I am talking about."

★ ★ ★

There were several online galleries of Dody's artwork, pencil drawings so intricate and so crowded it was difficult to make out what they were of. Cutlery, clock parts, buttons and safety pins. The kind of small, cheap trinkets you find in Christmas crackers. One of the drawings was actually entitled *Christmas Cracker*.

There was another that looked at first like a pile of autumn leaves, the individual elements overlapping and bunching and drifting against one another in an endless juxtaposition of similar forms. When she enlarged a section of the image, Deb realised the forms were not leaves after all, but moths' wings. The drawing was called *Everlasting Love*. There was an option to add to basket, but when Deb attempted to do so the gallery informed her that this particular print was out of stock.

Searching online for 'playground shootings', Deb read about a case that had happened in America; a doctor had paid her cousin to murder her husband. The husband had been fighting her for custody of their child. The husband, who was a dentist, was shot in the chest, just outside the entrance to a children's playground.

His blood was streaming from his wounds, Deb read, *soaking through his clothing and staining the asphalt.*

Not just wanting him dead, but needing to watch. After the man was shot, the woman who had ordered the killing rushed to his side and attempted to give mouth-to-mouth resuscitation. Deb found it difficult to imagine becoming prey to such irrational impulses, even through the medium of fiction. And surely this was what Barbara had meant about making a story count. Deb's unwillingness to imagine was a falling short, a reluctance to grapple with danger that would forever mark out her work as inauthentic, skating across life's surfaces instead of diving in.

Fiction that involved no risk, either for the reader or for herself.

She examined the photograph of the woman who had been convicted. She stared straight at the camera, unaffected and seemingly unafraid. As if she had no regrets about what she had done, even now. She reminded Deb of Saint Barbara, whose fiery revenge had been conjured out of the depths of total erasure. From a pain so brutally enforced Deb could imagine that for Saint Barbara as for the American doctor there had been nothing left to lose.

A joy in bringing down the house, a rediscovery of the power of the letter 'i'.

I, Deb mouthed under her breath. Such a steely little word, like an ice pick, and if I write Barbara into this sentence, she is here with me, too.

This is what it is, to say how I feel.

This is how we brought down the house.

This is what happened next.

* * *

It's not my car, Barbara said. I stole it.

Stole it?

Well, borrowed it. We can take it back later. The people who own it are in the Canaries until the end of January. They won't even know it's gone. And their alibi will be solid.

Alibi?

Even if the car is traced, they were never here. She pulled away from the junction and on to the dual carriageway. She drove with confidence, which surprised me. The fact that she knew how to drive at all surprised me. I always imagined her on trains, buses, on foot in her well kept brogues, in those frumpy Fifties outfits of hers, like the costumes worn by actors in BBC dramas set just after the war.

Soldiers who never came home. Lovers unmasked as spies. Traders in the misfortunes of other people.

I knew so little about her, really.

The day was blank and grey, one of the vacant spaces between Christmas and New Year. There was nothing on the roads, or very little. I thought of the families hunkered down around their gas fires, desperate for movement, desperate for life, desperate to kick-start a war, even a small one between each other. Time worn thin, like an old pillowslip, I wrote later, liking the sense of the words even though I could not ascribe an exact meaning to them. Only a colour, a particular shade of grey, or off-white, the pallor of linen that has been washed so many times you can see gaps between the threads.

I'm going to fetch Chloe, Barbara had said, when she called me earlier. I need to get her away from there. Do you want to come with me?

The stories I write at this time of year are always the same: yellow-leaved and restless, with a side-serve of bleak. The murder rate rises at Christmas, did you know that?

Of course I said yes. I would follow her anywhere. I don't care what she does.

The town centre was more or less deserted. Most of the shops were shut, or boarded up. In the windows of the Tesco Metro, anoraked figures moved slowly behind the glass like fish in a tank.

I hate this place, Barbara said. I'd like to blow it sky high.

How did you meet? I asked her. You and Dody?

I bumped into her at the butcher's. Does it matter? Her eyes were fixed on the road. She went around a roundabout, the three spindly conifers at its centre strung with flashing blue lights. The street looked like it did in the photographs. In the downstairs windows, the glimmer of Christmas lights and TVs, that chilly electric glow, and I thought about Clive and me, how it had never really been anything, just a boring chance encounter between his ego and my need.

How miraculous life is, and how vast. What a ghastly mess we make of things.

Whatever happens, I said to Barbara.

Don't say it, she said. Wait here. This shouldn't take long.

She parked the car behind an unmarked transit van, then reached for her handbag, the same one she had been carrying the night we met. When I saw what she was taking out of it I felt the world shift sideways.

I'm assuming that's a replica, I said, though even as I spoke the words I realised I didn't care, that I was only trying to cover myself, to get it on the record that whatever was about to happen had not been my idea.

My heart was racing.

Wait here, Barbara repeated. She slid the gun into the right-hand pocket of her jacket and stepped out of the car. I watched as she walked towards one of the houses, a single upright figure on an otherwise empty street. As she reached the front door it opened, and a child appeared. She was dressed for the outside, in jeans and trainers and a blue Parka. There was a rucksack strapped to her back. Barbara pulled the girl towards her for a second then pointed towards the car. I got out of the passenger side and came around to the pavement. So I could open the car door for her, I reasoned, help her with her stuff, I could do that at least, only before I had time to do anything a man started shouting.

Get back inside. Right now.

He was standing in the doorway of the house the child had just come out of, yelling and waving his fist at her as if she was a dog that had slipped its leash. I noticed he was wearing carpet slippers, the tartan kind you get from M&S, a comfortable, grandfatherly detail that seemed entirely out of kilter with the way he was shouting.

The child ignored him and kept on walking, hunching her shoulders and dipping her head as if battling a strong wind. The man on the doorstep took a step forward and then stopped abruptly – perhaps he'd only just realised he was still wearing slippers. Then he rounded on Barbara.

I warned you to stay away. I'm calling the police.

I saw Barbara smile. The lipsticked, rapier smile of a wicked queen who has just handed over the poisoned apple. She spoke too quietly for me to hear what she said to him but it must have been spectacular. He shoved his face at hers, his lip curled, his features twisted in that same expression of outrage, of barely concealed hatred you will see on the face of any man who has been contradicted by a woman and is trying to work out whether he can get away with belting her one. The slipper-wearing grandfather was gone, or rather revealed for the casual deception he had always been.

Another figure appeared in the doorway, a small, grey-haired woman in tracksuit bottoms and an oversized Smurfs sweatshirt. The Smurfs were all wearing Santa hats, embroidered with red sequins.

What's going on? she said. The man reached out his arm to block the doorway but she barged on through. We said no, she barked, glaring at Barbara. You're to stay away.

Go inside and call the police, Lilian, the man said. He did not so much as glance at her. The woman seemed not to hear. She swivelled her head, looking up and down the street. When she caught sight of the child she started screaming.

Chloe, you get back here this minute.

Barbara was reaching into her pocket. The man in the slippers seemed so intent on trying to stare her down he failed to notice. Barbara pulled out the gun. She aimed it straight at his chest. She looks like Ruth Ellis, I remember thinking – Ruth Ellis, as played by Miranda Richardson in *Dance With A Stranger*.

Ruth Ellis who had been in love, and paid the price for it.

The two of them, locked in the moment, and as Barbara's finger tightened around the trigger there came the rumbling of thunder, the sound of the sky being ripped apart like a plastic shower curtain, the sullen light of the afternoon exploding in platinum fire.

White lightning, and the clatter of wings. Gargoyles streaking from ruined turrets, as in a painting by Bosch. Barbara threw back her head and laughed. She fired the gun in the air, and in front of her on the pathway the man in the tartan slippers burst into flames.

He went up like a firework. There's no other way of putting it. The woman shrieked, her hands cupped around her mouth like a Hollywood scream queen's. Then she dashed back inside. The door swung back on its hinges. I could see the doormat, a section of carpet. From somewhere inside I could hear the theme tune to *Strictly Come Dancing*.

Barbara basked in the light from the fire, the gun plainly visible in her right hand. Smoke clung to her back in long drifts. When I finally took my eyes from her, there was Chloe.

We gazed into each other's faces. Her eyes, ageless as rainclouds, her cheek bruised with smuts.

I'm sorry you had to see that, I said. My voice was trembling slightly.

She shrugged. Don't worry about it, she said. They had to go.

She went to the car and sprung the boot, threw in her rucksack. Then she opened the passenger door and climbed in. I hesitated, just for a second, then got in the back.

My clothes and hair were thick with the stench of barbecue.

Barbara put on her seatbelt and started the engine. Not a bad little car, this, she said. I stared out of the window: the shop fronts, the headlights and pavements and street signs, all the London things I loved. The haloed shimmer of Christmas lights, of advertising hoardings, of planes passing over our heads, swiftly, silently into the unknown.

Chloe and Barbara chatted together in the front of the car, their voices soft and companionable, with the occasional laugh. Their words were inaudible above the traffic but I did not mind.

It was beginning to get dark, but I felt shielded and cheered by the knowledge that the year was on the turn.

I always feel better after the solstice.

I could hear the sound of sirens, but they seemed far away.

HARE MOON

H.V. Patterson

Mom's ragged scream woke me. I turned over in bed and locked eyes with my twin sister, Lia, as the scream became a wail. And then I heard Dad's voice, a rumbling baritone, comforting her.

"Jana?" Lia whispered, voice taut with fear.

"It'll be okay," I said, getting out of bed. "Come on."

Lia, ever my shadow, followed me to the front door. It was slightly ajar, and our parents huddled just inside, clinging to each other. They didn't stop us when we stepped onto the porch. We'd turned twenty last week; we were old enough to see.

The headless hare hung from the door, a nail through each paw. Its blood was dry already, hours old. A jagged line ran down its belly, and its eviscerated guts and organs lay coiled in a stinking spiral on the welcome mat. Flies and ants feasted on the hare. Their quiet buzzing jarred my ears.

Two guards stood at the foot of the porch. They nodded at me, rifles respectfully lowered. I pulled Lia back inside, shutting the door behind us.

"No!" she said. "Why us? Why our family?"

"It's Ostara's will," said Dad. He and Mom reached for her, but she turned to me.

"You said it would be okay!" Lia said, starting to cry. "You lied!"

"I'm sorry," I said.

I held out my arms, and she collapsed into me. I held tightly while she wept, her tears dampening my nightshirt. Mom and Dad closed in around us, and the four of us huddled together, mourning.

Eventually, the shock wore off. Lia was the first to break from our huddle.

"I want to bury Harvey," she said.

I hadn't recognised Harvey without his head, but I'd never cared for the hares like Lia did. Lia had raised Harvey when his mother rejected him, and he'd been her special pet. I thought it was a mistake to name the hares, to grow so attached to something you knew would die to feed you. Besides, the hares unnerved me. When they stretched, they were longer than seemed decent, and when they stared at you, they saw too much.

"Sweetheart, are you sure?" Dad said. "You don't have to."

"I have to do something," Lia muttered, sniffling.

Lia wore her heart on her sleeve for the whole world to see. I felt things as deeply as she did; I just hid my emotions better. It was hard to be strong all the time. But I was the older sister, even if only by a handful of minutes, and it was my responsibility to make the tough choices.

"I'll help," I said. Unlike me, Lia wasn't used to handling dead bodies.

"I want to do it myself," she said.

"Fine," I said, a little shortly.

Our hands were the only thing about us not identical: Lia's were soft, her palms smooth; mine were calloused and rough from my lessons with Dr. Fetch and working in the fields. Digging would hurt Lia's delicate hands. She'd regret not accepting my help.

While Lia dug Harvey's grave, I helped Mom make pancakes with huckleberry syrup and fatty strips of salty bacon. I savoured the tastes of smoke, salt, sugar on my tongue.

We ate no hare. No one ate hare on the sacred day of Hare Moon.

After breakfast, we spent the day together, playing board games and downing endless cups of coffee, tea, and cocoa. We didn't say much, but our eyes spoke volumes, every glance a declaration of love. Instead of lunch, we wandered in and out of the kitchen, nibbling on cheese and crusty bread with butter. Somehow, I'd never realised before how lovely salted butter was, the blessing of it spread on soft bread. I licked my fingers, savouring the sensation.

In the afternoon, I made cookies, desperate for something to do with my nervous hands. Baking wasn't as satisfying as practising stitches under Dr. Fetch's astute eye or grinding up plants for medicine. Dr. Fetch taught me anatomy as part of my training. She'd shown me skeletons of hares, humans, cats, and dogs, pointing out the similarities in structure all mammals share. Harvey's paws and my hands both possess carpals, metacarpals, and phalanges. I loved watching the miracle of my fingers, my flexor tendons beneath my skin, all fifty-four bones and forty joints in my hands and wrists working together as one, just as every member of our community did.

As God in his Heaven and Ostara in the Earth willed it. Amen.

The hours bled through my fingers more quickly than I thought possible. Soon, the sun was a searing ball of orange fire setting the tops of the hawthorn trees alight. We dressed in our finest clothes and headed for Church, flanked by our guards.

I couldn't help looking back over my shoulder. The moon was rising behind our house, painting it silver. Lia squeezed my left hand, and Mom took my right as Dad pressed gently against my shoulders, urging me onward. We were all thinking the same thing as our home vanished from sight: one of us would never see it again.

* * *

We walked into our Church's cool vestibule, down the centre aisle to the very front of the congregation. As I settled into my seat, I held myself straight and tall, my thoracic vertebrae pressing against the hard, juniper pew. My mind turned over what would come, what Dr. Fetch had whispered would happen if our family was selected. What I needed to do to survive. I wasn't sure if I could make the choice if the moment came. My heart beat quickly, in time to my racing thoughts, and I was grateful no one could see the fear and grief lurking beneath my composure.

A stranger, a young man about my age, pulled me from my thoughts. He smiled widely as he seated himself in the pew beside me. Outsiders were rare, but we received them graciously when they arrived in our community, guided by the hand of Ostara.

"Hello! I'm Isaac," he said.

"Hello," I replied. He waited, but I didn't give him my name.

"I'm really excited to be here today, on the Feast of Ostara! I'm writing an article about it," he said, gazing around the Church. "This is a gorgeous building. It's so similar to my grandparents' Church!"

I smiled politely. I don't interact with many outsiders, but Dr. Fetch said they're always surprised that our Church looks so familiar. I don't know why. Our ancestors were Christian, and we still honour God the Father who created the world and Christ the Son who died that our souls might be redeemed. We sing the same hymns and read the same Bible our forefathers brought ashore after The Second Flood.

Dr. Fetch arrived, clothed in dark grey, and sat on Isaac's other side. Her silver-white hair was swept into an elegant bun at the nape of her neck, and her worn but vital hands were folded devoutly in her lap. Isaac introduced himself and started asking her questions about the Church and the significance of 'Saint Ostara'. Dr. Fetch answered politely and neither of us corrected him, though it was hard to sit there hearing the Holy Mother stripped of Her divinity. Rendered a mere saint.

"The Crucifix is…interesting," he said, gesturing to where it hung above the pulpit. "Do you know how old it is? Who carved it? It's very…expressive."

"It's been with us since the founding," Dr. Fetch said.

During my lessons, Dr. Fetch often spoke to me about suffering. She'd told me that many outsiders shy away from Christ's suffering. They minimise the holiness of pain, rendering Christ's body without the stigmata or even displaying a bare cross without a body. Our Christ doesn't hide the truth, the holy agony of his death. His face is contorted, and his crown of thorns drips painted blood. The wound at his side gapes wide, a loop of intestine trailing from it, slithering down his left leg, like the serpent twisting round the Tree of Knowledge.

Reverend entered, cutting short Isaac's impertinent questions. The congregation hushed. Reverend wasn't a harsh man, but his very presence demanded respect. He'd led us through many trials and tribulations, as had his father before him, and his father's father, and his father's father's father, all the way back to the second drowning of the world. His brown eyes were kind but firm. The rustling of his black vestments was the only sound as he ascended to the pulpit and began to speak.

"Brethren, we are gathered here on this most Holy Day of Hare Moon, when we give thanks not only to God in his Heaven and

Christ the Redeemer, but to Ostara, the Hare Mother, the Earth Mother, the Warren Mother, whose bounty nurtures us in this life, on this Earth."

"Hail Ostara, the merciful," we chanted as one.

"Ostara feeds us—"

"—and we feed Ostara," the words slipped from my lips. Beside me, Isaac scribbled furiously in a notebook, and I tried to ignore the disrespect, the blasphemy. He would be punished soon enough.

After Hare Moon service, everyone filed out of the nave and into the community hall in the basement where the feast lay waiting. Despite my trepidation, the hall was still a cozy, protected space, filled with the delectable scents of food. Great platters dripping with every kind of meat but hare. Bottles of wine, cheeses, nuts, loaves of fresh bread. Salads heaped with all the bounty of the Earth, great steaming plates of roasted vegetables. Eggs in every form. The dessert table groaned beneath a wealth of cakes, cookies, brownies, and even specially imported chocolates.

But I couldn't enjoy myself because this year wasn't like other years. My family walked to the raised dais at the front of the hall and sat at the table of honour with Reverend, Dr. Fetch, and Isaac. The guards brought us platters of food that I didn't feel like eating. No one at our table had much of an appetite. Except Isaac, who sat between Lia and me and wouldn't stop stuffing food and wine into his mouth, smiling between bites.

"I haven't eaten a meal this good in years," he said, grease dripping down his chin.

"I'm glad you're enjoying it," Lia said, looking down at her plate.

He probably thought her shy, but I could see the tears shimmering at the corners of her eyes. My heart twisted. How could I bear to lose Lia today, to lose any of them? I silently prayed to Ostara to make Her will known without my intercession, to take the choice from me.

Our guards returned with dessert: piles of cakes, cookies, chocolates, and sweet wine. I bit into a chocolate. It was chalky and bitter on my tongue.

There was no clock in the community hall, but I felt the press of time, of minutes passing. Some people danced, unable to control their exuberance. The young children started to fuss, their faces and fine clothes stained with chocolate. A couple argued, faces flushed with wine. A chair clattered to the floor. Grease and crumbs and icing smeared the walls, the ground, the very air. From the dais, above and apart from it all, the scene grew increasingly nauseating to behold.

I was relieved when the bell rang, silencing the hall. A thousand pairs of anxious, curious eyes turned to us, wondering who wouldn't return. Reverend stood and made a short speech I didn't pay attention to. Finally, the hall drained, leaving us alone on the dais.

"Isaac, we're having a special afterparty celebration," Reverend said. "Would you be so kind as to join us?" His benign smile didn't reach his eyes.

"Sure," Isaac said, swaying a little as he stood. "I think I'm a little drunk."

"It won't take long," Reverend said, holding out his hand.

Isaac beamed back at Reverend with all the trust a boy has for his father. He took Reverend's hand, sealing his fate.

Reverend led Isaac to a small door half-hidden by shadows. Dr. Fetch and my family followed, and the guards trailed behind. It was an ancient door hewn from white oak and secured with a padlock. An image of three hares running in a circle was burned into the door. Their sightless, ancient eyes watched us approach. I'd seen this door dozens of times, but I'd never seen it opened before.

"Remove your shoes, everyone," said Reverend, letting go of Isaac's hand.

We obeyed. Isaac fumbled with his laces and needed help.

When all were barefoot, Reverend pulled out a brass key and forced it into the battered lock. The door creaked on rusted hinges. Lia grasped my hand and squeezed. I squeezed back. We saw a dark, narrow tunnel sloping downwards into the earth. Dad wrapped his arm around Mom, and she sagged against him. They looked as if they'd aged ten years in a single day. I gazed into Lia's haunted eyes, identical to my own. My future grief looked back at me.

Ostara, please, I thought. *Please spare her.*

"Single-file," Reverend announced, lighting a lantern. Behind us, the guards and Dr. Fetch lit lanterns as well.

I dropped Lia's hand as Reverend started down the tunnel first, followed by Isaac. I took a deep breath and followed.

Reverend's lantern flickered, casting fantastic shadows on the walls as we descended. The tunnel wound in a tight spiral, like a serpent coiling deeper and deeper into the earth. It smelled strange, not like dirt or musty air, but like dew-drenched clover on an early spring morning.

Finally, we entered a small, roughly oval room. At the far end stood two wooden thrones and a small table. The thrones were tilted back, like lawn chairs. On the table were four small boxes wrapped in green and silver paper, a tray of Dr. Fetch's surgical equipment, freshly sterilised and gleaming, and a large, golden wine glass. Reverend led Isaac to one of the thrones. Isaac blinked and opened his mouth to speak, but Dr. Fetch stepped forward smoothly and pressed a small, liquid-filled vial between his slack lips. Startled, he coughed, then swallowed.

"What—" he tried to rise, but Dr. Fetch pushed him and he slumped onto the throne. Dr. Fetch's tinctures worked quickly. Her scalpels gleamed in the lantern light. I knew Isaac would not rise again.

Reverend set his lantern on the table and gestured for us to stand before it. The guards stood behind us, illuminating the room. I could see a half-dozen tunnels, none of them more than three feet high, branching out around us. I wondered where they led. I hoped we wouldn't have to crawl through them; the very thought made my skin prickle.

"We are gathered here beneath to give thanks to Ostara, the Hare Mother, Queen of the Earth," Reverend said. "Blessed be God in Heaven, and Blessed be Ostara in the Earth."

"Blessed be Ostara," we said.

"We honour and love you, Ostara. We obey your Word and eat of your Flesh. For you, the flowers grow. For you, the Earth is fruitful. You are the nourishing of our bodies."

"Blessed be Ostara."

"We remember your mercy, Ostara. We were cold and adrift on the sea, and you rescued us. We have fed from your bounty, and now we will feed you."

He nodded to Dr. Fetch, who began threading a suturing needle.

"We sew shut the mouth of the Outsider," proclaimed Reverend. "We sew shut his eyes and his ears, for these secrets are not his to speak, his to behold, his to hear."

Isaac's eyes widened, but he couldn't move. Dr. Fetch started with his mouth. I admired her skill, the precision of her stitching. I'd practised on leather, cuts of meat, and the occasional injured animal. It wasn't easy work. But her weathered hands were clever and sure, never missing a stitch. She only stopped occasionally to dab blood from her fingers. Blood is slippery. I'd dropped more than one blood-coated suturing needle during my training.

She sewed up his pretty eyes next, and I wasn't sorry. He kept staring beseechingly at Lia, and though she stood steadily beside me, I could hear the uneven catch in her breath. It was hard for her, hard for all of us. But that was the nature of sacrifice: it wasn't supposed to be easy.

A few quick stitches closed his ears.

"We now sanctify this offering," said Reverend. Dr. Fetch picked up her scissors and cut away Isaac's shirt. His chest was startlingly white and hairless, like a boy's. Dr. Fetch grasped her scalpel and began the incisions.

I admired her work as she made a long, smooth cut from navel to groin. She cut through epidermis, dermis, subcutaneous fat, and muscle, then made a few vertical slits and carefully pulled the skin and abdominal muscle back in two flaps. Isaac's exposed viscera glistened, untouched by the scalpel. Only the angle of the throne kept everything from spilling out onto the floor. Isaac was still living when Dr. Fetch dipped her hand into his abdomen and carefully examined the intestines. After a few minutes, she turned and smiled approvingly to Reverend, who nodded back. Whatever she'd seen augured well. Someday, I too would gaze into the hidden, secret places of a living, breathing body and discern what lay ahead: a good year, or a hard one.

Carefully, she slid Isaac's intestines from his body and arranged them in a spiralling coil on his lap. The smell of dying overwhelmed the room. My parents winced, and Lia covered her nose and mouth. I didn't move; I was accustomed to the stench of death.

"Have you sanctified this offering?" Reverend asked.

"I have, praise Ostara," Dr. Fetch said.

"Then proceed."

She picked up the knife, and Reverend picked up the cup. She stepped to Isaac's side and drew the knife across his carotid artery. As his life's blood poured out, Reverend caught it in the cup, filling it almost to the brim. Isaac died sightless, unhearing, and in great agony.

"Blessed be Ostara," Reverend said.

"Blessed be Ostara," we repeated.

Reverend turned to us next.

"Martha Abraham, Mathias Abraham, Jana Abraham, Lia Abraham. Do you come here, to the sacred Warren of the Hare Mother, of your own free will?"

"We do."

"Do you accept the fate Ostara decrees for you?"

"We do."

"Then step forward, Martha, and choose."

He gestured to the four boxes on the table behind him. Mom walked forward with her head held high, but I saw her hands trembling as she chose a box and returned to her original position.

"Step forward, Mathias, and choose."

I swallowed as Dad stepped forward, steeling myself. In my chest, my heart raced like a hunted hare, but I kept my face composed and my breathing even. I was the elder daughter. Only by a handful of minutes, but the elder still. I was next.

Please, merciful Ostara. Take the choice from me.

"Step forward, Jana, and choose."

I walked to the two remaining boxes. They were covered in a pattern of green leaves and grass intertwined with leaping, silver hares. I stared hard at the boxes, praying that they were identical. At first, they seemed to be, and I felt something loosen in my chest. But then, I saw the left-hand one had a single speck of dark red on its lid.

My hands clenched and unclenched. The red drop of blood watched me unblinkingly, waiting to see what I'd do. I could feel Dr. Fetch's eyes burning into me, could hear her whispered instructions. The marked box held death; the other held life. This ritual was supposed to be a game of chance, fate directed by Ostara's will, but Dr. Fetch had interceded for me. And now, despite my prayers, I was being punished by Ostara: mine was the hand which held my sister's fate.

I wanted to stop time, to reveal the deception, to demand we start over. But I knew better. We'd begun the ritual, and we must see it through. My heart thudded painfully in my chest, a snared hare. It broke something inside me to make the choice, to know that Lia stood behind me, waiting her turn. I reached for the marked box, hesitated, then picked the unmarked box instead. I stepped back, avoiding Lia's eyes.

"Step forward, Lia, and accept what remains."

Lia took the last box and walked, trembling, back to her place.

Reverend nodded to Mom, and she opened her box and pulled out a bright, red apple. Next, Dad opened his box. It held a loaf of bread.

Reverend turned to me. I reached into my box and pulled out two large, white eggs.

Lia looked at me, understanding and anger in her face. She knew that I'd cheated, somehow. She opened her mouth as if to speak, but hesitated. Her face became still and resolved. Guilt, fear, and sadness rushed through me. But someone had to die, and it couldn't be me. Lia had to understand that, didn't she? The community needed me to replace Dr. Fetch when Ostara called her body to the earth, and God took her spirit heavenward. Would Lia understand, or would she halt the offering?

Lia pressed her lips firmly together and looked away from me. She reached inside the box. Slowly, hands shaking, she pulled the hare's head out by one ear. His eyes were half-closed, his mouth open in surprise. Through blood-clotted fur, I could see the pink-white edges of cervical vertebrae.

When Harvey was born, he'd been the runt of the litter. Lia had bottle-fed and tended him before he'd even opened his eyes. Now, she held his severed head.

Tears ran down her face, down Mom's and Dad's faces. My own cheeks were dry, though I knew the tears would come later. Behind my ribcage, my heart shuddered. Bile flooded me, and I hated myself, hated that Dr. Fetch's cheating and my desire to live had sealed my sister's fate. But even as my heart broke, I curled my fingers tightly around my box and did not regret my choice.

Reverend and Dr. Fetch moved towards Lia. She trembled but didn't flee. Reverend offered the cup to Dr. Fetch, and she added a medicine I recognised, one I'd helped make. It removed pain from the body and made the mind go calm and far away.

"Do you, Lia Abraham, of your own free will, take this cup?" Reverend held the cup filled with Isaac's blood and Dr. Fetch's medicine to her lips. "Do you, of your own free will, accept the death within it?"

"I do," Lia said, voice barely a whisper.

"Then take it and drink."

Hands shaking, she reached out. Her nose wrinkled at the taste and smell, but she drank.

Reverend offered the cup to Mom, Dad, and then me. His eyes were firm, but kindness softened the firmness.

"Do you, Jana Abraham, of your own free will, take this cup? Will you bear witness to the death of Lia Abraham?"

"I will," I said.

"Then take it and drink."

Despite all the times I'd assisted Dr. Fetch while she set a bone or pulled a child from a screaming mother's womb, I'd never tasted blood before. The blood was warm and thicker than I'd expected, thicker than water. The ancient saying was true. Salt coated my tongue and throat. I pushed down my nausea as I swallowed. A wave of calm washed over me. Reverend walked past me and offered the cup to the guards. Only he and Dr. Fetch didn't drink.

"Lia, please step forward," he said, gesturing to the empty throne opposite Isaac's remains.

Lia looked at me again. Love, anger, and resentment burned in her gaze. Then she turned away. Reverend took the box and Harvey's head from her and set them carefully on the table. Lia stood, gaze unfocused, as Dr. Fetch picked up her scissors and carefully slit her dress open from hem to collar. Barefoot and wearing only her undergarments, she must've been cold, but Lia didn't shiver. Dr. Fetch guided her onto the unoccupied throne.

"The Hare Mother honours your sacrifice, daughter," Reverend said. "She does not wish you to suffer unnecessary pain."

He held the cup to her lips again, and Lia drank deeply until her eyes went soft and unfocused, and she sank against the back of the throne.

Dr. Fetch stepped to the table and picked up a clean scalpel. Reverend bowed his head, hands folded in front of him. Lia stared straight ahead as Dr. Fetch's practised hands moved down her stomach, and the scalpel slid through her skin like it was butter. Blood trickled out in red rivulets. Dr. Fetch made three precise cuts, forming a rectangular window around her belly button, much smaller and neater than the hole she'd made in Isaac. When she eased the skin and muscle away, I could see Lia's stomach. Dr. Fetch gently pushed it aside, leaving a bloody cavity. Reverend stepped forward and handed her Harvey's head.

The head fit into the cavity like a child curled inside its mother's womb. Dr. Fetch took up a new suturing needle and stitched Lia closed with care. My own fingers twitched at my sides, my hands mirroring her movements. Someday my hands would be that skilled and precise.

The entire time, Lia didn't look at Dr. Fetch or at any of us. Her breathing quickened as her body slid into shock, probably from blood loss, but her face was blank, serene. I'd never noticed before how large and dark our eyes were, the colour of earth after a summer storm.

Dr. Fetch finished the stitches and took up her sharpest knife. The light gleamed off its unsullied edge. Her arm moved in a single, decisive slash across Lia's throat. Lia convulsed once, twice – then went still.

Seeing my twin dead before me, her sightless eyes still gazing serenely at the dirt ceiling, should have throbbed like an open wound. I knew that tomorrow I'd mourn her, that I'd despise myself, that I wouldn't be able to look Dr. Fetch in the eye. Tomorrow, the whole community would honour and mourn Lia. Her funeral would be beautiful, though the casket would be empty.

But now Dr. Fetch's medicine filled me, leaving room for nothing but the taste of salt and the smell of blood. It was done;

there was no turning back time. We had done what was best for all. Praise Ostara.

Reverend began a familiar scripture, one I'd heard so many times my lips moved in tandem as he spoke.

"In the beginning was the world, and the world was wicked," he said. "And so, God sent a flood, and humankind was humbled. But we forgot the lesson, and so God sent a second flood, humbling us further. If not for the mercy of the Hare Mother, our ancestors would have perished."

"Hail Ostara, the merciful," we recited automatically.

"Ostara sent us to this rich and fecund land."

"Hail Ostara of the Fields."

"She sent us braces of hares to eat."

"Hail Ostara, Hare Mother."

"As the hares have fed us, so too do we feed the hares."

"Accept our sacrifice, Dread Ostara."

"Amen."

Reverend fell silent. My gaze drifted from Lia's body to the dark corners of the room. To the tunnels, spiralling off into darkness. I wondered how far they went: how far out, and how far down.

The sounds were faint at first, so faint I thought I was imagining them. The scuffle of small bodies moving steadily across the dirt floor. Then I saw eyes gleaming in the lantern light, one pair, two, a dozen, a multitude. Hares poured into the room, hares of every colour. They surrounded Lia and Isaac, concentric circles of hares, spiralling unending lines of hares. Hundreds of gleaming eyes studied us. And more kept coming, pouring from the tunnels.

Reverend bowed low to the hares. I found myself folding too, my spine curling against my will. And then Reverend was retreating, and we fell into step behind him, heading back the way we'd come.

As she headed past me, Dr. Fetch paused to whisper in my ear.

"I know it's hard, Jana, but you made the right decision. The community needs a doctor, and I am too weary to train another. Ostara understands and honours your sacrifice." She squeezed my wrist then turned and followed the others out of the room.

I was the last to leave, and though I knew I shouldn't, like Lot's wife I looked back. Lia was covered in an undulating sea of twitching fur. I could hear the hares gnawing at her, see the blood staining their paws and twitching noses. From the tunnels, thousands of bright eyes approached, waiting for their turn at communion. I turned and followed the others, my mouth dry and coated with salt.

UNDER COVER OF DARKNESS

Stephen Volk

We thought the best plan would be to remove it discreetly, quietly, causing the minimum of fuss or attention. The story was, as far as the press were concerned, that the family had requested it after the allegations had come to light 'out of respect to the public' – but in reality I was the one who had got the ball rolling. As soon as the Met announced there were over seventy-five separate lines of enquiry, and upwards of twenty more victims had spoken out, it became pretty clear, to me anyway, that something had to be done.

There was a creeping realisation, after decades of gossip and innuendo, that these accusations were not going to be swept under the carpet as they might have been in previous years. The perpetrator was no longer around to use his influence with those in power, or to threaten those he had sexually abused with legal action. That he had operated like that for so long was a cause of horror and mystification for many, while others, with twenty/twenty hindsight, basted themselves with the congratulatory knowledge he was always a 'wrong 'un' – yet what had they done to prevent anything? Precious little. It was a whole sorry mess for all concerned, and all concerned unfortunately included me.

Tragically – if one can use such a word; perhaps ironically would be better – the headstone had only been unveiled in January, a mere three weeks before I went to the council to get permission to have it removed. Eleven months after his death. During which time numerous reports had emerged which painted a horrendous picture of the former national treasure as an appalling and habitual molester of underage girls.

Simmy Noble.

As I explained to the council officers round the table, his name had already been taken off an inscription to the great and the good in Clayton Civic Hall. His name on a local footpath had been removed. His holiday cottage on the Isle of Wight had been sprayed with graffiti.

"Hell, a plaque outside his flat in Oxworth has had to be taken down after the words *Rapist* and *Paedophile* were written on it… It's only a matter of time before the headstone gets the same treatment," I said. "Pro or con."

A pot-bellied man in a rugby club tie stiffened his back and asked me what I meant – "Pro?"

"Some tearaway who wants to outrage the public," I said. "You hear about swastikas daubed on gravestones. Young men get up to all sorts of vile nonsense to get noticed."

Someone I'd forgotten the name of from the Burial and Cemeteries Team was cleaning his glasses with a lint cloth.

"Is it our job, though?"

I fixed him with my eyes. "I think it's mine. I buried the feller."

He said, what he meant was, wasn't it the responsibility of the police, and the family? The police if it was a criminal act, and the family, well…

"I'm happy to talk to the police and I'm happy to talk to the family," I said. Having arranged Noble's funeral, they weren't strangers to me and it would be better coming from someone they knew rather than a council jobsworth. That could have the worst possible effect. I thought they'd have to agree with that, and they did. At that point coffee, tea and biscuits arrived on a rather quaint hostess trolley, which I thought incongruous given the discussion we were having.

"It's not a question of that," a Thatcheresque woman said when I implied they were procrastinating. "It's a question of things going wrong. What if it attracts more publicity? We don't want that for the city."

I laughed. "Well, you've got it if you do nothing. *Bad* publicity."

Someone concurred with me on that, thank goodness. Another person backed him up, and soon there were no naysayers, though the one with the Thatcher helmet of hair still sat on the fence somewhat.

"Look," I told her straight. "We have got to do something. We can't eradicate the grave, but we can stop *advertising* it."

Luckily, that word hit home. Nobody argued the toss after that, and all we had to do was forge through the details in plodding, semi-disgruntled fashion. Like all politicians, they were primarily concerned with diverting the flak, keeping their heads down, and maintaining their jobs. At no point did I get any gratitude for coming to them and alerting them to a potential disaster – which was fine. All I was bothered about was the site becoming some kind of horrid tourist attraction for ghoulish visitors. The kind of rubberneckers who slow down at car crashes, or those who go out of their way to attach themselves to even the vilest examples of fame. I had little doubt there were some out there, even, who refused to believe he had done anything wicked – that it was all malicious lies by greedy young women – so dedicated were they to an image of Simmy Noble as some kind of secular stained-glass window saint. I said I did not want to give those people a point of pilgrimage.

"God help us," said the man responsible for grounds maintenance, setting off shuffles of rumps and nods of agreement.

I knew most of them by name, in fact. It had been a rigmarole to comply with cemetery regulations for what was a substantial funerary edifice. The monumental mason had to be signed up with the council's registration scheme, which ours was, and the application had to include a design approved to proceed to the cemetery supervisor. You had to set a date for an initial stability test (not before thirty days after installation) and the stability had to be guaranteed in writing by the mason (with the exception of malicious damage, severe storm, or subsidence). Paperwork, paperwork – and all for what? Now we were going to pull it down and use its fragments as landfill.

The plan was to do it covertly and under the radar, for expediency's sake and to avoid a media circus. Issue a press release telling them it would be done on the Wednesday, but – my suggestion – actually do it on the Tuesday night, before anybody noticed. Basically, get it done quickly and get out of there. No prior warning to anybody except those directly involved. In fairness, once this was decided, nobody questioned the logic of getting it done, sooner rather than later. Our conversation thereafter was a technical one.

I visited the family. Talked through the problem much the same way I had with the council and they were fine with it. Relieved, I think, at the thought of somebody else taking control. I think they trusted me. They were decent enough people, battered and bruised by the storm of events around them, through no fault of their own. They didn't see me as the enemy. I hope not, anyway.

I conceived the wording of their statement with their solicitor and we released it to all branches of the media: 'The family have made the decision to remove the gravestone because of the impact it would continue to have on the dignity and sanctity of the cemetery for those who tend graves of their loved ones and visit them.'

The white lie that we were doing it on the Wednesday was something I'd have to deal with when appropriate, and roll with the punches, if necessary.

On the Tuesday afternoon I closed the office at 4:30 and drove home to try to get a few hours' sleep as it was going to be a long night. That turned out to be a vain hope. My wife always found it easy to have an afternoon snooze but I never could, and this proved to be the case. After tossing and turning in my bed I got up and watched afternoon TV, which was a rare joy I wasn't used to. Quiz shows with smarmy comedians exhibiting the same kind of unctuous charm the deceased used in his prime. Consequently I found them hard to watch. My wife said I was so twitchy I was making her twitchy too.

"Sorry," I said.

At 8:30 p.m. – still way too early – I changed out of my house pants and T-shirt and said I'd better make a move. She stood up and kissed me on the cheek, saying she hoped it would go well. I said I was sure it would.

Barney and Megan were glued to the television screen. My imminent departure made my son look up, startled. "Where are you going?"

Before I could answer, my wife said I had a meeting.

"What, now?"

"Boring," I said, kissing each of them on the top of their heads. The boy had just got out of the shower and smelled of posh shampoo. Stealing his mother's. He was that age, the devil.

Megan held out her hand and we fist-bumped. "Smash it, Dad."

She had no idea that's what I would be doing. Literally.

I drove my own car, not the business vehicle which was a grey personal ambulance, what we call a deceased removal vehicle. I decided to dress in the pleated, striped trousers, herringbone jacket and doeskin waistcoat I wore for funerals, rather than my first instinct, which was sweatshirt and jeans. If anyone were to spot me I didn't want anyone badmouthing the firm based on lack of decorum or insensitivity. That would be bad for business. I didn't want to look slovenly anyway, out of regard for my profession as much as anything.

I thought I'd drive around for a bit and clear my mind. I turned on the radio but the kids had tuned it to a station of their choice and it blared out Alvin Stardust singing 'My Coo Ca Choo' – which I could only stand for a few seconds before poking the OFF button. It was just the sort of pop song Noble would have played during his breakfast show in his heyday, interspersed with inane banter and moronic catch phrases. The background banality to all our lives.

With time to kill, I found myself aimlessly circling the district of town near where I was brought up. I always say, the feeling of being raised in a Christian household was like being given the antidote for a poison you didn't know yet.

I found myself passing what used to be our local church. I envisaged sitting in a pew and having some quiet time with my thoughts. I should have known the door would be locked due to the ever-present possibility of vandalism. So, as it was, I sat in my car with the heating turned up, in all the comfort of Swedish engineering.

At about half past nine I pulled in and filled up with petrol, picking up a Crunchie at the counter, since I hadn't been able to face the big dinner of lasagne the rest of the family were having earlier but now needed the energy boost of some sugar. I stopped to eat it in a side road beside a discount carpet warehouse and sat with my eyes closed, before realising it was daft putting off the inevitable and silly driving in circles.

Twenty minutes later I flipped my indicator and took the inside lane coming off the familiar roundabout, turning right past the old hotel. At the entrance to the cemetery a policeman standing next to his motorbike waved me on. They were in place and expecting us. Good.

I drove up the narrow single-track road that followed the circumference of the graveyard, up a gentle slope to the East Gate where there were a few empty parking spaces, a line of three stopcocks for filling vases with water and a bin for the disposal of dead flowers. I was glad to see the media had gone and the police were as good as their word in keeping the location sealed off and sacrosanct. Two officers stood either side of the gates, yellow Hi-Viz tabards shining brightly in my headlights. One extended her right arm to direct me to the flat upper road overlooking the tiers of headstones that populated the various terraces zigzagging to the chapel below. I pointed the car towards the familiar obelisk where the paths met, the cenotaph where the dead of two world wars were recorded. Halfway along, framed in my windscreen and off to the left, I made out two arc lights on tall, extendable stalks, the kind you see casting their beams downwards when there are roadworks on the motorway at night. They illuminated a group of almost static silhouettes that took on more definition as I moved closer.

I recognised our work vehicle, the grey Renault Trafic. I'd asked three of my employees to be in attendance. The floodlights picked out Tod's shaved head in an unforgiving way, like a white ball on a billiard table. Marta was wearing a green cagoule over her black suit. Ever practical.

I got out of my car and put on the black overcoat that was folded on the back seat. Immediately I could hear the hum of a generator, and saw a JCB lurking in anticipation, like an actor in the wings waiting for his cue. I also noticed grounds contractors with spades and picks, squarely built chaps in Hi-Viz smocks and wellies, guys used to getting their hands dirty. Though this was a dirty job in a way far beyond getting muck under your fingernails. We were all aware of that.

Nods were exchanged.

I shook hands with a uniformed senior police officer who gave me his name. I gave him mine. I wished I'd brought gloves, as he had, and instead sank my hands into my overcoat pockets.

The weather was cold – colder that you'd expect in February.

You could see your breath. It seemed to emphasise that we were the living.

Only the most cursory orders needed to be given. We all knew why we were there. It seemed slightly ironic that the dead man's entire career was based on his gift of the gab, and here we were, hardly exchanging a syllable between us.

The headstone was a triptych, extended over three plots, its central rectangle having two wings either side, akin to the covers of an open book: something he never was. The grandeur of the thing was the kind you'd expect of captains of industry or tinpot dictators – a massive display of ego that now made me feel queasy. I'm sure I wasn't alone in that. Normally I consider black granite offers a sense of dignified contemplation, but that night all I could think was: they say black sucks in the light.

The middle block was emblazoned with his full name in gold and that of his parents, long gone, mercifully saved the ignominy of their son's abhorrent crimes. To right and left, etched portraits. The trademark 'bandido' moustache, the trademark glasses. All over, a list of his many glorious achievements. The benevolent causes, the charities he had supported or ennobled. Laurels conferred by royalty. A dubious record of his many visits to Buckingham Palace and Downing Street over half a century or more, hobnobbing and cosying up to the powerful who needed to bask in the sunlight of his radiance. Not knowing his ulterior motive for doing so. On the plinth below, that glib parting remark it was impossible to read now without disdain or anger:

"Make your last laugh a good 'un!"

It seemed grotesquely triumphant. Premeditatedly so. Rubbing in the fact that the star's greatness was now irredeemably gone. The apogee of not only fame and success but also altruistic goodness now transformed into the lowest of the low.

Activity around me almost took on the aspect of a mime show. People moved to their positions and went about their appointed tasks. Since my team and I were attending in a supervisory capacity, we mostly stood back in the customary stance of undertakers, one hand over the other, feet apart. At ease, yet anything but.

I felt for the neighbouring residents as the pneumatic drill went to work, its operator's eardrums protected. The surrounding householders hadn't been informed. I felt bad, but this had to be hush-hush if it was to be carried out efficiently. We couldn't afford someone to know in advance and ring the *Daily Mail* or *The Sun*.

Short, piercing bursts like machine gun fire emitted from the instrument, stone dust coughing up like smoke from gun barrels, or the decrepit mouth of an ancient celebrity with a penchant for cigars.

I was conscious that, underneath the monument, he lay in his golden coffin like some Egyptian Pharaoh of light entertainment. That was why he was encased in concrete, so I was told – to stop grave robbers digging him up. I could vouch for the fact he was buried resplendent in bling – the gold neck chains and jewellery that had become his daily attire. When I had talked to the council, we had given consideration to moving the body, but the cost involved would have been £20,000 and that would have had to have been covered by the family, and they were unwilling to do so, as they believed (rightly, in my view) the money was supposed to go to good causes.

Marta got mud on her shoes and wiped the sides of them in the long grass. She caught me looking at her but didn't smile. It wasn't a smiling night.

Platinum blonde and tiny, though anything but fragile, she had responded to my call out for an apprentice, and I count my lucky stars she walked through my door. She soon proved to have a rare openness and empathy perfect for the job. Perhaps it was her Polish upbringing that gave her a no-nonsense work ethic combined with dedication. I don't know. She could run the business when I was gone, I had absolutely no doubt of that, and it pleased me.

As the night wore on it became clear there wasn't an awful lot for us to do on a practical level. So it was a case of, as Mark Twain said: "I like hard work. I could watch it all day."

Soon my nose really did feel like ice. Occasionally, I'd pace up and down, just to exercise my legs and give my arms a ridiculous-looking swing or two, or blow into my cupped hands. From that high vantage point I could look out over the community of Clayton, seeing the lights in the windows, the rooftops as people slept.

I'd stare off into the shadows. If there was wildlife hereabouts – foxes, owls – they were keeping a low profile, perhaps intimidated by the presence of the arch-predator in the ground.

At around midnight the council workers took a short break. I wondered what the union rules were regarding the dismantling of a prolific sex offender's memorial. One of them sidled closer, shook his cigarette packet in my direction, offering me one.

"No, thanks."

He lit up. "Ever smoked?"

"Tried it when I was about sixteen. Could never get on with the things. Just gave me a sore throat. Could never understand what pleasure you'd get."

He semi-chuckled as he took a substantial drag. "Tried it once, didn't like it. Like girls, eh?" The only thing said that night that even remotely passed for humour.

"Hardly," I said. "Got a wife and two kids back home."

He asked what age.

I told him.

He said his three had flown the nest.

When he finished the cigarette he tossed the stub away. I watched the glow of it go out.

He made me think of my wife tucked up under the duvet in our double bed. I could see her head against the pillow patterned with roses. I wanted to be there lying next to her, not out in a cemetery freezing my so-and-sos off.

The drilling continued. Fissures appeared and black chunks fell away like calving glaciers.

Turning my back briefly, I saw a Thermos flask sitting in the foot well of the graveyard workers' vehicle. I wished I'd brought a Thermos too, and started to fantasise about the taste of really strong coffee. Then I thought not. In some deep sense I felt I deserved the punishment of the cold. I'd put him in the ground, after all. I was an associate of sorts, in some people's eyes. I was complicit in the charade.

It was well-known locally that I was the funeral director who had taken on his burial, but I had not asked for it. The family had come to me. Noble's father had been buried by us and he must have thought we'd done a good job, as *John Absalom & Son* was specified in his will. I admit – pre-revelations – we were flattered.

Not that his dad's service wasn't a bizarre affair. I'd observed at a distance his keening and tears, how Simeon Jr. had knelt in silent contemplation and prayer for hours. Was it possible for such a man to be pious and a devoted Christian considering what we later found out he had done over decades? I had no idea, and still don't. It's not my judgement to call. It's for Him upstairs to do that.

At the time, my own father had dealt with the TV star directly and I hadn't. I remember asking him after their first meeting what he made of the celebrity. Never given to passing judgement on anybody, my father summed him up in one telling word: "Grubby."

It was the literal filth of the creature that had struck him most forcibly. Rather than anything of actual worth, up close his personal accessories seemed more like costume jewellery. His Rolex, thick in dirt, had flakes of dry, discarded skin trapped between the links, festering with a greenish mould, he said. The bottle-bottom glasses were chipped and repaired with dabs of paint. Everything about him reeked of the unclean. Crumbs and detritus had gathered in the hairs of his moustache, the whole effigy of him soiled and matted, diametrically opposed to the gold-lamé apparition captured by the TV cameras.

Perhaps, like many people before and since, Dad had perceived him as projecting a strong-willed and upbeat persona that masked a fiercely narcissistic inner core. An individual used to getting his own way, by hook or by crook. Or maybe I'm just needlessly floundering around the word *evil*.

Not that I saw him as evil growing up, when I was a fan of his TV shows like every other child my age, though I never particularly found him a lovable presence. I found him creepy in a way that few of us could really explain. And, yes, there were rumours flying around throughout my journey to adulthood, yet nobody had any concrete proof of sexual abuse at the time he died, so his funeral was simply seen by us as a feather in our cap. Like anyone in my trade, my prime concern was that I wanted the family to be happy the service went smoothly and appropriately.

Then the allegations began to emerge, and I found myself being looked at with sideways glances, heard muttering comments behind my back. The association with fame had been tarnished, then poisoned, as the stories of the victims became more and more awful and heartrending. The image of the cheery, anarchic clown in his coat of many colours grew ever more monstrous and sickening.

It's my belief that every human being deserves dignity in death, but thinking back to his funeral, as I did that cold February night, I couldn't help but feel guilty that I had been a part of it. I asked myself, if I could go back, would I have taken on the job, knowing what I knew now? I'd have to answer: Yes, I would. Because even the worst of us is entitled to a communal ritual at their passing and the possibility of grace. I know many would say that some individuals deserve no respect or dignity at all, when their debased and selfish actions so denied the respect and dignity of others. And it's hard to argue that they're wrong. But if you don't believe in the possibility of grace in the next life as a Christian, what do you believe?

I stared up at the night sky.

Low cloud cover, no stars. The only star was in the ground.

The red dot of another cigarette end was flicked into the shadows.

Around me, things were winding down.

I looked at my watch. A cheap, unostentatious one. Christmas present from my son the year before. Bought with his own money, bless him.

We had started at 11:00 p.m. and were finished by 1:30. No mistakes. No surprises. No gawkers. A sense of completion was palpable. Everyone moved around more easily. Limbs looser.

The council team piled the pieces of black granite into a truck. Wheelbarrows of soil did some filling in surprisingly quickly, then sections of turf were laid over in the bare earth that was left. Rolled out like carpet runners.

Shortly after I'd arrived I'd moved aside half a dozen small bouquets that had lain beside the headstone. The cheap plastic wrapping seemed appropriately shoddy. Now I put them back in place upon the freshly embedded segments of lawn. I let them lie there not due to any respect for the dead man but rather to those who had left them, his grieving family and friends. Grief is universal, and so is pain. I equally knew that when those last, paltry floral tributes were gone, the grave would remain unmarked.

I quietly told Marta and the others to go home. Marta was typically thoughtful. "Are you sure, boss?"

I nodded that I was.

"Thank you. Thank you everybody."

Under normal circumstances I might have asked them to stand at the graveside and bow their heads in respect. But these were not normal circumstances.

Watching them drive off towards the East Gate, I caught my dim reflection in the side window of my car and saw the silvery glisten of morning dew on the shoulders of my overcoat. I ran my fingers through my hair and found it wet.

I followed the council van to our monumental mason's yard, not far from our sister office, a drive of an hour and a half away. His instructions were to grind off the inscriptions – name, dates, litany of achievements; most of all the odious, chirpy innuendo on the plinth. I wasn't obliged to accompany them, but I was adamant I wanted to see it done, first hand. I wanted no possibility that any fraction of the memorial would remain. That anything would be missed, done wrongly, or put to one side to inadvertently end up as some sort of trophy on eBay, or in some warped mind's private museum.

The stonemason, whom I trusted implicitly, switched on the grinder and got to work without hesitation. The room filled with a thick, toxic cloud. The workshop became opaque, like a New York street after 9/11. Eddie was an old friend of my dad. Chain smoker. Never wore a mask. I dreaded to think what the stone dust was doing to his lungs. I had a feeling I'd find out one day.

"Thank you for coming in," I said, hours later, when he'd finished, and the material had been, ostensibly, pulverised. "Go home and get your beauty sleep."

The object had been reduced to the smallest possible fragments, bagged up and dumped in a skip. In the early hours of Wednesday, it gave me pleasure to watch it being hoisted up on rattling chains, taken off to its final destination.

The encrusted hands shook mine.

"Good riddance," the old man with stone dust in his beard said, turning away.

I was grateful when the sun started to peek out as I drove home, gradually lightening the world as it lightened me. Little paintbrush strokes began to delineate buildings, outlining the cityscape as dawn prodded it awake. Something I didn't remember experiencing before, except for all-nighters during my mis-spent youth: the day stirring. Morning seemed to belong to rubbish collectors in green overalls trundling wheelie bins. Frowning runners urgently consulting their watches. Girls in swishing ponytails pausing to lean against lamp-posts to stretch their hamstrings.

Needing a soundtrack, I didn't want the radio on but instead reached into the glove compartment, took out a CD and slid it into the slot in the dashboard. I let John Dunstable's incredible *Veni Sancte Spiritus* envelop me with its magical counterpoint and sweetness, asking the Holy Spirit to come and save us from Purgatory. It elevated me immediately as it always did. My wife was bored of hearing me say this was the music I wanted at my funeral.

I parked in the driveway, careful not to slam the car door. The bedroom curtains were still drawn, as I knew they would be. The idea of my russet-haired Rhinemaiden lying rested and toasty against her pillow was so absorbing that cuddling into her was an intoxicating prospect which excited me for a second, but what time was it? 5:30 a.m. – far too early to wake her. Let her sleep. Let everybody sleep.

I took off my overcoat and hung it in the hall. I noticed the sleeves were covered in a layer of powder. The stone dust. I tried to brush it off with the flat of my hand but it just smeared. It would have to go to the dry cleaner's.

I dropped my car keys on one of the kitchen surfaces. Took off my jacket and put it on the back of a chair, the grey waistcoat over it. I filled and switched on the kettle, loosened my tie and undid the top button of my shirt. It was still pretty dark outside the kitchen window, that ailing conifer a ghost of green and brown.

The silence suddenly struck me. This was usually the noisiest room in the house and it didn't seem right for it to be calm and peaceful, devoid of domestic turbulence. I actually wanted some of that turbulence – craved it, actually. The babble of voices arguing over the inconsequential. *Where's this? Where's that? Under your nose, where it usually is.* The hum of the hair dryer in the hall. *Mum? Dad? What? Do it yourself!*

Before I forgot, I took out my phone and emailed the family, as I promised I would. Nothing flowery, just informing them it had been done. Somehow, that small action of pressing SEND did for me.

The sudden relief was overwhelming. Exhaustion hit me and I sat at the kitchen table, immobile, with my face in my hands. The weight of all the tension I'd carried lifted from my shoulders like a massive boulder. A millstone of responsibility.

It was over.

After a good five minutes I stood up, my legs like jelly from tiredness, poured myself a glass of Jameson's and knocked it back in one. Most unlike me. I didn't even like spirits most of the time, but it did its job. I needed to drive to the press conference at midday – for that I needed a clear head and a few hours' kip, and the whiskey would help, I hoped.

As the sharpness anaesthetised the back of my throat a voice inside me told me I should pray. Not for him, not for me. I don't know who for.

Clasping my hands together, for some reason I thought of the words from Luke 17 in the King James version: *And if he trespass against thee seven times in a day, and seven times in a day turn again to thee, saying, I repent; thou shalt forgive him.* But it was a passage in Ephesians I had used in many a service for the dead that came to my lips:

"Let all bitterness, and wrath, and anger, and clamour, and evil speaking, be put away from you, with all malice. And be ye kind one to another, tender-hearted, forgiving one another, even as God for Christ's sake hath forgiven you."

I sat in silence, watching the shade lift from the colourless garden.

I waited until 6:15 a.m. before making a cup of tea to take up to my wife. She'd be rousing then, or thereabouts; she always did, wide awake while I snored for Britain, as she never ceased telling me. Larks and owls, we were. Yin and yang.

I whirlpooled the tea bag with a spoon. Splash of milk. No sugar. She liked it strong, borderline stewed. Soon it would be time to rouse Megan and get her ready for school, which her dad would do for once. I took out boxes of cereal and placed them on the kitchen table. The bowl she insisted on, ready for madam. Sunlight tentatively filled the room. It would be a day like any other day. The darkness had been dispelled.

Mug in my hand, I placed one foot on the first step of the staircase when a groggy, muffled voice came from above.

"Daaad?"

The voice of my ten-year-old daughter, just breaking the surface of deep sleep. I conjured the image of her little arms stretching up in her pyjama sleeves before she opened her eyes. It was what she said next that turned my blood to ice and froze me to the staircase like an enchanted statue in a fairy tale. And I want to disbelieve it now, just as I tried to deny I'd heard it then, even though the earth opened beneath me.

"Daa-aa-aaad? Why did you kiss me on the back of my neck just now?"

DUSK

Angela Slatter

Sommerset House is enormous. A white rectangle, two storeys and an attic high, columns wrapping all sides, sash windows, dark shutters. Manicured lawns. Innocent-looking as if its history is nothing to do with it; the outbuildings dismantled some while ago. *Nothing to see here.* Rather like a man pretending he hasn't just stepped in dog shit. But that stink just never goes away.

About a forty-minute drive from anywhere useful.

A lot of the surrounding land – out past the gardens – is much wetter than it used to be. Rising water levels, climate change, no matter how much it's denied. More swamp, more bayou, the paths that wind through the estate getting more picturesque, but also less visible, less reliable, than they once were. Mists creep in morning and night like cats slinking, not there one moment then suddenly thick and present as can be. Daylight burns them off, but only temporarily.

Sissy likes watching them from the verandahs, happy at a distance; does not wish to wander in them. Right now, staring out the kitchen window as the last tail of white shrivels in the sun, waiting for the kettle to boil and the egg in the saucepan beside it, she takes a moment to be pleased with herself.

A lot of nurses wouldn't have taken this job – and a lot of them didn't, she knows – but Sissy isn't a lot of nurses. She's not afraid of hard work, troublesome patients, remote locations, and being without any kind of backup or supervision. In fact, she works best without anyone else looking over her shoulder.

As if on cue, the door swings open to reveal Henrietta Beaulieu – Mrs. B, as Sissy has dubbed her. And Sissy knows this just pisses her off – she could tell by the way the woman's shoulders went back a little further, her chin lifted a little higher when she'd introduced herself, that the housekeeper was proud of her name. That's okay, Sissy is sure to make herself helpful, which is especially handy at this very moment when Sommerset House is down a maid, and Mrs. B isn't so proud that she wants to be doing all the labour herself. So, if she has to suck on an annoying nickname like a bitter lozenge for a while, then so she will. Sissy doesn't push it, though, no need to poke the bear. Although, in places like these, Sissy always ensures the patients like her, because in places like these the infirm rich hold sway.

"Morning, Mrs. Beaulieu," – *let's not start the day by pushing it* – "I hope you slept well."

"Good morning, Sissy." Polite, reluctant. Sissy insists on going by her first name, insists no one call her 'Nurse Symanski'. One of those tricks to get folk to like you; don't rub your title in their face, makes you seem approachable. Benign. "Yes, thank you. And yourself?"

"Not too shabby. Now, can I make you something? Kettle's almost boiled." Up until Sissy arrived, the housekeeper had been spending her nights dozing on a chaise in the patient's room in case anything was required. The nurse's hiring means she's got some of her life back – a lack of sleep will erode even the most long-term devotions, and Henrietta Beaulieu had boasted to Sissy that she'd worked for Mrs. Sommerset for almost thirty years.

"That's kind, but no, thank you." A thin twitch of the lips, passing for a smile. Then Mrs. B leaves; Sissy grins. The housekeeper will return the moment Sissy's gone. Doesn't want to stay lest she have to endure more polite conversation. Sissy's watched her scurry back in when she thinks the nurse has disappeared. Probably checking the number of teabags to make sure Sissy's not stealing those. Long-term staff sometimes come to regard their employers' possessions as an extension of their own – things no one else is going to steal except them.

Sissy can't imagine staying in one job, in one place for so very long. Luckily, she's patient, but that's because she knows there's a pot of gold at the end of this dim and dusty rainbow.

The kettle whistles and the toaster pops at the same time. Both appliances are ancient – the former goes on top of the stove, and the latter is big and heavy, one of those brands they don't make any more because the products were just too long-lasting. While there's a lot of money in this house, there's also a tendency towards not wasting things; no replacements just for the sake of it and if anything can be fixed, it will be. Just about everything's old-fashioned, from the antique furniture to the bone china teapot Sissy fills with hot water, drowning all the loose leaves. She's careful with the three-minute egg, quickly runs it under the cold water tap, then into the eggcup. The toast goes onto a matching plate (so fine she can see the light through it); she scrapes on a little butter, then swirls a whole lot of honey. Sissy loads the polished wooden tray, adds the slender white vase with the single yellow rose to the array, and heads out.

Sissy's movements are slow and sure, almost meditative. She tends towards the methodical, finds it calms the people around her. Calms her too, and she's better, smarter in those calm times – and Lord knows she's been given to panic in the past and hasn't that cost her? So now, she likes to take her leisure, get all her ducks in a row, and all those other clichés that help her feel okay about what she's doing.

She's been here three weeks now and wishes she had more time.

The staircase is monumental, but she doesn't mind because both sides are a gentle curve upwards. Sissy likes the stately walk she can affect. The chandelier hanging in the foyer tinkles. Sissy pauses, looks back: the front door's open. Mrs. B will be out on the verandah, overseeing the three gardeners whose names Sissy hasn't bothered to learn. The dangling crystals throw prisms of light on the walls and stairs and that enchanted moment is something Sissy looks forward to every day; she thinks Stevie would like it too.

And those noises have stopped bothering her. Working in hospitals in her early days she became used to all manner of *susurrations* – she knows the word's meant for 'whispering' but for the longest time it's been Sissy's hold-all for the sorts of indistinct-sounds-seemingly-with-no-source that flutter around corridors in the middle of the night. The things that seem to brush by you when nothing's to be seen, the *kiss* of something that's just passed through a doorway either real or otherwise. Things that may or may not be there.

A soft something slips past her – the first time it happened she'd thought it a very quick cat, but now she thinks of it as the something-on-the-stairs. There's no harm in it. Just that gentle *whoosh* as she steps onto the landing and along to Mrs. Sommerset's master suite.

The tall doors, pristine white, creak a little as Sissy pushes her way in – the latch has been pinned back for ease of ingress and exit. Better when your hands are full; a tray, medical supplies, fresh linen and all. The housekeeper is technically in charge of changing the beds, but Sissy always insists on dealing with her patient's, making sure the old lady's not jostled too much or disturbed. And she's also been helping Mrs. B with the rest of the beds in all those rooms kept for Mrs. Sommerset's five children, just in case they come to visit (which they have not done so far during Sissy's tenure, nor any time in the recent past as far as she can tell). Sheets are changed every week, as are the flowers, and the spaces aired so they don't get stale. Same with the guest room that little lawyer uses once a week, because he generally arrives in the afternoon and spends dinnertime with his client, then stays the night. He drives the forty minutes back to Temple Cove at dawn.

"Morning, Mrs. Sommerset," Sissy calls gently, and steps behind the silk privacy screens. The high-tech bed is at odds with the antique furniture (Louis Quatorze, if she's not very much mistaken). Carpets thick underfoot dampen the noise of footsteps, even though polished wood would be more hygienic. There's just the hum of the refrigerator in one corner, and a little birdsong from the windows Mrs. B must have opened earlier.

The figure in the bed is wrapped in sheets and shawls like a mummy. The room's warm but the old lady's got no meat on her; she'd be cold in full sunlight on a summer's day in the Sahara. Mrs. Sommerset is seventy but could pass for a centenarian. In her preferred white nightgowns with high button-up necks, embroidered yokes and long sleeves, she looks like she's from another era. A cream silk scarf covers her bald head, and her face is furrowed and mostly immobile. Sissy's fascinated that someone whose only nutrition comes in liquid form is so desiccated.

"Morning, you," she says. And waits for those bright green eyes to flicker open, which they do, but more slowly than usual. "I brought your breakfast, I hope you're hungry."

This is the little show they do each morning. Sissy places the tray on the mahogany table beside the bed, makes sure it's close enough for the aroma of food to waft towards Mrs. Sommerset's nose. Carefully, Sissy decapitates the soft-boiled egg, feels the old lady's gaze on her. Pours the tea into the floral cup. Not that any of this matters: her patient can't drink or eat. All sustenance comes via the PICC line, but the lady of the house does like the *form* of how life once was – the ritual – to be observed, and she's rich enough that all her whims are obeyed.

Which is why that lawyer of hers (tiny weasel of a man Sissy can't bear) comes out once a week, just in case the grand dame decides to change her will (scratching messages on a notepad). Which she's done with some frequency, Sissy'd heard, this child and that removed from the inheritance, later reinstated and another banished from their mother's affections – like a game of chess that only Mrs. Sommerset knows the rules of. Just to keep everyone on their toes.

Money, thinks Sissy, tends to make folk into assholes.

"Did you sleep well?" she asks as she checks the drip on the stand, the PICC line that's been the only thing keeping Mrs. Sommerset alive for many years. A repeated question, a safe question, and one she already knows the answer to: *yes, thoroughly drugged.* A soft grunt in assent.

Next she goes to the refrigerator – incongruous against the antique decor, the heavy ice-blue damask curtains, another chandelier suspended above – and selects a fresh bag of parenteral nutrition. It's not like it matters (*the chicken or the beef?*) but she makes a show of choosing anyway. While she's hooking it up, she jokes, "A fine vintage, I think Madam will like it. Pairs nicely with fish."

There's a sound from the bed that Sissy recognises as a laugh, and she smiles at the woman in her care. Sissy does all the necessary things to ensure her employer is clean and comfortable. When these duties are performed, she takes a seat and picks up the book from the beside table.

"A little more *Rebecca* today? Or would you like to switch to *Jamaica Inn*?" Mrs. Sommerset loves a gothic novel and Du Maurier fits the bill. A bit too grim for Sissy's tastes but it's not for her pleasure, is it? There's a noise that's recognisable even though it's not really a word, but the shape of it, the rhythm of it, a kind of hum from the throat rather than the lips.

"*Rebecca* it is then."

A lot of nurses wouldn't do this, but Sissy isn't a lot of nurses.

Truth be told, she's not a nurse at all.

★ ★ ★

Sissy likes to think that all her troubles started when she met Stevie, but she knows that's nowhere near the truth.

The only thing he made her want to do was settle down. And it had been good for a truly respectable while, almost two years – which for someone like her, who moved on a lot, was practically a lifetime. She *liked* Temple Cove and being by the water. She liked the little townhouse, the kindly neighbours who kept to themselves. She even liked the waitressing job at the little café. She really liked that her family didn't know where she was and that no one else had tracked her down after all these years. She'd been on, if not the straight and narrow, at least not the entirely twisted and wide spectrum of what was legal. And she hadn't been near a betting shop, racetrack, or poker game in that time. She liked that Stevie believed she was a better person than she was, so it made her *try*.

She'd also liked being able to make a living as a private nurse to rich folk – and really, wasn't 'nurse' such a broad term? It was a caregiver, right? And Sissy certainly had given care. She was smart, she'd picked up a lot working in hospitals after she'd first dropped out of school. Starting in the kitchens, doing cleaning jobs, helping anywhere and everywhere people would let her, and she'd listened – Sissy's a great listener – and asked questions. Learning. She might not have a degree or formal training, but by god, she had a mind like a steel trap and knew enough to live the lie. But she *really* was trying to be better.

When the demons took their claws out of her, Sissy was a model citizen, or looked like one at least. But the problem with demons is that they slink back like alley cats you've made the mistake of feeding. One moment everything had been going along fine, then just the tiniest speedbump – a fight with Stevie, pointless and barely memorable – got Sissy Louise Symanski all het-up and her ingrained *I'll-show-you* DNA kicked in. A sports bar and a bunch of bets later, a loan from a guy called Paulie the Shark (the name, in hindsight, might have been a warning sign), left her owing more than she had a chance of paying back in a month of Sundays.

She'd bought herself some time with promises and lies, taking Stevie's savings from the lockbox beneath their bed as a downpayment – better to beg forgiveness than ask permission – but there was no way legal she was going to get out of this. And yes, she could have cut and run, but that would leave Stevie behind and Paulie the Shark somehow knew about Stevie and was happy to offer threats as incentives.

So, Sissy told Paulie she had a way to get the cash, but she needed him to be patient. It would take a couple of months, but she'd get him his money back with interest. And Paulie, observing that she seemed like a good kid, had *promised* to be patient.

Now, Sissy's outside, earbuds in but there's no music playing – it's just an excuse to ignore anyone speaking to her: Mrs. B calling from the house, the gardeners warning her about not leaving the paths. This is Sissy's breaktime and she's determined not to have it stolen. The old lady had a disturbed night, and therefore so did Sissy, and now she's got one of those tired headaches, tight behind the eyes, lethargic. She needs the fresh air for a while.

When she's out of earshot she'll try calling Stevie again. He hasn't picked up the last twenty-four hours, which is not unusual in itself – he's still processing what she did, what she's planning to do – but she wants to hear his voice. Ask him again if he's forgiven her – just the same way she did when she'd confessed, clinging to him and weeping until he said *yes*. Sissy wants to tell him she'll be home soonish. That she's got the situation well in hand.

The thing about rich people is that they've got *so much stuff*.

Sissy's got a system, tried and tested in her previous life, her BS era (Before Stevie, thank you very much). She starts by moving items around, just a little out of place, a few inches to the left or right, just to get a slight disruption going in what people expected to see as a matter of habit. Then after maybe a week, a statuette or trinket box or bronze bust, a Fabergé Egg or ormolu clock or Ming vase is shifted across a room, from a mantlepiece to a sideboard or a dining table or another plinth. If that first phase goes without a hitch (the oldies, who *really* did not like change, noticed such *adjustments* quickly), she begins properly hiding things – behind something else in the same room, or in another room (not in *her* room because she's not stupid), and if no one notices or mentions it after a month or so, then she taps a girl she knows. Annika works in an antiques store that's not too fussy about provenance – it's still reputable enough, but something like that only lasts so long – and sends a courier to whichever city Sissy might happen to be working in. Even though it'd been two years since they'd had any contact, Annika immediately replied to Sissy's text. That makes her kind of proud – that Annika knew she could be relied upon for quality merchandise.

Sissy's foot sinks and she's up to her ankle in muddy water; she almost loses her balance. Swearing, she steps back, looks around, focuses. She's wandered off the path; almost where the swamp begins. No *almost* about it – there it is, water and weeds and cypress trees with their damp skirts, things hiding beneath the surface, bubbling, bursting upwards where something breathes. She can't be seen from the house now, but then *she* also can't see the house; hyper-focusing makes her walk hyper-fast. Sissy takes her bearings and a deep breath, recognises the stone flowerpots with the last of their purple blooms; the gardeners will be replanting soon. She turns around and starts back towards the building with its columns and shutters and all those valuable and very portable treasures.

After her down payment meeting with Paulie the Shark, she'd gone somewhere to think (not drink, not again) and listen. The Salty Dog wasn't a dive bar but in a dim light it might be mistaken for one, being just on the border where 'the boardwalk' turned into 'the docks'. It was one of those places where conversations flowed over and around you, nuggets of gossip and truth that a good listener could pick out of the air. People under the influence of alcohol let their secrets slip like old pets they irrationally trusted not to wander. And that was where she'd heard the ex-Sommerset maid muttering to the bored-eyed barman dark and drunken snippets about the house, the old lady, and all the things inside those white, white walls that no one might miss. How they were hard-pressed to keep domestic staff, and couldn't get a nurse to stay. How she was sometimes late for work because she got lost in the gardens or coming up the drive; how things *moved*. Sissy decided the maid probably spent too much time drinking before work, and/or not sobering up from the night before.

So Sissy'd bought the girl drinks, asked some questions, bought more drinks, enough to ensure any memories of said questions and their answers would be hazy at best, non-existent at worst. Didn't bother asking *why* they have trouble keeping a nurse – she's done the job enough that she knows how fractious old people, sick people, rich people can be. Combine those three elements? It's a wonder anyone takes up nursing at all.

It was then just a matter of contacting the agency tasked with finding someone to look after the old lady (a name dropped by the ex-maid), dusting off her impressively forged resumé, and priming a couple of old associates to give glowing references. Sissy always makes a good first impression, and desperation to get a body out to the Sommerset estate meant that far fewer questions were asked of her than she'd asked of the ex-maid. Sissy'd resigned from the coffee shop – it would have been nice to just take leave, but who was she kidding? – and packed her bags. Stevie drove her out there because he still needed the car for work; that was okay, he'll collect her whenever she's ready.

Just before she steps back onto the front lawn, before she lets herself be seen again, she hits Stevie's name in her contacts list. Listens to it dialling, dialling, dialling. Sometimes she thinks it sounds like an insistent purr; doesn't find it so appealing as it goes through to voicemail. Her tone is terse when she leaves a message, telling him to get back to her, then starts moving ahead again.

It's getting on for time to make a decision: which piece to take?

There are smaller things around, less likely to be missed, easier to conceal, but there's also that huge vase in the formal dining room, smack-bang in the middle of that loooong polished walnut table. Not really a vase so much as a jar, because it's got one of those cute little lids. Sissy's willing to bet it's a Qing Dynasty Famille Rose piece. Usually these things come in pairs, but this seems to be an only child. And Sissy just happens to know, because she likes to stay abreast of such things, that one just like this sold in Hong Kong last year for almost ten million pounds on account of the rare glazes. To the untrained eye, it's simply pink and blue, but the pigments for that particular object were made from ingredients no one's been able to identify. Ever. So, they look different, if you know what you're looking for – and rich people love to own something unique just so no one else can have it. This one here might be a twin to that Hong Kong orphan. A fraction of almost ten million pounds would pay back Paulie the Shark, and let her and Stevie take an extended vacation.

She's moved it a couple of times, up and down the table a little, but no one's moved it back; it and a few other small items in different parts of the house, just to get an idea if someone's watching. Next step is to try it in a new spot – there's another vase, similar though not the same, that she can use to replace it. Such a big piece, though, so noticeable. It's dangerous, she knows – but then, Sissy recognises that even though this whole escapade is stressful, there's something she likes about the risk.

She tells herself, too, that no one's going to be hurt by this theft. Mrs. Sommerset has so much; her children won't miss that tiny bit of an inheritance when the old lady's gone. But bad things will happen to her and Stevie if she doesn't take it. So, really, she's like Robin Hood, stealing from the rich to give to the poor. She just happens to number herself among the latter.

* * *

It's late in the day when Sissy comes down the stairs, bearing the tray of food Mrs. Sommerset can't eat. She passes by the open door of the formal dining room, that Qing vase, those rare hues of pink and blue, catching at the corner of her eye. Tomorrow, she thinks, tomorrow she'll swap it for the other one, the one that's not quite so valuable. See how that goes.

Through the swinging door and into the cool of the kitchen, where Mrs. Henrietta Beaulieu sits at the table, partaking of a solitary meal. She never offers to make something for Sissy, even though it would be no extra trouble. Sissy's just filed that away. Mrs. B's doing the night shift; if Sissy were planning on staying, on embedding herself in this home, she'd insist another nurse be hired. Neither she nor the housekeeper are superhuman and the rest they're getting isn't really enough. Maybe she'll suggest it anyway: that sets up a good reason to leave (when she finally does) and also makes it sound like she's planning to settle in.

"Evening, Mrs. B."

"Sissy. How's the patient?" Mrs. Beaulieu almost manages to hide her distaste by sipping at the single glass of red wine she allows herself each evening. Sissy admires the restraint.

"No change, good or bad. I guess that's the best to be hoped for?" Sissy wonders how long Mrs. B is going to hang around, then decides she's hungry and doesn't care. She sets the tray onto the table and sits across from Henrietta Beaulieu. There's the medium-rare steak with baked potatoes and blanched French beans the housekeeper had prepared for Mrs. Sommerset earlier, and a glass of Chateau d'Yquem Sauternes 2019 (because the old lady doesn't care for pairing red wine with red meat). Sissy enjoys the scandalised look from Mrs. B as the nurse cuts into the steak, which will teach the old bitch to be so selfish. "Waste not, want not."

She puts a sliver of tender albeit lukewarm meat into her mouth and smiles around it. "Perfection, Mrs. B."

The housekeeper's eyes narrow into a Clint Eastwood squint, and Sissy figures she'd better make nice. "It's such a pity Mrs. Sommerset's kids don't visit."

The change of topic seems to throw the woman. "What do you mean?"

"Well, she seems like a nice old lady. And don't you think they'd be interested in their inheritance?" Sissy gestures around the kitchen by way of illustration. "All these nice things?"

The housekeeper's gaze shifts again, focuses and seems to settle on a kind of barely repressed rage. She hisses: "I know what you've been doing."

Sissy feels cold rush through her, but she's been keeping secrets for a long while and she's no amateur to overreact. She's definitely regretting baiting the housekeeper though. "Mrs. Beaulieu, I just don't—"

"I know you've been moving things around," – *which is evidence of nothing* – "trying to make me think I'm going mad."

Huh?

"You want *my* job? You've got no idea what I've had to do. But this is *my* place and you'll take it over my cold dead body."

Oh.

"Oh, Mrs. Beaulieu! You've got me wrong. I have no desire for your job! You do it so well, and Lord knows it's demanding." She summons an expression of embarrassment, shame. "I...the moving things. I...it's a problem with me, a compulsion. It's just – I had a very disrupted childhood and I'm told that this is a way of trying to exert a little influence over my environment – the sort I lacked as a kid." She hangs her head, looks away. "It's nothing to do with anyone else, and I'm so sorry that it upset you." As the final touch on her performance, she mutters: "I'm so ashamed."

There's a long pause, and she doesn't look up until she's got some tears to brim. The housekeeper's staring, stunned, as if not sure to believe her. But Sissy knows that the admission is just stupid enough and embarrassing enough to be credible. Childhood trauma has helped her weasel out of trouble more than once.

"Well," says Mrs. Beaulieu. "Well."

"I am genuinely sorry, and I will do my level best to keep the urge under control. It's such a silly thing, after all."

The housekeeper rises, takes her plate and glass over to the sink, scrapes any leftover food into the bin, pours wine dregs down the drain, rinses them and stacks the dishwasher. "Just so you...' Henrietta says, then: "the children..."

But she doesn't finish. Whatever kinder instinct was so briefly birthed is rapidly extinguished. Mrs. B shakes her head, and her expression turns brittle again. She dries her hands on a tea towel and exits. Sissy listens as her footsteps grow fainter, then lets out a sigh of relief. That was a close one, and will teach her not to get too cocky.

* * *

A little later, when Sissy's walking up the stairs to her own little room, the mobile in her pocket vibrates. The screen flashes Stevie's name. Sissy's awash with equal measures of joy and irritation. She clicks to take the call, is raising the phone to her ear and still isn't sure if she's going to be sweet or sour, when she hears the screams coming over the line.

Sissy freezes. Even without words she can tell it's him. Stevie. Screaming like a baby. She doesn't need to hear much of it to know she'll do anything she can to make it stop – but she still hears far more than she wants to.

Eventually, Paulie starts talking – but the screaming's too loud, so then he's shouting at whoever's hurting Stevie to "lay off, why dontcha?"

"Sorry about that," he says and he sounds sincere. "Now, you know why this is happening, right? You're taking too long, Ms. Symanski."

"But you said you'd wait!"

"I did, I did. But you know about big fish-little fish?"

Sissy stammers that she doesn't, although if her mind weren't so jangled by Stevie's screams she might be able to figure it out.

"So, you're a little fish – a tiny little minnow. I'm a much bigger fish – I eat minnows for breakfast. But you gotta understand, Ms. Symanski, that there are even bigger fish than me and *they're* gonna eat *me* for breakfast if I don't honour my debts. And me being soft and telling you I'd be patient coz you got that sweet face? Well, some of the bigger fish are less patient than I and of a far less pleasant disposition."

"Please, don't hurt him any more—"

"That all depends on you getting here with what you owe me plus interest for inconvenience caused." He names a figure, which wouldn't be a problem if she'd already passed that Qing vase onto Annika, but *is* an enormous problem right at this moment. And again, if Sissy was thinking straight, she wouldn't say what she says.

"I can get it to you. But I don't have a car. You'll have to come to me. I'll meet you out on the highway – don't come to the house. But only you. You come and get me, Paulie." Because she's going to have to do some fast talking and doesn't want to have to explain the value of the vase to one of Paulie's idiot henchmen. And if she tries to tell Paulie over the phone, he's going to hurt Stevie again. If she can only talk to Paulie face to face, get through to him how much money they'll have on their hands, then she can save Stevie. Can save herself. Sissy blurts out the address.

"Ms. Symanski, you sound genuine but you better not be screwing with me or it isn't going to go well for anybody."

Sissy swears she's not and he hangs up.

She's partway up the curved staircase, bending over to catch her breath and not vomit. When she's steady enough, Sissy straightens. The chandelier's not on, and the dusky glow filtering in from outside is the only illumination. Sissy tilts her head, listens carefully. No sound from above or below. Mrs. Beaulieu will be ensconced with her employer, and the gardeners will have gone home. If she goes now, there's just enough light to show her through the grounds, but not enough she'll be seen.

⋆ ⋆ ⋆

The vase is heavier than she remembered, but then, she's only ever slid it along the table, not actually picked it up, hefted it, taken it for a walk.

It was okay at first, sneaking across the lawns until she could connect up with the sealed drive where it went beyond sight of the house. It was okay. But then the driveway seems to be awfully long, so much longer than it should be, and she feels a fresh drop of panic in her brain, which joins the rest of the pool of panic that's already there given the events of the evening. Makes things worse.

The dusk light is mostly gone and the trees are closing in, making the lane narrower and narrower.

It's definitely getting heavier, this vase. The heavier it gets, the harder she finds walking and carrying. And though it takes a while, at some point she realises the vase isn't actually empty. Something's shifting about inside. She's resisting the urge to try and take off the lid, just to satisfy her curiosity.

Then she starts to wonder *why* a vase has a *lid*.

Sissy thinks back to that article about the Qing vase in Hong Kong, about those almost ten million reasons why she thought this was a good idea. And she remembers that the word 'vase' wasn't used at all.

It was 'urn'.

Funerary urn. Those needs lids, don't they? To keep things *in.*

It begins like butterflies, feathers. Soft laps against the skin. Pleasant.

Then less so.

More cumbersome. Like humidity clinging in high summer, sinking in until your very bones weigh a ton. And now, Sissy's feet are wet and she's sinking too. The driveway is no longer there, somehow she got turned around. Somehow, she left the path. Somehow she's in the middle of the fucking swamp, those cypress trees like prison guards, and there are mists creeping through.

She notices that the water and mud around her feet aren't so much pulling her in as the things like butterflies and feathers are pushing her down. Her steps falter, Sissy surrenders to gravity, still holding onto the urn.

The whispers start then, or perhaps they've been going for some while and she's only now listening. She thinks of the something-on-the-stairs and wonders if she's brought it out of the house with her.

Momma.

Momma.

Momma.

Momma.

Momma.

Distinct voices, she thinks. Five. Hollow. Echoing inside a porcelain funerary urn. Young. Infants? Babies? She thinks of the children who don't visit their mother. Realises she's never asked about them, where they are now, how long they'd lived. Why they don't come home.

They're already there.

The voices are bubbles in her ears.

The rushing of air from a thing trying to breathe underwater.

Maybe, maybe, maybe it's just the sound of her own drowning.

A FACE LEAVING NO TRACES

Brian Evenson

I awoke with a start, with that kind of deep indrawing of breath that comes from forgetting to, or being coaxed not to, breathe. I could feel sharp pains on the side of my neck, exactly two of them, very acute, and when I lifted my hand to touch them I was sure it would come away wet with blood. But even in the dark, I could tell it came away dry.

My wife was still asleep beside me, undisturbed, her body radiating heat. She was in no danger of awakening, so it seemed to me.

I left the bed, hand pressed to my neck, and took my phone from where it was charging. I thumbed the screen on and risked holding it close to her face: yes, it was her all right, her face relaxed, placid. Her eyelids didn't react to the blue light radiating softly off the screen, didn't tighten at all. I pressed the button on the phone's side and turned the screen off.

In the bathroom, I closed the door and turned on both lights, tilted my head for a better look. I was sure I had been bitten, had awoken certain of that fact. I could still feel the pain there on the jugular vein, one higher and one lower, where two sharp teeth had plunged in. But there was no mark at all, no tear or gap, no redness, no abrasion, nothing, nothing, nothing.

I probably should have simply gone back to bed, deciding what I had experienced must be a dream. I probably could, I realised, talk myself into believing it to be a dream. I can, when I choose to, pretend to be a person just like anyone else, can make the common decision not to pay attention to all that is wrong around me. But there has also long been something of the prophetic in me, a residue left by the strict religion I grew up in and eventually deserted. And so, whether it was a dream or not, whether it was real or not, whether it had happened or not, I had to believe it meant something. That it was, at the very least, a premonition.

And so I found myself wandering the dark and empty house, my body moving slowly and without discernible purpose, aimless, as I struggled to get my bearings. There had been a dream, I was sure of that, even if the details of it escaped me now. But I was also sure, somehow, that the dream was not of me being bitten, but of something else. *A dream of a face*, I came to believe, as I moved from the kitchen to the living room as if sleepwalking, *coming unbidden, unfocused and too close*. Or no, not that exactly. I ran my hand along the wallpaper, in the darkness feeling the slight irregularities that in the light I would be unable to see. It was more a slippery face, a face which left no traces. Or even more than that: a face-like seeming of a face, and not in fact an actual human face at all.

I stayed there, meditative, running my fingertips over the wallpaper, letting the vague tactile pleasure of the act tug me away from my thoughts. When, fingers buzzing, I returned to them, I was alarmed to find myself thinking of J.

⋆ ⋆ ⋆

Let me explain. I was at that point perhaps only half awake, confused. I was alarmed because in the past thinking of J. had always seemed eventually to summon her, almost supernaturally – had always returned her to my life precisely at moments when she would inflict the most damage. I had been committed, for years, to blocking all conscious thought of J. from my mind. This was the first time I had broken that rule.

I was more awake now, uncomfortably so. I told myself that I must not think about J., that this was the last thing I should do, but of course this only made me think of her all the more. She had seemed, when I first met her, like an ordinary person. She had a laugh, which had, at first, in those initial days of our connection, struck me as extraordinary and welcoming, but which, over time, seemed increasingly false. It came to resemble for me a fingernail scratching along the surface of my eye. When a colleague of mine who had paid her no heed before began, out of nowhere, to announce every time she laughed how great her laugh was, how wonderful, I began to realise the laugh was less a laugh and more a spell of some kind, and that the spell had largely stopped working on me.

J. and I had been together for a long time, years in fact, and I had managed to break my connection with her only at so-called great personal cost. I had, indeed, lost a thumb, which J. had severed by surprise during what I thought was a period of détente during a fight, but this felt like the least of my losses. By this time, I had come to believe that J. was not quite human. Or, rather, had once been human and no longer was. It had gotten bad enough that, once I had severed our connection, I felt I had to place wards around my house so as to prevent her from returning and trying to re-enter my life.

Which is why I found myself moving through the darkened living room, parting the drapes and looking out. I saw only the quiet and deserted night street, the sodium light of the streetlight throwing down a slightly tainted glow, its buzz just audible through the pane. Everything felt wrong, off. I couldn't see the wards I had made, nor, curiously enough, could I remember quite what the wards were or how I had made them. Disturbed, I drifted through the room and on to the kitchen, peering through first one window, then the other. I saw nothing through either that struck me as a ward, and I felt panic begin to rise. *Perhaps the gardener has picked them up and thrown them away by accident*, I thought, and then thought, *Gardener?* And suddenly I realised it had been years since I had had a gardener, years since I had lived in a house with a large enough yard to merit one. It was that house, the house with the twice-a-week gardener, which had had the wards. This was why, I told myself, reassured myself, everything had felt wrong, off. It was only that, nothing more. I did not need wards at this house for the simple reason that J. was dead, had died several years before, in circumstances I preferred not to ponder. *Even if you think about her*, I told myself, *she cannot come back.*

Of course, I did not believe this. If anyone could come back from the dead, it was J. No, even with her dead it was better not to think about her. And perhaps not a bad idea, even now, to fashion new wards, just in case. Not for J. necessarily, but for all the other things out there that might be looking for a way in. J. had died, I believed, in such a way that she would be unable to come back, but then again she had always seemed to show up in the most unlikely ways. She was very determined: who was she to allow a simple thing like death to prevent her?

But what would my wife think if I were to suddenly encircle the property with a line of salt? Or if I were to bind sticks together with twine, and place them on our front and back porches? Or if I were to begin once again to fashion the doll-like figures I used to make with paper and scissors, their bodies covered with words that were more than words, and began affixing them with iron nails above the frame of each room's door? Would she think I had gone mad? How would she respond when she realised these dolls fluttered slowly where they had been pinned despite there being no current of air?

I rubbed my neck, felt it tingle.

No, better to wait until morning when I was less disoriented, when I could see things more clearly, and make a decision then. It was a mistake to do anything now.

My hand, I suddenly realised, was resting gently on the handle of the front door. I was not sure exactly how it had gotten there, nor even, for a brief moment, if the hand belonged to me. Not knowing what else to do, and not willing yet to return to bed, I turned the handle and left the house.

* * *

It was colder outside than I'd anticipated, the air brisk. *I should go back inside for a jacket,* I thought, but instead stepped off the porch. I wouldn't be outside long, I told myself, and if my wife woke up and saw I was missing, it would be one thing for her to find me outside in my pyjamas and quite another if I was wearing my jacket. There was less spontaneity if I was wearing a jacket, more premeditation, and it would worry her and would require more explanation from me. Since I could not explain what I was doing even to myself, it seemed wiser not to go back for a jacket.

At first, I simply moved aimlessly around the front yard, as if vaguely searching for something, or as if investigating the source of a noise heard earlier from inside. And then, once this started to feel too contrived, I began slowly to circle the house. I moved as if I were someone else, a stranger coming upon the house for the first time, considering whether this was a house he had some reason to enter. *Yes*, I thought, *new wards are a good idea.* I was as silent as I could be and kept, best I could, to the shadows. There were a lot of shadows in my yard, I couldn't help but notice. Two or even three men could have hidden in them at the same time without glimpsing one another, or being glimpsed from the street, or from the house. Nevertheless, I was careful when I brought my face up just against the bedroom window. Would my face be visible from the inside? No, I didn't think so, but something would be, a face which left no traces – or not even that, a vague shape that might in fact be nothing at all. If my wife awoke and cried out on seeing me I would, I told myself, hurry back into the house, tell her I had heard, or thought I had heard, a noise, but there had been nothing there, there was no reason to be alarmed, I was sorry to have startled her. How quickly these lies spring unbidden to the mind, well before they are required!

But my wife did not wake up, or if she did she was not facing the window, or if she was facing the window she did not notice me, or if she noticed me she did not cry out but simply watched, watched, perhaps trying to decide if anything was really there at all or if it was just her imagination.

* * *

I circled the house nearly seven times, returning each time to the bedroom window. My bare feet were wet from the grass and tight with cold, and the cuffs of my pyjamas were sodden too. *Enough of this*, I thought, and moved the rest of the way around the house to the front porch. But then, instead of going inside, I found myself moving down the front walk and to the sidewalk beyond.

It was, perhaps, 3:30 in the morning. We live in a quiet suburb, and the chances of me meeting anyone at that hour were next to nothing. I followed the sidewalk to the end of my cul de sac and onto one of the paseos, the large paved paths for pedestrians here that run beside and behind the houses. I started down it. On the paseo, I told myself, I was even less likely to be seen.

I do not know what I was trying to do. I supposed I was trying to clear my head, though there was also still that now distant double throb in the side of my neck and perhaps I could not imagine lying back down until it was gone. On some level it felt to me as if I wasn't making the decisions I was making but that they were being made for me, but by what I would have been at a loss to say.

My feet had begun to ache from the cold, their soles sore from slapping against the pavement. I kept walking. I would, I told myself, walk until the end of the paseo, until I reached the black metal gate that separated the paseo from the dirt paths in the wash just beyond, and then I would turn around and walk back, re-enter the house, re-enter my bedroom, and go back to sleep.

In fact, I did not make it as far as the gate. There is, two blocks before the paseo reaches the gate, an intersection that has always struck me as strange. As I approached, I could see movement, many tiny shapes passing rapidly over the pavement just below the streetlight. *What am I seeing?* I wondered. As I got closer, I realised what I was seeing was dozens of cockroaches, big as thumbs, rushing first in one direction and then another. I had never encountered anything like it on the paseo before. I came right up to the edge of the circle the light made, and from there watched them. Was there a pattern to their movement? If there was, I couldn't make it out. For a while I just stood there watching in silence, and then I stepped into the light and began, with my bare feet, to crush them.

They crunched as I stepped on them. For a moment the other roaches kept pursuing their same irregular patterns, and then, all at once, as if suddenly now a single organism, they fled. They flowed out of the circle of light, off the paseo, into the adjoining cul de sac and towards the right half of a duplex. They scuttled up the driveway, burrowed beneath the garage door, and were, abruptly, gone.

★ ★ ★

For some time I stayed there, staring at the duplex. There was, on the house, hanging near the basketball hoop, just above the garage door, a political flag touting an ex-leader who I detested – which no doubt had some influence on my belief that there was something wrong with that duplex, or rather with that half of the duplex: I had no opinion about the other half since there was no political flag there, and no roaches, at least none that I had seen, had streamed under its garage door.

I was halfway up the driveway before I realised I had moved at all. Not long after that, I had my ear pressed to the garage door. Did I hear anything? Yes, I did – or at least am almost certain I did. There was, so it seemed to me, a rustling noise, whispery and nearly inaudible, and I imagined, on the other side of the door, the roaches slowly clambering on top of one another, slowly moulding together to form something else – what exactly, I could not say, but whatever it was I was certain it wasn't good.

I made my way into the side yard, slowly moving in a half circle around that half of the duplex. There were a few windows and I peered into them, but I saw nothing out of the ordinary. There was a bedroom window, a blind drawn over it, but there were enough gaps in the blinds that if I pressed my face to the glass and held very still and cupped my hands around my face, I could begin to see shapes within. There was a bed, two forms in it, either sleeping or dead. *Are they merely inanimate?* I wondered. Would there be a moment when the gooey mass of what had been roaches would slip under the bedroom door and flow up the side of the bed and then split in two, half flowing into the mouth of one of the forms and half into the mouth of the other? And then the forms would suddenly sit up, as if alive? Or was I imagining all of it, making something out of nothing?

I kept watch, waiting to see what would happen, if the bodies would move at all, if something would flow into or out of them. But I must have nodded off for a moment, as strange as that sounds – standing, my head pressed against the glass – because suddenly the light within the room came on bright enough to blind me and someone within, or maybe two people within, was (were?) screaming.

★ ★ ★

When I reached home, I sat down on my front steps. At first I did this only to catch my breath since I had run for so long. But once I'd been there a little while, I realised I should wash the remains of the dead roaches off my feet before going inside. I uncoiled the hose and turned it on low and then lifted one foot and looked at its sole, but there was nothing there. *Perhaps*, I thought, *I crushed them all with my other foot.* But there was nothing on the bottom of that foot either.

I was still puzzling over this, which somehow disturbed me more than anything else that had happened over the course of the evening, when I heard, behind me, my wife open the front door.

"Honey?" she said, voice drowsy. "What are you doing out here?"

"I didn't mean to wake you," I said.

"Where have you been?"

"Nowhere," I claimed.

I couldn't see her because she was behind me, but I could feel her there, waiting for more.

"I...thought I heard something," I offered. I turned around and saw her standing there, her arms folded tight as a way of keeping warm. "In the bushes. But it turned out to be nothing."

"Come back to bed," she said, and then turned around and went back into the house. After a moment, I stood up and followed her in.

* * *

She was already back in bed by the time I entered the bedroom, and seemed asleep too, which made me feel that the time it had taken to move from the front door to the bedroom had somehow been much longer for me than it had been for her. I climbed into the bed and under the blankets. With a sigh she moved so she was pressed against me.

"You're as cold as the dead," she murmured, and slid further against me.

"Am I?"

Her body was very warm, hot even, almost unnaturally so, and in this, too, I couldn't help but feel that she had somehow spent several minutes lying in bed during the twenty or so seconds it had taken me to walk from the front door to the bedroom.

J. was like that too, I couldn't help but think before I could stop myself. Unnaturally warm whenever she had been in the bed for even a few minutes. Almost out of reflex, I blocked the thought out.

I looked over at my wife, her placid, relaxed face. If I looked at it long enough, what would happen? What would I see in it?

I looked quickly away, staring up at the ceiling.

Eventually, I knew, I would have to let my guard down and fall asleep.

Without warning, I quickly looked back to my wife. Still the same peaceful, relaxed face. There was not, so I told myself, anything to be worried about. I stared at the face as long as I dared and then looked away again. And then, so as to stop myself from looking again, rolled over onto my side and stared at the night-blackened window.

I could feel my wife's breath on the back of my neck, not far from where I had been bitten. Or, rather, apparently, hadn't been bitten, at least not physically. I tried not to imagine what her face was becoming when I wasn't looking at it.

And there, through the blackened pane, a sudden and fleeting glimpse of what could have been a face. But before I could decide that that was what it actually was, it was gone.

Morning will come eventually, I told myself. It always does. Close your eyes. Don't look at the window. Don't turn around.

I lay there, in the dark, eyes tightly clenched shut, neck tingling. I waited.

GOOD BONES

Sarah Read

The porch leaned one way, the gables another, and the door hung crooked so that Jim could see the shadow of the old woman's feet through the gap at the bottom, standing at the threshold. The whole house sagged like a slow song on a warped record. He stepped up onto the bowing boards of the porch, boot laces catching on the splintered wood as if they were trying to stop him, hold him back. He was convinced the porch would fold under him, that the entablature above would come down like a rotten blanket to smother him. He held his breath as he crossed the boards, as if it would make him buoyant. Perhaps it worked. He made it, at least, to the twisted door with the twisted toes showing beneath. It was for the best that she stood so close, he guessed, as he only had to knock gently. Too hard and the whole thing might collapse.

The wood felt soft under his knuckles, but the door swung open without a sound.

My health isn't good, and I need a few things done around the house, she'd said on his voicemail. Both were understatements. The woman leaned as the house leaned and seemed just as likely to fall. Her skin hung sallow and spotted like damp wallpaper, her hair a tangled wisp of cobweb.

My kids are all gone away, so I've got to hire some help. The Allens at church said you needed work.

Sympathy overcame his hesitation. Imagine being left in this state, with no one willing to help. And he did need the work, badly, and there was enough work to be done here to keep him busy for years. If he could even stand the thought of charging her for it.

"Mrs…"

"Mrs. Kelsey," she said. Her voice was muffled as if she spoke around a wad of cotton.

"Mrs. Kelsey, I'm Jim. Here to do some work for you." He nodded in a friendly way and clutched his toolbox handle. He never offered his hand to shake. His hands were always stained with paint and oil, rough with scrapes. No one wanted to touch them, and it felt rude to compel them to.

"Oh yes, come in, mind the step here."

There wasn't a step there, or there wasn't meant to be. What there was, was a hole where a board should have been, and a line of old bricks stacked to fill the space.

Jim stepped over the bricks into the house and felt the damp, cool air settle onto him. He wanted a shower, and he hadn't even started work yet.

He followed the woman down a tilted hall, past a sitting room that smelled of mushrooms and dog, though there was no dog to be seen or heard, and into a kitchen as dark as if it were late evening. Scum coated the windows, which glowed a dull amber colour. In the centre of a crooked table sat a camping lantern, the only source of light, that clearly needed fresh batteries.

Light could have only made the room worse, as it would have illuminated the sources of the many smells that burned the back of Jim's throat.

"Is there something specific you'd like me to start on? Do you have a list?"

"Well, I think probably the first thing is that the oven doesn't work. It hasn't for a while, and I miss a fresh meal. Can't figure out what's wrong with it." She sank onto a spindle chair that tucked under the rocking table.

Jim could not see much that was right with it. He set his toolbox on the table, rocking the whole surface back toward him, and pulled out his flashlight to take a better look.

"Before you get too busy with that, can I ask what you charge for your work?" A bent hand with long nails slipped into the pocket of her spotted polyester pants.

Jim's anxiety spiked. He hated quoting prices. It felt too much like asking for money, felt presumptuous, like a confrontation. Perhaps that was why he was in the trouble he was.

"I charge fifteen an hour for small jobs. Or seventy-five for a whole day's work. For longer term projects, we could probably work something out..."

"Oh, I don't plan ahead much any more," she said, pulling a billfold from her pocket. She put a few bills on the table. "Just do whatever you can for today."

He slipped the money into his toolbox. "Sure thing. I'll let you know how progress goes."

The woman smiled and pushed herself up from the chair, tipping the table back again, and made her way through the hallway toward the sitting room they'd passed on the way in. Jim stared at the fresh footsteps her bare feet left in the damp dust. His boot prints were there, too. Clearly she hadn't come this way in a while. Weeks, it would seem, for that much dust to have collected. But the lantern…

He shook his head and turned back to the stove. It was an electric unit with no spark of life. None of the electrics seemed to be working, at least in this room.

"Can you tell me where your fuse box is?" he called down the corridor where the woman had disappeared. He realised he'd forgotten her name already and flushed with embarrassment at having to call for her so rudely. She didn't answer.

He crept down the dusty hallway, following her shuffled footprints back to a den clad in brown shag carpet. A lumpy corduroy chair of indeterminable colour sat like a mound in the corner, and the woman sat like a mound in the chair, her head pressed into the stained headrest, eyes closed. Jim blinked hard to see through the haze of dust and cobwebs that filled the air. Had she died? Had the effort of answering the door for him been her last burst of life? A low groan from her vicinity reassured him that she was exhausted only in the living sense. He didn't want to wake her. Fuse boxes were predictable. He'd find it himself.

He picked up the lantern from the kitchen table and scanned the room for other doors, perhaps a basement or cellar. The only door that led from the room went to the back yard. He could tell because the window pane in it had fallen in and shattered on the floor below. In the square of light let in by that broken window, Jim saw a row of planks, bent like twisted teeth, set into the curling linoleum floor. A loop of rope stuck up from a hole in one of the planks.

An old root cellar. A strand of web floated down from the ceiling and brushed the hairs standing on the back of his neck, sending a current down his spine that might have started the stove if he'd been holding onto the wires.

It was the most likely place for the fuse box. He grabbed his toolbox and carried it and the lantern to the trapdoor. He set them at its edge and pulled at the boards by their rope handle. The hinge popped and separated from the wood in a puff of old splinters. Jim lifted the door away and leaned it against the wall, adding *fix cellar door* to his growing mental to-do list for the house.

The stairs leading down were made from the same plank wood as the door had been and were likely just as rotted. Jim lowered the lantern into the space as far as his arm would go. Its fading light skimmed the packed dirt floor below. It wasn't a far drop, but he'd need a way back up if the stairs wouldn't hold him. He grabbed the chair from the kitchen table and carried it under one arm, his toolbox in his other hand, and the lantern handle clenched in his teeth as he made his way gingerly onto the first step. It bowed and groaned, the same noise the sleeping woman had made in the den down the hall. But it held. For now. He set the chair down by the bottom step, his toolbox on top of it.

The fuse box was in the corner, wires snaking from it along the floor joists, most of it knob and tube, its frayed fabric disconcertingly charred at the joins. The fuses were all intact, which was good, because he hadn't brought any replacements for a system this old. *This whole house needs to be rewired. This isn't even safe.* Jim turned in a circle, inspecting the beams and boards that held the floor above him. Nothing looked as solid as he'd like, nothing as square. Still, the house had somehow remained standing for seventy or more years. *They don't make them like this any more.* For all its issues, to still be here, it must have good bones. He just needed to find them and shore it all up.

He shut off power to the kitchen and crawled back up the rickety plank steps, leaving the chair behind in case he needed to return to the cellar and start that rewiring.

He needed to get to the stove's outlet, see if it was one of the few updated ones, check its connections. He rocked the stove, scooting it out of its narrow space between the cabinets, dragging it through the debris on the floor. It was practically glued in place by spiderwebs and ancient food spills. A pile of rodent droppings lay in the corner.

The stove's cord dangled loosely from a broken outlet plate. From its face, Jim doubted he'd find good news behind it.

He pulled the cord from the plug, dragged the stove all the way into the room to give himself space to work, and waved his screwdriver like a wand through the curtain of web, winding it in a sticky cocoon to pull it away.

The screws in the faceplate were stripped, but it hardly mattered. The plastic plate broke away from the metal and he was able to pull the rest out with pliers.

The plug unit stuck in the wall and Jim pulled it away, exposing a thick cloth of web stretched along the corded wires. He pulled harder, and the web unravelled, dropping debris to the filthy floor. Small bones, as delicate as matchsticks, fell at his knees. He dropped the outlet and let it hang by its wires. His flashlight beam shook in a trembling wave across more bones stacked there, web-wrapped and layered like cottage thatch. There were narrow teeth like needles and gaping eye sockets, and somewhere in the mass, something moved.

Jim scrambled back from the hole, hitting his head on the sticky back of the stove. He reached for the edge of the counter, pulling himself to stand, ignoring the sour tide rising in the back of his throat.

Traps. This house needs traps or spray or both – something. He stood, breathing slowly through his nose till the wave of nausea passed. He wondered again if the house could even be saved. If it was even worth pulling it apart and rebuilding it scrap by scrap. But where would the old woman go? He turned to glance back down the dark hallway and screamed.

Eyes, the sclera red and inflamed, lashes coated in web, peered into his from inches away. A mouth stretched wide with teeth as delicate as the wall-bones, opening in front of him.

"Did you find the problem?" The old woman stood next to the stove, blocking his exit from the dirty cubby.

Jim switched off his flashlight so the wavering beam wouldn't give away the shaking in his hands.

"Yes." He couldn't manage to say more. She smiled again and nodded. The smell that came from her mouth turned his already tender stomach, and he fought once again to keep the sick down.

She continued to nod, to smile, but didn't move away. Jim looked down at his boots, anywhere but the red of her eyes or the dark of her mouth. Instead, he saw her feet. What toes she had were purple, nails brown and uncut, twisting like withered leaves. And the toes she didn't have, in the places where toes should have been, gnarled skin blackened over protruding bone limned in old blood.

Jim felt his own mouth open, a sound spilling out that he didn't recognise, like a scream, but dropping into the pit of his stomach, like a penny falling down a well.

Finally, the woman moved, her truncated feet shuffling back through the dust. As soon as she cleared the gap between the stove and the counter, Jim pushed past her, rushing to the table, wishing he'd brought up the chair to collapse into. Though maybe it's the old woman who should sit.

He leaned on the rocking table and panted. "Does anyone…? Do the Allens, or anyone from church, ever check on you? Take you to the doctor?" It was none of his business. He was just the handyman. He shouldn't pry. It was a lesson learned long ago, the hard way.

But she didn't answer. She was already heading back down the hall, to the den with brown carpet. Had he upset her? He'd screamed in her face, twice, but she hadn't even flinched. Perhaps she was hard of hearing. Or he'd scared her.

But not as much as she'd scared him.

His chest still ached from where his heart had jumped and hammered, burned from all the acid stewing in his throat.

He couldn't solve this woman's life. He couldn't even solve his own.

But he could fix her stove. He could help in the only way he knew how, the only way he was any good for.

He made his way back to the front door, across the sagging porch, and out to his truck, where there were more tools, spools of wire, and a shop vac he could use to suck up some of this dust and web. And all the small bones falling out of the wall.

He thought again of the bones sticking out from the old woman's feet and he shuddered. *Mind your own business, Jim.*

He carried the supplies back to the house in several small trips, not wanting to weigh himself down so much that he'd fall clear through. He covered the table in everything he needed.

There was nothing left to do but face the task, though he dreaded staring back into that dark space.

He crawled back around the old stove, into the gap in the counter, where the outlet still hung like an eye from a socket, its optic nerve a frayed braided wire and strands of filth-studded web. He'd fetched his headlamp to keep his hands free as he worked, and its bright beam cut further into the dark than his small penlight had. The wall was filled with webs of small bones as far as he could see. Packed, like insulation.

He'd need to clear it all away to work on the wires, and to keep this nest from spreading and doing more damage.

He slid a small hacksaw into the space to expand the hole, but the old plaster fell away with little effort. The more he removed, the better he could see, further into the wall. The strange nest continued, a graveyard of voles and squirrels caught in filament.

A scratching noise grew louder as he worked his way higher up the wall. His hands began to shake again. What would he find? A mouse fighting for its life? Or the thing that had spun the web?

Jim lowered his hands, let the saw drop into the pile of soft plaster on the floor.

Maybe I'm not even good for this. Maybe even this is beyond me. He began to rehearse, in his mind, how he would tell the old woman. Show her the giant hole he had made in her wall, her busted stove and broken cellar door, and tell her…what? That he had somehow made everything worse, and she would have to find someone better to come in and set it all right? If he did that, he was finished. He'd deserve his cold nights in his truck and the empty stomach chewing on his insides.

No, he could fix this. It would take time, and steeled nerves, but he had the skill if he could summon the will. He had to believe in himself, and in this house that seemed determined to keep standing. If it could, he could. He had good bones, too.

He picked the saw back up from the floor, but his shaking hand slipped, and his palm slid across the thin blade, opening a line of red, clotted with the dust and filth of the wall.

"Shit." He hurried over to the sink to rinse the wound. It didn't hurt yet, and it couldn't be too deep, but the thought of all that disgusting mess creeping into his bloodstream soaked him in a cold sweat.

He twisted on the tap knob and a bubbling spray of brown water sputtered out in a stream that seemed to move slower than water should.

He drew his hands back to his chest, then reached out and shut off the water. *Fix kitchen plumbing*, he added to his list. There must be a bathroom somewhere, one with clear pipes, he hoped.

Jim made his way back down the hall toward the den. "Ma'am?"

The woman didn't answer. The den was empty.

There were three doorways leading from the room. Jim tried the first and found only a closet full of tattered linens. The second doorway led to what appeared to have once been a guest room, but it had been filled with boxes and piles of books and clothing. A tiled enclosure at the far side of the room promised a bathroom, but there was no way of accessing it without digging his way through. He backed away and closed the door, adding that task to his list as well.

The third door led to the stairs, a narrow, enclosed space. He had to angle his feet sideways to fit them on the treads.

"Ma'am?" he called out as he cleared the landing, not wanting to frighten her as he moved through this more private space, uninvited. "I'm just looking for the bathroom."

The upstairs landing was small, with two bedroom doors facing each other toward the back of the house, and the bathroom clearly visible in front of him. He sensed the lean of the house more clearly at this elevation, and though the stairs had seemed solid, the floors here felt thin under his feet. The spine of the floor joists ran in waves between the sagging boards, and he focused his steps there, relying on those old limbs to hold him.

The light was better up here, the windows more plentiful and not as dirty.

The bathroom would have been charming if it had been clean. It had clearly had a mid-century makeover at one point, and boasted an authentic vintage façade that people were paying fortunes to recreate. It was beautiful, minus the mould clinging to the ceiling, rusty water clouding the bottom of the tub, and the green film coating the mirror. Cobweb stretched across the vanity, tying an old brush to a dusty bottle, and then to the faucet, which had not been touched in months.

Jim picked up the brush and used it to sweep the webbing off the faucet. He didn't have much hope that this sink would work any better than the one downstairs, and his fears were confirmed when turning the knob did nothing at all. There wasn't a drop of water, not even the hiss or gurgle of a broken pipe trying to work.

He stepped back onto the landing. The doors to the two bedrooms stood open. The woman must be in one of them, as there was nowhere left in the house to go, and he hoped that one of the rooms might have an ensuite, like the room below had, as unlikely as that would be in a house of this age and size. *There must be clean running water somewhere.*

His hand had finally started to hurt, the cut burning as he cupped his fingers around the growing pool of blood in his palm. He stood on the landing between the two bedrooms, looking first into one, then the other. Both were empty, beds made, quilts carpeted in dust and mildew. There were no footprints in the dust on the floor, and webbing strung across the open space like a rope maze. There was no sign of the old woman. But one of the rooms had another door.

Jim stepped into the room, and as he did, he heard scraping overhead, like the scratching noise from the kitchen, but louder, closer. *Is there an attic?* He supposed there must be, given the pitch of the roof. It sounded like that might be the source of the pest problem. The source of all those tiny bones.

The brass doorknob was freezing, the cold stinging his hand even through the glove of cobweb that coated it. He twisted and pulled, separating the web like a veil as the door swung open.

It was not a bathroom, or a closet, but the stairs to the attic. He could only see the bottom few steps in the dim light from the bedroom windows. He didn't care to see more. With the door open, the scratching sound had become more like a thrashing. He swung the door shut quickly, boards squeaking with friction before the latch even caught. The scratching silenced.

Jim backed away from the door, turning slowly back toward the landing. A new sound, like the shush of a silk curtain surrounded him. His hands shook, scattering droplets of blood to the dusty floor.

The old woman's face swung in front of him, upside down, her needled black mouth aligned with his eyes. His scream stuck in his chest, squeezing his heart. She gaped and the scratching sound bellowed from her chest.

Jim shoved at her narrow shoulder. Her body swung, suspended in the webbing that stretched from the ceiling. He pushed past, fighting the grip of web, feeling the long rake of the woman's nails sawing at his neck.

The narrow tunnel of stairs seemed to squeeze him like a throat as he rushed down. The den below had grown more hazy, strung with sticky cord, and he fought his way through to the hallway, back toward the kitchen.

The walls around him seethed. A chittering, scratching sound overwhelmed him. He spun, trying to focus, vision blurred, unable to settle on one shape as long, chitinous legs waved like meadow grass across every wall. Creatures, spider-like, but coated with stiff fur, and each leg ending in a grasping hand like a rodent's, climbed the cabinets and spun a milky filament across the ceiling. The prick of forked clenching feet stung through the fabric of his jeans as the surge of creatures moved up his legs. Jim stomped his boots and grabbed his hammer from the table, swinging it at the brown, bristled bodies plucking at his shirt.

His hammer made contact with a crunch and the chittering in the room went quiet as a million red-bead eyes turned to him.

More of the beasts poured from the hole in the wall, an unending tide. Jim turned to run for the door, stumbling over the crisp carapaces scattering the floor. Their exoskeletons snapped under his feet like seashells, their grasping legs clinging to his boots even as a milky yellow mucus oozed from the cracks in their bodies.

The old woman stood in front of the door. Her head cocked to one side, mouth and eyes open as the creatures moved over her, chewing at her toes and burrowing into her open mouth. The skin of her neck bulged as the creatures moved beneath it.

Jim bellowed and raised the hammer, swinging it down with all the force he could summon into the woman's chest.

Her old bones caved, as brittle as the plaster, and a cloud of dust billowed from the cavity, followed by a tumble of needle bones as fine as toothpicks, the skulls of voles and squirrels collecting at their feet as her ribs crumbled. The open shell of her chest gaped, her spine visible through a veil of the creature's spun cloth, studded with plump egg sacs.

Jim swung the hammer again. The blow echoed through the house, and the creatures stilled. The sudden silence raised a ringing in his ears that sent his head spinning. Then a splitting creak shattered the silence, the groan and wail of straining timbers, of breaking bones.

He reached past the broken woman to the door and flung it open just as the frame collapsed. He rolled across the deck and scrambled back through the yard as the whole house came down, folding in on itself and crumbling, sending out a wave of dust that stuck in Jim's throat, choking him.

He curled up against the flying debris, coughing and catching his breath as it all finally settled into silence. Or nearly silence. He could still hear the scratching, quiet, muffled, incessant.

Jim lifted his head. Dust and debris fell from his hair and clung to his lips and eyelashes. The house was only a pile of splintered lumber and plaster dust as fine as ash. Nothing moved save the powder blowing away in the breeze. Still the scratching, chewing noise persisted. He pressed his hands over his ears and the sound grew, echoed, like waves in a seashell.

He pulled his hands away and shook them, yelping as the pain in his palm spiked, the cut pulled wide. He looked down at his wound. The skin at the edges of the gash had blackened into a deep bruise, the blood thickened into a crust, and somewhere deep in the dark of the muscle, something moved.

FACTS CONCERNING THE DISAPPEARANCE OF THE ORLOFF SIX

Alyssa C. Greene

On August 12, 1997, six people disappeared during a three-week backcountry hiking trip in northern Maine. The names of the Six: Joshua Orloff, 23; Analiese Wieland, 21; Chris Ferreira, 22; Lia Donnell, 22; Trevor 'Rex' Carter, 21; and David Auerbach, 19.

David Auerbach, the least understood and most maligned figure in the case, was my cousin.

★ ★ ★

Early in film school, I mentioned that I was related to David Auerbach. Just once, hoping to seem interesting. After that, it was the only thing people knew about me. Strangers greeted me with, 'You're the Auerbach girl!' instead of 'hello'.

Fellow students tried to ingratiate themselves with me when they learned about my connection to the famous cold case. After a while I felt like I couldn't trust anything, not even the empty politeness of grocery store cashiers. Only one person was bold enough to say what they all meant: "God, you're lucky. To be so close to such an important story." That was the first time I met Bonnie.

Bonnie's boldness – crassness, some might say – made me respect her. I knew exactly what she wanted, and that was a relief.

★ ★ ★

David Auerbach has always been the outlier in the Orloff case. The other hikers were experienced outdoors people; David was not. Five were students at or recent graduates of the University of Massachusetts Amherst; David lived in the area but was not affiliated with the school. The original five had been friends with one another for a number of years, but it's unclear when David first met the group, or how.

David's oddness among them has always been a point of contention for enthusiasts of the case. In 2002, a popular crime writer published *The Orloff Five*, a shoddily researched account of the mystery of the missing hikers, arguing that David Auerbach had lured five upstanding college kids to their deaths, and that he was probably still alive and still murdering. The book relied on unsubstantiated rumours that David had been a drug dealer, had been in love with Analiese Wieland, had killed a child while still a child himself. For most of the world, our family's refusal to speak with the book's author constituted proof positive of David's guilt. The book became a national bestseller.

When I asked my mother why Aunt Emilia wouldn't just tell her side of it to the press, my mother looked furious. "Because she doesn't owe anyone her dead son's story."

Only later would I come to understand another reason: Aunt Emilia's words would do nothing to dissuade those who had already made up their minds about David.

* * *

Bonnie and I collaborated on assignments, and eventually on our theses. After we'd graduated, she told me about her next project: she wanted to solve the disappearance of the long-missing hikers. "I don't just want to make movies," she told me. "I want justice." She called it my chance "to set the record straight. For David."

Bonnie was my only friend. I didn't want to disappoint her. And I wasn't prepared to find out whether our friendship would survive my refusal.

That's what I told myself. It's what I resolved to tell anyone who asked, and it's what I told myself during our miserable hike, during our futile attempts at escape. But now, struggling to grip pen and paper in my bleeding, blistered hands, I need the record as complete as possible. Otherwise, it was all for nothing.

While it's true that I agreed to do this out of friendship, it's not the entire truth.

I did want justice for my cousin. But more than anything, I was tired of the speculation, the intrusions into my family's private life. I wanted an end to the wild, baseless speculation devoid of any connection to evidence. I wanted a normal life.

The one thing I denied Bonnie was an on-camera interview. "I was not there," I told her, "and therefore have nothing to contribute."

What I meant was, I've seen how the spotlight can tear a life apart.

Bonnie never mentioned it again. I knew what it meant to her, how much she wanted this film to launch her name, her career. I never told her – I never knew how – that her respect for my boundaries meant everything to me, that I thought the story might finally be in the right hands. In return, I took over planning the hike.

★ ★ ★

At sixteen, I began compiling the known facts of the Orloff Six's disappearance. I held my facts to a rigorous standard. No one else's interpretations. No eyewitness accounts. I didn't want to have to deal with people.

Having all the information, I believed, would allow me to succeed where others had failed.

It didn't.

Removing the human element left almost nothing to work with.

★ ★ ★

In my baby book is a photo of David Auerbach holding me, three months old, in his arms. He wears a white and blue striped shirt. He smiles for the camera. In the corner, a time stamp says 10 10 95. My mother keeps it hidden beneath her mattress.

We have no other pictures of David. In 2002, a few weeks after the publication of *The Orloff Five*, a person or persons unknown broke into our house and stole family photographs. They took albums from shelves, pictures from walls. Photos of David soon appeared on eBay, under the title ORLOFF SIX DAVID AUERBACK [*sic*] PICTURES DISAPPEARANCE MURDER ABDUCTION. My mother reported the sale to the site and to law enforcement but never recovered any photos.

★ ★ ★

One year and thirty-seven miles from the Six's point of departure, hikers found a weathered notebook with a map stuffed inside. Upon further examination, they discovered Joshua Orloff's name written on the front inside cover. His mother would later confirm this was "without a doubt" his handwriting.

Some consider Orloff's notebook a hoax. How convenient, they argue, how perfect, to have discovered such a clear record of the Six's journey. Others insist on the veracity of the Orloff notebook precisely *because* of its oddness. A mantra commonly found on forums dedicated to the case: *Truth is stranger than fiction.*

The Orloff map shows the group's planned route in pencil, its actual route traced over in red Sharpie. The dates and locations they camped at each night are accompanied by anecdotes. 'D. scared by bunny'; 'L. told ghost stories'. Many argue that these are obvious misleads, designed to throw truth-seekers off the trail.

Joshua Orloff's mother told reporters that he planned to propose to Analiese Wieland at the end of the trip. The map, she said, was going to be a keepsake, a memory of what should have been the beginning of their lives together. It had been her idea.

Investigators traced the route outlined on the map. They found nothing.

★ ★ ★

If the map is to be believed, the Orloff Six only hiked for five days out of the intended twenty-one. Bonnie wanted to replicate the Six's progress exactly, hiking anywhere between ten and thirteen miles each day.

We were a crew of four: Bonnie Wells (director), James Leahy (assistant director, grip, emotional support boyfriend), Lyle Durand (sound), and me (camera). By the end of our first day, it was clear that unpractised bodies lugging heavy rental equipment would not keep pace with the Orloff group. Each day we didn't hit our target mileage, Bonnie fretted over late fees.

I did not tell my mother where I was going, only that I was travelling to shoot a documentary. If I'd told her the full story, she would have done everything in her power to stop me.

Once, a cousin announced to Aunt Emilia that he planned to hike the Orloff trail and leave a marker for David at the place where he vanished. "If you want to know what it was like," my mother said of Emilia's reaction, "go nuke some tomatoes in the microwave."

★ ★ ★

Before departing, Bonnie and I studied every photo and video of the path we could find.

After the map's discovery, someone marked the trail with blue spray paint. We followed the blue blazes precisely. Everything we saw matched exactly the places and things others had seen before us.

Bonnie programmed the GPS co-ordinates of the Six's last-known location into her smartwatch. On our eighth day of walking, we were less than a mile from our destination when we came to the narrow valley. The valley appeared on no maps, nor was it mentioned in any of the hundreds of personal accounts of people who'd done the Orloff hike.

The valley stretched maybe a half-mile long by a quarter-mile wide. Maybe. I couldn't judge the distance very well then, and there's no sense in trying to now.

We should have been able to walk straight across a relatively flat terrain to arrive at our terminus. We were already discussing when to begin filming.

Correction: *they* were already discussing when to begin filming.

When overwhelmed, I retreat into silence. It's not a choice so much as an involuntary shut-down process. The sun, the sluggish trudging through the hills, the constant company – it had all proved too much. By the fifth day of our hike, I could barely speak. I missed privacy. I missed my bed. I missed the days when I'd simply refused to answer questions about the Six, about David, about my family. By the time we approached the valley, I had barely spoken in thirty-seven hours.

Bonnie took my silence for insolence. The men kept their heads down each time she exploded at me. It was as if some contract between us had been broken. She began turning her GoPro on me, asking abrupt questions, as if she might surprise an answer out of me.

If this account is to reflect the facts, then it must be said: under other circumstances, I might have answered. The years of silence, even a self-protective silence, were heavy. My life withering in the shadow of someone else's.

* * *

The valley's grass looked a deeper blue-green than the grass we stood on. The colour might have made more sense undersea. Its shape gave the illusion of undulation, but in fact it remained perfectly still, even in the slight, merciful breeze.

Lyle dropped to a squat and reached a hand across what seemed to be a dividing line between the environment in which we'd trekked for eight miserable days and this other ecosystem. Watching him, my hands could feel what he felt: grass like oily, unwashed hair, stiff with gel.

Bonnie asked for the map, and I handed it over reluctantly. It made me too nervous to allow anyone else to carry it. The map had been the first sign of what I should've known but couldn't admit: I didn't trust them.

There was nothing mysterious or nefarious about it. I simply observed their competence in nature, their awareness of their surroundings. They couldn't help me survive.

They, apparently, considered this rude.

* * *

I filmed Bonnie and James hunched over their map at the edge of the valley. They rehashed a conversation we'd already had off camera, debating what to do. In truth there was never anything to do but move forward, to press on until we reached our destination.

Framing the shot, checking the light, watching their pretend conversation through the camera: the work calmed me. I felt my throat relax.

"Got it," I said after we finished the take. My voice sounded flimsy, as if it had atrophied from disuse.

Bonnie looked up in surprise. I turned away, unprepared for her attention, and focused instead on packing up the equipment.

Lyle and I hiked down first, stepping carefully over the large rocks jutting from the ground. The earth gave differently under my boots: springier, more elastic somehow. The basin was narrow – a slow-moving creek, grassy banks on either side.

"Not much down here, is there?" Lyle said. He was right; only grass, rocks, and blackberry bushes. Unlike the rest of the trail, there were no weeds, no wildflowers poking up their heads, no trees or tangled roots. Only those bushes, heavy with deep purple fruit.

⋆ ⋆ ⋆

Vanished (2017), the most recent documentary on the Six, argues that all credible evidence points to a routine hiking tragedy. Lost, injured, out of supplies. Bad luck, bad weather. Eventually, animals.

David Auerbach's lack of experience in nature factors into many theories about the Six. Some argue that he couldn't keep up, that he injured himself, or wandered off, and the others got lost searching for him. Others argue that some action or inaction of his doomed the rest of the group – they fell victim to his basic ignorance. Still others say that Auerbach's inexperience is proof that the group never went hiking at all, and the map is merely a distraction from the truth.

I read every book I could find about survival in the wilderness. I wanted to be sure I could do it, should the need arise. During film school, I embarked on my first camping trip. Those first few steps into the woods were delicious, a middle finger to fate. But that night, soaked through and bug-bitten, listening to the rain pound my tent, I realised I hated the outdoors. I didn't camp again until the documentary.

But even this limited experience made me the most experienced outdoors person in the group.

⋆ ⋆ ⋆

As we filmed Bonnie and James climbing down, I noticed that the air around us had grown hotter, thicker. Quieter, too. Even the slow-moving creek at my feet added little to the soundscape. The rest of the world felt far away.

"It's beautiful here," Bonnie said when they reached the basin. She held her head high, her back straight. She knew how to command a scene. I loved to film her.

James bent down and pointed at the blackberries. "They look like jewels." Only when I examined them myself did I see he meant it literally. Through the camera, they looked like extra-large, deep-purple blackberries. Up close, however, their drupelets weren't perfectly rounded – they were faceted. Small, flat, polygonal surfaces, giving the illusion of spheres.

I suggested we get some footage of the two of them walking by the creek. Bonnie agreed but avoided looking at me. We'd only gone a few steps when Bonnie's watch beeped and vibrated, announcing she had reached her destination – the last known location of the Orloff Six.

⋆ ⋆ ⋆

For many years, Aunt Emilia accepted that her son David was likely dead. She never stopped grieving, but still more or less participated in family life.

In 2007, a man claiming to be both psychic and ex-CIA contacted Emilia and told her that her son was still alive. The man's name was Rufus. He spoke of false flag operations, government cover-ups. Many such people had contacted Emilia over the years. It's unclear to me, or anyone else, why this was the one she chose to believe.

Within six months of meeting Rufus, Aunt Emilia asked her husband for a divorce and invited Rufus to live with her. The two of them dedicated themselves to David's story, which, over the years, grew ever-more elaborate, involving black sites, chemtrails, nuclear weapons, and other topical flotsam. When Aunt Emilia died in 2016, Rufus inherited her house, her belongings, and what was left of her money. He continues to hawk their self-published books and churn out new ones of his own. The rest of the family does not speak to him.

★ ★ ★

I walked along the banks of the creek while Bonnie tried to figure out where we were. Something in the water glinted.

I called to Bonnie and filmed her approach, pointing as best I could to where I wanted her to look. She stepped forward, gingerly at first. I saw her eyes widen. Then she splashed into the water with abandon, as if the object might at any moment scurry away, instead of lying exactly where it must have been for well over two decades.

Bonnie held up for the camera the face of a watch, frozen at two minutes to twelve. Carefully, she spun it around so I could film the inscription. *Joshua Adrian Orloff. May 5, 1995. Happy graduation. Love, Mom & Dad.*

★ ★ ★

Joshua Orloff's parents had often described the watch in interviews. Pictures were reproduced in the papers. Because it was never recovered, the Orloffs, unlike the rest of the Six's families, have held out hope that their son may yet still be alive.

Once Aunt Emilia made it known she believed David was still alive too, the Orloffs reached out to her. For a while, they became allies. They were the only families, they said in a joint statement, 'who haven't given up hope'.

I'm told that the Orloffs quietly distanced themselves from Emilia and Rufus just a few months later. Apparently, they found the pair 'a bit much'.

★ ★ ★

Bonnie wanted to camp in the valley basin. I advised against it, my voice still weak. She glared at me and said, "We're not walking away from the biggest breakthrough this case has ever seen."

My choice was this: stay, or walk away from the project, and from the only friend I've ever really had. One night in sub-optimal camping conditions seemed a small price to pay for the repair of our relationship.

We pitched our tents by the water, then gathered around the cookstove for dinner.

"Think those berries are edible?" James asked. Everyone looked at me.

"Blackberry lookalikes usually are," I said. Clustered skin, purple colour – everything I'd read told me they should be fine. Still, panic hit me when James cavalierly threw handfuls of them into our rehydrating mush. Everyone seemed grateful to have some variety. It seemed too late to express my reservations, so I didn't.

"Can you believe," Lyle said, "that some people do this for fun?"

★ ★ ★

My first thought the next morning was that there was too much blood in my head. I sat up and realised I had somehow manoeuvred myself into an awkward position as I slept. My legs lay up the slope of the hill, my head below. Then I remembered that I had pitched my tent on a level surface, not a hill.

All of our tents were tilted like that.

Even standing up, even caffeinated, I felt groggy. The ground beneath our feet sloped in a way it hadn't the day before – I'm sure of it. The sides of the valley looked steeper. Not only steeper, but concave. The rocks, previously as unremarkable as any rocks, had a darker, glassy sheen to them. The blue-green grass looked slicker, no longer frozen but rolling and twitching.

Bonnie emerged sleepily from her tent. She cocked her head and stared at the creek. The water seemed to have risen higher overnight. "Did it rain?" she asked, yawning. It hadn't.

James didn't leave the tent he shared with Bonnie. She crawled back in to rouse him. "Go away," we heard him moan. "I need to sleep."

"I think I'm allergic to something," Bonnie said as we made breakfast. She pulled up the cuffs of her pants. Her ankles were red and raw. We all itched, but she had the worst of it.

"How the hell did we even get down here?" Lyle said. I think what he meant was, *How the hell do we get back up there?*

"We should go home," I said quietly. I was ready for Bonnie to fly off the handle. "The late fees on the equipment," I added when she didn't respond.

She shrugged, sluggish. "What's the rush?" She wandered off before the oatmeal finished cooking.

* * *

Lyle and I prepped our equipment and were ready to shoot. "Let's get this over with," he muttered under his breath. We stood by the campsite waiting for our stars, trying not to itch the rashes that were spreading on our bodies.

After an hour I crawled into the last-remaining tent and shook James as hard as I could. He groaned and buried himself in his sleeping bag.

Lyle shook his head when I crawled out. "You need to get the boss lady."

I looked around for Bonnie. She sat by a shrub a short distance away, close to the creek. She'd taken off her shoes and was soaking her feet in the water. They were red and so covered with blisters that I wasn't sure how she'd be able to walk.

She didn't seem to notice. Mindlessly, she pulled berries off the bush and put them into her mouth. Her fingers were stained purple, slicked with drool. "They make it itch less," she said.

* * *

Lyle and I waited by the remains of the campfire, packs on our back, like two children forgotten at school. "We could go for help," he said. "Send someone after them."

It's this moment I replay over and over. I knew what would happen to Bonnie and James if we left. And I remembered what it was like for our family, to be associated with the person blamed for a tragedy. "I'm not abandoning them," I said.

I told Lyle he was free to go without me, that I wouldn't hold it against him. He chose to stay.

I'll admit it wasn't a choice between two equal options. I was the most experienced outdoors person in the group, he the least. He made the logical decision.

⋆ ⋆ ⋆

On the third day in the valley it seemed that, rather than saving two people, I had condemned four.

I awoke in the corner of my tent to the sound of Lyle screaming, "*Fuck*," over and over again. When I tried to stand, I immediately lost my footing and fell back down. The ground rose at an even steeper gradient.

Outside, everything seemed wetter. The grass felt slick. It moved more freely, though not with any wind I could sense.

The valley was smaller than it had been before. Narrower. Less a valley and more of a ravine. The gently sloping ground had turned into walls, trapping us.

The water had risen again. Bonnie and James's tent had tipped into the drink. Lyle's screams were coming from inside.

He was crouched in front of James's sleeping bag, half-submerged. We pulled him out together, struggling with his dead weight.

Much of James's face was gone, as if it had simply melted away. No sense of struggle, of motion, of energy. Perfectly still, static.

I screamed for Bonnie and heard moans in response. She had fallen asleep in the grass. Her skin was covered in weeping blisters. She struggled to form words. I did what I could, but our first aid supplies were wholly inadequate to the task.

⋆ ⋆ ⋆

The rocks that littered the ground when we entered the valley had not moved, even though physics dictated that they should have fallen when the ground rose up. They were still embedded in the same spots, only now they shimmered, dark like volcano glass.

Lyle and I attempted to use the rocks as handholds to climb out, but they were sharp, cutting us as we tried to form a grip or hoist ourselves up. Blood slicked our hands, and we fell. The grass posed a problem, too. Any skin that touched it felt as though it had been embraced by a man o' war.

By nightfall we were in too much pain to keep trying. Neither of us made it more than twenty feet off the ground.

★ ★ ★

Day four, the valley had become less of a ravine and more of a crevasse, a tight little split in the earth. Lyle and I paced it separately, each avoiding the other's gaze, squeezing awkwardly past one another whenever our paths intersected.

It was darker, colder, though it should have been the hottest part of summer. Little sun filtered down. I used a lighter to aid my way.

Something glinted, and I knelt down to find it: a diamond ring. The gold setting was warped and scratched, but the diamond remained intact. It lay next to an obsidian rock into which someone had once etched, *HELP*.

I collapsed to the ground beside it, allowed myself to understand this frantic searching would not save us. I took out my notebook – the same kind Joshua Orloff once purchased, all those years ago – and began the only thing I know how to do. Putting down the facts as I know them. This time I've decided not to ignore the human element.

★ ★ ★

Nothing is certain; evidence remains scant. Nonetheless, I have drawn my conclusions about the fate of the Orloff Six. Admittedly, I still cannot say with one hundred per cent certainty what happened to the Six. Not yet.

I'm not sure whether the walls are moving in faster, or if it's my own fear, and the darkness, playing tricks. I'm also not sure whether they're moving in and out, in and out, in a slowly accelerating rhythm, almost like respiration. Rapturous breath.

At this point it feels ridiculous to lie. Discovering an answer that not a single one of the so-called Orloff Truthers anticipated, even in their wildest fantasies, is exciting.

Looking at the evidence, an outside observer would draw an easy conclusion: that I wanted to insert myself into the story, just like so many others. That I felt I had a special claim to that story, because my whole life was swallowed up by someone who died when I was a baby.

I don't know if that's true.

I don't know if it's wrong, either.

Meanwhile, I can't help but wonder if today's daylight was the last I'll ever see. It stands to reason that there will soon come a night in which the sky vanishes entirely. I'll collect my facts as long as the light holds out, or as long as my burning hands can grip a pen. When I've finished, I'll throw this notebook in the creek. Though I cannot be certain, I suspect it may one day wash up, approximately thirty-seven miles from where we lie.

* * *

"Was it a mistake," Bonnie wheezed, "to think that we could ever know?" She lay sprawled beside me, eyes wet, skin raw and pooling, almost liquid.

Of course, I said no. As much as I believe in truth, even I know it's more important to comfort a dying friend.

What I wish I could have said to her, to anyone: It was a mistake to think that all this was ever about them, when it was only ever about us.

HE WASN'T THERE AGAIN TODAY

Peter Atkins

I'd been nursing my coffee at a sidewalk table outside the Atwater Village taco stand for about ten minutes when Dino finally pulled into a parking spot.

His royal blue PT Cruiser was hardly a '57 Corvette, but it was the first car he'd let himself buy since he got his licence back, and Dino loved it. He'd picked it up from a customer out in Palmdale for a thousand cash and the rest in morphine and, first time he showed it to me, he'd walked me around it as proud as if he'd bought a fucking house.

As a rule, drug dealers are hard to like – you either resent them or are scared of them, maybe both, depending on what kind of drug dealer you've been stupid enough to get yourself involved with – but, unless you're the kind of dick who wakes up every day desperate to dislike *somebody*, it was really pretty hard to dislike Dino. This was partly because he never seemed to be doing any better than any of his customers, and partly because, no matter how deep in the hole you were, he'd never cut you off if he saw you were hurting. You know, now that I say it out loud, I see that reason B kind of explains reason A.

Anyway, I watched Dino feed his meter, throw his Cruiser an anxious look like he'd just dropped it off for its first day at big-boy school, and walk to my table. He was beaming at me, like finding me here was a happy accident instead of an appointment he'd made.

"Kitty Donnelly," he said, in case I'd forgotten my name. "Let me buy you breakfast."

"I'm good," I said, lifting my coffee mug.

"No food?" he said. "Really?" A little troubled, like I'd put a crimp in his plans. "But you're still Irish, right?"

"From shamrock to shillelagh," I said, trusting that the eyeroll was implicit.

"So let me buy you a beer."

"It's nine o'clock in the fucking morning, Dino," I said. "Racist much?"

He shrugged. "I'm going to get something, though," he said, and strolled to the service window, where he made short work of ordering a fully loaded burrito.

"You met Andrea that one time, didn't you?" he said, once he was back, sitting down with his food. "At Angie's party?" Angie, Dino's sister, was an Andrea too, but the one he meant was her daughter, his niece. She was the reason he'd asked me to meet him.

"She was still a kid," I said. "Maybe twelve, thirteen?"

"Still a kid now," he said, nodding. "But at college, you know? Freshman."

I nodded too, took a sip of coffee. Dino didn't say anything else right away. Bit a chunk off his burrito instead, chewed for a moment, looked around at the other customers. It was okay. He'd tell me when he was ready.

Eventually he swallowed and brought his eyes back to mine.

"You have to help her," he said. "She's being haunted."

★ ★ ★

The thing about living off-campus, Andrea had discovered – one of the things, anyway – was that there was no dorm monitor or student counsellor to give a shit about your fucked-up stairwell lights.

Los Angeles tended to favour the bungalow approach to housing – high-rises being maybe not the greatest idea in a city built on fault-lines – but the only affordable no-roommate sitch that Andrea'd been able to find for herself was at the top of a six-storey walk-up at the sketchy end of Silverlake.

It had been built in 1928 – "As old as the talkies," the renting agent had said with the rhythm of a joke, though Andrea'd had to Google it – and it didn't look like Southern California at all, looked instead like it had got lost on its way to Greenwich Village or the Bowery. It was built from bricks, for a start – try getting that *past contemporary LA's earthquake codes and zoning restrictions – and had a fire escape zigzagging down the streetside exterior wall like it was waiting for an impromptu performance of West Side fucking Story to break out.*

The stairwell was windowless, and the lights had been out on all but the top floor for more than a month. Every time Andrea came home at night, once she'd rounded the stairwell's first curve and left behind any overspill from the lobby's not-generous-to-begin-with hanging lamp, her climb to her sixth-floor nest could only be illuminated by the occasional thin escape of light from behind other people's doors. If they were home. And – her hand to God – it seemed like nobody was ever *home, so when it was dark it was, like,* dark.

But it was fine. Well, had always been *fine, at least. There was nothing in the dark. There was never anything in the dark. Or, as she liked to joke to her friends, if there* was *anything in the dark, it had so far failed to display any interest in attracting her attention. Which was exactly the kind of working relationship that Andrea favoured having with whatever kind of thing it might be that might choose to live in the dark.*

Andrea's policy was to take each flight briskly and to stay in the centre of each step, taking pride in the nights she could crest a whole flight without stretching out an arm to tap at the wall to check how she was doing. That's what she'd done tonight – a little wobbly maybe, one shot too many at Taylor's karaoke bash perhaps – and here she was, all but out of the darkness, rounding the corner triumphantly onto the last flight, the flight that led up to her floor, the flight with the bulb that worked. It was particularly handy that the bulb was working tonight, because it allowed Andrea to see very clearly the man who was standing on the stairs, about nine steps above her.

Andrea stopped short. She heard her own gasp, but was already telling herself that she wasn't alarmed, she was just surprised. It was true she'd not heard any movement on the stairs, but that was okay. People tread softly. And she wouldn't have heard anything anyway, would she? It's not like he was walking, either up or down. He was just standing there, looking down at her. Well, not even at her, really. Kind of past her. Kind of through her, maybe.

Even though it crossed her mind that he must have been not walking for quite some time for her not to have heard him at all as she'd made her way up in the dark, Andrea wasn't frightened. Not at first. She wasn't frightened until his mouth fell open. There was something wrong with the slow and disturbing slackness of its movement, and she might have dwelt on that, might have tried to work out what it was that was wrong with it, except that she was busy finally realising why her stomach was trying to crawl into her throat.

The problem wasn't that there was a man on the stairs. The problem was that Andrea could see right through him. The water stains and wallpaper scuffs on the stairwell wall behind him were as blurrily visible as if she were looking through a rain-soaked window.

He cocked his head and furrowed his brow as if he too was beginning to understand that something unusual was going on, and his eyes came back from whatever they'd been looking at to finally lock on hers.

And then he disappeared.

* * *

"...and then he disappeared," Dino said.

He trickled a little more hot sauce over his close-to-collapsing burrito and raised it gingerly to his face. It was practically in his mouth before the thought occurred to him that, while cliffhangers might well have their place, this was maybe just rude, and he managed to make himself pause before actually taking a bite.

"I mean, bad enough, right?" he said. "But it was when it happened again the next night that she thought, you know, something was up."

This fucking guy. "Something was *up*?"

He bit down on his burrito's ruin, other hand raised at me in a cool-your-jets kind of way.

"She's working her way through college," he finally said, still chewing. "Waitressing at *Palladio* – you know, that shit-show for rich idiots who think that what they're eating is Italian? They've got her on the lunch shift today. Go see her, would you? For me? For old times' sake? She's a nice girl. Go see her."

That last little repeat was what did it. Go see her. I could hear his concern and his confusion. He loved his niece, was worried for her, had no idea what the fuck to do, and wanted someone who might.

Look, if I'm being honest, that *old times' sake* was kind of pushing it. Dino had at least twenty years on me, and we'd only been in the same profession for those ten stupid months I'd spent running candy for Paulie Benson, and that was three years ago now. But we'd liked each other enough, made each other laugh sometimes, and, let's face it, how many other reluctant occult detectives was the poor bastard likely to have in his Rolodex? So I nodded a yes over my mug's rim and broke eye contact before he could say something sentimental, looking over to where a neighbouring table was being cleared like I was checking out the busgirl's legs.

"Okay. Good," he said, after a moment. And there he was, back to stoic. Like a trouper. "Thanks. And for Chrissake, eat something while you're there, wouldya? Skipping breakfast and everything."

"You said the food was crap there," I reminded him.

Again with the shrug. I felt vaguely insulted but elected to rise above it.

* * *

I'd decided against food but was living up to Dino's earlier ethnic stereotyping by having a drink at the bar while Andrea was finishing up her shift. That single shot of Jameson's – which, to be fair, included an ice cube the size of a baseball – cost eighteen dollars, for which I very much looked forward to invoicing her uncle.

The table she was working was occupied by a little prick in a blazer and two significantly younger women, one of whom was kind of a knockout but who, truth be told, didn't quite live up to the beret she was wearing at a rehearsed angle. I couldn't hear what they were saying when Andrea brought them the menus, but I could pretty much read the closed captioning. Little Prick looked her up and down and said something condescending that pretended to be a joke. Andrea said something back which, even though she clipped its wings with a non-threatening smile, was quick and clever enough to win a giggle from Ambitious Beret Girl. Li'l Prick smiled too, but it was surprised and unsure, the kind of smile you'd give to a monkey making a finger painting. If you were an asshole.

The restaurant was at least within walking distance of her college and, as we headed back to campus for her afternoon classes, I told her that, while her charm and composure were admirable given the circumstances, I'd have driven his fork right through his fucking hand.

She gave a whatcha-gonna-do shrug. "I need the tips," she said.

"But you spit in his food, right?"

"Yeah, he *wishes* it was spit."

"Attagirl," I said. I thought for a moment about getting his address from a credit card scan but I'm in therapy now and Juliana is trying to impress upon me that they don't *all* have to die. "Hey," I said to Andrea. "I want to check something. No judgement, but has your uncle been giving you and your friends any free merchandise lately?" Dino was usually careful about the quality of his stock but, you know, accidents happen.

"Seriously?" she said, in that mock-offended way they do now. "No. Not stoned. Not tripping. Not anything." She paused. "Well, a little drunk."

"Sure. And you were scared, right?"

"Of course I was scared," she said.

"But scared because it was *weird*? Or like, scared as in you felt threatened?"

Andrea gave that some thought. "Look, I don't want the memo to be misunderstood," she said. "I was *plenty* fucking scared. But I guess I didn't feel directly *threatened*. Partly because he looked kind of confused and scared himself."

"And he saw you too, you said?"

"Right at the end, he did, yeah. He looked at me, like he maybe wanted to say something, and then he just...wasn't there. He just...I don't know...faded out."

"Just gone?"

"Gone. Like a ghost."

"And the second night was kind of the same thing?"

We'd reached the college grounds by now and crossed on a light toward the quad.

"*Exactly* the same thing," Andrea said. "Like I was watching a fucking rerun."

"Right. And after he was gone, did—" I stopped myself. Went back to something she'd said. "Wait. Why'd you say *like* a ghost? You think it wasn't a ghost?"

"Well, I mean, it couldn't be, could it?"

She was losing me. "What? Shit you've gone through the past couple of days, you don't believe in ghosts?"

"Huh?" she said. "Oh, no. I didn't mean that. I mean, I don't know, I'm not sure that I believe *per se*, but I guess there has to be *something* that happens after we—"

"Let's stay focused, Andrea."

"Right. Sorry. What I meant was that it couldn't be *his* ghost."

"Whose?"

"Professor Dunham's."

"Okay. Name's useful. First I've fucking heard. More to the point, why not?"

She pointed across the quad at some middle-aged but trim guy trotting up the stone steps of what the sign told me was the English & Modern Languages Department. "Because he's not dead," she said. "That's him over there."

Fuck me. "You ever hear the phrase *burying the lead*?" I asked her.

* * *

Professor Jack Dunham was very much not dead. What he was was a busy senior lecturer with a loaded desk and a full schedule, but one who was nevertheless willing to give me ten minutes once I'd knocked on his office door and asked politely.

Andrea'd already told me she wasn't enrolled in any of his classes – knew him only by sight and by reputation and by, you know, the whole haunting thing – so I had no reason to disbelieve him when he told me he had no real idea who she was, either by name or by the photo that I'd taken three minutes earlier on my phone. I'd just put it away when his own phone rang – the office landline, not his cell – and he took the call on speaker. Maybe in some spirit of full disclosure, maybe because he hated to waste an audience.

"Am I speaking to Jack Dunham?" said the male voice from the speaker. Bit of a spin on it. Just short of aggressive, like its owner was already impatient with the bullshit it hadn't yet heard.

"You are," said Dunham. "And to whom am *I* speaking?"

"My name doesn't matter, Mr. Dunham. I—"

"Come, come," Dunham interrupted. "You mustn't think so little of yourself." He winked at me across the desk, let me know I was in on the fun.

The voice didn't rise to the bait. "I represent the Clarion Collection Agency," it said. "Your debt to our client, Edwards and Sons, is ninety days past due and the case has been referred to us. I'd advise you to take care of this matter immediately. Collecting debts is what we *do*, Mr. Dunham. And we *will* collect this debt."

"I see," Dunham said. "Well, perhaps you'll have better luck with someone more amused by your self-importance than I am." He killed the call.

I was starting to like the guy.

"Now, how may I help you, Ms. Donnelly?" he said.

Weirdly, I wasn't sure that he needed to any more, other than to maybe confirm what I was already getting a very strong hunch about. I'd been looking around his room while he had his fun with the collection agency schmuck, and had been registering a few things about him. One, he was a guy who ran up debts. Two, he was a guy who had a sense of fun but not so much a sense of consequences. Three, there was an ashtray on his desk, a heavy glass souvenir from Paris, Las Vegas, which he obviously could no longer legally use in his office, so it must have been there simply because he was fond of it.

Now, you can call my next question to him jumping to conclusions, if you like, but that's why I'm Kitty Donnelly, Girl Detective, and you're not.

"You're a gambler," I said.

He looked quizzical for a second, and then a little annoyed. "Oh, God," he said. "You're not another debt collector, are you?"

"I'm not," I said. "But I'll take that as a yes."

"Well," he said. "*Gambler* implies someone with a problem, wouldn't you say? I might prefer to phrase it as that I'm someone who's fond of games of chance."

"Preference noted," I said. "*Debts* are a problem, though, wouldn't you say?"

"Oh, everything's paid eventually."

No shit, Jack. "Let me ask you something," I said, doubling down on my hunch. "You ever make a really *stupid* bet? Like, something ridiculous?"

He cocked his head at me, curious that I should have asked. "Interesting," he said. "Not a bet, so much as a deal."

"Yeah? What did it cost you?"

"No, no," he said. "*I* was paid." He was trying to keep the laughter out of his voice. "And it was money for *nothing*. I was teaching somebody credulous a lesson."

Poor bastard. Poor stupid bastard.

* * *

The thing about people who are way too into secret shit is that they can't keep their fucking mouths shut. Ufologists, conspiracy theorists, flat-earthers, they're all the same. And occultists are the worst. The *worst*. Like, the literal meaning of 'occult' is 'hidden', but you wouldn't think so from the non-stop rumours, bragging, and bitch-fests that constitute most of the dark web's Satanist message-boards.

I realised that I might actually have already heard whispers about the guy to whose apartment Andrea and I had headed after leaving the campus. The Gatherer. That's what he called himself, he and his online acolytes. I know, I know. The fucking names they come up with. Probably first thought of it back when he was rolling a twenty-seven-sided dice in his mom's basement. Bastard should've stayed there. Wouldn't have drawn my attention.

All I'd needed was to ask Andrea one very simple question – "Any particularly creepy neighbours in your building?" – and she hadn't even needed time to think. Billy Z in 3F was the hands-down winner. Billy Z wasn't in his apartment right now. But Andrea and I were, because not a single one of Billy Z's three high-security locks from Best Buy had stood a chance against Mrs. Donnelly's Youngest and her mad skills at housebreaking.

Billy Z was The Gatherer, all right. His taste in pictures and posters was exactly as you'd expect, and a quick scan of his bookshelves revealed all the usual suspects: Crowley, LaVey, Jack Parsons, a couple of genuine *grimoires*, and a *Necronomicon* bound in human skin. Huh. Fourth I'd seen this year. Must be a factory somewhere.

But it was neither the books nor the vintage signed photos of Madame Blavatsky and Jimmy Page that told me Billy was the one we were looking for.

"Jesus Christ," I said. "There they are."

I was pointing to a special display shelf he'd had fitted above his desk, and more specifically to the nine bell jars all in a row atop it. The jars were high-end fancy, each of them twelve inches of cylindrical clear glass perched on a dark wooden plinth. The kind of expensive display item you reserve for your very favourite creepy shit, whether that be taxidermied animals, puzzle boxes that open the gates of Hell, or homunculi in the shapes of devils and ballerinas. There was nothing visible to the naked eye in any of these ones, though.

"They're all empty," Andrea said, which was a perfectly reasonable conclusion for her to draw. But not the right one.

"They're not empty," I said.

"Huh?"

"He'll have a blu-light somewhere. See if you can see it."

"A what?"

"A UV flashlight," I said. "You know, like in the forensic cop shows. The thing you shine on the crime scene when you need to know where all the blood landed. The thing you never want to shine on a motel bedspread."

"Oof," she said, but pointed at a thin strip-light fixture in a fancy brass housing that ran above the shelf. "Won't that be it?" she said. "But why would he need—"

"He'd want to see them, want to gloat."

"Want to see *what*?" she asked.

I flipped the little toggle on the side of the fixture, and suddenly Andrea and I weren't alone any more. Within the jars, bathed in the eerie blue light, were wisps of weighty smoke, each of them revolving slowly, each of them rising and falling as if straining against invisible tides.

"They're twirling," Andrea said, in a tone that implied she wasn't entirely sure whether to be entranced or disturbed.

"You're cute," I said. "They're not twirling. They're writhing."

"Oh, Christ," she said. No ambiguity in the tone this time.

I didn't mean to upset her, but I wasn't kidding. We were looking at that which The Gatherer had gathered. Nine stolen souls. Trapped. Terrified. Lost. If they weren't in Hell, they were in the next best thing.

I neither knew nor gave a shit whether nine had some ritualistic significance or whether it was just the maximum size of Ikea shelf that Billy Z could fit in his fucking car; I just knew that these were what he'd managed to collect for himself, by various means – bargained for, bid for, wagered for, inherited from other assholes, whatever. These were the fruits of his Gathering, and I did my best to explain as much to Andrea.

"One of them's Dunham's?" she asked and, in response to my nod, "We have to help him. Help all of them. What can we do?"

I turned the UV off, so that the jars looked empty again. Cosmetic fix, I know, but it made us both feel a tiny bit better.

"Thank Christ this prick's a memorabilia collector," I said. I nodded at the wall that held the Blavatsky photo. Next to it, a baseball bat stood on display beneath a framed Phillies shirt.

"The fuck?" Andrea said. "I wouldn't have put Billy down as a Jock."

"Number Ten," I said, pointing at the shirt and its embroidered number. "Darren Daulton. Catcher for the Phillies and practising occultist."

"You're kidding me," Andrea said, as I crossed to the case and grabbed the bat.

"Nope," I said. "This shit's *everywhere.*"

I hoisted the bat, wanting to test it for weight, and got an eyeline on the bell jars.

Tell you the truth, I was hoping to impress Andrea by shattering all nine in a single swing, but it took me two. It made a satisfying mess on the bastard's floor, but I wasn't the only one who knew that that wasn't going to be enough.

"The jars were just *where* he kept them," Andrea said. "Not *how* he kept them. Smashing the jars can't have freed them."

"No," I said, impressed by how quickly she was grasping the underlying metaphysics here. "You're right. A deal's a deal, lifetime of the owner kind of thing. Felt good though."

Something else was troubling Andrea. "Dunham shows up for work every day," she said. "Talks to people, does his job, lives his life. How does he not *know*? How does he not feel something's missing?"

"Have you *met* the twenty-first century?" I said. "For most people, losing a soul is like losing a fucking passport. You don't even know it's gone until you need it. And by then it's always too late."

She nodded. "But smashing this asshole's stupid jars," she said. "That was only…I don't know…only *symbolic* or something. It didn't really *help*."

She sounded upset. Can you blame her? I was pretty mad myself.

"Yeah, that's true," I said. "Smashing the jars didn't really help. But then, smashing the jars isn't really what I wanted the bat for."

There was a little pause then, a little moment of silence, while Andrea looked at me. It's possible she was remembering what I'd said about the lifetime-of-the-owner aspect of these kind of deals. It's possible too that she was maybe remembering certain stories she might have heard about me at the occasional family gathering, if her Uncle Dino had been a little loose lipped and careless – which, on occasion, I knew he was capable of being.

"Andrea, honey," I said, in my kindest voice. "Why don't you go see Dino? He was worried about you. Go have dinner with your uncle. He'd love that. I'll finish up here."

I locked the door behind her. Wondered if I should have a drink while I waited for Billy.

★ ★ ★

Later – quite a bit later, after quite a lot of cleaning up – I thought about Andrea and pondered the question of whether I should tell her something about herself or not.

The thing is, I doubted Billy Z had been in the habit of letting his little pets out for walkies. Andrea hadn't seen what she'd seen on the stairs because The Gatherer had popped a jar off its plinth, she'd seen it because she *could*. Because she *knew* Dunham, however slightly. Because she could feel his sundered soul's proximity. Because she was close to it, could sense it and see it. See it trying to scream. Because she was somebody who could tune in to the kind of things that a certain type of person could tune in to.

I decided it was probably better to let her eventually realise that on her own, but I did make a mental note about a government contact I had in the UK, an old friend of my grandfather's, who – though very much on the side of the angels – was kind of a gatherer too, a gatherer of a certain type of person, and I wondered whether Andrea had given much thought yet as to what line of work she might be interested in once college was done.

DODGER

Carly Holmes

Lorna sat in the jagged shade of the church's ruined wall, legs stretched out before her and one hand slanted against her brow to keep the late afternoon sun from finding her eyes. The steady trample of passersby kicked up a dust that swirled and spurted from the heels of trainers, settled like ash on naked toes. She watched the march of strangers' feet from her quiet patch of grass and pulled long channels of smoke into her lungs, whistled it out through barely parted lips. Music crashed in the distance; children shrieked and galloped by, tugging on garish balloons.

Lorna glanced at her watch and guessed she had another five minutes before she'd need to stand up, insert herself into the crowd and find her husband. But there were at least three more drags left on the cigarette and she was going to idle here for now and savour every one.

The little boy wailed from the spiralling dust like a tiny stampeding bull and charged at her. His face was a crushed cherry from crying, the flesh from his peephole eyes down to his chin silted and slimy with mucus. His shadow flowed ahead of him, leapt the warm grass and pounced. Before she could move, raise a hand to ward it, him, off, he'd barrelled into her and knocked her backwards, pinning her to the ground. She lay there with the cigarette smouldering beside her, gazing up at a sky that was faded and unreachable, purest baby blue, while the child squirmed and bellowed against her chest. His soaked face oozed against her neck, sticking her skin to his and making her stomach clench with nausea. She tried to flip herself free but couldn't manage more than a weak convulsion. She was too winded to speak.

"Mummy," he sobbed.

The woman who'd been following him stood over them both, fists worrying at her hips. "Thank god," she snapped. "He was beside himself." She ground her trainer into the cigarette, taking her time to make sure it was out, then crouched and patted the boy's heaving shoulder. "All's well that ends well," she said in a high singsong. "I told you we'd find your mummy. You really need to keep a better eye on your child." The last sentence was sharp and just for Lorna, who nodded weakly, shook her head. She flailed onto her elbow and tried to say something, but the boy scrambled up her raised body and grabbed at her desperately, pushing his fingers into her mouth and twisting her bottom lip. He began to roar with relieved fury. Warmth flooded her thighs and she thought he must have wet himself.

"Goodbye, darling. Be a good boy for Mummy," the woman said. She gave Lorna another long, narrow look of disapproval and turned away. Beyond the retreating body, Lorna caught a glimpse of her husband Phil at the other side of the abbey grounds. He'd seen her, was running towards them with arms stiffly outstretched and mouth glossy and wide. He might have been laughing and she couldn't blame him. *Only you, Lorna darling, could get embroiled in such bizarre situations.* She tried to lift her arms in response, urge him on, but the boy had his legs wrapped around her, heels drumming painfully against her pinned wrists. She could taste salt, something bitter beneath it, and tried to spit his fingers out of her mouth.

When Phil reached her side and plucked the child from her lap she jackknifed onto her hip and retched, scrubbing at her cheeks with her palms. "God, thank you," she said hoarsely. "God. I have to wash my face." She reached out a hand to her husband, a mute gesture for him to help her up, but he wasn't looking at her. His expression was hidden, buried against the neck of the boy. His arms were tightly wrapped around the solid little body and his shoulders shook. The boy screamed and sobbed against his chest.

"Where did you find him?" he asked finally, raising his head. His gaze was blind and inverted, pupils flickering between unspooling nightmares. He dipped down again and again to kiss the boy wherever he could, pecking at an ear, a tip of nose, landing a smacking cheek kiss that was almost cannibalistic. "I looked everywhere. I had to check the pond..." His voice cracked and he sucked a deep breath in, held it, grinned shakily at her. "Shit, Lorna, that's the most scared I've ever been in my life, I can barely stand up. I need a sugar hit, like, now. Hey, let's go to Oscars and eat ice cream. What do you reckon, Dodger?" He held the boy out at arms' length, dangling from the armpits. "It's okay, Jack, Mummy found you safe and sound. You can stop crying now. What do you say to three whole scoops of ice cream, one for every year of your life?"

He set the child on the ground and finally reached for Lorna, wrapping her hands between his huge palms, hauling her upright. She tugged herself loose and stepped back, rocking on her feet, staring from him to the boy who was smiling now at the prospect of a treat, tugging at Phil's legs.

"I have to wash my face," she said, her voice shrill. "I want to go home."

Her husband leaned close, an arm heavy around her shoulders. "It's okay, darling," he whispered into her ear, "it wasn't your fault. Don't look so broken. You take your eye off them for a second and that's all it takes; nobody would blame you. Let's go straight home then, and you and Jack can clean up while I pop out and get something nice." He winked down at the boy. "I'm going to get *all* the ice cream, Dodger. Every flavour in the whole world. That's what we're having for dinner tonight."

They walked, the three of them, through the park, past the squeal of happy families and the detritus of the village fête, out through the gate. Phil held one of Lorna's hands and the boy took the other, swinging it with wild enthusiasm as he jogged beside her, grinding her arm back and forth in its socket. Every step jerked a startled moan from her, a swift grimace down at him. She smiled falteringly when they chattered to her, but she didn't speak. Beside them, their linked shadows clung and hobbled, indistinguishable one from the other.

* * *

Lorna locked herself in the bathroom and stripped off her clothes, unpeeled the soaked jeans from her legs and kicked them towards the laundry basket. She turned the shower on and waited until steam lapped against her throat and the mirror clouded. She pushed the plug into the drainage hole, stepped into the bath and scrubbed herself with soap and flannel beneath the jet of scalding water. She used an exfoliating scrub on her face, a cleanser, the scrub again, opened her mouth and swilled fragrant gritty water until she gagged and gasped for air.

Something sharp snagged the side of her foot when she waded backwards to hook the shampoo from its rack, forcing a stumble that almost tipped her over. She bent and flailed a hand beneath the murky water, scooped up a red plastic fire engine. One of its wheels was missing and its roof was dented: a well-loved toy. She dropped it and watched it float for a moment, bobbing on its side valiantly and then flipping over onto its roof before it sank slowly through the fruity foam of her sloughed shower gel, and down. It left a hole in its wake, a perfect rectangle that cut scarlet through the sludgy residue and didn't close even after she splashed it with her toes; it pressed like a wound against the bottom of the bath.

She hugged herself close and looked around. Scattered along the edge of the bath were a small tractor, a truck, several stout plastic figures in bright primary colours. A parade of yellow ducks, mould trimming their pursed beaks, were lined up beside the taps. She reached out to touch them, drew her hand back and pressed it against her stomach. Smooth flesh, taut. No creping of the skin below the bellybutton, no scar. She remembered the shock of seeing her mother's body when she was young, the sag of it, being told *she'd* done that. But this body she cradled now was unmarked, still hers. Her womb had never swollen and stretched to accommodate another life. She would have known if it had.

Beyond the door, Phil rattled the handle and called her name; the boy pounded with his fists and howled something unintelligible. Lorna held her breath and stood still, a hand over her mouth, waiting, but they didn't go. After only a few seconds' silence the banging started again, the name-calling, the outraged need for her. She turned the water off and towelled her body roughly, wrapped herself in a hooded dressing gown and released the lock, letting them into the room.

"Why did you lock it?" Phil swung the half-naked child past her briskly and planted him on the toilet, steadying him with a hand on his back as the boy slithered and then settled onto the misty seat with a dreamy frown of concentration, baggy shorts cascading from his bare feet. "I can't find the potty and he's been doing so well. We don't want an accident, do we? Do we, Jack? No, sir, we don't. Undo all the good work."

"He already had an accident, all over me." Lorna wrapped a towel around her hair and kicked a leg sharply towards the sodden clothes she'd discarded. She half turned away from the hunched figure of the grunting child, crouched squat and gnome-like on his throne of white porcelain. Her husband's body was folded in half and hidden from her as he attended to the boy. She felt a stab of wild, desperate rage and tied the dressing gown tighter around her waist. "I'll open the window."

There was no mistaking the dense, almost hollow thud of solid matter hitting the water in the toilet bowl, the sudden violent stench of other people's bodily waste. Lorna gagged again, flapped a hand in front of her and waved away the fistful of toilet paper Phil held out to her. "Your turn, I think," he said with a smirk. She shook her head and backed out of the room, crossed the landing to their bedroom at a run and shut the door. Blood throbbed and knocked against her temples; her vision starting to clot and waver. Her migraine tablets were downstairs in the top cupboard in the kitchen, safely shut away high above the counter. She could picture them, too many steps away from where she was. She didn't know why they'd be secreted so carefully, so far from her, when she needed them now, here.

A cheer ricocheted from the bathroom, the sound of the toilet flushing and then the tap briefly running. Lorna scrambled into clean shorts and T-shirt and met her husband as he emerged, flushed and grinning. He gave her a double thumbs up and knocked a clenched fist against his heart. "First time on the grown-up toilet," he exclaimed. "What a pro!"

She smiled weakly, embarrassed for him, by him. The boy ran full tilt over the rug and tangled himself between her thighs, spun around and around her and crowed with pride. His hands were damp against her bare legs, hot and greasy. The fine hairs on her calves prickled as his fingertips scraped over them. She thought of fleas, spiders, the bedbugs that had infested her home when she was a child, and she had to force herself to stand still and not slap the imaginary creatures off.

"Right, I'd better go." Phil kissed her quickly and laid a hand on the boy's forehead. "I'll be as quick as I can. Be a good boy for your mummy, Jack, and hop in the bath without any fuss." He ran down the stairs and turned to wave. Lorna trailed after him, stopped halfway and lowered herself slowly onto a step. She bent her head forward and whispered into her lap. "Phil."

The word left her mouth as a soft purr, tentative and wispy as a dandelion clock. She swallowed hard and spoke again, louder. "Phil?"

He turned then, house keys in hand, bouncing on the soles of his feet. "What is it, darling?" He planted one foot on the bottom step, and she willed him up, willed him to come back to her and put his arms around her, laugh at the ludicrous joke he'd played on her, or just divine her unspoken question without questions of his own; without judgement.

As he waited for her to answer he tossed the jangle of keys from palm to palm, glancing around him at the front door, and then from behind her the child called out in a high gleeful shout and dropped something, or threw something, and she jerked around.

"Text me!" Phil said, turning away. "I've got to get there before they close." The door swung shut behind him and she heard the slap of his trainers on the tarmac as he started to jog away.

Lorna pulled herself upright, gripping the banister, using it to haul herself back to the landing, one careful step at a time. "You need a bath," she told the boy.

He led the way to the bathroom, strutting and blowing an imaginary trumpet. He lifted the toilet seat and slammed it down over and over while she ran water and squirted bubble bath, swept the plastic toys into a bright heap to join the ducks by the taps. She could do this, one simple chore at a time. *Test the water temperature, collect a large towel and a small one, lay them in a neatly folded pile on the side of the sink. Keep going, one foot in front of the other, and things will get back to the way they were.*

"In you get," she said, pointing. The child looked at her uncertainly for a moment, then tried to scramble over the side of the bath. His naked buttocks floated, creamy pale as mushroom caps, as he sprawled, caught on the rim, then wriggled free and heaved himself belly-down into the tub. Water surged over the side onto the mat as he rolled onto his back and sat up, spluttering.

"Good boy," Lorna murmured. She closed the lid of the toilet and perched on it, watching him as he busied himself with his toys, chattering to her and himself as he staged peril and then rescue with the firemen. She nodded and smiled, gasped when it seemed warranted, and all the time she searched his face, his frowning concentration and his quick, triumphant glances up at her from eyes as sludge-grey and heavy-lashed as her husband's.

"Have a proper wash, please," she said. "Phil will be home soon." Could she run to the kitchen quickly and get her migraine tablets? She'd be there and back in under two minutes if she hurried. She stood up, edged towards the door.

The boy tugged the flannel from where he'd draped it on the top of his head and stretched a hand out to her. "Where are you going, Mummy?"

"Nowhere. You need to scrub harder than that if you're going to get rid of all the dirt." Lorna moved to his side and took the flannel in her fist, pummelled it with soap. "Lean forward." She watched her hand float through the steam – it could have been a stranger's hand – before she placed it firmly on his slippery neck, touching him of her own volition. She felt the bones there, delicate as quills, shift beneath her palm. She pushed down a little, just a little, and sensed his immediate resistance, the warmth and solidity of his existence as he reared back against her and craned his head away. "Ow, Mummy," he said. "That hurt."

"Sorry. Lift your arms."

He was blotched a deep pink when she declared him clean and wrapped him in the larger towel, lifted him from the bath. *Pull the plug, sluice clean water around the tub, dry the sides off with the small towel, push the window wide to let the steam out. Just keep going for a little while longer.*

He rubbed his finger along his forearm and let out a short, rasping squeal that made her jump. "Squeaky clean and good as new," he announced, grinning at her expectantly. She groped for a response, the response he was looking for, and settled for nodding briskly and herding him towards the door. "Indeed. Yes, you are."

* * *

Late that night Lorna slid out of bed and settled in the chair by the window. She opened the curtains just enough to let the streetlamps smudge the darkness in the room a faint orange. From her corner, tucked partly behind the chest of drawers, she looked across at Phil's curled body, the milky blur of his face on the pillow. She couldn't make out if his eyes were open or shut, didn't know if he was watching her. The more she stared at him the less like Phil he looked.

The room seemed different from this perspective, unfamiliar. Or it might have been she who felt skewed, adrift from the safe and knowable landscape of her home and her life. Every tiny sound beyond the bedroom door – the house ticking as the day's heat left it; the night-time creatures rustling in the garden hedge – drove a pin through her carefully controlled breaths and unstitched them; brought her stomach reeling sharply up to the level of her heart, her heart to the level of her mouth. She needed a cigarette. She needed a cigarette. She needed a cigarette.

She began to cry, covering her face with a cushion to keep the sound contained. She used to go and sit on the top stair when she needed to do this but she didn't dare risk going out there, rousing the child who now slept in the room across the landing. He'd taken an age to get off to sleep, three stories and any number of I-spy games, though Phil had cheerfully taken charge of all that while she'd stood helplessly in the doorway and gaped at the sheer amount of *stuff* the room held. It would have been an impossibility to walk across to the bed or the window without treading on something, being forced to negotiate a way over or around it. Plastic toys lay heaped on the rug; teddies spilled from the cupboard. And the state of the walls. They were striped with thick crayon in every colour, the lovely green paintwork ruined.

"Lorna? What's wrong?" Phil was at her side now; she could feel his muggy breath on her scalp, his hands scrabbling to prise the cushion from her face. She shook her head, clung to it with fierce panic.

"Have I gone mad?"

He knelt between her legs and held her close, rocking her as he tried to soothe the rising sobs. "I knew you were upset about today; I knew it. Of course you're not mad, darling. It's okay, I promise you. It's going to be okay." He stroked the back of her neck. "You've been behaving a bit…oddly, recently, since you went back to work. A bit vague. Maybe it was too soon? Maybe you need more time off?"

She raised herself up in the chair, wiped her cheeks with the cushion, and pushed him away gently. "No, I'm fine. Really. I'm probably just overtired. I'm going to pop into the garden for a cigarette and then I'll come back to bed."

He sat back on his haunches and stared at her. "What?"

"What?" His tone made her instantly defensive, her voice now chilly as she stood up and walked past him to the door.

"Are you joking?" Phil asked. "You gave up smoking four years ago when we found out we were pregnant."

The door handle against her palm was sticky with humidity. She held onto it, squeezing until it hurt, concentrating on the dig of metal against her skin. "Oh, fuck off, Phil," she said softly, turning her head slightly to address the room behind her. "*We?* Why do you have to be so bloody priggish all the time?"

The cigarette smoke was silk in her mouth, the rush of poison to her head a beautiful, giddy pleasure. Lorna smoked two, lighting one from the butt of the other, standing directly beneath the bedroom window so that Phil would smell it and know what she was doing. She waited until the bedside lamp was switched off, and then she moved to the garden lounger and settled down on it and smoked another.

⋆ ⋆ ⋆

The boy refused to eat the cereal Lorna set in front of him the next morning, pushing his bowl away with an expression close to shock on his face. "Mummy!" he whined. "You know what day it is!"

Phil came into the kitchen, dressed in a suit. He gasped theatrically as he swept the bowl up. "It's Eggy Bread Monday!" he said. "That's what day it is. What a forgetful Mummy! Don't worry, Dodger, I'll take care of it." He bent and whispered something quickly into the child's ear, sliding a sly look at Lorna. They both laughed, the sound harsh and malicious, too loud in the white humming space, and then Phil straightened to look at her fully, clashing gazes. He leaned in again and murmured something else and the boy clapped a hand over his mouth and nodded vigorously, crowing with delight, his eyes crinkles of mirth.

Lorna cupped her mug of coffee close to her chest and fumbled in her dressing gown pocket for her cigarettes. Not there. Had Phil found them earlier this morning, hidden them somewhere? Or had she left them beside the lounger?

She walked to the French door that opened onto the back garden and looked out, affecting interest in the scorched grass ringing the trampoline. Her neck was stiff with exhaustion, her eye sockets tender. The rage she felt towards Phil was a vicious thing, barely containable, and she was scared of what she might say, of what she might do. She could hear the spiky hiss and buzz of their whispers behind her, knew they were watching her, but when she turned sharply to confront them Phil was at the stove and the boy was scratching at the worn surface of the table with his spoon. Both figures seemed blurred, their outlines slightly out of focus, as if they'd been in the act of moving and had frozen in response to her sudden attention.

Phil glanced over. "Did you manage to get any sleep in the end?"

She shrugged, shook her head. "What were you saying about me?" she asked. "Just now, you were talking about me."

Her husband slid golden slices of fried eggy bread onto plates and carried them over to the table. "There you go, Jack. Ketchup on the way. I can't remember," he said to her, over his shoulder. "Just silliness." He sighed. "Oh, Lorna, do cheer up, please. Sit down and eat your breakfast."

"I've got to get ready for work," she said. "Maybe when I come home this afternoon you might have decided this—" she waved her hand vaguely around the room, pausing at the table with a flourish of the wrist and then sweeping on "—sick joke, this cruel trick, has gone on long enough."

She left the room as Phil started to say something, closed the kitchen door behind her with a brisk click that wasn't quite a slam and felt a spiteful pleasure in cutting him off mid-sentence, a smug sense of achievement in her own self-control. She was halfway up the stairs when he called to her from the hallway. "Do you have to go in today? Maybe you could take the day off. And you have remembered you've got to take Jack to nursery, haven't you? I haven't got the time."

Lorna stumbled, swivelled round to stare down at him. "Yes," she said. "I know. You don't have to keep going on about it."

* * *

The nursery at the end of their road was one Lorna always walked past on her way to and from work, edging nervously around the extravagant farewells and the tiny howls of anguish.

She hovered at the gate for a moment, hoping somebody would approach her and take charge of the situation, at the very least appear to recognise her so that she knew she was in the right place, but the parents were too preoccupied and the staff too busy counting children in through the door to notice her hesitation. It was as though her true self had become invisible: her sense of who she was, or who she had thought she was, hacked down to no more than a heap of splinters. They could re-form into the rough shape of a person, of *her*, if squeezed hard enough in a strong enough fist, but they were no longer the original thing.

She steered the boy in through the gate and stood in the busy yard, clasping his hand and grimacing hopefully at every adult who passed. The day's heat was already gathering itself, forcing sweat in a greasy rush through the thin cotton of her blouse. A man nudged into her as he passed, woebegone child dangling from the crook of his arm. He nodded a curt apology but didn't look at her. Lorna tugged her hand free and blotted it on the inside hem of her skirt, glanced at her watch. She needed to leave now if she was going to stop at the newsagents for cigarettes before she got to the office.

The boy pressed himself tighter against her side when she tried to step away, peeking shyly at the milling children. Lorna nudged him slightly towards a small girl who'd stopped to wave frantically at him – "Hi Jack!" – but he clung even closer and hooked an arm around her knee. His bottom lip trembled; his eyes narrowed to paper cuts. She knew he was going to start crying any second now and she couldn't bear it.

"There you are! Did you have a nice time at the fair yesterday?" A woman in the nursery staff uniform of yellow T-shirt and black shorts, smile radiant, stopped in front of them. Lorna let out a hollow laugh and was about to speak when she realised that the woman wasn't talking to her. She'd crouched in front of the boy and now applied herself to loosening his grip on Lorna's legs, chattering cheerfully about the fun they were going to have, gently transferring his attention to herself. "There we go, Jack!" she said, straightening up and beaming at Lorna. "We're going to have a lovely time! Say goodbye to Mummy before we go inside."

Lorna crouched beside the child and leaned slowly into him, watching his face swim closer to hers until he filled her entire world and panic seized her, a sour flood of saliva filling her mouth. She swallowed hard, forced it back down into her stomach to burn there.

"Have a lovely day, darling. Be good," she said. She leaned close as if to kiss his cheek, turned her head slightly at the last second and found his ear. She whispered, softly, "I hate you."

He jerked as if she'd slapped him, eyes huge and blank with brimming tears. "Pardon, Mummy? What did you say, Mummy?" He scrabbled towards her, but the nursery worker kept a tight hold of his hand and nodded at Lorna kindly. *Best you just go.* Lorna thought about saying it one more time, saying it louder this time, but didn't.

She straightened and smiled gratefully at the woman who was going to make this all go away for a few hours, then patted the boy's head quickly and turned her back on them both. She felt the air heave and resettle behind her as a small body clawed away from his carer and was pulled firmly into line. Her steps quickened as she neared the gate. She didn't look, but she could hear the rising wail, feel the child's throbbing need as a sharp, pinching knot between her shoulder blades that tried to tug her back.

It was only when she stepped out of the nursery's yard and onto the street, swung right briskly and strode away – the tobacconist at the corner of the main street her urgent objective – that the pain lessened and she was able to suck a breath in deeply, hold it in her lungs as a blessing and release it in a long whistle. Every step she took away from the boy, every step towards the office and the knowable mundane routines awaiting her there, returned her to herself. There, she would have a name. There, people would call her Lorna. And when they looked at her, they would *see* her.

She felt a pang, just briefly, when the hot breeze sailed over the suburban garden walls at the crossroads and brought with it a faint cry. Probably a gull. Or another child. Not something she need concern herself with.

⋆ ⋆ ⋆

By the morning break Lorna wished she'd taken Phil's advice and stayed at home. It wasn't that she felt ill as such, just a bit *vague.* Hadn't he used that word, last night? She was sure he'd accused her of being vague. The sun drilled mercilessly in through the large windows and Polly had moved the only fan to her corner of the room, mantling over it with feral possessiveness.

Lorna's desk, which she was sure she had left neat and clean last Friday afternoon, was a clutter of screwed-up pieces of paper, lidless biros oozing ink in navy clots, and last week's coffee mugs. She knew some of the mugs weren't hers – she always washed up at the end of every day – but Polly shook her head impatiently when accused. She didn't even bother to look away from her computer screen. Watching her frown over her emails, tendrils of hair wafting merrily around in the cooling breeze of the fan, Lorna felt that vast rage crashing through her again. She imagined slapping the woman until her cheeks were purpled, tender and raw as mashed kidneys, then pushing through the building and out onto the street. Not walking towards home but away. The where didn't matter.

When her phone rang, she was checking the figures for the monthly report and chewing absently on a sandwich. She ignored it, ignored Polly's tutting, and then ignored her mobile when it started to trill in her handbag. Working on the columns of numbers had soothed her and she was almost cheerful, determined to hang onto that. Once she'd finished this task she was going to reward herself with a cigarette and catch up on the office gossip, always the spiciest and most up to date in smokers' corner.

She leaned back in her chair while she finished her lunch, strangely pleased with just how irritating the duet of landline and mobile phones were. They continued to ring, and she continued to chew and swallow, take another bite, chew and swallow. Polly got up and swept out, muttering. Lorna considered dashing over to her side of the room and stealing the fan back but couldn't summon the energy.

The framed photograph of her and Phil, taken on their honeymoon, was toppled over and dull with dust. She used a tissue to wipe the glass clean and righted it, looked for a moment at the young, happy faces. Her cheeks had been fuller back then, her eyes wider and her gaze steadier. Phil's grin was huge, infectious. She felt an urge, a sudden choked need, to see him and put her arms around him, try to dance them both back to that place and hold them safely there. When her mobile rang again and she saw the call was from him she dropped the apple she'd been gnawing on and answered it immediately, warmly. "Darling, hello!"

"I've been trying you for ages," he said. "Why didn't you pick up? You need to get Jack."

"Jack?" She stared at the computer screen with its calming rows of numbers, tried hard not to bridle at his tone.

"Yes. Jack. Your son." There was a long beat of silence, and then he said in a clipped, end-of-my-tether voice, "Jesus, Lorna, what the hell is going on with you? Jack's had a complete meltdown at nursery and you need to go and get him. Now. This is *your* department, we agreed that when he was a baby. Why are you suddenly making this so hard?"

She reached a hand out and moved the mouse, clicked it a couple of times and corrected a small error on the screen in front of her. There, done. Once she'd emailed it over to her manager she could nip out for a cigarette. "I'm busy right now," she said. "Can't it wait?"

"No. It can't fucking wait." He sounded close to hating her and that gave her a twisted, bitter satisfaction. The thrill was almost sexual. "Lorna. You need to leave right now and collect our child. Right. Now. He's been desperate for the last hour. Inconsolable. He needs his fucking mother."

She laughed then, high and hysterical, covered her mouth quickly to hide the sound. "Fine," she said. "I'll speak to Rob and leave in a minute. Okay? Happy?"

Phil sighed. "No, not happy. But thank you, Lorna. I'll let them know to expect you in the next half an hour, and I'll see you at home later."

* * *

The walk back to the nursery was hotter, brighter, slower than the walk from it had been a few hours earlier. Lorna dawdled along the quiet streets, paused for a few moments in the deep shadow of a horse chestnut tree to smoke a cigarette. The late-summer sunshine blushed the drooping leaves of the tree a deep rose gold, its bristling conker cases glowing the fresh green of peridot.

Phil phoned her again while she was stubbing out her cigarette; added another message to the voicemail pileup. She didn't bother to listen to it, switched her mobile off and dropped it into her bag.

The gate leading into the nursery yard was locked. She had to press a button and speak into the intercom, wait while someone was sent to let her in. Faraway voices wailed and groaned tinnily through the little machine as she spoke to the faceless gatekeeper. It sounded like an entire village of ghostly children were queued up in the nursery corridors, all desperate to be let out.

A different woman from this morning emerged from the building and crossed the yard. She held the yelling boy against her chest, his small body writhing and bucking, making forward progress difficult. "Look, Jack, there's Mummy!" she exclaimed, pointing. He twisted round and saw Lorna, let out one long piercing scream, then half leapt, half fell out of the woman's hold and ran across the yard to the gate. He tried to climb it as the key was wrestled into the lock, clawed a frantic path over and dived into Lorna's arms. His teeth against her throat were sharp and hungry, nipping along her collar bone. He wanted to devour her.

She crouched to try and loosen his grip, heard the cotton of her blouse rip as he thrust his face against it, blindly lipping at her chest. The woman towered over them both. "He's been like this for a couple of hours," she said. "He hadn't seemed right since he arrived but then after their morning snack he got a lot worse." She bent to help Lorna, tugging the child back and hanging onto him. "Has anything happened to unsettle him over the last few days?" she asked.

Lorna stood and rebuttoned her chewed blouse. Apricot lace peeked through the torn cloth and she saw the woman glance at it, divined unspoken disapproval at the unmotherly choice of bra. "No," she said. "He's been fine."

She reached for the straining child and held him by the shoulders. "You need to calm down," she told him. "The longer you scream, the longer it will take us to leave here." She nodded at the woman. "Thank you for letting us know. I'm sorry he's being difficult."

The woman started to back away through the gate, relief plain on her face. "He's at that age," she said. "And probably just overtired and missed his mummy." She locked the gate quickly behind her. "He'll be right as rain after a nap."

Lorna nodded and watched her go. She wondered how on earth they did it, these people, day after day. The boy leaned against her leg, exhausted. His head jerked back and forth as sobs rattled through him, slower now. His left thumb crept into his mouth and with his right hand he twisted the hem of Lorna's skirt into a ball, hobbling her. "Come on," she said. "I'd better carry you."

His weight in her arms, the loose swing of his leg against her waist, made the walk to the park harder in the afternoon heat. Lorna paused a couple of times to rest and catch her breath, hoisting the sleeping boy back up to her chest when he slithered down. His head nestled into her neck, his mouth a snuffling creature pressed against her skin. Something about his smell reminded her of Phil or reminded her of home. She kept her face turned away as much as possible, craning to see where she was going and breathing through her mouth.

The park was empty, the end of the school day still a couple of hours away. A man walked a small dog on a lead in the distance and a young couple dozed and kissed on a rug under a tree, but nobody paid any attention to Lorna as she crossed the hot grass towards the tucked-away shade of the ruined church wall. She lowered the boy gently down and sat beside him, resting a hand on the tight curl of his body so that he would sense her presence and not startle awake.

She smoked a cigarette and gazed out across the park. There were still patches of churned earth from the weekend's fête, a few wrappers tangling around the swing set. Against her back the wall stood cool and sharp, grounding her.

Phil shouldn't be back from work until 6:00 p.m., maybe even a little later if traffic was bad. If she left now she'd be home in ten minutes, have hours to herself. She could lie in a cool bath, tackle the weeding, read a novel. When she got home everything there would be just as it was, just as it should be.

She closed her eyes and saw herself standing in the driveway, opening the front door, stepping inside. Her home and her life returned to her and this terrible interlude, that had started right here, scrubbed out.

Lorna loosened the thin cotton belt from her skirt and slipped it free. She shuffled to kneel beside the boy and watched him for a moment. His eyelids shimmered, pearlescent as the inside of abalone shells; his sucking mouth crumpled around his thumb. She looped the strip of fabric around his ankles, looped it round and round and tied a knot. Tied another, and another. His socks bunched above and below the tether. She wouldn't be able to undo it now even if she wanted to.

He muttered something in his sleep, tried to kick out his legs. Lorna stroked his head and hushed him, settled him back into a dreaming state. She gathered her bag and edged away, got slowly to her feet.

When she reached the gate that led to the street, she knew that if she looked back now there would be nothing to see. The boy would be gone. Because the boy had never been.

She unlatched the gate and stepped through, pulled it carefully closed behind her, walked away. She didn't look back.

FROM THE MAN-SEAT

Reggie Oliver

Unlike some people, I do not in the least mind going into clothes shops with my wife, always provided that there is what I call a 'man-seat'.

Most of the really good ones seem to have them. They are the comfortable armchairs tucked away in a corner of the shop where you can sit down while your partner browses through the racks and shelves. There you can read, or consult your mobile, or, as I usually do, just sit and look at the world going by. If you pay attention, even the most banal activity of your fellow human beings can become fascinating to watch. Interactions between staff and customers are particularly worth studying. So, my experiences in shops with a man-seat have been rewarding, and, up until a certain event this year, my friend Fergus Moore might have agreed with me. When I visited him in hospital, just after he had undergone a second eye operation, he told me what had happened.

You may have heard of Fergus Moore. He is an opera director, particularly well-known for his productions of contemporary work by the likes of Ligeti, Poul Ruders, Turnage, and Thomas Adès. Of course, that world may be a closed book to you, but it really doesn't matter. Fergus is about my age, yet looks considerably younger. He seems as fit and trim as when we first knew each other as young actors thirty or so years ago. Unlike me, he is not married, but has enjoyed a number of relationships, mostly with dancers and opera singers. Every time I saw him, Fergus seemed to be with someone younger and more glamorous. I have always liked his girlfriends, and when they and Fergus part, as they always do, there is rarely any acrimony – or so he tells me. It is just the way things are in his world; people are constantly on the move from opera house to theatre across the globe, so bonds of communication fray and snap.

When I called on him in Moorfields last week, he was sitting up in bed with his eyes bandaged, but he knew who I was as soon as I came into his room. He did not at first seem to me particularly downcast, but he was in a febrile, agitated mood. When I asked him how he was, he waved my commonplace enquiry aside. Fergus, in any case, is never one for small talk. It was clear that he urgently wanted to tell me something, and so, after putting a bag of seedless grapes into his hands, I let him.

This last summer Fergus was in Alderness directing an opera for the Music Festival there. It was Donizetti's *Don Pasquale*, as it happens. The classic operatic repertoire was not his usual territory, but, by all accounts, he made a good fist of it. Being unattached at the time, he began to befriend a cellist in the Alderness Festival Orchestra called Anna.

"Not my usual type," Fergus told me, "I am generally drawn to the singers. Anna is not unattractive; far from it, but she is not, you know, obviously…well, glamorous like some of the others. But we just got on, went out together on long walks, when we were free: that kind of thing. I began to feel that this could be someone I might actually want to, you know – oh, God, what's the ghastly phrase? – 'settle down with'."

"What became of the last girlfriend, Gina, wasn't it? The soprano. I rather liked her."

"Oh, she was lovely, yes. Unfortunately, after she was runner-up at Cardiff Singer of the Year, she became a sort of celebrity which rather spoiled her. Gina even wrote a bad children's book, as these celebs do. *Mrs. Fighole's Marvellous Sock*, it was called. The most frightful ullage. Ever come across it?"

"No." I write an occasional book review for the papers, but children's fiction by minor celebrities is not my field of expertise.

"Frightful ullage…" Fergus paused to contemplate Gina's aberration while he reached into the bag for a grape. The silence continued as he savoured the fruit. Finally he said: "I'd better tell you the whole thing. You're the one person who might possibly believe me."

"What makes you think that?"

"Well, you write that sort of stuff, don't you?"

"What sort of 'stuff' are you referring to?" I felt mildly offended.

"Just listen. Okay?" He had suddenly become very agitated and irritable. I sensed fear, and the fear was infectious.

"All right! All right!"

"Well, one afternoon Anna and I were both free, so we decided to go into Alderness. We'd just had the first night of *Pasquale*, and I was staying on to monitor subsequent performances, and for a bit of a holiday. Also, of course, because of Anna... As you know, most of the Alderness Festival actually takes place inland at a place called Froston Manor where there's the theatre and rehearsal rooms and so on. Alderness on the coast is the nearest big town and one or two of the festival's concerts are also held there. Are you listening?"

I nodded, then, remembering that he could not see me, murmured some kind of assent.

"We had a coffee and wandered along the sea front. It was getting a bit windy. I don't know whether you know Alderness. It's basically an old fishing village, now grown into a sedate and respectable seaside town. Retired solicitors go there to yacht and play golf. Quite picturesque, but it can appear rather bleak at times. Rough seas, stony beach, no dogs allowed on it between May and September, that sort of thing. The tide was coming in; there were big angry grey waves. Then it started to spit with rain. We decided to go back to the High Street and get under cover somewhere. That was when we started looking at the shops.

"Anna spotted one which she said she hadn't seen before. She comes every year to play at the festival, so she knows the place pretty well, you see. And she told me the shop hadn't been there last year; in fact, what had been where the shop now stood was an old-fashioned undertakers, with, she informed me, a 'Chapel of Rest'.

"Then I said something like, 'Ah! Chapel of Rest, just what I need.' It was a sort of joke, but it was a stupid thing to say, because she hugged me and said: 'Oh, you poor old thing!'

"Sweet of her, I know. And Anna is a sweet girl, but I hated her saying it because it reminded me that I am rather older than her. To be honest, about twenty years. Or thereabouts. I was rather hoping that we could forget about that. It's the kind of thing which shouldn't really make a difference, these days, should it?"

"I'm sure it doesn't," I said, as convincingly as I could.

"Yes... Well... This was a new shop and had just opened. It was called *Seahorse* and was obviously designed to reflect the fishing village aspect of Alderness. You know: artistic piece of driftwood and a rusty anchor in the front window display. It sold smart casual clothes with a slightly nautical feel: stone-washed denim, cable knit sweaters, striped fisherman's jerseys. Lots of woolly stuff. The sort of thing you might wear on a yacht, if you had one, or aspired to have one. Anyway, Anna said she wanted to take a look, and, as it was still spitting, I didn't object. Anything to get out of the rain; so we went in.

"Anna liked the look of the place, but for some reason I didn't. I can't quite explain. It may have been the light, which seemed unnecessarily subdued. The nautical theme of the shop was pursued by the murals, more or less in the manner of post-war artists like Craxton and Minton: slightly stylised depictions of coastal scenes with muscular sailors, coils of rope, and dead fish with gaping mouths and staring eyes lying on stone jetties.

"There was piped music, of course, but it was not the usual light pop. It sounded like an organ, and reminded me of the lugubrious murmurations you hear from the instrument in a crematorium chapel before the service begins. Normally that would have been preferable to light pop – for me, anything would! – but somehow not on this occasion.

"Luckily, or perhaps unluckily as it turned out, this shop had one of those chairs you can sit on while your partner browses."

"Yes. I know what you mean."

"Right. Well, this one was situated at the back of the shop, not far from the sales counter and next to a couple of changing rooms where people could try things on. You know, those little cubicles with curtains in front of them? The cubicle curtains in this shop were rather heavy looking: they went right down to the floor and were a sort of greyish colour decorated with the shop's seahorse logo. I would have much preferred it if my chair had not been so close to the changing rooms, but it was the only seat available, so I sat down. Anna saw me do so and smiled."

Fergus hesitated.

"That smile. It was a kind smile, meant to reassure me, but there was something about it, and the way her body was only half turned towards me as she smiled, that filled me with an almost uncontrollable desire. I suppose you might call it lust: well, possibly, but I don't like that word. So bloody moralistic! At the same time I felt a sort of terrible despair, that I would never have her, didn't deserve her, was too old for her. At one and the same moment she never seemed more desirable, never more unattainable.

"I was beginning to feel sorry for myself, and I suppose I must have looked it, because I suddenly noticed the two shop assistants at the counter staring at me, and not in a friendly way. One of them was blonde, petite and – what's that awful polite phrase? – 'well endowed'. The other was tall and thin with a beaky nose. Looked like one of those wading birds that haunt the estuaries around Alderness. The Blonde kept calling her 'Trace': presumably an abbreviation of 'Tracey'. Trace was clearly the dominant partner."

"The alpha female."

"Yes, well, I don't want to sound sexist or superior or anything, but that was the gist of it. They looked at me with disapproval. Older man with young girlfriend, that sort of thing, I suppose. Am I sounding paranoid? Well, I just waved at them in a friendly way and pretended to study my mobile, but secretly I listened in on their conversation. They talked pretty loudly so I had no difficulty in hearing. It was mostly the usual girly stuff—"

Fergus then went into a full impersonation of Trace and the Blonde. It reminded me what a good actor he had once been before he entered the more rarefied world of opera direction.

"'So Trace, did you see Gary last night?' 'Yeah, I saw Gary.' 'Where d'you go?' 'Down Saltbridge. That place called *Ghoolies*.' 'Oh, yeah. Cool. The music's cool.' 'Saw that Teegan.' 'Did you? I think he's weird, Trace.' 'He's cool.' 'Yeah, he's cool, Trace, but he's weird. Looks like one of them Zombos, like in that *Zombo Acopalypse* on the Netflix.' 'It's *Zombie*, lame-brain. Zombie.' 'So did Gary try anything, Trace?' 'What d'you mean?' 'You know. "Lerve."' 'I told him where to shove it.' 'Oh, yeah? Where was that then, Trace?'

"And so on… I can't vouch for the absolute accuracy of that rendering, but that's what it sounded like to me. Anyway, just as they were gabbing away, this woman came up to the counter. She was elderly, foreign, not very agreeable looking. She plonked a garment on the counter and said: 'I wish to try on. Where?'

"Trace and the Blonde just stared at her for a while. I must say the woman had sounded rather abrupt, but I thought you were supposed to put up with that sort of thing if you were serving in a shop. There was quite a long silence until finally the old lady snapped: 'Come! I have not all day!' Trace looked at the Blonde, who nodded, and said to the lady in a very formal, affected voice: 'If you would go to that changing cubicle there, madam. Nearest to where the old gentleman is sitting.' My God! Old gentleman! Me! I nearly threw something at Trace.

"The elderly lady said: 'Why not the other?' And Trace said: 'That one is currently occupied, madam.' Now, I happened to know it was not, because as I came to sit down in the chair, I saw someone coming out of the changing cubicle furthest from me. I'm pretty sure Trace and the Blonde had seen them too. So the woman went in through the curtain nearest to me. I had a brief glimpse of what lay beyond. It seemed perfectly normal except rather more dimly lit than expected, and the mirror reflected an oblong of pure darkness. I only had the briefest of glances, though, and I turned my attention surreptitiously back to the two shop assistants.

"The Blonde looked at Trace, who said: 'She can go to Hell and fuck herself there.' Now I reckon to be pretty unshockable, but this was said in such a cool, matter-of-fact voice that it shook even me. I studied my mobile intently and tried hard to pretend I had not heard what Trace had said. I doubt whether they noticed, though, because by that time they were attending to another client.

"Shortly afterwards I heard this cry, more of a wail if you know what I mean. It was quite faint, seemed to come from a long way away, but definitely from behind the curtain of that changing cubicle. The curtain started to move, as if someone was fumbling behind it, trying desperately to get out. This movement was accompanied by a whimpering sound, more like a dog's than a human being's. Then the curtain parted and it burst out.

"What surprises me most in retrospect is that nobody else in the shop apart from me appeared to pay it much attention. It was the old lady who went into the cubicle, but she had changed. The head, partly covered by a piece of dirty grey cloth, was twisted and elongated, so that her features were barely recognisable. The face was bestial, half-human, half like that of a goat, and the eyes were bulging. I noticed that the pupils were not humanly round but slitted, like a cat's. She was making a faint animal whining sound. No distinguishable words were uttered. She staggered on two thin and sinewy legs. They were bare, sprinkled with coarse grey hairs, and several times she almost fell. I realised why this was. Her right leg was so twisted that the foot, shod in a heavy brown leather sandal, was back to front, its scaly heel facing forward. What clothes it had on were no more than rags, and all black.

"I realised, even then, that this must be some kind of hallucination, but that did not make it any less terrifying. What was happening to me? I must be ill, having a weird sort of seizure. I could barely get to my feet but I did so to follow this monstrosity in the hope that my eyes would somehow adjust and I would see properly again. I blinked hard, each time expecting my sight to return to normal, but it didn't.

"The creature stumbled through the shop while I followed. It went out of the door and into the street where it collapsed onto the pavement outside. The rain had stopped and some fitful sunlight was breaking through. I thought of going out and doing something to help, but what could I do? Fortunately for me, by the time I had got to the shop door, a considerable crowd had gathered around the body, obscuring it from view. What they were seeing I don't know, and frankly I don't want to.

"I began to breathe hard, trying to restore a sense of normality to myself. It must have been a waking dream of some kind. I was certainly feeling very exhausted. As I was going back to my chair, I saw Anna at the counter with a blouse on a hanger, and Trace point towards the changing cubicles. As Anna turned in that direction, I hurried to catch up with her. I did not want to cause a disturbance, but I was determined at all costs to prevent her going into the cubicle from which that thing – that creature – had emerged. I opened my mouth to speak but nothing came out. She did go into that cubicle; I could swear to it. I saw the curtain shake, and I could do nothing but follow her and try to save her. I pulled aside the curtain and went in after her.

"I could not see her anywhere, but it was all rather dim. I called out to Anna and thought I heard a faint answer from somewhere.

There was a mirror on one wall, yet when I looked at it there seemed to be no reflection of me in the glass, though I could see the curtain behind me. My eyesight – or the room – was darkening by the second now. The space I was in, by contrast, looked as though it was getting larger, but perhaps this was the fading light. Then I was in complete darkness.

"I knew by that time that I must be suffering from something physical, as well as mental: perhaps a heart attack. I could see nothing, and began to grope my way towards the curtain, or what I guessed was my way because I had lost all sense of direction. I was uttering those whimpering animal sounds that I had heard coming from the old lady. My hands met something that at first I thought was the curtain. It was certainly cloth of some kind, but thinner, almost muslin, and beneath the cloth was a shape which felt like a head. There was a round smooth cranium and then below it two indentations, as if it might be two eye sockets. I know it said something to me in a low, sort of jabbering voice which I cannot now remember, but it put me into a further state of shock, after which I can remember barely anything at all until, somehow, I staggered out of that cubicle, stone bloody blind, as you see me now."

Fergus stopped to take in a great gulp of air; beads of sweat were coursing down his forehead into the bandages over his eyes.

"I don't quite know what happened next, but Anna was there. She was safe, at least, thank God! According to her, she hadn't gone into my changing cubicle; she'd gone into the other one, and she had heard me calling out, but only very indistinctly. Anyway, they summoned an ambulance and I was carted off. Anna was very sweet; went with me in the ambulance and all that, but I could tell she was just doing it out of kindness. Not more than that. After all, in her eyes, we were just friends.

"So, she has gone off on tour with the Alderness Festival Orchestra, and I've been here mostly. They tell me that I should be able to see, more or less, after this operation. That, if you will excuse the rather dull play upon words, remains to be seen."

I got the impression that Fergus felt even more deeply about Anna's absence than he was letting on, so I decided to contact her to let her know. Fergus and I went on talking, but we said nothing of great interest. I knew he didn't want me to go, while I felt guilty about my desperate urge to get away from him. Even as we talked about the old times at the Grand Theatre, Tudno Bay, where we had first met as young actors, my thoughts kept straying to that shop in Alderness. I had never seen it, but it was clear in my mind's eye.

I obtained Anna's address from the Alderness Festival people and have emailed asking her to visit Fergus and hinting at the strength of his feelings for her. I am quite sure Fergus would not have wanted me to do that, but it seems necessary. She is currently in Bratislava with the Festival Orchestra and I have yet to hear from her.

Yesterday, I went to Alderness. I did not tell my wife what I was doing. I said I was off on a research trip for my new book. It was a lame excuse and I am not sure she quite believed me, but it would have been too difficult to explain. I am not even sure if I can explain it to myself, just that I owed it to my friend to try to disentangle illusion from reality, if that is at all possible.

It was a white, damp day in Alderness, so misty that you could not tell where exactly the sea met the sky. I walked along the High Street and there was *Seahorse*, just as Fergus had described it with its arrangement of driftwood and rusty anchors in the shop window, denim yachting caps and cable-knit sweaters draped over them in an artistic manner. I went in.

I was surprised, in fact disturbed, by the way that my image of the place culled from Fergus's description almost exactly corresponded with the reality of the shop itself. It was as if I were seeing the place with his eyes. There on the walls were the fake Craxtons with their assemblies of staring sea-creatures lying dead in the foreground. Only the piped music was different: it was the regulation light pop, and not the moans of some sepulchral organ.

I recognised the two shop assistants from Fergus's descriptions: Trace, the senior partner, and the Blonde. I did not want to talk to them, at least not yet. I was afraid, so I decided to make a general tour of the shop before addressing them; but as I passed by the counter where Trace and the Blonde were, I heard Trace say:

"I can't stand all these dead people, can you? Makes you sick."

To which the Blonde, who was filing her nails, replied: "No, Trace. Dead people are the pits."

I was so astonished by this snatch of conversation that I could not prevent myself from stopping in my tracks and turning to stare at Trace and the Blonde. They noticed me and stared back.

Trace said: "Excuse me, sir, were you wanting anything?" It was not a friendly enquiry; I thought there was a hint of mockery in it.

I explained haltingly that I was a friend of Fergus Moore, who some weeks previously had 'had an accident' in this shop, and that I wanted to see for myself, and find out what had happened. It sounded very lame: it was. I was beginning to wonder what on earth had driven me to come here. Trace and the Blonde looked at each other and then me with suspicion.

Trace said: "Oh, I remember. The old man who went blind. Was that him?"

I nodded.

"Poor old man," said the Blonde, a slender note of sympathy in her voice. Trace gave her a hard glance, after which the Blonde was mute. I explained that Fergus would appear to have lost his sight in one of the changing cubicles at the back of the shop. Trace looked at me blankly.

"What d'you mean 'one of'? There's only one." The Blonde nodded her agreement; then it was my turn to look blank.

Suddenly and very decisively Trace came out from behind the counter, took me by the arm, and guided me to the back of the shop. She spoke no word as she did so. I felt like a small boy being taken unceremoniously by a schoolteacher towards an unknown punishment.

The back of the shop was as Fergus had described, but not quite. There was the 'man-seat', but next to it there were not two curtained alcoves for trying on clothes, but only one. I told Trace that Fergus had specifically stated that there were two.

Trace insisted, rather irritably, that there had never been a second changing room and pointed to the fact that the place where Fergus had said it had been was marked by a door and not a curtain. The door looked to me as if it had been very recently installed, but Trace told me emphatically that it had 'always been there'. When I asked what was beyond that door Trace gave a very vague response, something about it being 'the old part'; then she said, with what seemed to me like a touch of menace:

"Would you like to see for yourself, sir?"

I shook my head.

THE SERVICE

Ally Wilkes

"Not you, Karolina. You'll be doing the Bell family's private service."

A waft of humid air at the kitchen door. Dinner starts in ten minutes, and guests at the Mount Hotel tend to be punctual. Come sundown, there's little to do in the seaside town except drift through the neon patches of light from arcade to arcade, coins chiming like thousands of silver bells. This place had started dying long before the boom in online gambling.

Karolina sighs.

"They'll like you," the host says. Leans in, a little: "You don't look too obviously foreign."

Most of the Mount's waitresses are Spanish – immigrant workers pulled in by the recruitment agencies, washing up disoriented on these pebbled shores. They're lined up now in the thin strip separating the kitchen from the dining room, their world from the guests' world. Carla applies her lipstick briskly. It's good for tips. She presses her lips together, gives Karolina a scarlet smile and a wave.

"They're racist, then," Karolina says.

The host shrugs. "They are what they are." He reaches out and adjusts her little black-and-gold bow tie. It never sits straight; makes them all look like clowns about to tell a rather unfunny joke. She sighs, and follows him into the kitchen. She knows her English is crisp and precise enough for her to be mistaken for a native speaker.

Twenty side salads are plated up ready to go. Twenty bread baskets teeter on the trolleys. They're not meant to take unused rolls from one basket and put them in the next, but Karolina has been shouted at for failing to do exactly that, and now does it every night without thinking. Guests at her tables are sometimes five times removed from the bread's original recipient, poppy seeds spreading like spores. A lot of penny-pinching goes on.

Fat Sandor, the enormous head chef, gives her a suspicious look as she enters his greasy kingdom. "She's doing the service," the host says, and he grins with a flash of yellow molar.

They pause where the poor pastry chef is shivering over his cream horns. "Right, here are the rules. Number one: you stay in that room the whole time, okay? Unless you're fetching the food. You need a bathroom break – tough. You stay in the room and stand against the wall and stay silent. That's rule number two. You don't talk to the Bells. Don't ask if they want water, or if they're enjoying their meal. You're just there to fetch and carry. Number three, you'll lay the table exactly as I show you. Everything has to be perfect."

The pastry chef gives Karolina a glance of mingled fear and envy; he's clearly heard this speech before.

It's like walking through a portal into another dimension: the private dining room beyond the gleaming pastry station is crowded and brown. Beige. *So* much beige. The wallpaper has an undulating pattern of ribbon-tied wheatsheaves and beady-eyed field mice. There's too much furniture, and not a single window. The five-bulb tulip chandelier is a nightmare designed by someone who's never seen a tulip before.

Karolina laughs out loud. "It's like the Seventies," she says.

"They've owned the hotel since then, yes," the host snaps. "Now, look, I'll show you."

The Bells have special cutlery, oddly blunt and gold-tinged, and large willow-pattern plates depicting ships, storms at sea. Their table has three settings, and everything has to be at right angles. The salt is in a little ceramic jar; there's no pepper, or any other condiments. The doilies come from a catering pack tucked away in the top drawer of the massive dark-wooden dresser. "A fresh doily for each course," the host says firmly. "Understand? They're very particular. And—"

"Stay in the room, stay silent, I know," Karolina finishes. She's a fast learner.

Service begins.

A bell rings in the kitchen, and in the small room a grandfather clock ticks out the time in loud, annoying seconds. The door opens at the far end, and the Bells shuffle in.

The old man leads his wife by the arm. He's very thin, skin stretched tight over his face, and his eyes appear lidless and unblinking. She's bent nearly double, and doesn't walk too well. They must be ancient, Karolina thinks, and stifles the urge to pity them. They don't like the Spanish girls waiting on them? Bloody racists. Behind the old couple, the son wears dark glasses – she's been warned about this, there's something wrong with his eyes, light sensitive – and has hands so massive and slab-like they remind her of shrink-wrapped meat.

They sit.

The first course is grapefruit salad served in little cut-glass goblets, a maraschino cherry gleaming crimson. Karolina approaches the table to set it down, then retreats. They push it about. They don't speak, not even to each other. The silence grows.

The second course is "lamb!" (Sandor had barked it at her). Brown, overcooked meat, which the Bells saw at with their blunt knives and forks. It comes with potatoes and cabbage, although they don't eat those. The clock ticks away oppressively. The silence grows.

Karolina nearly forgets to put down fresh doilies for the dessert, because she's lost the capacity to feel time passing – the clock and the silence must have put her into a sort of fugue state. Tick tick tick. There's just the farty smell of cabbage and the gleaming eyes of the field mice and the sound of the Bells chewing. The service is endless.

Dessert is crumble with custard. They don't eat it.

"We like that one," the old man says to the host as they shuffle back out into their private hallway. The son turns around, and for a minute he stares through his dark glasses almost directly at Karolina. "She does things properly." The door closes and she's left to clear the dishes and fend off the superstitious stares of that anaemic-looking pastry chef.

Then she goes back to her room, a single bed surrounded by thin walls, the fluorescent light above the sink winking on and off, and sleeps straight through for twenty-four hours as if she's had a bad case of the flu.

* * *

Karolina doesn't get in the trouble she'd expected for missing her Tuesday shift. On Wednesday afternoon the host puts his hand on her forehead, business-like, and says, "Well, it looks like you're over whatever it was." There's something sideways about the way he looks at her. He tells her to come back in time for the Bells' private service that evening.

She fills the hour by walking down to the beach, past the off-licences with fortified windows and photos of wine bottles bleached bluish-grey by the sunlight. She'd liked the idea of living somewhere with a beach, even a pebbled one. But the pebbles are sharp rocks, ready to turn her ankle, and everywhere she looks the power station is on the horizon. She'd bought a few postcards for her grandmother; she's poor enough and far enough from home that her mobile phone is a small smooth stone with five pounds' credit for emergencies. But all the postcards were terrible, the power station looming in each one. The water had looked contaminated. She stares at it now, and shivers.

Some of the Spanish girls go down to the beach after service to sit on the rocks and drink, and smoke, and chat – little bright sparks in all that grey – but she can't imagine doing the same. She only really knows Carla, and one of the others had said, wafting a cigarette, "Ay, it doesn't matter," when Karolina had asked her name. The hotel has a high turnover of waitresses and chambermaids. Only Fat Sandor has been here forever, and the androgynous amber-eyed host.

The hotel crouches on the cliffs like a demon squatting over the town.

"Come on – you're late!" the host hisses when she returns, and shoves her towards the pastry area so fast she hits her thigh on the sharp corner of the work surface. It'll come up blue: she's been so pale since she moved here.

Karolina enters the room. In her hurry to get out the doilies, place the cutlery, fill the water jug, the walls whirl around her like the boarded-up carousel on the esplanade, and she wonders just how *over it* she really is. She fastens her hair with a clip – it smells faintly of smoke and salt – and takes her place in the corner of the room. It has one too many corners. It's a pentagon, and something about that makes the skin prickle on the back of her neck, like she's been out in the sun and entered a cool underpass.

The Bell family troop in, and there's a flicker of satisfied recognition on the old man's face, his eyebrows high and thin. She serves the first course (tomato soup, little hard explosions of croutons from a ten-kilo sack by the pantry door) and time just…stops.

She comes to when the old man says something to the son, sharply and with malice in his voice, but she can't quite understand what he's saying. There's a tabloid paper on the dresser, shouting about immigrants and borders and the flood. The Bell family has owned the Mount since the Seventies. They must be English, but for some reason it sounds garbled coming from those thin lips.

There's a pause, and Karolina finds herself wondering if they can hear what she's thinking. The old woman wipes her mouth. The grandfather clock ticks on.

When it's over, the cold air on her face makes her swallow bile, gives her a sharp tickling behind her eyes, as if her body is preparing for an assault, and she only just makes it to the staff toilet before she throws up. Her chest aches. Her forehead feels slick with sweat, and she unclips her hair, clips it up again, remembering a fragment from all that lost time: how the old woman had looked up when Karolina served her meat.

Looked up with her china-blue eyes and *sniffed*.

The headache is worse than before. The chills make her pile her coat and towel on top of her covers, then thrash it all off in the night, as if she's being devoured.

★ ★ ★

"Have you ever seen them outside the hotel?" Karolina asks. She's in the Koffee Korner – aggressively low couches and a perpetually looping lounge-music track – pulling the last usable meat off chicken carcasses. It's a slow afternoon, so she's been sent upstairs, away from Sandor's towering mood. It's impossible to get all the flesh off with gloves on, so she's using her bare hands to pick and scrape and tweeze out the little scraps that will go into chicken mayo sandwiches. It gets under her nails, and smells.

She's a vegetarian.

"Sometimes the son – Billy, I think?" the Koffee Korner girl answers. She's Australian, on a better contract than the rest, which is how she's escaped the dining room. "Billy Bell. It sounds like a joke, right? The girl before me used to see him around town, sometimes. But then he stopped."

"That's when he got his...condition?" Karolina says. "The glasses." The sun is already edging behind the privet bushes. For a hotel on top of the cliffs, the Mount is surprisingly dark.

"Right. About the time that girl went missing."

Karolina doesn't ask which one.

She's called downstairs into the linen cage to fold tablecloths until the smell of starch gets too much, and she ducks out into the staff 'garden' at the bottom of the ventilation shaft. One of the Spanish girls – she thinks her name is Rosa – refuses to lend her a cigarette, and is then asked to put it out; it's wafting up towards the guest areas. Karolina eyes the ponderous concrete of the staff area's underbelly and thinks about the location of the five-cornered room.

It's at the centre of the hotel. No windows. The second door leads to a private hallway containing a lift and staircase. The Bells live in the attic.

Karolina finds the conference suite upstairs; empty chairs look at her accusingly. That room must be right underneath. She finds a loose tile of carpet, prises it up. Bare floorboards. And – yes – a knothole. She's looking down onto the Bells' table, left waiting, expectant. One room from the west. One room from the east.

Dead centre, in fact.

That prickling feeling again. She feels superstitious, and it reminds her of her grandmother. Round-framed spectacles, squat TV quietly churning to itself in the corner as unsuitable stories were told to an impressionable girl. The feeling that monsters were real, shadows were watching, and the world was several shades darker, the woods several shades deeper, than they had any right to be.

The sunset is hazy pink from the pollution around the power station. It's like being inside one of her grandmother's polyester skirt suits.

When she goes to Carla's room, out in the accommodation block, the door is open, and a girl is efficiently removing the curtains. Carla had sewed them herself, lush and red, and the girl pulls each ring down with a small plastic *snap*.

"Where's Carla?"

"Gone," the girl shrugs. "Took everything with her."

The bed still has its hotel-issued blankets and pillows, the soap dispenser is still bolted to the wall above the tiny sink. But there aren't any clothes in the wardrobe, or thrown over the single chair, and all Carla's shoes are missing.

"When?"

"Yesterday," the girl says.

Karolina realises she didn't know Carla's last name, or her plans. She didn't know if she wanted to go to college in England, or return home and marry and have children. She only knew Carla was kind, and no one else here was.

"I'm sorry," Karolina says, meaninglessly, and goes outside to cry.

There's a high turnover at the Mount Hotel.

She wonders about the chewy overcooked meat Sandor dishes up to the Bell family, night after night, with all the accompaniments from a Seventies cookbook – accompaniments which never get eaten. Drying her face and checking her mascara, she slips downstairs where they're getting ready for service, shining down cutlery at ice-buckets filled with boiling water and vinegar. The dining room smells like a chip shop.

It's almost too ridiculous, but she does it anyway. "Sandor," she says, leaning against the pass so her tits are perfectly framed by her arms, "could I ask you something? Like really, truly? Where does the meat come from?"

He gives her a suspicious look. "Now you wanna eat the meat?" Somehow it comes out dirty. She isn't surprised.

"No, I mean…" She takes a calculated risk. "It's local, right?"

The suspicious look curdles, and he turns away, arms wobbling threateningly. She can feel her pulse in her wrists. The rumours are true. Once every few months, meat arrives overnight in the fridges without going through the checklists, and the girls say there's a personal connection to the slaughterhouse.

She looks for Carla everywhere, but doesn't find her.

★ ★ ★

Karolina takes iron for the fatigue. Metallic-tasting juice from the town's only health-food store, a woman yawning widely on the carton. She's never been so tired as when performing private service for the Bells. She skips almost every other shift, and the host never says anything about it, even though she's seen him lock someone into the walk-in freezer ("Just a joke! Just a joke! Don't sue me!") for missed overtime before.

She realises it's expected. The girls who attend that five-cornered room, who stand still and quiet and wait, are always drained.

Better that, she supposes, than the ones who disappear.

She finds herself looking dully at the sous-chef's mise-en-place, chopped into little stainless-steel bowls, everything in its own separated world. There's not much call for what their guests would describe as "fancy cooking": herbs other than parsley or rosemary are viewed with suspicion, let alone the bright smoky paprika that stained her grandmother's fingers red. There's grated nutmeg to sweeten the bland white sauce, and a few sad cloves of chopped garlic. The Mount has one vegetarian option, a deep-fried spring roll – a single fat one like a crispy battleship – sitting on a bed of rice with violent sweet-and-sour sauce.

She dips her fingers into the garlic, feeling it sting her bitten nail-beds. It's the work of a moment to smear it over the pallid chops waiting to be grilled.

In the five-cornered room, the Bells don't even pick up their gold cutlery. "What's this?" the old man says, turning up his nose in an exaggerated tenting of distaste.

The old lady coughs. A single thread of saliva glistens at the corner of her mouth. She pulls out a handkerchief and wipes it away. "Disgusting."

"Sandor knows better," the old man says petulantly. "He must have got it mixed up. Girl!"

It's the first time the Bells have addressed Karolina directly, and it makes her shrivel inside, her skin crawl. She looks at the old man's sharp fingernails, the son's dark-hidden eyes. The room is crowded and beige-and-brown and the clock ticks on and on, and she's sure no one could possibly have tasted that single smear of garlic, let alone smelled it.

"Girl," the old man says again, and she widens her eyes, as if she's only just heard him. She doesn't breathe. It seems important he doesn't *know* how aware she is. "Take this – foreign rubbish – away. Tell them to make it again."

And they clatter their cutlery onto the plates, rip and ball up the doilies, as if it's all been contaminated, as if that little fingertip of garlic has ruined everything.

She gets the sous-chef to prepare more meat, sits shivering on the pastry table while she does so, her arse making a shadow in the dusting of icing sugar. The pastry chef is pale as death, keeps giving frightened glances towards the five-cornered room. The shivering starts at her toes and moves all the way up to her cleavage, her breastbone, her bony clavicle, where she'd taken another fingertip of garlic and pressed it – once – against her beating vein.

She's a girl. She knows about all sorts of vampires.

★ ★ ★

Karolina treks to the phone box on the esplanade. Above her, the Mount is shrouded in mist, its greying façade blending with the cliffs, and the rain finds its way inside her boots until she's squelching with each step. She doesn't have the energy to run, or even break into a jog. "You're getting pale!" Rosa – maybe – had said to her, and she'd tried some tanning moisturiser, the sort that smells like biscuits and leaves traitorous smears between the fingers.

Karolina knows she's getting pale, and getting tired, and it's all connected to the Bells. They'd reached down from their attic and plucked her from the waiting staff. Time passes differently in their five-cornered room, and they don't eat garlic, or the potatoes Sandor slams onto the counter like a personal insult. They've been here for over forty years, and something of their ancient silence has infected the town as well.

She blinks rain out of her eyes, and ducks into the piss-smelling box. Around her, women with orange skin spread their legs, fleshy and alluring. The phone eats all her coins, and doesn't offer any answers to where Carla has gone. The receiver moulds to her ear like a sweaty mouth.

The despair almost surprises her. Gives way to anger just as quickly.

How dare they take her? How *dare* they.

Back at the hotel, a new girl has joined the waitresses in that concrete ventilation shaft. She's got honey-coloured hair, light eyes, a delicate upturned nose. She's wearing a little crucifix on a gold chain, and the host tells her to take it off, personal religious convictions aren't welcome in the workplace. She hesitates, chewing her lip, and Karolina can see her weighing up whether it's worth it to resist. But she's come all the way from Northern Ireland, through some byzantine process of the recruitment agencies.

Her name is Mary. She doesn't look 'too foreign'. Karolina's unsurprised when the host says, "Will you help me show her how we do the private service? She can cover for you – when you're under the weather."

She pauses in her shining of the silver. A moist breath of hot vinegar floats up. "What happened to the girl who did service before me?"

The host shrugs. "Morning shift. You know what they're like."

An appeal to ancient prejudice. Back when Karolina still got up for breakfast – leftovers from the hot buffet and sliced fruit that wouldn't survive another day before going fizzy – the morning girls would gather together on one side of the room, shunning the evening shift and being shunned in turn. They were all native to the town. Karolina wondered that any of them would set foot in the Mount after the pink-tinged sunset.

"No, really. Where did she go?"

The host puffs out his cheeks. "Uni, I suppose. Now get back to work."

Karolina stares at the glinting cutlery, wickedly hot out of the bucket. Remembers Carla being pulled aside, the host asking her to fill in, telling her to wipe off that lipstick and put her hair up neatly. The new girl comes over, and Karolina wants to tell her to run. To leave the hotel while it's sunlight, and keep running, before the Mount gets its claws into her.

She stares at the silver.

"You don't want to wait on the Bells," she says quietly. "Take it from me."

Mary laughs. "Oh, they're just some old people, aren't they? I've heard about them. Poor weird things."

"No – really."

"Worried I'll take your place?" Mary says sweetly. "Must be an easy ride." She glances with her fresh new-girl eyes at the crammed dining room, the flock wallpaper, the low ceilings, the useless bar in the corner where the card machine never gets a signal.

"Wear your crucifix," Karolina says. "Seriously, I mean it."

"Karolina!" the host hisses, and wrenches her away by the arm. "Don't think you're doing her any favours. Where do you think she'll go, if she makes trouble? There aren't any other jobs. You've seen the town. And where will she live? Think she's got enough money to get back to Ireland?"

Karolina shakes her head.

"Think you've got enough money to get home?"

And Karolina sees a boat – a sailing-ship, like the ones on the Bells' willow-pattern crockery – docking in the harbour. Canvas crackling, rigging pregnant with movement, and a box on the deck. An oddly shaped box, and maybe that's how the Bells got here, years and years ago. They've been hiding in plain sight ever since. She wonders whether she'll be shipped home in a coffin. Whether Mary will. Whether Carla has been. Or whether they'll all disappear into thin air.

The walk-in fridges. The pale, undercooked meat.

Whatever they're taking from her in the five-cornered room, however they're sustaining themselves, it's – abominable. She sees the hotel built on a foundation of blood and shadows, and she pushes the host away and walks off to get ready for the service.

* * *

It doesn't take her long to come up with a plan.

Mary has the flu, after her first night in the five-cornered room, and Karolina grabs the pastry chef and hisses, "What happened? How was she?"

"Pale," he stutters. "Well – paler than before. Sweating. Peaky."

Karolina wonders how many girls have come through his frigid domain on the way to service, and makes sure to sweep over a platter of choux buns as she stalks off. Sandor bellows with the rage and pain of a stuck animal.

She waits for the morning to dawn grey and dingy over the town, and goes back to that health-food store. They sell it to her without any questions. The liquid is clear, and comes in a brown bottle. When she unscrews the cap, she almost expects the fish-and-chips smell of the polishing station, but it's odourless.

Colloidal silver. Invisible to the eye, the microscopic particles swimming around in suspension like silverfish. She knows the Bells can smell garlic, but this looks harmless as water.

Mary staggers in for service like she's just left a sauna; pink-cheeked and vague when spoken to. Karolina checks whether she's wearing the crucifix, and is unsurprised to hear that the host has confiscated it, put it in the little red-and-black lockbox housing their cash tips. There's still a crumpled envelope in there with Carla's name, passed over every Friday night when the disbursement is done. Carla would have leapt on it and cooed with delight at the thought of more cigarettes, more lipstick, maybe a trip to the cinema. She and Karolina had shared popcorn, half salt, half sweet.

Karolina doesn't want to get Mary into trouble, but it's better – in case this doesn't succeed – if the attempt can't be traced back to her. So she dumps the colloidal silver into the Bells' cut-glass water jug, fills it to the brim from the cold pot wash tap, and places it on the doily and walks out.

Dinner service passes. Guests mouth at scalding tomato soup. Wine is presented with a flourish. Someone presses a tip on her in coppers that, when counted, is exactly seventy-six pence and a handful of euros. Every time she goes into the kitchen, she listens for sounds from the five-cornered room, but they're drowned out, if there are any sounds at all, by the clatter and bang of Sandor picking on his minions.

She waits until she can't bear it, then slips upstairs – pretending they need a cash float from the Koffee Korner – and into the empty conference suite, turning the sign around behind her to 'meeting in progress'. Her bitten fingernails hurt as she yanks up the carpet, lies on her side to press her face to the knothole. The table underneath her is a perfect circle, a single lidless eye.

The water jug is nearly empty, and the old man is coughing. It's a rattling sound, like wind trying sash windows – the staff accommodation is draughty, rabbit-warren narrow – and he's gripping the tablecloth with bony fingers. Karolina's heart jumps when she sees that his long nails are turning silver-purple. He looks like he's struggling to breathe. A cough, then a slaughtering sound, as he fights for air. She'd put the whole bottle in. Beside him, the old woman is trying to stand up, making a low sound, and from the jittering of her knees Karolina understands she's having some sort of fit.

Mary is pinned to the wall, opposite the clock. Her wide eyes are fixed on the clock. She seems to be in a trance. The Bells don't want their girls to notice too much.

The old man wheezes, thumps a limp hand against his chest. He reaches out for water and spills his glass on the table. He drinks noisily, messily, from the jug. Coughs again. Says something pleading to the old woman, not recognisable as English at all.

The son sits immobile.

With a whistle, the old man stops breathing. The old woman clutches her chest, a clawed hand over her heart, and falls sideways. There's a crunch. Old bones.

Mary remains frozen.

The son stands up. He's so big – nearly seven feet tall, and from this angle Karolina can just see his slicked-over hair, the ashen fall of dandruff on his shoulders. It's so oddly human it makes her ball up her hand and cram it into her mouth to stop herself making a sound. He's moving, slowly, towards Mary. She thinks about vampire stories. She imagines the son picking delicate little Mary up with those meaty hands, pulling her blonde hair to the side. Sinking his tombstone-like teeth into her neck. Sunglasses jiggling as she struggles.

Karolina hesitates.

Then spits out her own fist and hisses, through the hole, "Mary! Mary, *wake up*!"

The son looks around sharply, trying to see where the voice comes from. Then kneels next to the old man, cradles his head, lets out a grunt. Then a howl, and it's that howl – an ululation, thin and piercing – which brings the host running through the kitchen door.

The spell is broken. Mary's chest heaves, and she goes to clutch a crucifix that's no longer there. The host screams, "Call an ambulance!"

Karolina replaces the carpet tile quietly, and swallows.

* * *

Lingering by the pigeonholes in the back office, Karolina brushes her fingers softly over the one marked CARLA with a little heart. The reception girls are gossiping.

"Blue all over," one is saying. "By the time he got to the hospital!"

"Poor thing," the other says, pleasantly scandalised. "To see her husband like that. It's no wonder her heart gave out."

The consensus is the Bells were ancient – in their late nineties, perhaps – although no one can pin down their exact age. Karolina thinks all the guesses are wide of the mark, because she's crept out to look at the photos in the little back hallway, behind that dreadful pentagon room, seat of their power. The photos are framed discreetly to draw no attention; a lost member of staff might think them harmless. But Karolina is sure she sees the old man's face in a picture from the 1920s, when the hotel was first built. The son shaking the mayor's hand at its grand opening. The old woman serving the first afternoon tea in a round hat with a ribbon, her pale eyes sharp and knowing.

Perhaps all old people look the same. Perhaps black and white is a terrible medium through which to compare faces. Perhaps.

No one knows if they're dead, despite the police coming in and out with cameras and a sleepy, disbelieving air. The host forbids gossip – he's more angular and dreadful than ever, an usher to the damned, the gold flecks in his eyes echoing those stupid bow ties – and makes them deep clean the pot wash instead. Karolina rolls up her sleeves and gets to work. The rubber gloves are wide and floppy as skin torn off a rabbit.

Mary is very quiet, gives her a tentative smile. "I heard you. Calling my name. Thank you."

Whatever happens, Karolina thinks, she has one more job to do.

Two days go by and still the older Bells aren't out of hospital. She hears the word 'deteriorating' and is fiercely glad. She learns the area around that private staircase, her feet soft and quiet on the deep pile of the undisturbed plum-coloured carpet. Three flights, the caged maw of the lift opening on each hallway. The son takes his meals in his room, and doesn't come down. She listens at his door.

She hopes he's grieving, to whatever extent those things can grieve.

She buys the necessary items: petrol in a can with a handle, so she can lift it. Chains and padlocks from the DIY store in the next town over, using a precious afternoon off to take the little clifftop bus, each seat stained with the imprint of hopelessness.

And she waits.

Eventually the host calls Mary aside and tells her, voice like syrup, that she'll be performing private service that evening. She has the vigour – really, Karolina didn't think she had it in her – to say, "What's happened to old man Bell? And his missus?"

The host sighs. Looks around. Doesn't see Karolina behind the fridges, lowers his voice. "They're gone. Better get back to normal, as normal as we can, for the last one's sake."

Karolina hugs this to herself. Skips out through the pass feeling weightless. She hasn't packed her things, but – reflecting on it – there's nothing in this place she'd miss.

⋆ ⋆ ⋆

The petrol makes her cough, but she covers it afterwards with magnolia-scented Shake and Vac from the cleaning cupboard, layers and layers of the stuff until it smells like a harem girl has died on that landing. She hopes it'll be enough. They'd smelled the garlic, but not the silver. They're not infallible.

When the son comes out of his room, it's after sundown, long shadows reaching their fingers through the staircase windows. He's a dark bite taken out of the world, and enters the lift with his head bowed. Preoccupied.

Karolina steps out from behind the curtain.

The lift starts moving with a clattering exhale. It's jerky, and old, and there's a moment where everything seems utterly still. The son looks up, sunglasses glinting in the dying light, and catches sight of her. But he's on his way down, and doesn't perceive the threat.

Her heart is hammering in her chest like it's trying to get out. She pulls the final chain from her blouse, warmed by the heat of her blood, and fastens it around the doors, barring them on this level too. Then turns in one swift movement to smash the little square of glass on the fire alarm panel.

The sirens start.

The lift stops.

She can see the top of his head, the peaked black hair, the dome-like forehead. He looks so much *more* like her grandmother's stories than the other ones.

The vampire looks around.

She thumbs the lighter open.

When she drops it with a thud into the locked cage of the lift, time starts up again. There's a thick *whumph* of ignition. Heat, and dancing yellow light, and the creature presses itself back against the padded leatherette, trying to avoid the flickering stream of flames. But it's such a small space. The sirens drown the noises it makes – not screams, she expected screams, but a disbelieving guttural cawing. It smashes the mirror with one sledgehammer hand in its panic and confusion. Such a large creature for such a small space. Petrol soaked into every inch of that lift, and no way out.

She thinks she sees its sunglasses pop in the heat, melt onto its face.

And then there are blue lights winking through the windows, in that horrible peach-and-pollution sunset, and she has to run.

⋆ ⋆ ⋆

Two postcards.

Her grandmother's apartment is in a tall cool building with mosaic tiles in the echoing entrance hall. From outside, Karolina can hear the honking of car horns and a busker playing the trumpet. Her grandmother sometimes loses things, has lost the mailbox key, and Karolina has to waggle her fingers around in the slot to get the mail, keeping her nails long to assist.

One postcard shows a spill of dark hexagons and pentagons, sending a shiver down her spine. Then she realises it's the Giant's Causeway, and turns it over to read – in careful, childish handwriting – the thanks of Mary.

The other is tacky as anything, a flamenco dancer with a ruffled skirt of some highly flammable fabric. Crimson like Valentine hearts.

Karolina feels the first prickling of doubt.

The hallway is still, dust motes floating in the breeze. The busker is singing a folk-song, choking a little on the high notes.

The postcard has taken a long time to arrive. The address has been annotated several times, as the author had only the surname and the town. But it's a small enough place, and her grandmother has lived here for sixty-four years, ever since she moved down from the mountains. Eventually it found them.

"KARO!" it reads. "Don't be angry at me. My boyfriend told me he wanted to marry me—" and there's a crude drawing of a woman in a veil, holding up a hand to show a ring that radiates like a lump of uranium, like the foam on that sickly power-station beach.

"But in case you've left the HOTEL, I'll never forget you.

XOXO, CARLA."

THE LATE MRS. APPLEGARTH

Mark Gatiss

The tablecloth was stark and white as a blank page. Ken drew a pattern on it with his fork, like sled tracks in the snow. Like in that film he saw years ago. The film he saw with Anna. There'd been wine. Hands brushing. Then a kiss. It was perfect.

Too perfect.

"Ready to order, sir?"

Ken ordered what he always ordered. The fish for him, veal for her.

When it came he told himself to slow down or he'd gobble it all up in fifteen minutes flat.

⋆ ⋆ ⋆

The empty chair across from him was like an accusation. When Anna was alive, he'd never been good with marking anniversaries. Garage bouquets. Impersonal chocolates. Hastily scrawled cards. Now he marked the passing years with this meal. This lonely vigil. Pointless, he knew. Like saving her number on his phone. But what else did he have? What else was left of her?

At last, the waiter, tired of bumping into the chair, pushed it in so it slid snugly under the table. Ken opened his mouth to say something but didn't. What was the point? She was gone.

He glanced over at Anna's untouched plate, cutlery just as it had been laid out, gravy congealing around the chop like old brown blood.

Out of habit, he dabbed his mouth with a crisp napkin, pushed back his chair and made for the Gents.

The light in the lavatory was harsh and white, almost painful. Idly, he watched the stream of his piss rocking the little blue disinfectant tablet from side to side. He stared through a tiny window at the black night outside. Sighed hugely. He should go. Settle the bill. Get home. This would be the last time. Five years of memorialising. Of 'celebrating' a life. Making up for all the things he'd never done for her. But this would be the end. It was time to move on.

When he got back to the table, Anna's plate was empty.

Not cleared away. Empty. The potatoes and carrots gone, the gravy scooped up, the veal chop only a rind of dun-coloured fat.

Ken frowned.

"Excuse me?"

"Yes, sir?"

Ken pointed at the empty plate. The waiter scanned the room. Peered at the bobbing heads, the laughing families, the lonely singletons.

"Oh. She *was* here."

"Who?"

"Your friend."

"I wasn't... I'm not expecting anyone."

"Well, she seemed to know you. I'm sure she'll be back any time now."

Ken felt suddenly cold. It passed over him like a prickling wave. His scalp shifted as though it had come unmoored.

"Who...did she say she was?"

"Didn't say, sir. Just apologised."

"What for?"

The waiter smiled. "Being late."

THE FIG TREE

Lucie McKnight Hardy

It had been Gareth's idea that they spend the final week of the holidays in Wales – something to do with a vague Welsh connection on his mother's side. They'd found the house online, and it looked idyllic – a three-bedroom cottage that bordered a brook in a pretty village with a pub and a shop. Bella had booked it there and then, surprised that it was still available over the August bank holiday weekend, and a week later they'd braved the heatwave and left their house in the Bristol suburbs and had travelled along the M4, before heading north into the wilderness of the Brecon Beacons.

They'd found the cottage easily enough from the directions in the email: follow the road through the village, over the little bridge, past the shop and there it was on the left-hand side, set back slightly from the road and next door to the pub. Gareth had parked in the narrow front drive and they'd got out, Bella peeling herself from the passenger seat, grateful to be out of the sticky confines of the car. Sweating from the exertion, she extracted the sleeping Oliver, still strapped into his car seat, from the back. A wasp buzzed up against her hair, and she flapped a hand at it to ward it away, even though she knew it was the wrong thing to do. It hung, indolent, in the still air, and it was only when she swiped at it again that it bounced lazily away. Margot climbed out and stood silently next to Bella, her small hand clammy when it grasped her mother's.

The house was small, and even though the internet listing had called it 'bijou' and 'cosy', Bella thought that 'tiny' was a fairer description. But it was very pretty, she couldn't deny that. It was made of red brick, the same as the pub, and an arched door, painted in the ubiquitous Farrow & Ball green, gave the impression of a schoolhouse or chapel; the diamond-shaped panes of leaded glass in the windows reinforced this impression. Bella skirted the car and walked around to the side of the property, where a carved stone plaque set into the wall at the apex announced: '1863'.

"It's nice," Bella said to Gareth as he joined her. "Even nicer than it looked on the website."

"I think you're right. I still don't know why it was available this late in the summer, especially over a bank holiday weekend," said Gareth. "You'd think it would have been snapped up."

"Perhaps they had a cancellation, I don't know. Anyway, their loss is our gain." Bella took out her phone and scrolled through her emails.

"Right, it says here we need to collect the keys from the pub." She nodded at the building next door – squat, slightly shabby, with loose slates threatening to slip from the roof and small, grubby windows. "Ready to face the wrath of the locals?" Gareth shook his head, but he was smiling.

"As someone of – admittedly dubious – Welsh heritage, I resent your accusation that all the locals will be hostile. That's a stereotype, a sad trope invented by the English to explain their unpopularity around these parts."

"Yeah, whatever. Bet we'll still get withering looks and everyone will start speaking Welsh as soon as we go in." Bella looked at her watch. "We're a bit early. It says we can collect the keys from two o'clock onwards."

"Shall we have a look around, then?" asked Gareth, stretching his arms above his head. "We can check out the garden, and then head over to the pub for lunch. By the time we've finished it'll be time to pick up the keys."

Bella nodded her assent and picked up the car seat containing the still-sleeping Oliver. She became conscious of Margot wrapping her arms around her thighs, clingy as ever, and looked down into her daughter's broad, open face.

"What do you think, sweetheart?" she asked.

Margot took time to consider her answer, reticent as ever, but wanting to please.

"It's okay, I guess," she said, biting her lip, and Bella knew this was the best answer she could hope for.

★ ★ ★

The fig tree was tucked into the right angle where the porch adjoined the kitchen wall. It was a vast thing, its branches spreading outwards and upwards, and the healthiest plant Bella had seen in the weeks-long drought. Its leaves were a solid, vibrant green, stark against the red bricks. The fruit hung heavy from the branches, obscenely testicular in the way they swung on the branches, jammily plump and purple, waiting to burst. One of the hottest and driest summers on record and they were still fat and juicy.

"We could make chutney," Gareth said, now that they'd exhausted their inspection of the outside of the house. "Or jam."

Bella snorted.

"I'm not exactly known for my skills in the kitchen. Besides, they'll be good for nothing in a couple of days. Look at them – already starting to rot." And it was true: here and there the fruits were shrivelled, balled up into themselves, like discarded socks. "I think we should try and enjoy the last week of the holidays, without expecting me to come over all Mary Berry." This elicited a small smile from Gareth.

The garden was evidently suffering from the drought. A friable, yellow lawn filled the space between the back of the house and a small stream, reduced to little more than a trickle now. A couple of puny shrubs slunk despondently to one side. The fig tree was the only sign of vitality, its limbs broad and strong, leaves bright and verdant.

Gareth extricated Oliver from the car seat and started wrestling him into the sling which he wore on his front. The baby looked around for a moment before settling into his father's chest with a sigh. He was a good baby; he slept well and fed easily, unlike Margot, who had been three before she had slept through the night and was a fussy eater, even now at the age of six.

Bella threw her head back, face up to the cloudless blue sky, and took a perverse pleasure in breathing in the arid air, the slight tang of rotting fruit. She reached out to touch one of the fig leaves, inexplicably drawn to the texture of its surface, glossy and smooth, and held it between her thumb and forefinger. A sharp stabbing pain made her yelp and yank her finger away, and a fat wasp darted angrily into the still air. Bella waved it away in panic, swatting it to the ground. It flailed there a couple of times, its wings convulsing, before she dragged her trainer over it, leaving just a smear of yellow and brown innards.

★ ★ ★

Bella was still sucking her finger in an attempt to remove the poison from the wasp sting as they walked the few steps to the pub. Gareth cradled the sleeping Oliver with both hands around the sling and pushed the door open with his hip. When it creaked he turned to Bella and raised his eyebrows, smiling sardonically.

"Beware of the hostile locals," he whispered. She managed a weak smile in return.

The inside of the pub was dark – gloomy, even – on one of the hottest days of the year. The grubby windows let in precious little light, and this was augmented by a sole strip light that hung over a scuffed pool table. A man in his fifties, wearing a sweat-stained T-shirt, was hunched over the table, about to take a shot, but stopped when the family entered and stood up, nudging his opponent who stood at his side. There were other customers – men in flat caps and women in cardigans – seated around tables, who all quickly stopped talking and looked to where the family stood at the door. Bella braced herself for a belligerent reception; to her surprise, the atmosphere became suddenly jovial.

The pool players placed their cues down on the table and picked up their drinks, which they raised in the direction of Bella and her family with broad smiles. The other customers also raised their glasses in hearty salutes, and Bella found herself smiling foolishly at them. She looked around her, at the huge inglenook fireplace, the fire mercifully unlit, adorned with horse brasses and some metal implements whose names she didn't know, but which were undoubtedly to do with farming.

The countryside they had passed when they got close to the village spoke of an agricultural community: large metal barns with gaping, open fronts, tractors parked in farmyards. There were quadbikes abandoned at the sides of fields, and grain silos standing stark against the sky. But the heatwave had desiccated the crops; the fields were sallow and fragile, and the random sheep they passed were skinny and gazed back at them, blank-eyed. Bella had felt a tug of sympathy for the community, so obviously dependent upon the whims of the weather for a living, and now having to turn to tourism to survive.

One wall was adorned with framed photographs – some sepia or black and white, others more recent and in faded colour. They all appeared to show a group of people – she assumed the pub's regulars – and she recognised the house in the background as the cottage they had rented; she could just about make out the fig tree in the background. Her interest was piqued by how the tree grew bigger as the photographs became more recent, and she inspected the text that was printed on the mounts below the photographs: 'August Bank Holiday,' it said each time, but then a different year – 1884, 1911, and onwards, through 1976, 1983 to the more recent 1995 and 2012. In each photograph the clothing and hairstyles changed, depending on the fashions of the time, but each picture depicted the people standing outside the cottage and raising their glasses in a celebratory fashion. The people all looked surprisingly similar to those in the pub, and Bella quelled a snort of derision as she realised it must be a very tightly knit community. As she inspected the photographs one by one, a little dog – a chihuahua, she thought – appeared at her ankles and wagged its tail manically, before running back to an old lady who sat at one of the tables and jumping up onto her lap. The lady beamed a toothy grin at Bella. And then Bella turned to the bar in the far corner, where a woman – she assumed the pub landlady – was looking delightedly at her, a half-poured pint of beer abandoned in her hand. It seemed the entire pub was joyfully transfixed by Bella and her family.

She walked over to the bar, conscious of the muttered greetings from the locals – "Welcome," "Nice to see you," "Enjoy your stay" – and smiling briefly at each well-wisher in turn. Bella was about to address the landlady, to explain that they'd come to collect the keys for the cottage next door, but the woman spoke before she could.

"Oh, how lovely that you've arrived. We've been expecting you." The woman's high-pitched voice suited her appearance – her small, compact frame, the candyfloss tufts of dyed orange hair that surrounded her angular face. Her wide-stretched lips, adorned with lavish magenta lipstick, put Bella in mind of a moray eel that had terrified her in a book at primary school. The landlady was surveying the rest of Bella's family – Gareth standing next to her clutching Oliver in his sling, Margot a little way off, transfixed by the photographs on the wall. The chihuahua was sniffing at her ankles, and Margot bent down to pet it.

"And this is everyone, is it? Mam and Dad and little girl and baby boy?" The woman sounded positively elated at the family's arrival, and Bella shifted uncomfortably.

"Yes. This is us!" Her voice was too high and falsely cheerful, in an effort to match the landlady's own enthusiasm. "We've popped in to pick up the keys. We've just arrived."

"Well, why don't you stay and have a drink – on the house, of course?" As she spoke, the woman's eyes were darting over the sleeping Oliver, occasionally landing on his pudgy thighs, or his chubby arms where they appeared from the sleeves of his sleepsuit. She licked her lips.

"How old is your little one?" she asked, not taking her eyes off the infant.

"He's six months," said Bella.

"Perfect!" exclaimed the landlady, and she clapped her hands, gold rings gleaming in the glare of the strip light. "Just perfect." She reached over the bar and stroked one of Oliver's bare arms with the back of her hand. "Oh, he's just perfect," she said again and her mouth widened into a grin, lipstick bleeding into the corners of her mouth.

Bella felt herself draw back a little. She looked around and saw that Margot was talking to the old lady with the chihuahua. Or, rather, the old lady was talking to Margot, her whiskery chin up close to the little girl's ear, whispering.

"Now, what can I get you? You must be thirsty, a long drive like that. It's so hot out there, isn't it? In years to come they'll be talking about the heatwave of 2022, you mark my words. Now, what will you have?" Bella didn't want to be rude, but she didn't know how to turn down the landlady's offer, and so she was glad when Gareth spoke up.

"That's very kind of you," he said in a firm voice, "but if we could just have the keys, we'll go and let ourselves in and unpack. We just really want to get settled in." A flicker of annoyance passed across the landlady's face, and then quickly retreated.

"Of course!" she said, turning to a hook on the wall behind her and lifting down a single key which she handed across to him. "There you are, now. That's the only one you'll need. That does the front door and the back door." Her voice trailed off for a moment and then she repeated, "The only one you'll need."

"Thank you very much." Just as Gareth pocketed the key, the landlady moved swiftly and reached over the bar. A scrawny, veined hand with long, sharp, vermilion nails came to rest on Oliver's plump thigh, the flesh whitening as she squeezed.

"Oh, he's just perfect."

* * *

That night, sleep eluded Bella. Recently she had been enjoying the odd glass of wine or G&T of an evening, and had found the effect to be one of delicious somnolence, at least until Oliver decided it was time for a feed. But she must have overdone it tonight, because she found herself at midnight, one o'clock and then two o'clock, agitated and sweaty, her heart racing, unable to switch off.

She thought back to Margot's uncustomary excitement when they'd finally let themselves into the cottage that afternoon. The hallway had been dark, the air dry and still, and Gareth had set about opening the windows.

"Smells like there's been no one in here for weeks, if not months," he'd muttered, as the casements were flung open. Hot air from outside the house mingled with the hot air inside the house, with the effect of no discernible change in temperature or air quality. They'd set about exploring – a sparsely furnished yet comfortable living room, and a spotless kitchen downstairs, and a bathroom and three bedrooms upstairs. Margot had taken an instant liking to the cottage, running from room to room and exclaiming in delight at each.

"I love it here!" she'd cried. "It's like something from a fairy tale!" She'd run up the stairs and called over the banisters almost immediately. "Can I have this room? This little one?" Bella had followed her up and stood on the landing. The room was barely big enough for a single bed and a nightstand, with most of the room given over to a built-in cupboard that faced the window.

"Yes, yes, I suppose so," Bella said, smiling at her daughter's enthusiasm. "It's smaller than the other two, though. Really tiny. Are you sure it's big enough? I was going to put Olly's travel cot in here."

Margot jumped and clapped her hands.

"Yes, of course it's big enough. Thank you, Mummy, you're the best," she said, wrapping her arms around Bella's waist and squeezing. Bella was surprised; her daughter was usually quiet and reticent, not given to outbursts of emotion.

* * *

When Bella's phone eventually told her it was 2:35 a.m., she pulled back the duvet and stood for a moment, conscious of the sweat pooling on her skin, before slipping on her dressing gown. Oliver was lying on his back in the travel cot in the front bedroom, illuminated by the light from the hall. She satisfied herself that his breathing was shallow and regular, and stepped back out onto the landing. The door to Margot's room was ajar, and she tiptoed in, glad of the pale glow from the nightlight. She leaned over and tucked the duvet over her daughter's bare arm. A small smile had settled on Margot's lips, and her mouth was moving slightly, muttering. Bella strained to listen, but the words were mumbled and faint, and then they merged into another sound, a gentle buzzing, a barely audible hum that she couldn't quite pin down. It might have been the stream that trickled along the edge of the garden, the sound making its way in through the open window, but she didn't think so. This was softer, more layered, as though a hundred separate voices were joined in a chorus. It seemed to be coming from the cupboard set into the wall on the other side of the room, and she was about to go to it when another sound caused her to stop abruptly.

Tap. Tap-tap-tap. Tap.

This time, it was coming from the window, a soft, insistent rapping. Bella turned and flung back the curtain. The fig tree. A rare breeze was causing it to brush up against the window, the fruit bashing rudely against the glass. Bella pulled the window shut and turned back to the room. The buzzing sound had ceased, and the room sat in silence again. She pulled her dressing gown tighter around her shoulders, despite the warmth of the night, and went back to bed.

★ ★ ★

"Yeuch! Imagine eating a wasp!" Margot's face was contorted into a mask of disgust and incredulity. Gareth stood before her, a fig in one hand.

"No, it's okay, there's an enzyme in it that dissolves the wasp. Look." He raised the fig to his mouth and took a bite, letting the juices gather on his chin. Margot was visibly sickened.

"But the enzyme is still in there? The enzyme that's come from the fig is still in there, so the wasp is still in there?"

Gareth swallowed and wiped the back of his hand across his mouth.

"Well, it's there and it's not there. You see, the female wasp crawls inside the fig and if it's a male fig, she'll lay her eggs in there. The eggs hatch into larvae – you know what they are, right?" Margot nodded solemnly. "And the larvae burrow out and turn into wasps. But if it's a female fig that the wasp goes into, she can't lay her eggs and she dies."

"Why doesn't she just leave? Why does she stay there and die?"

Gareth hesitated, but then ploughed on.

"Because the hole that she crawls in through is so narrow that her wings get pulled off," he said. Margot took a moment to digest this new information.

"So she dies anyway? Whether she lays her eggs or not?"

"I'm afraid so, love. Nature is cruel like that."

Margot looked thoughtful, as though she was reconciling herself to this fact. After a couple of seconds she shrugged.

"Well, I won't be eating figs anyway, just in case."

Bella smiled at this, and reached for her glass. The sun was high in the sky now, and the air around them was ripe with the scent of sun cream. Oliver sat on the playmat next to her, under the shade of the fig tree, a plastic rattle held in his pudgy hand. Gareth offered Bella a fig, but she grimaced and smiled and shook her head. She leaned back in the deckchair and closed her eyes. There was perfect bucolic silence, broken only by the tinkle of the stream, which flowed ten feet to her left, much dissipated now by the heatwave, but still a couple of feet deep. Perfectly set against it was a blackbird's trilled lullaby.

She was woken by Gareth shouting. He was leaning out of the upstairs window, the one in Margot's room, stretching his arm through the leaves of the fig tree, and pointing towards the stream. Oliver was sitting on the grass, six inches from the edge, seemingly transfixed by the flow of water. The canvas of the deckchair thwarted Bella's efforts to stand and it was a moment before she was on her feet. She grabbed her son, and hoisted him onto her hip just as Gareth appeared at the back door, breathless.

"What happened?" Bella asked, trying to shush the bawling infant. Gareth's face was like parchment.

"He was sitting there. Right at the edge of the river. He was about to fall in when I looked out of the window and saw him."

"What? How did he get there?" Bella felt a hot flush of fear rise through her. "He was on the playmat. How did he get over there?"

"I don't know, do I? I was upstairs with Margot, trying to fix her cupboard, when I looked out of the window and there he was. You were asleep." Almost, but not quite, an accusation.

"Shit." Bella pushed her hand through her hair. She hugged her son tighter, but this only served to make him cry louder, great wailing sobs that made him gulp for air. Gareth wiped his hands on his jeans and attempted a smile.

"It's all okay. It could have been worse." Bella was grateful for his attempt at reconciliation, and she nodded.

"At least we know he's crawling now," she said and looked around for Margot. A tapping from above made her look up, and her daughter was there, looking down at them from her bedroom window. She was smiling.

* * *

It was late and the children were in bed. The night air was still and heavy and rank with the day's heat. There was a barely perceptible smell, ripe and fruity, which Margot thought might be from the over-ripe figs on the tree outside the kitchen window. She resolved that the next day she would strip the fruit from the tree and throw it in the bin. Gareth topped up her glass of lager and then wiped a crust of naan bread around his plate to gather the last of the curry.

"What did you mean about Margot's cupboard?" Bella asked him.

"Eh? You what?"

"When...when Olly crawled over to the river, you said that you'd gone upstairs to look at Margot's cupboard."

"Oh, right. Yeah. She wanted me to see if I could open it. She said she wanted to see what was in there. Wouldn't stop going on about it – seems to think there's something important in there, but I don't know where she's got that idea from – the door's locked tighter than a gnat's chuff." He took a swig from his glass. "And she kept going on about the photos – the ones on the wall at the pub. Did you notice them?"

"Briefly." Bella shrugged. "Looked like they were pictures of a carnival or a fête or something. All the locals celebrating. I didn't pay them much attention, to be honest."

"No, me neither, but Margot was very taken by them. Said she was looking forward to the celebration. It's tomorrow, apparently – on the bank holiday."

"Well, I just hope it doesn't go on too late. I don't want them keeping Olly awake."

Gareth was looking at his watch; he wasn't really listening, she could tell, so she let the subject drop.

"Go and watch the match, then. I'll clear up in here." She started to gather the plates.

"Thanks, love," said Gareth, and grabbed another can of lager from the fridge before making his way into the living room. Bella placed the plates in the sink and opened the dishwasher, and that was when she heard it – a very faint tapping sound. She peered through the window, expecting to see one of the branches of the fig tree knocking against the glass, but it wasn't that. She heard it again – tap, tap-tap-tap – and looked up at the ceiling. It was coming from upstairs.

She wiped her hands on a tea towel and went out into the hall. She craned her neck to look up the stairs, but it was quiet there, and the only illumination was that which emanated from the nightlight in her daughter's bedroom. But there it was again – a quiet yet insistent knocking, which disturbed and intrigued her in equal measure – and she started up the stairs.

In Margot's room, all was as it should be. A jumble of limbs under the duvet, her daughter was lying on her side with one arm thrown out. Her lips were moving faintly, mumbling in her sleep, and Bella leaned forward, trying to make out what she was saying. The sounds were intelligible as words – she could make out a variety of vowels and consonants – but it didn't sound like English.

Bella stood up straight and listened for the tapping sound, but there was nothing. Almost nothing. At the periphery of her hearing was a low buzzing sound, a gentle hum, barely audible. It was the same as the sound she had heard in here the previous night, and now it grew louder as she approached the built-in cupboard in the corner. The brass handle was cool to the touch, and impossible to turn. It stayed stubbornly in its place, above the keyhole with its shiny surround.

The first wasp struggled slightly as it crawled out from under the door. It was a tiny thing, with vivid yellow and black stripes, its wings folded back against its body. Then another appeared, and another, and another, and soon there were dozens of the creatures wandering drunkenly in circles over the floorboards. Bella shuffled backwards, and then rushed down the stairs, shrieking for Gareth.

* * *

"We just need the key to the cupboard in the little bedroom," said Bella, trying to speak slowly and quietly to mask her panic. The landlady smiled at her and looked down at the pint she was pouring, and then back at Bella.

"I don't know anything about another key, I'm afraid," she said and placed the beer on the bar in front of one of the locals, who picked it up silently, tilted it in Bella's direction with a toothless smile, and returned to his chair by the inglenook. "The only key I was given is the one I handed over to you yesterday."

"Well, there's no key for the cupboard. Can you ask the owner about it?" asked Bella, determined. "Could you give him a ring? There are...wasps, you see. Lots of them. I think there must be a nest in there." The landlady looked up at her sharply, and then a broad smile spread over her face.

"Well, why didn't you say? I'll give him a call right away." From under the bar she pulled out a battered red leather bag and from it withdrew an ancient mobile phone. She squinted at it and then pressed a couple of buttons. She turned away from Bella, and when she started to speak, Bella could make out harsh, guttural consonants combined with long, rounded vowels. Welsh.

The landlady ended the conversation and turned back to Bella.

"He says there is no key. He's never had one, ever since he bought the house." She replaced the phone in her bag and stashed it under the bar again. "Never been able to open that cupboard. He says if you're worried about wasps in there the best thing to do is to block up the gaps and he'll come over and have a look next weekend."

"The weekend?" Bella was aghast. "We'll be gone by then. We're only staying until Tuesday."

"Well, sorry, but that's the way it is. He's working away, you see." The landlady kept looking at Margot, the smile still anchored into place. Then, as if remembering something, she reached under the bar and brought out a roll of brown packing tape.

"Use that – to block the gaps. Just until you leave." She placed the tape on the bar in front of Bella. Then she retrieved something else from under the bar: a bottle of whisky. "Have that on me – to say sorry, like, for the inconvenience." Bella was about to refuse the whisky – she hated the stuff – but then she remembered that Gareth was quite partial to it, and she didn't want to appear rude. She picked it up from the sticky surface of the bar together with the roll of packing tape and muttered a thank you. She was walking towards the door when the landlady called out to her.

"And your little boy? How is he?"

Bella turned back. She found this an incongruous and slightly irritating question, but managed to mutter, "Fine, thank you."

"Good." She could hear the warmth in the landlady's voice. As Bella continued to walk to the door, the locals stopped talking and looked up from their drinks, and smiled affably in her direction.

* * *

It was gone midnight by the time they got the children to bed. They'd made up a bed for Margot on the floor of their bedroom, using the cushions from the armchairs in the living room. Even though there had been no further evidence of any wasps by then, between them she and Gareth had used the packing tape to construct a makeshift seal around the edge of the cupboard door in Margot's room, paying particular attention to the gap where the timber didn't quite meet the floorboards. They'd retreated, and closed the door behind them.

Now, Bella lay in bed, listening to the muffled sounds of the television from downstairs, where Gareth was sitting, somnolent, on the sofa, the bottle of whisky and a glass his only companions. She shuddered at the thought of the wasps, their legs running over her flesh, their wings tickling her skin, the low-pitched, insistent hum. She thought of the female wasps, entering the figs to try to lay their eggs, but instead dying there, their wings ripped from their bodies.

When she woke up Gareth was in bed next to her, soporose from the whisky, acrid exhalations punctuating his snores. And beyond that, something else. Bella listened, straining her ears to hear what was on the periphery of her auditory perception.

The first thing she registered when she got out of bed was that Margot was not in her makeshift bed; the sheet had been thrown back and the cushions were in disarray. In Oliver's room the cot was empty.

Bella went straight to her daughter's room, where the door stood wide open. Margot was standing in front of the cupboard, leaning against the door, illuminated by the gentle glow of the nightlight. She had her ear up against the timber, and a smile on her lips. She did not seem surprised to see her mother; in fact, quite the opposite.

Her smile widened and she lifted a finger to her lips: silence. Then she beckoned Bella over and made way for her to stand at the door. Bella assumed her daughter's place and stance, and listened at the door of the cupboard.

At first, she heard nothing. But as she listened, there came the sound of a low murmur, a drone that increased in volume the more she craned to listen. Her gaze was focused on the gap at the bottom of the door, the packing tape removed now, and lying in redundant curls on the floorboards. The sound was hypnotic, and her sense of weary calm was broken only when the crying started.

Oliver's whimpers were low at first as they escaped under the cupboard door, and then they became indignant cries, as though he couldn't believe what was happening to him. Bella shook the door handle, but even in her panic she knew that it would be locked. She turned the metal again, her son's anger translated now into terrified screams, which even in their intensity failed to completely mask the sound of the wasps, a loud, relentless buzz which filled the room. She looked around her, desperate for something with which to break open the door, but finding nothing. Margot was no longer there.

And then, beyond it all, from outside the window, the tap-tap-tap of the fig tree. Bella flung open the curtains and looked out through the open window. Below her, gathered on the patch of grass at the back of the cottage, were a dozen or so regulars from the pub. She recognised the pool players, and the old woman clutching her little dog, and the landlady, who stood at the front of the group, her mouth wide in a vivid gash which appeared blue under the moonlight. When they saw Bella, a roar went up through the crowd, and arms were thrust heavenwards. Each person held an empty glass – a pint glass or a tankard, and in the case of some of the women, a brandy balloon or a wine glass. As Oliver's screams increased in volume and intensity, the crowd quietened, and an expectant air sat upon them. Then Margot appeared, ushered through the crowd, the pub-goers standing back reverently to let her through. Bella watched as her daughter took her place at the side of the landlady, and the woman placed a possessive hand on Margot's shoulder. Oliver's continued screaming cut Bella to the quick, and she had already turned back to the cupboard, to try by any means to get him out, when she heard it.

Tap. Tap-tap-tap.

But this time, it was not the sound of the fig tree. It was the thud of the first drops of rain, falling fat and heavy against the window panes. Another roar went up from the crowd, and the glasses were raised again, as the villagers collected the first rain to have fallen there all summer. It came down in a deluge then, in biblical proportions, and Margot was smiling up at Bella as her nightie clung to her and her hair hung in wet tendrils around her pale face. And then, when they were all soaked to the skin and their glasses full, as though at some unheard signal, the villagers turned away from Bella and stood with their backs to the cottage. The landlady had crossed to the other side of the garden, her back to the stream, and was facing the villagers and Bella. Her scrawny arms raised an old-fashioned camera up in front of her, and she counted, "One, two, three." The crowd erupted into a deafening, celebratory cheer, and the last thing Bella saw before she was blinded by the flash was Margot, her skinny arms raised above her head, clutching a glass overflowing with water.

IF YOUR SOUL WERE A PITCHFORK, I'D DESPISE YOU

Eric LaRocca

February 15, 2021

If you want to truly and unmistakeably unravel a person – hurt them and then let them live.

February 16, 2021

If your soul were a pitchfork, I'd despise you.

Not because I truly detested you or because I wished you unwell. Quite the contrary. I'd loathe you entirely because it would be that much more difficult to finally possess you, to fully and utterly bewitch you and make you mine. Of course, I'd happily pluck the shiny bits of gore from the weapon's teeth and save them to be artefacts warehoused in the museum of our love. But I'm delighted to know that your spirit is uncaged and eager to be possessed by the first presence willing to charm it.

There are times when I think of you and wonder if you truly understand me and what I desire to be. It's difficult to even consider how the two of us might exchange words with one another, how you might receive me once you've issued an invitation to the dance.

I've already told you that the love you seek is unnatural, that it's abhorrent. The idea of two men coupling – it's repugnant in every aspect of the word.

But your soul is free to be possessed. The fact of the matter is that everything in this world wants to hurt you. It's unequivocal and unmistakeable in the way that the world seems to delight in the destruction of small, delicate things. It takes pleasure in torturing you.

Perhaps your soul should have been a pitchfork. Perhaps then you might have had a fighting chance to be free.

But you don't.

That's why you so completely and so wholly belong to me.

It's a bit unfair when you think about it, isn't it? I'll always be able to hurt you more than you could ever dream of harming me. If only your soul were a pitchfork…

February 17, 2021

I don't know whether I'll plan to write in this diary every day or not. It seems like a shame to waste such a handsome notebook. My mother bought it for me at a local shop for my twenty-first birthday a few years ago and I only just rediscovered it when I went to New Hampshire to visit her for the weekend.

I'm glad I found it.

There's an unearned familiarity you seem to associate with any item you recognise after something terrible has happened to you.

I never used to pay much attention to the row of neatly polished teapots my mother keeps above the dining room fireplace. Now, for some reason, I count each of them when I enter the room and touch each of their handles as if I were introducing myself to them for the first time.

"I'm still alive. I'm still here," I tell each of the teapots, as if fearing they were somehow concerned, as if they somehow knew what had happened to me and how I had been completely and utterly changed since the last time I had visited.

I'm not ready to write about what happened yet. But, for the sake of clarity, in case anybody ends up reading this, I'll refer to what happened as 'the birthday'.

I'm not referring to the horrible event as a birthday because I consider that the day when I was born for the second time. Nothing as dramatic or as impossibly pretentious as that. I'm referring to it as 'the birthday' simply because I prefer to view the event as a living thing – as if it had skin as shiny as an alligator's and teeth like a grinning chimpanzee and the antlers of a young buck. I refuse to think of it as a day when I was changed, but rather as a day when the whole world around me changed – a day when a new kind of creature was brought into existence. Something that I helped to create.

I wonder if I think of it like that because I'm queer and I've been taught for most of my life that I'll never have children of my own despite the fact that I have a loving and devoted partner. Of course, we can adopt. We can try to apply for a surrogate as well. But it goes without saying that the two of us can never conceive and procreate the same way that a man and woman can. I think that's the most inequitable aspect of being a faggot – the simple fact that a child seems so impossible, so unlikely.

I'm not sure I would even want one now. Not after what happened. Not after knowing what some people are truly capable of.

February 18, 2021

"If your soul were a pitchfork, I'd despise you."

I think I've perhaps misheard them. They speak so softly that I can scarcely understand what they're saying, especially late at night when I'm drowsy and ready for sleep.

"What soul?" I ask. "Mine?"

"This body has been used many times," they tell me. *"You'd do well to honour it better."*

I search every corner of my bedroom – the dark where the walls meet – and I don't see anything. The voices seem to arrive suddenly in my mind as if they were already gently swirling there, as if they had already been planted deep inside me by invisible hands so loving and so tender.

"I can't honour what's been hurt," I tell them. "He took most of me with him when he left. There's more of me on the outside than there is left on the inside."

The voices hiss at me, and I nearly retch at the unbearable sound of their shrill, metallic murmurs whirling in the space between my ears.

"He left us in your care because he knew you could handle it," the voices say. *"You'd be wise to respect the honour."*

I nearly laugh at them, but I control myself as much as I possibly can.

"Should I respect what he did to me?" I ask them. "Am I supposed to be grateful for how he let me live?"

My head throbs, the voices churning inside my mind like melted butter in a pot.

"We were always supposed to find you," they tell me. *"This skin once belonged to us. We're overjoyed to find it again."*

I sense my stomach curling at the thought of them staying, of them taking up residence inside me, of them claiming me the same way he had once claimed me and smeared himself upon me.

"There's nothing I can do to change your minds?" I ask them.

"Why would we leave you?" they ask me. *"We were always supposed to find you. Your body is our home."*

It feels unusual to hear them say this – to know that I'm considered 'home' to someone, something else, when I've struggled to call any place 'home' since I was a child.

I think there's something that happens when you grow up and move out of your parents' house – you feel as if you don't belong anywhere. It's a fine art – to create a place you can call 'home'. Even though I love Yusuf with all my heart, there's a part of me that wonders if I'll ever be truly content with him. There's a part of me that wonders if I'll be brave enough to consider him my 'home'.

It's a strange feeling to know that there are things living inside me that have known me before, that consider my body their home – their sanctuary, their refuge.

Who am I to deprive them of that comfort?

February 19, 2021

I woke up this morning and discovered that my teeth had turned black, something dark oozing from my gums as shiny and as black as motor oil.

"Something's wrong," I told Yusuf, spitting broken bits of teeth like tiny black buttons. "There's something inside my mouth."

I called my dentist and begged him to schedule an appointment for me as soon as he could. Yusuf wanted to take me to the emergency room. Naturally, I thought about it. But hospitals have always scared me. Not to mention, I'm forever convinced that once I enter a hospital, I'll never come back out. That's what had happened to my grandfather, after all. He went to the ER for a minor heart palpitation and then two days later he was pronounced dead.

I went to my dentist and the most peculiar thing happened. He didn't seem alarmed by the sight of my teeth. He didn't shy away or flinch in revulsion as I had expected him to. In fact, he seemed to acknowledge the decaying teeth with a look of matter-of-factness that all dentists seem to possess when they're confronted with the ordinary or, even worse, the inevitable.

"You don't think there's anything to be worried about?" I asked him, my mouth stuffed with bits of gauze to reduce some of the swelling.

He glanced at his masked assistant, rolling his eyes. "Surely you could have expressed concern while it was happening."

I sensed my face scrunching at him, confused. "I was sleeping when it happened. I woke up and I found them like this."

"You don't expect me to believe that," he said. "There's no possible way you were sleeping while it was happening."

I could hardly understand him. "While what was happening?"

It was then I began to wonder, my mind racing. *Does he know? Does he know what happened to me? How could he have possibly found out?*

Then it dawned on me. When something horrible happens to you, other monsters are acutely aware that you've been marked, that you're an easy target. Perhaps that's what I was to him. After all, I had heard some rumours that he preferred the company of younger men. But I had never seen him on any of the apps. Still, it made me wonder if he knew because he was capable of doing the same unspeakable thing to me. Perhaps he wanted to.

More than anything, I knew I had to leave.

I went home, my mouth swollen with gauze, and fell on the couch where I cried for hours until Yusuf finally came home.

He held me in his arms, and we pretended that we were two small birds roosting in the rafters of an old barn – mated for life, our hearts tethered by a thin netting of chicken wire and softly beating together as one.

February 20, 2021

There's a small boy named Ezekiel who lives inside me and tells me that I'm unnatural – that I'm repugnant, that I'm a vile, obscene thing undeserving of comfort or grace.

I've decided to let him write this diary entry:

One of the main problems with sex between two men is the horrendous smell. There's nothing forgiving about male body odour. But when it comes to the male sex organ being generously oiled and shoved inside another's ass, you must admit that the actual act is grossly abnormal – an abomination of the very integrity of nature, a manmade perversion of cosmic proportions.

Two men cannot truly love one another the same way that a man and a woman can fall in love. This is not only evident in the fact that most gay couples are non-monogamous, but it is also clear in the fact that procreation is not possible between the same sexes. Of course, some might argue that this is a trite and overused example of why homosexual couples should not retain the same rights as heterosexual couples; however, to discredit such a fact is to corrode the very integrity of a union between man and wife.

Circling back to the obviously offensive smell of anal sex between two cisgender men, one must acknowledge the simple fact that sex has been and always must be a pure act. The mere thought of two male bodies coupling in such an aberrant and objectionable way – it's enough to deter anyone mentally fragile enough from considering such a destructive and repugnant lifestyle.

The fact of the matter is that only those who are weak of mind and spirit are easy to influence into becoming a faggot. It gives me no pleasure to write this, to tell you that you are destined for the pit of eternal suffering if you continue subscribing to this harmful lifestyle.

Ezekiel's finished writing now. It's me again. Oscar.

He doesn't always mean the things he says. It's just that he cares so much about me and doesn't want to see me hurt by anyone or anything. Even though sometimes I often wonder if he'd hurt me if he had the chance.

February 21, 2021

It's been a few days since it happened – 'the birthday' – and I think I'm finally ready to write about it. I've torn out several pages from this journal, trying to decide where to begin – wondering how to efficiently tell you how everything began without draining myself entirely, and completely undoing my resolve to follow through with the story.

He came over to our apartment late one night after we had texted for most of the day. I had told him that Yusuf was working late and that he wouldn't be home until after midnight. He asked if he could stop by because there was something he needed to tell me. I knew what that meant. There wasn't anything he wanted to tell me. What could he have possibly wanted to tell me? It was a ruse – an excuse for him to come over and take exactly what he wanted from me.

He arrived and wore a dark, baggy sweatshirt that stretched down to his knees. I'll never forget how he smelled – how he reeked of cheap cologne barely disguising the stench of a recently finished cigarette. As soon as I pried open the door, he threw himself at me and forced his tongue down my throat. I didn't wince or shrink away when he did this. I had asked him to kiss me when he first arrived. I had wanted him to do it.

He asked me where the bedroom was, and I showed him the way. It wasn't long before our clothes were torn off and I was on my knees, my head bobbing at his groin like the obedient bitch he wanted me to be.

This is what you wanted, I kept reminding myself. *This is what you asked for.*

I didn't ask for him to pin me against the wall, to shove two oiled fingers inside me so that I would open up for him. I certainly never asked him to shove himself inside me again and again, his fists pummelling my head because I was squirming too much or because I was begging him to let me go. I might have asked for that once. I might have once dreamed of an encounter when he and I were together and bound in a permanent embrace.

This is what you wanted, I repeated over and over inside my mind.

Finally, he emptied himself in me, slime dripping from between my cheeks. However, it felt different than whenever I was with Yusuf. It somehow felt as though he had drained himself entirely of all his insecurities, his fears, his reservations, and had sent them pulsing through me and filling each and every empty corner inside my body the same way a flood will plug shallow pockets of marshland. That's what my body was now – a swamp, a fetid place where all useless things might collect and eventually yellow with antiquity.

After he wiped himself clean, he dressed. I walked him to the door and kissed him goodbye. Then, once he was gone, I climbed into the shower and twisted the faucet until the water was scalding hot. I scrubbed myself until I wondered if I might strip the skin from my bone.

And that's when I heard it – the very first time I heard them utter those words to me, those terrible, spirit-splitting words that seemed to bud from deep within me:

"If your soul were a pitchfork, I'd despise you. Thankfully, it's not. So, I'm free to hurt you."

February 22, 2021

I once almost drowned when I was a boy.

I should have died that day.

I was visiting my grandparents in upstate New York when I was eleven or twelve. They had rented a small cabin on the shore of a lake, and we often spent the hot afternoons reclining in the shade of a nearby grove of trees or swimming in the shallow water near the docks where my grandfather kept his boat.

I'll never forget how one afternoon when I decided to venture out into the deeper water, something caught my foot. It felt slimy like the tail of an eel. Just as I began to reach underwater to see what had grabbed me, something pulled me under and kept me there for what felt like hours. I resisted as much as I could, my vision beginning to blur as soon as I opened my eyes. I tried to swim toward the surface, but something pulled me down deeper and deeper until it felt as though my feet were touching the very bottom of the lake.

I floated there for a moment, and it suddenly felt like something had slipped inside me, a slime-covered rope as thin as a telephone cord coiling inside my belly button and creating pressure there until I could hardly bear it any longer.

Finally, the invisible concrete brick that had been weighing me down suddenly seemed to be removed from my shoulders. I could move again. I was free. I shot up from the depths of the lake and eventually arrived at the surface – gasping, choking for breath.

My grandparents found me when I finally had the strength to swim to shore, dragging myself out of the water and heaving myself onto the sand. It felt peculiar – having survived the ordeal, I mean. I felt as though I were a different person, as though something had happened to me at the bottom of the lake and I had been replaced by someone, something else.

"There's something different about Oscar," I would hear my grandparents say about me, whispering to one another in the kitchen as they cleaned dishes. "I wonder if his mother will say anything to us."

Of course, there was something different about me. Eleven or twelve is the exact age when a young boy starts to realise that he fancies the camaraderie of other boys, that he would much prefer a sexual partner with the same equipment and appetite as him.

Yes, there was something different about me. It had happened in that brief, wondrous moment at the bottom of the lake near my grandparents' cabin. I had finally realised who I was, and I was completely and utterly unafraid of what I was to become.

We all become possessed by our sexual desires – our urges, our yearnings – eventually. After waiting for most of my life, it had finally happened to me.

February 23, 2021

Don't ask me why I did it, but today I typed in the search bar on my work laptop: 'Big Black Cock Fucks Tight Virgin Ass.'

I didn't realise I was doing it until it finally happened, until I watched the results leach across the page and fill the entire frame of the computer monitor with various images of young men and their freshly bleached assholes being teased by massive specimens of manhood.

It felt as though something else had forced me to type those words into the search bar, as if my mind had been temporarily disconnected while something else took control.

I don't expect you to believe me. They didn't believe me at work and asked me to return my laptop as soon as possible, considering the fact I would no longer be employed there.

It's strange. I've thought about searching for pornography on my work laptop many times before. But I've never acted on it. I've never contemplated the possibility of actually going through with it.

Today, that changed forever.

I told Yusuf what I had done, and he could hardly believe me.

I told him how sorry I was, and he seemed to feel bad for me. He promised that he'll pick up extra shifts on the weekend until I get a new job so that we can get by with paying the rent.

He also promised me that we'll be okay.

But I don't know if I truly believe him.

February 24, 2021

This morning I woke up and discovered I had sprouted a pair of antlers as intricately ornate and as fine-looking as an Ancient Egyptian headdress.

I touched them and I winced a little. They hurt for some reason. My skin around the area – tender and blistered bright red.

"What are they?" Yusuf asked me – far too cautious to touch them, too afraid of what they might be and if they might somehow be infectious.

"I don't know," I told him, gazing at myself in the mirror and wondering the same thing.

"But why are they suddenly here?"

"Because I survived," I told him, my voice breaking apart and disintegrating as if it were wet straw. "Because my soul isn't a pitchfork."

February 25, 2021

I've finally come to the horrible realisation that this was always supposed to happen to me. He was always supposed to hurt me and completely undo me until I was a totally different person – a person that enjoys being possessed, being controlled and manipulated by others.

I was so easy to possess, after all. I made it so comfortable for them to slip inside me, for them to take ownership of my body, my integrity, my sexuality. Yes, my sexuality. That's the reason this happened in the first place. This would have never happened if I had preferred women instead, if I had suppressed these terrible urges, these feelings, as my father once begged me to.

But I'm a faggot.

To be a faggot is to relinquish control of your body and to allow others to desecrate it.

Perhaps Ezekiel is right. Perhaps the others are right as well.

This is a truly monstrous lifestyle.

February 26, 2021

This morning, I told Yusuf that I did not love him.

It's not that I stopped loving him, but rather that I was never completely in love with him in the first place. He always loved me more than I cared for him, and I think a small, quiet part of him always knew this to be true. I think he recognised this fact and came to terms with it a while ago but never wanted to actually address it in case I might have a change of heart.

He stared at me for the longest time, his mouth opening and closing with muted words.

"Is it because of what happened?" he asked me, his voice brittle-thin and trembling.

"It's because everything's changed for me now," I told him. "It was always supposed to be like this."

February 27, 2021

Yusuf decided to pack some of his things and spend some time at his mother's house over the weekend. I don't have much else to write today.

February 28, 2021

Rape is a living thing.

It has eyes and ears and a nose and a mouth.

What they don't tell you about rape or any kind of sexual assault in general is that it can create something in the aftermath of its existence.

It flowers deep inside both people – both the transgressor and the victim – and spreads roots there as if it were a rare tropical plant.

Rape is a living thing.

March 1, 2021

Yusuf returned home today and locked me in the bedroom. He sealed the windows shut and now passes a tray of food underneath the door when I tell him that the voices inside my head are hungry.

"What's your name?" he asks me.

I can hear his voice quivering – as if he already knows the dreadful answer, as if he were already certain that I was quite and irreparably gone.

"What's your name?" he asks again when I won't answer.

"Ezekiel," I tell him, more bits of broken teeth dripping from between my lips like carpenter ants. *"Please let me out."*

"Why won't you leave us?" he asks me, his voice strained as if pleading.

I laugh, another set of voices hardening in the pit of my throat. *"If your soul were a pitchfork, I'd despise you. Thankfully, it's not."*

I can tell for certain that Yusuf wants to hurt me. He'd bash me over the head with a crowbar or he'd shove a screwdriver inside my ear if he could. But he won't. Not yet. Perhaps not ever.

He wants this to hurt me as much as possible.

He's going to let me live.

"We're going to sharpen your spirit today, Ezekiel," Yusuf says, the fear and uncertainty in his voice nearly hollowing me out like a spade shovelling a weed-filled flowerbed. "Now. Let's begin."

HEEBIE JEEBIES

Amanda Cecelia Lang

Charlie was five when Nona introduced him to the Heebie Jeebies that lived inside his crevices. Carrying a single suitcase between them, he and his mother came to Nona from a Greyhound bus in the midnight snow. The slippery walk from the depot stretched on and on through slushy sidewalks and unfamiliar small-town neighbourhoods. By the time they reached a gigantic iron gate, Charlie's feet felt soggy and numb and his teeth wouldn't stop chit-chit-chittering. He'd rarely been out of his bed this late at night, and never in the blustery cold. And now Nona's ancient, thick-boned house loomed two-storeys large, too monstrous not to contain monsters.

Charlie buried his face against his mother's hip.

"We must be brave for once." But his mother stood on the sidewalk for a very long time, watching the sleepy house with cold, faraway eyes.

Only when Charlie asked with an earnest shiver if they were going to sleep in the snow, did she finally ring the doorbell.

It took Nona a long time to answer. Charlie's mother had to ring twice more before they heard footsteps creaking toward the door. The sickly yellow porchlight snapped on, scattering the darkness, and Nona peered out at them. She was old, older than anyone Charlie had ever seen. Her eyes wrinkled, and she didn't seem to recognise her own daughter standing there.

Finally, his mother stepped into the light, revealing her suitcase and split lip, and Nona mumbled something Charlie didn't understand. After a slow hesitation, she shuffled aside and let them in from the cold. The vast, unkempt rooms were cluttered with over-fat furniture and peculiar odds and ends. Every antique edge and corner hung heavy with cobwebs and dust motes. Every shadow moved, full of skittering shapes and tiny, glittery eyes.

Those first nights after running from his father, after his mother swallowed her mangled pride and asked Nona if they could stay awhile, Charlie felt the house crawling all around him. Chitters and whispers in the moon-washed gloom. Unfamiliar scritches and scratches. Shadows with spiders and spookies and things that go bump. He wanted to be brave for his mother's sake. He tried to keep his big imagination small. But hiding under a musty quilt on a creaky brass bed in an echoey bedroom was never going to make the strangeness of his new life go away.

Inevitably, the bad dreams scurried over him and turned into shrill, petrified sobs – just like when he used to wake up the whole damn-blasted house with his night terrors and enrage his father. *Little sissy-boy!* Charlie clapped his hand over his mouth, but too late.

Heavy, shuffling footsteps chased his whimpers down the hallway and filled his open doorway with the nightgowned silhouette of his mother. She swept to the edge of his bed, but as the window's moonbeam caught her face, Charlie's relief twisted into a wild, gape-eyed horror.

His mother's smooth, familiar beauty had grizzled while she slept and standing above him was the husk of a living corpse! Just like the ones in the bedtime stories his father liked to tell. Spidery shadows skittered in and out of those sunken eyes. The undead thing closed skeleton fingers around his shoulder, and only when it hushed his cries with a voice of raspy velvet did Charlie recognise Nona's face smiling down upon him.

"Poor child, you truly are a skittish one, aren't you? Seems us nervous-nellies come in all sizes."

Charlie burrowed deeper into his quilt, hot tears streaming. Back then, Nona was still a stranger and Charlie never spoke to strangers. Especially because he might say cowardly words and get himself booted out onto more icy streets. His own father didn't care what happened to him – so why should Nona?

"I know exactly what you're feeling," Nona said. "Deep-down spooky ideas squirming like buggies. You don't live half your life in a big, empty house and not feel the Heebie Jeebies creeping under your skin."

Heebie Jeebies? Charlie mouthed the words, and a prickle ran down his neck. *Heebie Jeebies.* Yes, that sounded right. He pulled his quilt tighter and peered out at Nona, breath held fast to listen.

"Your mother never believed in them, but they're very real indeed. Nasty little pests. They burrow around your nerves and crevices, freezing you up with scary, ugly worries. Simply horrid. But you wanna know a secret?" Nona tapped the tip of Charlie's nose with a sly finger. "Jeebies can be *vanquished* – caught and released."

Charlie shifted inside his bundle. "They can?"

"Oh yes." Nona's watery grey eyes sparkled. "May I show you my trick?"

He sniffled and nodded solemnly.

"Sit up straight then, and hold still." She wiggled her fingertips like a fortune teller examining a crystal ball. Humming a curious singsong, she closed her eyes and raked the air around Charlie with wavery hands.

It was all rather dreamy and bewildering – a wrinkled old woman putting on such an elaborate show at his midnight bedside – and he couldn't help but wobble a grin.

Nona cracked an eye at him. "Oh, my stars, a most dreadful infestation...*right here!*"

She corkscrewed her fingertips into Charlie's underarm, surprising him – and his Jeebies, too!

"That's right, I gotcha, you little nerve-chewers!" She tickled away, chasing those buggers until Charlie rolled backwards, wriggling and giggling. "That's it! Oh goodness, so many Jeebies! Hold on, dear boy! It's easiest to snag their tippy-toes."

Just when he thought he might burst from so much squirmy-wormy laughter, Nona cupped her wrinkled hands together. "Got 'em!"

Charlie sat up, wiping at tears of delight. "You caught my Jeebies? May I see them?"

"Oh, dear me, no! Never look a Jeebie in its beady little eyes. Jeebies are never to be seen, Charlie, especially freshly plucked. Never give them that power." Nona's smile turned serious. "You understand? Promise me."

"Cross my heart."

"Good boy. Now..." Nona held out her cupped hands to him. "Whisper the bad feelings into my hands. Remind those Jeebies what they are, all the awful things that frighten you."

Charlie regarded Nona uncertainly. Tell his Jeebies *that*? Though...he *did* feel braver without their nervous toes whispering all through him.

He leaned forward, hesitantly, and Nona nodded, encouraging him.

He thought he heard their spiny legs scritch-scratching at her palms.

With a gulp and a deep, daring breath, he told his Jeebies about the monsters that go bump – especially his angry, unhappy father. Being away from the man with his tattooed knuckles and mean bedtime stories felt happy and scary all at once. His father liked to tell Charlie about zombies eating the eyeballs of gutless pansy-boys, and green hands under the beds of crybabies. But scariest was his promise that without his roof and his pay cheque, Charlie and his no-good mother would freeze to icicles in the winter streets. Scariest because it almost came true. Now that Charlie thought about it, that other bad feeling scritch-scratching inside him wasn't from Nona's big, cobwebby house – but the fear that she might toss them out of it.

But when he sat back, having told his Jeebies everything, Nona smiled at him with the warmth of a fireplace.

"Never worry, my boy. You and your mother are always welcome here. And your father most certainly is *not*." She paused. "Now, Charlie, one last step. Are you ready?"

Charlie nodded.

"You must shut your eyes and let your Jeebies go. Here, wrap your hands around mine." He did so and closed his eyes. "On the count of three. One...two...three!"

Together they opened their hands.

And, with a scritch-and-a-scratch across the quilt, then the floorboards, Charlie's Heebie Jeebies scurried away into the deepest shadows of the house and were forgotten.

* * *

Over that long fairytale winter and into the next, Charlie and Nona grew to be the cosiest of buddies.

Nona never kicked him and his mother out into the icy streets – just like she promised. And in return, they dusted away the cobwebs full of moth husks and replaced all the smoky, burned-out lightbulbs that Nona had been too rickety to reach. The house was still big and old and full of spiders, but now it glowed like it had when his mother was a kid.

Sometimes, though, Charlie sensed an unhappy distance looming between Nona and his mother. They'd had a big fight a long time ago, way before Charlie was born, Nona told him one night. But when Charlie asked what the fight was about, Nona said sometimes it's best not to dig up nasty memories.

Best to just forget.

While his mother was busy bettering herself – working a second shift at the diner or taking night classes at the college – Nona taught Charlie how to bake ginger cake and the difference between a fuzzy wolf spider and a deadly brown recluse. In exchange, Charlie showed Nona how to make snow angels and catch daddy-long-legs in jars. He helped her tie her shoelaces whenever her spine ached too much. And after the doctor told her no heavy lifting on account of her upset old heartbeat, Charlie always carried their trays of cookies and glass bottles of Coke from the kitchen to the parlour.

And, of course, whenever his imagination stretched the shadows into ghouls, sending prickly toes racing up his spine, Nona helped him vanquish his Heebie Jeebies.

Catch and release.

She was an expert at Jeebie hunting. Like on Halloween when Charlie saw his first zombie during trick-or-treat, and later that night heard a torso groaning up the long staircase. Or the evening of the town's big snowstorm when the power went dark and the candles tossed distorted shadows all across the walls, scorpions and furious father-faces. That same winter, the wind and wet snow snapped the tree branch outside his window, and Charlie's imagination was certain he heard Nona falling down the stairs, cracking her fragile old bones, all her cola-stained teeth knocked right out of her.

But all his mean dreams, all his many-legged worries, small and big.

They were no match for Nona.

In the menace of the night, whenever Charlie needed her, Nona came shuffling down the hallway, fast as her old bones could move, ready to wrangle those Jeebies right up. Some liked to hide between his toes and the giggly landscape of his ribs. But the hairiest Jeebies – like the frights about his father – hid under his arms where he was most ticklish.

"Nona, what're your worst Jeebies?" Charlie asked one wind-whistle-y evening as she bundled his quilt around his chin. "I mean the ickiest ones with lots of bristly legs."

"Oh, that's easy." Nona tapped his nose and sat on the side of his bed. "The Jeebies that promised I'd never meet my grandson or see my daughter again. But looksie, here you both are. All those years of worrying and sadness for nothing."

Charlie beamed, though something about Nona's answer prickled the pit of his stomach. "You felt those Jeebies for years? Didn't you have anyone to catch them for you?"

"Well, no…I suppose it was just me."

"You caught your own Jeebies?"

"Wasn't always easy, I'm afraid."

Charlie hadn't even been sure it was *possible*. Once, when Nona had seemed extra sleepy from their day, he'd tried plucking a big plump meanie from between his toes – only he wasn't so sure he vanquished it. The next day, his father appeared on Nona's front porch looking to sweet-talk his mother – just like Charlie had feared! Nona had refused to unlock the door for the man, but Charlie felt certain he'd appeared because of that elusive Heebie Jeebie. After that, Charlie left the Jeebie hunting to Nona.

"Sometimes, the worst Jeebies are the ones you catch alone," Nona went on, half-lost in squirmy faraway thoughts.

"Nona?" Charlie said. "If you ever need help with *your* Heebie Jeebies, just holler. Promise?"

"Such a dear. Of course, I promise."

After that, whenever the bug-bomb commercial came on the parlour TV – the one where roaches twitched across the screen with spiny legs and feelers – Nona would shudder and enlist Charlie's faithful help. Same whenever they sat in the waiting room at her poke-and-prod doctor's office. But even though she swore Charlie was a master at catching her Jeebies, he wasn't so sure. For one thing, he never felt their toes inside his clasped hands. And sometimes Nona's brave smile wobbled and shadows skittered behind her eyes.

Then came the evening when his father returned with roses.

This visit proved worse than the last, because it was already dark outside and his mother was home to unlock the door.

Even so, Nona refused to let the man inside and ordered Charlie to an early bed. But Charlie gripped the banister, trembling like a sissy-boy at the top of the staircase while his macho father stomped back and forth across the front porch.

That's when all the unhappy feelings hiding in the silence between his mother and grandmother came rushing out.

Shouts echoed up the front hall.

"I can stand on my own!" his mother cried. "I'm a different person now."

"And men like that never change!" Nona's brittle voice cracked. "Don't be that same foolish girl again. I'm begging."

"Christ's sake! It's only drinks at the roadhouse. To catch up. He came all this way."

"With satin-tongued promises, temper tucked away. Drinks, and then what? Another seedy motel room, a lifetime tied to trouble. Think about poor Charlie."

"You, Mother, of all people, don't get to tell me what to do with my child. *Remember*?"

Nona sucked in a sharp breath, then the front door opened and slammed.

Charlie's mother hadn't even kissed him goodnight.

Then came the slow, creaking footsteps of Nona making her way up the stairs. "I see your shadow lurking there, sweet boy. Come now, bedtime awaits."

From outside Charlie's bedroom window, his father's headlights sprayed across Nona's worried face, then spun away down the long driveway. "Had a nasty feeling since the day I met that man. But your mother never believed me about the Heebie Jeebies."

Without needing to be asked, Charlie tickled Nona's ribs. She giggled dustily, and he clasped his hands together.

Leaning in with a hand trembling against her chest, Nona whispered her deepest fear. When she finished, Charlie promised: "I won't let him take me away. Never ever."

Nona folded her hands around his, they closed their eyes… and released!

But as always, Charlie wasn't so sure he felt Nona's Jeebies crawl away.

And the shadow-shapes were back, scurrying behind her sunken eyes before she even dimmed his bedside lamp.

"Sleep tight, my boy," she rasped, becoming a stooped silhouette in the door, then footsteps scraping down the hallway.

Charlie felt his own Heebie Jeebies tippy-toeing around, old worries nesting beneath the tucked-in quilts of his thoughts. But tonight, of all bad nights, he wanted to be brave for Nona.

At last, the exhaustion of his father's visit swept Charlie under.

In the feverish imagination of his dreams, he saw the man strike his mother in the front seat of his old Camaro, splitting her lip again for daring to leave him and better herself. Then, howling, he cranked the wheel and squealed tyres back to Nona's house. No bitch was gonna lock him out! No sissy son of his was gonna cower from him! Then, in his dreams, Charlie was in his bed, whimpering as familiar footsteps stomped down the hall. Not Nona. The hulking silhouette of his father appeared in his doorway.

Charlie opened his eyes.

Awoke to a tearful sound. Sharp, bursting cries, echoing, fading…

Nona?

Had those sounds belonged to her? Or to Charlie?

He waited, breath sucked deep. In the moonlit stillness, an old spidery chill prickled his skin. He imagined his father on all fours, scuttling unseen through the shadows.

This time, the whimper *did* come from Charlie. Loud and awful.

He waited for the familiar shuffle down the hallway, waited for the golden sweep of light from his bedside lamp and Nona's soft hand on his cheek.

But tonight, she didn't come.

Charlie squirmed.

Maybe that first whimper *had* come from Nona's bedroom.

Maybe right now Nona's Heebie Jeebies had her frozen in place.

Charlie sat up in bed, determined, but also certain the instant he placed a bare foot on the floor, his father would reach out from under the mattress and grab his ankle.

Charlie leapt from his bed anyway.

Nothing grabbed out at him, and he found himself tiptoeing down the hallway. The nightlight Nona had installed for midnight bathroom trips scattered a faint starburst along the floor and ceiling and the stretched-out gloom.

Nona's door stood open at the end of the hallway.

Charlie crept inside the winter-cool bedroom. A beam of pale blue moonlight slanted in from the window, but didn't touch the murky outline of the bed or the lump resting under a pile of quilts and darkness.

"Nona?"

Silence.

Charlie inched ever closer. "I've come to vanquish your Jeebies."

Nona's silence stretched ever louder.

Standing in the moonbeam now, Charlie reached into the shadows and placed a hand on his grandmother's quilt.

Something shifted beneath. Writhing, squirming, chittering.

"Nona?"

The quilt fell away.

Like an egg sac hatching, Jeebies erupted from Nona's sleeping form, a buzzing wave of pincers and antennae and twitchy ghosts of the mind. Inky-slick exoskeletons, so pitch-black they stained the eye. They swarmed down the mattress and across the floor.

Across Charlie's bare feet!

He wailed and stumbled backward.

Not knowing what else to do, he did what Nona would do.

He flicked the bedside lamp. In the feeble glow, the creepers disappeared at once, faster than cockroaches scattering into secret corners. No Jeebies.

Only Nona lying there.

A warm, nightgowned bump, silver hair, wrinkles, huddled in on herself, a nervous-nellie if ever there was one.

"I'm still right here," Charlie whispered. "Don't you worry."

Ever faithful, he tickled away the last of Nona's Heebie Jeebies.

Tickled and tickled.

Until her tender warm ribs grew cold and stiff, until the darkest-before-dawn return of his father's headlights flashed down the driveway and across his trembling pansy-boy face.

★ ★ ★

Later that week, at Nona's funeral, Charlie fidgeted at the end of the church aisle. Drippy-nosed, tear-swollen, almost too infested to approach the coffin.

He knew Nona was in there. But during the pastor's prayers, Charlie had hunched low in the front pew, unable to see over the open edge of the polished white box. His father sat on the far side of his mother, costumed in his handsome blue eyes and best behaviour, a casual arm draped over her sobbing shoulder. These calm moments of the man petrified Charlie the most because they felt like a dare: go ahead, make his day. Charlie spent the service shrinking away from the grinning skulls tattooed on the man's jagged knuckles.

But now, the prayers were silent.

Time to say goodnight to Nona forever.

While his mother sobbed with old friends from town, Charlie tiptoed alone toward the open casket. Every step felt like that night in the hallway, a growing nest of Jeebies squirming inside his ribs, chewing up his heart.

He had let Nona die.

He'd let her Jeebies get her!

And now, a new hideous terror lodged inside his darkest crevices, a hard-shelled thing growing bigger with every step closer. He could see Nona's folded hands, the tip of her nose and her powdered, doughy wrinkles. Her smile stole his air, startlingly wrong, a tightlipped thing of pale moulding clay.

He wanted to turn and run right then.

But his father might be watching, with his narrowed gaze and yellowed, insectile smile.

Doggedly, Charlie hugged himself and tucked his hands into his underarms. His fingers wriggled, on a secret hunt for Jeebies.

And to his icy surprise, antennae tickled his fingertips.

A horrified giggle escaped him, a giggle despicably out of place beside Nona's coffin. Even so, Charlie cupped his hands together with a quick little clap.

As always, he wasn't certain he had a Jeebie in there. But, standing over Nona, he brought his hands to his mouth anyway, preparing to whisper his newest, ever-growing fear. The one where Nona whimpered from somewhere far-far away while his father stood over him, sneering with laughter. If he didn't spit the idea out soon it would become real. If only the words he needed didn't feel so enormous and twisty.

He opened his mouth.

And fell silent.

His father had crept up behind him.

He clamped his grease-moon fingernails onto Charlie's shoulder and squeezed until the bone ached. "No more tears now, Chuck, those are for the girls."

Charlie swallowed. Something inside his cupped hands circled his palm with tiny feelers, then spidery legs squirmed through a crack in his fingers.

Nona said never look a freshly plucked Jeebie in its beady little eyes.

Too late! The tiny monster sprung from Charlie's knuckles and landed on the edge of Nona's coffin with a hard, chitinous *thunk*.

Like Nona's clay smile, Charlie wanted to scream at the wrongness of it.

A bug but not a bug.

A centipede-sized ghoulie put together with different odd bits, like a cut-and-paste collage. Clicking legs made of greasy fingernail clippings, a thorax of yellowed tobacco teeth, folded wings of tattooed flesh. Dozens of devious, handsome blue eyes.

That thing came from Charlie?

With a twitch of leathery wings, the Jeebie flitted from the coffin lid onto Nona's folded hands. It crawled with the intent of a cockroach, gliding up her arm, then up her shoulder and the dough of her neck. Charlie froze, horrified, certain the thing would worm inside Nona's ear canal. Instead, it skittered across her mouth, spiny legs parting her lips in a grimace, revealing cola-stained teeth.

Choking on sick screaming horror, Charlie glanced up at his father.

Had he noticed?

If he had, he was too much of a manly man to react.

The Jeebie finished probing Nona's lips and wandered up the doughy curve of her cheek. It ruffled her eyelashes, made her eye wink.

Charlie's father checked his watch.

"Fun time's over." He clamped a hand on the lid, happy to close it and trap Nona in the infested darkness forever.

"Wait." But Charlie had never sounded so puny.

"Can't wait. The ground at the cemetery's too frozen to bury her." His father leaned in with whisky-hot breath. "Gotta get her back in the fridge right away, before the grave-bugs start squirting their eggs inside her."

With a flitter of fleshy wings, the Jeebie sprang off Nona's face. It darted through the air, its round, translucent belly shimmering fatly. Charlie saw the sac of tiny pulsing skulls as it landed on his father's cheek. Juicy with fresh terrors, it meandered across his bristled moustache.

A whimper echoed inside Charlie's bones. The stained-glass church seemed to tilt-a-whirl sideways, sweeping his and Nona's fairy-tale life clean away.

Hope was out of reach.

With a gleeful flick of feelers, the Jeebie folded its wings, then wiggle-wormed up inside his father's flaring, raging-bull nostril.

The man never even flinched.

He simply grinned at Charlie and closed the coffin up tight.

* * *

Charlie missed Nona. Missed her so horribly every thumpy beat inside his chest felt like waking from a nest of nightmares.

Except Nona wasn't around to shuffle down the hallway.

The lack of her was deafening. Every moment felt wrong and upset, and even in the very brightest rooms of her house, cobwebby shadows thickened and squirmed.

Charlie slept with the lights on now. Alone at every bedtime, he strained to hear the downstairs chatter of his babysitter's television. A volunteer from the neighbourhood, the young woman had plopped down in the centre of Nona's couch and acted exasperated whenever Charlie tried talking. And when he summoned the spit to tell her about his Heebie Jeebies, she'd only snorted. "Your mother warned me about you, kiddo. Buggies aren't real."

Really, the only comforting thing about the woman was that she wasn't Charlie's father.

After the funeral, the man hadn't been able to afford any more nights at the motel, and Charlie's mother wouldn't let him stay at Nona's house out of respect. Charlie expected him to rage at being told what he couldn't do. But he'd simply winked goodbye to Charlie and returned quietly to his grease-monkey job in the city.

With a Jeebie still lodged inside his nose.

Every morning since, he'd called Charlie's mother to check in. The phone would chime, Charlie's stomach would clench, and the way his mother sometimes giggled – as if she'd forgotten all the split lips and nasty middle-of-the-nights – made Charlie's spine crawl.

But his mother didn't believe in Heebie Jeebies.

"You're all the family we have left," she'd whispered into the phone just that morning, and Charlie missed Nona worse than ever.

Now, hidden under his quilt, he found himself infested. A mindscape of clay smiles and tattooed wings and coiled, nightgowned corpses. Gravediggers couldn't put Nona in the frozen ground, so Charlie's imagination stuffed her in the downstairs refrigerator between the glass bottles of Coke and the stiff remains of her last-ever ginger cake.

That awful scrunched-up image twitched inside his head, meaner and meaner, until glass bottles rattled and Charlie cried out.

Let it echo.

He waited for his babysitter's footsteps to trudge up the stairs, holding his breath as tiny monsters ran circles inside. But after what happened next to Nona's casket, he didn't want to catch his own Jeebies ever again.

Even as Charlie thought it, his armpit prickled.

Two bristly feelers licked out from the crevice and something plump wiggled loose.

Feathery legs twisted beneath his pyjama shirt.

The edge of his collar shuddered and lifted.

A bits-and-pieces monster appeared. Frozen grave dirt, cola-stained teeth, doughy wings, and eyes, eyes, eyes, the glued-shut eyes of Nona!

Charlie shrieked.

In the sickly yellow lamp-glow, the Jeebie took flight and thumped the wallpapered corner where the blackest dreams gathered. As it vanished into the inky murk, the darkness sprouted feelers, mandibles, legs, the shadows multiplied and slithered outward.

His forgotten Jeebies!

They skittered everywhere, dotting the walls and ceiling and floor!

Everywhere! Little feet clicked and chittered.

Every Jeebie Nona ever caught and released had returned.

Only who would protect him now?

Charlie cowered, wailed for Nona. At the breath's end of her name, a Jeebie skittered out across his tongue and hooked its pincer to the corner of his cheek.

He scream-spat and twisted from the bed. The quilt tangled around his legs and the ground rose up to knock the air from his lungs. The Jeebie fell loose and scurried past his nose.

Still, nobody came to save him.

Scrambling, barefoot, Charlie whimpered out into the hallway. At the top of the stairs, he paused to listen. The drone of the television haunted the lower floor.

Behind him, shadowy legs chittered and buzzed, spilling out of his bedroom door.

Afraid to look back, Charlie gripped the banister, white knuckles and tippy-toes all the way down.

In the parlour, every stained-glass lamp glowed at peak brightness. The commercial for the bug-bombs that used to give Nona the shivers hummed on the television. Shadowy little pests flitted across the screen as someone watched from the centre of the couch.

Not his babysitter.

Charlie clapped a hand over his mouth.

"That you making all that ruckus, Chuck?"

His father cricked his neck, stood from the couch, and turned with gleeful, red-shot eyes.

And oh creepers, he didn't look so hot.

Dark, crusty bruises caked the inflamed edges of the man's left nostril, and his whole body had a twitch about it.

"Sent the brat-sitter home. Done letting a gaggle of skirts raise my boy."

Charlie's throat had gone dry. His first big words came out as a rasp: "You shouldn't be here. Nona doesn't want you here!"

"*Nona* ain't kicking no more, is she?" his father barked with singsong laughter. Prickly shapes twisted in and out of his sharp-toothed grin. "But you're right. It's *not* my house. Know whose house it is, Chuck?"

Charlie didn't understand the question. It was Nona's house. It would always be Nona's house.

His father took a jagged step closer, swiped a backhand across his nostrils. "I grit and sweat my whole life to make rent on a lousy two-bedroom, and a pansy-boy like you tumbles skirts-first into a big fancy castle."

"Nona said I never have to leave here."

"Imagine that! And after the hissy-fit she threw when your mama got knocked-up." The man leaned in. His bruised eyelid bulged and peaked, something spiky prodding at the fine-veined skin. "Didn't think we'd make nice parents. She didn't want us to keep you."

"That's not true! She promised she'd never put me on the street."

"Not the street, Chuck. She wanted you scraped right out of your mama."

Charlie shook a sick dizziness from his head. Just more nasty-mean stories, lies to scare him. "She kept me safe from you!"

"Did she?" His eyelid rippled, but the man still refused to flinch, even as the lid split down the oozing centre. Hatching.

A Jeebie scurried loose. Made of blood-packed snow and steel scrapers and the tiny hands of babies-in-tummies. It glistened wetly and tracked a dotted red trail down his father's clenched jawline. "How's the old dead bitch gonna keep you safe now, Chuck?"

Charlie backed away and choked on a lump.

He screamed for Nona without a voice.

Behind his father, beyond the doorway, glass bottles rattled in the kitchen.

Then, with a magnetic-suction *pop,* the refrigerator door swung open. A rectangle of silver light cut across the checkered linoleum floor and a shadow filled the empty glow...

Wiggly fingers and a nightgowned silhouette.

Icy amazement prickled Charlie's spine and, despite his looming father, he froze.

Nona?

His father exhaled a bullish laugh, a threat Charlie knew too well. More wild Jeebies poked around inside the man's inflamed nostril and the bruised lump of his cheek. "Spineless runt. If I stomped on you, you wouldn't even *crunch.*"

In the kitchen, the slow slog of a bedroom slipper scraped along the linoleum.

It was her! Charlie's throat uncorked. "Nona!"

Rage cracked his father's face.

His five o'clock shadow contorted and tore open with a sickening wet *rip* – handsome eyelid to hard-cut jaw. A nest of writhing shapes squirmed across his face, larvae dripped free.

"You aren't scared, are you, Chuck?" The man's oozing gaze narrowed on Charlie. Fists balled, knuckles jagged.

Ready to pounce.

No! Charlie snapped the invisible webs holding him in place and ran toward the closest escape.

The staircase!

Up and up, gripping the infested banister as his father stomped after him and swiped at his heels. Up and up, as Jeebies spilled across his hand and crunched under his bare feet.

At the top, Nona's bedroom was nearest.

Charlie bolted for it.

Behind him, his father leapt off the staircase like a brown recluse spider, coming down hard on all-fours in the hallway. The nightlight smashed to black. The scattered stars fell away just as Charlie slammed Nona's door.

He scrabbled for the doorknob, twisting the skeleton key and bracing for his father's scuttling weight to slam against the door.

But the chaos in the hallway cut to silence.

Charlie backed away from the door, inched slowly through the dark of Nona's room. No moonlight tonight.

Prickles in his blood, nightmares crawling through every crevice.

Alone...but not alone.

Behind Charlie, the brass bedframe exhaled a slow screech.

Something shifted atop Nona's mattress. Uncurling, sitting up, swinging frozen legs over the side.

A thousand forgotten Jeebies loosened from the quilt and scurried to the floor.

Then two fast-shuffling slippers raced up behind him!

Nona!

Even so, Charlie choked back a wail and ran for the door. Too afraid to unlock it, he pressed his face against the wood and rode a chittering wave of bright white terror.

From behind, fridge-chilled fingers corkscrewed into the crevices beneath his arms.

Wiggled and tickled and hunted.

Finally, Charlie burst with a mind-crawly shriek of laughter.

Hands clapped together in the darkness.

"*Got that Jeebie,*" said a voice of raspy velvet, far-far away and drifting farther. "*Now, my boy, we vanquish him...*"

The key untwisted in the lock. The door cracked open. After a few thumpy heartbeats, Charlie realised it was *his* hand on the knob.

Listening with all his senses, he pulled the door open.

The long hallway beyond appeared empty. At the far end, the sickly yellow lamp-glow from Charlie's bedroom cut a dim path across the floor. The shadows barely even twitched.

Charlie crept forward, arms crossed, hands jammed in his armpits. A few steps from the stairs, he rose on tippy-toes, searching for movement down below.

Something uncurled on the high ceiling above him.

He didn't want to look.

A Heebie Jeebie dropped to the floorboards near his feet.

Then another, another, a hard-shelled rain. *Thunk, thunk...*

He looked anyway, rolled his eyes heavenward.

The spider-hunched shape of his father clung to the rafters in a squirming nest of cobwebs. Wearing a ghoulish, split-faced smile, the man sprang free and landed with a heavy, insectile *thunk* at the edge of the staircase.

Teetering, towering over Charlie.

He opened his mouth – "Gonna crush you, Chuck!" – and Nona's grave-bugs spilled out. Skulls, crossbones, monsters that go bump.

Charlie brought his hands together like a thunderclap.

Hands clasped, he stood tall and terrified and approached the maker of all his ugly-worst dreams.

"I'm done having you as my father!"

The man snickered, showed no fear.

But he should've been afraid.

Charlie opened his hands and something prickly and heavy and nasty sprung out.

Lucky this time, Charlie had his eyes squelched tight.

Never look a freshly plucked Jeebie in its beady little eyes.

His father roared, bellowed, then down and down he went. The house shook with a terrible tumble-clatter, ending hard with the chitinous *crunch* of bones.

Then silence.

Release.

Slowly, Charlie lowered his hands and gripped the banister. Dared to peek.

His father waited there, curled in a hell-bent heap at the bottom of the stairs. Jagged limbs and knuckles, swollen skull cracked down the middle.

A dark red mess leaked ever closer to the shadows. But nothing else moved.

A soft giggle escaped Charlie, a ghost-sigh of relief.

After all these years, Nona's house was finally pest-free.

KILLING BONES

Simon Clark

How did all this graveyard slaughter and mayhem get started?

It all began when some idiot tried to get themselves killed by running out into the path of our car, as we barrelled along a country road at midnight. There were three of us in the car: Scrotter (wasted on pills in the back), Zita driving (fifty days sober), and me riding shotgun (started literary life as a poet, performed my *Extro-Necro* saga live on TV, then – where do the years go? – narcotic oblivion for an entire decade. I'm being good now – too good for this world, huh?).

Picture this: car speeding, engine screaming, lights ripping open darkness – a deserted highway, where monster trees stretch out claw branches, wanting with all their sap-filled hearts to tear you apart. Then a woman running into the road, staring at us with eyes that blasted out raw terror. She stood there, hands gesturing '*Stop*!'

"Shit!" Zita pounded the brake.

The car began to skid, after maybe hitting a patch of slippery mud, or perhaps that big beast of a BMW simply broke free of Zita's control. In any event, tyres squealed as the car slid sideways, accompanied by thuds, bangs, crashes as German steel slammed into roadside bushes, gouging sprays of dark mud from the earth banking.

And we were screaming. An ear-battering combination of terror and anguish, because, as the car skidded along, venting blue smoke from tyre rubber, we saw the woman lying there on the blacktop behind us, absolutely still – corpse-like.

A second later, the vehicle skidded to a stop in the road. Zita switched off the engine – and, for a moment, the silence was so intense it hurt my ears.

A silence broken when Scrotter yelled: "Who was that crazy woman!"

"What was she doing in the road?" I looked back, trying to see what must undoubtedly be a mutilated body. However, I could now see nothing in the darkness.

"She just ran out in front of me," cried Zita. "I've killed her, haven't I? She's dead!"

Then Zita and me, we were scrambling out of the seats, me activating the flashlight on my phone, illuminating a human shape lying there, motionless.

Zita's lips were a slash of absolute black. Shock does that to you. Blackens your lips (and bulges your eyes) – sometimes shock even changes your life forever. Meanwhile, my phone illuminated the stranger. She wore jeans and a white T-shirt, and lay stretched out like a crucified martyr, eyes staring up into eternity.

"Oh, God," whispered Zita.

As I leaned over the corpse (no doubt, bones shattered, brain ruptured), it abruptly grabbed my sweatshirt collar and used my sorry garment to haul itself to its feet. What I'd assumed to be a lifeless cadaver actually fizzed with vitality.

The woman yelled into my face, so close I could smell peppermint on her breath: "Help me! It's fucking got hold of my boyfriend!"

Zita gasped with relief. "She's not dead. Thank God. I didn't kill her!"

"Must've dived out of the way," observed Scrotter, his prodigious intake of feel-good pills rendering him unsteady on his feet. "Gotta have thrown herself clear of the mojo…still took a damn good battering from all that hard stuff they make roads out of, though."

Indeed so. The woman must have dived clear of the car, before hitting the blacktop violently enough to knock herself senseless for a moment or two, giving me the impression she was dead. Her jaw was grazed, and she'd lost a chunk of skin from her knuckles, allowing speckles of blood to seep through the flesh.

Zita's relief mutated into anger. "Hey! Whoever you are! Why did you run out into the road? Me swerving like that to save your life nearly got us killed!"

The woman did not listen, because she was on a mission, and that mission was to grab hold of my already stupidly baggy sweatshirt and drag me into the trees.

"Please help me." Tears bled from her eyes. "It got hold of him. He was screaming!"

We ran through the night, she still clutching a fistful of my sweatshirt. Some residual hero instinct pumped thoughts into my poor, self-abused brain, urging me 'to do the right thing' and help the woman.

Moonlight painted with dabs of chrome light – illuminating the way ahead, between looming trees.

Zita ran alongside us, her eyes flashing amazement. "At least I didn't kill her. Everything's going to be all right."

A moment after Zita uttered those far from prophetic words, we saw for ourselves what had befallen the graveyard. Believe me, I've witnessed all kinds of horrors erupt from the ground after injecting lousy gear into my disintegrating veins, but nothing compared to this.

Of course, I did that thing where you stare at everything *but* the object of your horrified fascination. My eyes fixed on the graveyard, a third of its tombstones ripped apart, heaped into piles, stone angels decapitated; lawns gouged, exposing raw dirt. There was a family of dead rats near my right foot that had been expelled from their burrow so forcefully that their stomachs had burst, discharging pink spaghetti strands of innards onto the grass. Yes, I saw all that...but I resolutely did not see what the stranger was pointing at.

"Look," she was saying. "There he is."

Zita shuddered. "There...on the gravestone – the one shaped like a table – is that your boyfriend's...?"

"Yes." The woman gave a savage nod. "But where are his eyes?"

Finally, I looked at the monument that had been crafted from white marble to resemble a table. Moonlight, in a grim mood to shock, revealed red stuff, running all sticky and wet in the epitaph chiselled there: *WEEP NOT FOR ME, PARENTS DEAR. I AM NOT GONE. AND REMAIN QUITE NEAR...*

And resting on the marble table, a football. But it wasn't a ball you play a game with, was it? And, to be honest, it wasn't even a ball: because there were holes in the front.

Where the fucking eyes had been.

What happened next distracted me from that horrific object oozing there on the morbid slab of stone.

Because the ground convulsed in the graveyard's centre, the upheaval producing something not unlike a boil you find in a victim of a medieval disease – possibly a recherché comparison, I know, but that's the image that swelled with awful clarity in my brain. The earth rose up, the cemetery lawn splitting open, gravestones near the disturbance moving in a rippling effect, like corn being blown in a breeze – and then venting from a hole in the earthen abscess: bones. Thousands of human bones. But not a chaotic scattering of disconnected skeletons. No, all the bones had stuck together in linear form – a thighbone connected to an arm bone, a toe bone connected to a neck bone – so they formed something like flexible bone tentacles that rose into the moon-silvered air.

The next thing I knew, we'd raced back to the car. Dents in its front wings, mud splattering the paintwork, and leafy branches hanging from the radiator grille were ample evidence of our accident just minutes ago. And there was Scrotter, lying flat out on the road, dead to the world, adrift in a deeply narcotic sleep after, no doubt, consuming even more pills from the stash in his coat pocket.

"Scrotter!" I yelled. "Get in the car! We gotta go!"

Zita shouted, "Did we just see a monster?"

The stranger hollered, "That thing killed Jermaine! We've got to smash the fuck out of it! Make it suffer!"

* * *

Nobody can live in a state of hyper-terror for long. After the three of us returned to the car, wide-eyed with horror, images burned into our brains of an interconnected mutant skeleton erupting from the cemetery, our spirits crashed into a profound emotional slump. We leaned, exhausted, against the car (though Scrotter remained sitting in the road, his brain adrift on barbiturate seas). Zita, the stranger and I began muttering amongst ourselves: "What was that thing in the cemetery?" "All those bones." "How can bones come alive?"

Scrotter merely gave a drowsy smile. "I see crazy stuff all the time. Don't worry, it'll pass."

The stranger glared at Scrotter with enough contempt to grant me a clear insight into what she was thinking: that Scrotter was the kind of guy who always played the fool, while wearing a drug guzzler's smirk on his face. Of course, the expression someone habitually wears might be a mask to conceal what haunts them. Six months ago, Scrotter and his boyfriend got beaten up by kids who no doubt enjoyed demonstrating their power over homeless people. Tam ended up with an even harder place than the ground to rest his head that awful night, when the hospital porters laid him on the mortuary slab.

Yeah, Scrotter laughs a lot, he's always smiling. He's super-good at wearing the happy mask.

For a while, Zita, the stranger and I remained perfectly still, listening for any sign that the creature might be heading our way.

Eventually, Zita gave a nervy shrug. "I don't hear anything."

"It might have gone," I said.

The stranger spoke firmly. "Listen. We must kill that monster."

"That monster will kill us," Zita pointed out.

Her warning was enough to silence us for a spell as we stood there, the breeze wafting trees, eliciting a million sinister whispers – evil mandrake melodies messing with your head. That lump of meat in my chest hadn't beat as hard as it had tonight since I did my debut gig ten years ago on *The Lost Riff*, a rock and poetry programme that went out every Friday night, back when I aspired to be a purveyor of horror verse. So, live on TV, I performed *Extro-Necro* – a gruesome lyric about my *bona fide* obsession with graveyards, and whatever writhes so wet and utterly rotted within morbid tombs. Studio lights blazed, the camera glided in. The cable of the little mic pinned to my turquoise shirt ran down my chest like a graveyard worm as I began to—

"My name's Carmen," said the woman who we'd come within a cat's whisker of running over.

"Uh?" I disentangled myself from memories of my six minutes of fame.

Zita managed a polite smile. "Carmen, the guy on the ground is Scrotter. This is Lee."

Maybe our we've-lived-a-chemical-life eyeballs hinted that we weren't the usual midnight travellers you'd find on a country road. But then Carmen wasn't your usual nocturnal rambler, was she?

Which prompted me to ask, "What were you doing in a cemetery?"

"Jermaine and I were recording the soprano pipistrelle."

"What?" Zita stared at her.

Scrotter nodded. "Bats."

"Exactly," declared Carmen. "Soprano pipistrelle bats. We set up recording equipment in the cemetery to determine the range of their echolocation calls. You see, there is a barn nearby colonised by pipistrelle."

"Right." I gave Carmen an appraising look, which might have suggested that I didn't believe her to be entirely sane.

Carmen steamed on. "We'd been recording the pipistrelle when the ground in the centre of the graveyard began to heave, and gravestones fell over, just toppling one after another. Jermaine ran toward the disturbance, wanting to see what was happening. Then he screamed… I've never heard a scream like it." Carmen didn't weep. Instead she became angry; murder burned in her eyes. "Jermaine had been broken into pieces."

"So," I began, "it's time we reported all this to the cops."

"No," thundered Carmen. "The police won't believe us. It's down to us to kill the monster."

Scrotter gave a bemused smile. "Monster. What monster?"

Zita pointed through the trees. "There's a creature made out of skeletons."

"Yeah." Scrotter pushed more pills into his mouth. "I see stuff like that all the time, but the lady's right. Whenever I tell cops about monsters crawling through the streets, they just laugh at me. Bastards."

I walked to the car. "We're not fighting monsters, we're leaving."

"I'm staying," Carmen insisted.

"Your choice." I flumped down into the front passenger seat.

Carmen lunged toward me. "You must help me destroy that thing. What if it kills more people?"

Zita shrugged. "How do we nail a monster like that? We'd need flame-throwers."

That's when the phones began to ring. Lots of phones, all playing different tunes.

Carmen frowned. "Are those your phones? Where are they?"

I replied, "Hidden under the back seat."

Carmen's eyes went wide. "My God, you're drug dealers."

Scrotter climbed to his feet. "No, we're not. But the guy I stole the car from is. The phones belong to him." Angrily he added, "Pinner says I owe him money for pills he said he sold me but never did. So, we're gonna start a new life in Cornwall."

Carmen was amazed. "You stole a drug dealer's car?"

"Yep."

"Is there any gear inside?"

"Yep." Scrotter nodded. "Loads of vac-pack coke hidden inside the doors – y'know, in the cavities."

Phones still rang – ten of them at least.

Carmen's eyes narrowed. "You think this Pinner guy can't trace the phones?" Another thought struck her. "And won't he have hidden an electronic tracker in his car, just in case anybody was stupid enough to steal it?"

Admittedly, that possibility had never entered my head.

Suddenly, two cars came roaring toward us. Big Range Rovers with tinted windows, their drivers channelling sheer aggression into the way they drove.

Zita stated the obvious: "Here comes Pinner."

"Nope." Scrotter sobered up fast. "Here comes death."

Into the trees! Into shadow! Into darkness! We ran, trying to put ample distance between us and our pursuers.

"Problem!" I panted. "We're heading toward the cemetery… don't forget the monster!"

Carmen, running faster than us, shouted back, "I'm going to kill that thing. And you're going to help me!"

Scrotter, Zita and I bunched up close as we loped along, panting for breath.

Even so, I managed to whisper, "Carmen's psycho-obsessive, isn't she? How are we going to kill a…a creature made of bones?"

Scrotter had issues other than monsters on his mind. "What if Pinner just takes his car and leaves us alone?"

Events proved Scrotter's hopes to be woefully misplaced. Pinner and his drug-dealing henchmen began searching for us, moonlight revealing gleaming machetes and bone-cracking baseball bats clutched in fists. Then came the clincher.

Pinner, a big guy with a shaved head, yelled, "Scrotter! Lee! Zita! When I find you, I'm gonna fucking slaughter you!"

We ran a whole lot faster after that, enabling us to catch up with Carmen, who now stood at the cemetery fence, glaring at trashed graves and bloody bits of boyfriend strewn across churned dirt. We paused there, panting hard, hearing the crashing of Pinner's army as they surged through undergrowth.

"I've been thinking," Carmen said. "Forest trees are connected by mycelium: slender threads of fungus that act as both pipes and telephone wires. On a very rudimentary level, trees communicate with each other. And water can be channelled via mycelium to other trees during drought conditions."

Shouts in the forest – Pinner and his murder-squad were getting nearer.

Zita spoke curtly: "Bollocks to fungus. We *must* get away from here."

"Don't you see?" Carmen's eyes gleamed. "Trees linked by fungal threads, transforming forests into a single organism. What if these graves are connected by something similar? Thousands of graves becoming interconnected, and everything in the graves – bones, gut, hair, teeth – evolving into a single entity. One with a unified nervous system that—"

"*There they are*!" Pinner's cohorts had found us.

"Run!" Scrotter hauled himself over the fence, before loping away amid gravestones that glinted their own bleak horror in the light of a death's head moon.

Flashlight beams swung in our direction, as Pinner's gang moved toward us. Something that prompted us to quickly scramble over the fence.

Zita called out, "Scrotter – no! Avoid the centre! Follow the perimeter fence!"

Thankfully, Scrotter complied, skirting out toward the edge of the cemetery, well away from the centre – a centre comprising violated graves, churned-up soil, bones evicted from coffins – and in the middle of the detritus, a pit of darkness ten feet across and God knows how deep.

The thugs raced toward the cemetery, moonlight shimmering on dangerous machete blades.

And we were moving, too…

Run across the grass! Jump over riven tombstones! Sear your brain with nightmare images! Assorted cadaver parts: ripped out teeth littering grave dirt, grey bones *crunching* beneath my feet. A torn face, a brown mole protruding beneath one eye. A severed hand, fingers curled into its palm. Chunks of wood from destroyed caskets – a section of coffin lining (once pink satin, now streaked tawny by juices of post-mortem rot).

Exertion, jabbing pain into every quarter of my flesh. Lungs burning. Legs aching. Belly cramping. Stink of decaying cadavers polluting my nostrils with every breath. And my nerves turning supernova-bright with terror, because psychos were roaring my name.

"*Lee! We're gonna kill you*!"

And there…in the heart of darkness…in the graveyard's centre, the ground pulsating. Soil bulging. Tombstones trembling with every upward thrust of the Earth.

That's when I tripped and fell, arms sprawling outwards, momentum driving my body onward, my face sliding through lumps of matter that were cold and wet – *ugh!* I'd fallen onto corpse flesh, torn from bone.

And there, on the grass, a dead face near my face. A single eye, cherry-red, bulging from a rancid socket. Still lying on the ground, I retreated from that horrible relic, by rolling away from the lifeless eye, resulting in my face touching more scraps of wet flesh, which felt like cold kisses being planted on my cheeks and lips. My heart pounded as I lay in the grip of churning darkness. Rivers of dread thundered through the forlorn canyons of this addict heart of mine. I felt like crying for my mother. Yet I could not utter a word, because the terrible understanding that this was the end of my life punched the strength right out of me, allowing gravity to pin me down into that foul-smelling chaos of bone, human skin and ruined coffins. *This is where I die. My ambitions as a poet unfulfilled.* Hands grabbed me. *Pray that oblivion comes quickly.*

"Lee," yelled a voice. "Move!"

To my surprise, those hands belonged to Carmen, not to the murderous thugs of Pinner's gang. Within an instant of her pulling me to my feet, we were running again.

By the time I'd returned to at least a degree of rational thought, we were on the far side of the cemetery. Pinner's gang, meanwhile, had chosen the direct route, through the centre. Maybe their fury hadn't permitted them the opportunity to consider that it was unusual for a cemetery to be a scene of utter devastation.

We paused at the cemetery fence because…

"Look, it's back!" Zita pointed.

A hand made from bone appeared – a hand with fingers ten feet long. The hand was followed by an arm, by a bone shoulder, by a skull. Then the entire monstrosity emerged from its womb of filth.

Witnessing the thing squeezing itself upward, through a relatively small hole in the dirt, I screamed so hard that blood shot from my nose as veins burst within delicate nasal membranes.

The creature rose above the tomb-scape. Thirty feet in height, a grey colossus, built from thousands of shin bones, thigh bones, fragments of skull, jaw bones – all knitted together by forces I could not even begin to understand. Limbs were supple, with flexible joints. While set into its massive face, the eyes were twin pools of glistening gel that gleamed red in the moonlight.

The most stomach-churning spectacle of all, though, was the creature's mouth. Moistly pale lips, crafted from bowel and intestine, filched from the recently buried. And slipping wetly from its lips, a blood-red tongue, seemingly formed from the compressed tongues of hundreds of corpses. And when it began to lick its lips with an expression of greed-filled lust, a feeling of utter revulsion compelled me to press my fist against my own mouth.

Pinner and his gang had stopped just fifty paces from the creature, their flashlights playing across it. The monstrosity swayed in front of them, as if learning how to balance after whatever birthing process had expelled it from the cemetery dirt. For the first time, I saw fear on Pinner's face. The other men were scared, too, their body language changing from that of aggressive predators to cringing terror-struck children as they raised bats and machetes – but not to attack. No, to defend.

Then, with a loud crack, the creature's back split open from top to bottom, revealing a shiny, pearlescent substance within.

Carmen gasped, "My God. It's falling apart."

"No." Zita shook her head. "Not falling apart...something is coming out of it."

Zita spoke the truth because PVC-like sheets spilled out of the creature. The sheets quivered, shook, smoothing out creases, and I saw...

"Wings." I stared in astonishment. "It's grown wings."

The wings spread out – membrane-thin – attached to a framework of osseous material.

The wings were made from the putrid skin of bodies interred in this sad acre. And when Pinner's men shone their flashlights at the wings, light gleamed through membranes, revealing stretched out faces, panels of belly skin, complete with belly button whorls.

The men turned and fled back toward the forest. They nearly made it as far as the cemetery fence. Before they could get that far, however, the creature, with three slow strokes of its wings, made a short flight to land in their midst where, thereafter, its bone hands flashed in the moonlight, ripping, slashing. Human arms and legs were sent flying through the air in aerosol bursts of crimson as the men were slaughtered.

Pinner climbed onto the fence. There he stood, ready to jump down the other side. A second later, the top half of his body had parted from the lower half, as one of the monster's razor-sharp fingers cut him neatly in two. Pinner, now on the ground, and with his own life-force still burning bright within him, desperately used his hands to drag the top half of his body across the grass, abandoning his hips, buttocks and legs, and leaving a trail of wetness on the grass as blood vented through the colossal wound beneath his belly.

Without any fuss, a bone finger and thumb neatly pinched off the man's head. Pinner, reduced to three gory parts, lay still.

That was when the creature turned to fix its evil gaze on us.

"Okay." Carmen spoke calmly. "Now we destroy the monster. Any ideas?"

Zita's expression was grim. "No way can we kill it. And we'll never escape. That thing can fly."

The monster took a step in our direction, head tilting to one side, sizing us up. Like a dog taking its time to pounce on a wounded rabbit.

Then Scrotter uttered, "Cook it."

Zita pointed. "Watch out! It's trying to get airborne!"

Carmen pointed, too: not at the creature but at the wheatfield beyond the fence. "Cook it!"

Turning, I realised what they meant. Running across the field were the stark, marching figures of electricity pylons, all threaded together by cables that hummed with thousands of volts.

The four of us clambered over the fence before running toward the pylons, through waist-high corn. I realised I'd lost a shoe, and that stones were puncturing the sole of my right foot, but I didn't care. We had a plan to save our lives – and those hope-filled words pounded through my head to the rhythm of my running feet. *Cook it! Cook it! Cook it!*

From behind, a loud rustle as wings shaped from dead skin began to flap faster and faster.

Scrotter yelled, "It's taking off!"

Zita surged through the wheat. "Get to the power lines! Stop for nothing!"

That was when she fell.

We kept running, me yelling back, "Zita! Stay down! Hide in the corn!"

Scrotter flapped his arms, imitating wings. "Bone Boy! Come and get us!"

I glanced back as Zita's head bobbed down, out of sight, beneath the ears of wheat. The monster, vast wings flapping, bones making a ratcheting, clicking sound, flew about fifty feet above the ground, homing in on us – a missile crammed with lethal promise.

The distance we needed to cover to the power lines seemed never-ending. Scrotter went down, too, cartwheeling in a flurry of arms and legs before lying flat, concealed by a million undulating stalks.

Carmen and I charged across the field, willing our aching bodies ever closer to those pylons that always, to me, resemble chain gangs of sinister metal giants striding across the landscape.

The thing flew toward us, lit by the ghostly light of the moon, bone arms stretching out, fingers hooking into lethal claws.

Carmen and I screamed the same instruction to each other in a frenzy of terror: "*Run! Run! Run*!"

That grim flyer rose into the night sky, a predator carved from death, preparing to plummet down and tear us apart.

"We're too late." I slowed down, corn tangling around my ankles. "It's going to catch us."

We both screamed and threw ourselves flat into the wheat as the creature came diving toward us, murderous claws extending, eager to rip our flesh.

A deafening bang. The bluest of flashes. The stench of burning. A stink of something horrible being cooked.

Carmen and I lay in the wheatfield as smouldering bones – disconnected, fragmented, scorched – rained down upon us, to be joined by crispy flaps of seared skin that had once been wings.

I looked up.

Hanging from power cables, which flashed and cascaded showers of sparks, was a single massive bone arm that terminated in an equally vast hand, its fingers twitching with every jolt of electricity.

* * *

I thought: *Pinner's dead. His gang are dead. Pinner doesn't care what we do with his car.*

So, we abandoned the other vehicle (the one that Scrotter had stolen) and we travelled in style, in Pinner's luxurious new Range Rover, Zita driving. We were laughing and talking all the way – Zita, Scrotter, Carmen and me. Happily, we had only minor scratches to show for our battle with the flying Goliath. Carmen would soon grieve for her dead boyfriend, yet right now she was high on adrenaline, her eyes glittering, her laughter extravagantly loud in the confines of the car.

Scrotter grinned from ear-to-ear. "Did you see how that monster exploded when it flew into the power lines?"

"Jermaine is revenged." Carmen's voice rang with the conviction of a bishop declaring an ecclesiastical judgement.

"And Pinner can't bully us any more," added Zita.

We passed a church as a new dawn painted the sky red.

"Did anyone see that?" Hearing the fear in my voice, they all turned to look at me. "There was a big hole in the middle of the churchyard."

We rode in silence after that. And it was in that subdued mood I noticed that Pinner had left his gold Rolex on the dashboard – no doubt not wanting to get its glass face scratched while he beat me to death.

Cornfields gave way to houses. A caretaker in a Hi-Viz vest opened a set of school gates. However, a nasty little instinct told me the kids wouldn't be going there any more.

"The churchyard back there," I began, "the crater..."

But the words died on my lips as we glided past another cemetery, a huge municipal one, home to thirty thousand cadavers or more. And...yes...an abundance of craters violated the ground, wrecking gravestones, disgorging coffins.

Now, should anyone subject this testament to a forensic exegesis, I would point out that this is the crux of my tale: for there, above our own realm of mortality, which is so often full of pain and regret, the sun rose over rooftops and church spires to softly illuminate legions of bone monsters, soaring overhead on enormous wings.

As I leaned my head out through the open window, to gaze up at those macabre creatures, delineated against a blood-red sky, my body shivered in much the same way as the last of the Neanderthals must have shivered when they saw the newly arrived Homo Sapiens come boldly striding over the hill to inherit the Earth.

IL CREPUSCOLO

Helen Marshall

1.

Vitale Gallo was an endling, the last of the Venetians, the last of his kind, and the feeling – oh, the feeling was like a kind of settling darkness, twilight – *il crepuscolo*. A last look at the sun-kissed horizon.

He was born the old-fashioned way in a third-storey *piano nobile* overlooking the Rio del Trapolin canal, his family's home for so long. His mamma hadn't meant for it to happen in that place. She'd intended to evacuate with the others, but his father, a scholar of Dante, was away on conference. A foolish decision, leaving his wife alone, but she was stubborn and had insisted. Still, he had felt misgivings. There were so few left by that point, those who still lived in the city despite the dangers: *acqua alta*, the creep and crumble of decay.

But she was an architect. She loved the city and wouldn't leave to join him, loved the thankless job of shoring up her basilicas and bridges, loved caressing the city, brushing her fingers along the roof of the *sottoportico*, the bas-reliefs and bricks. And Tommaso Gallo loved *her*. He was a slave to her wishes.

And so he was in Rome when the waters rushed in, swamping her ground floor. The neighbours couldn't hear her screaming over the sirens. It was faster than she would have thought possible. One moment she was pregnant and fat as a seal, then her ankles were soaked with brine and eleven squeezes later – she counted them, of course she did – eleven squeezes, each worse than the last, and out came her little *passerotto*.

She swaddled Vitale in a blanket and clutched him close, as a motorboat laden with priceless Tizianos and Tintorettos carried her to *terra firma*. A treasure, amongst so many fine beautiful things. She always said it was the city wanting one last son for herself.

Gallo inherited two things from his mamma: her love of mathematics and the ghost feel of the city under his feet. He never walked Venice's piazzas, never stumbled through the Zattere or waved to a little *s'ciopon* as it ventured out into the lagoon, yet as a child it seemed there was a memory lodged within him: standing under the Dome of the Pentecost, staring up at all of creation arrayed above him in glittering mosaic. Under his feet lay a vast oaken raft, supported on stilts. Larch, alder, pine – they floated a forest, a forest, could you imagine it? – across the lagoon and then they hammered it upside down.

By the time Gallo was two, the last remains of the city had fallen. Houses, churches and palaces: their foundations had rotted away after years of neglect and patchy repairs. Just like that, his pappa said, *La Serenissima* went from salvation to salvage. It broke his mamma's heart. They sunk her ashes in the Adriatic where the waters of the lagoon poured out into the sea.

⋆ ⋆ ⋆

"Every city has a ghost within her," Gallo would say in the years that followed, "the ghost of the city she once was and the ghost of all the cities she could have been." He would know. He carried the ghost of Venice inside him through the bad years as Europe burned and ash choked his lungs, as the vineyards blistered, the Po dried up and waves of yellow fever, flu and hantavirus spread through the crowds of refugees.

During those decades of flood and fire he felt himself drifting – *per una selva oscura*, lost in the woods, the straight path abandoned. Bombai, Shanghai, Miami. Other cities drowned before the fragile peace took hold and the process of rebuilding began, but it was Venice that haunted him. When he dreamed he saw the gleam of candlelight on mosaic, heard the tinkling sound of a thousand shards of glass falling to the cobblestones, Christ surrounded by a glittering universe of gold. Ageless, beatific, as his mamma was now.

He never married. Never had children himself. How could you, this world being what it was? He devoted himself, not to the work of preservation, but to the work of discovery. He knew so much of the old world was vanishing, but there was a chance, he thought – he dreamed – a chance he might yet build something new.

He attended the Sapienza University of Rome where he studied materials engineering, ceramics and glassblowing. He was not the best of his classmates but he was driven, he worked hard. As he held the mandrel in the flame, he thought of the steady hands of the artisans of Murano and the things they had made, how the lagoon must have been littered with the kaleidoscopic dust of their workings. In Hawaii, as a second wave of disease ravaged the Old World, he climbed through collapsed craters and calderas, testing the peculiar qualities of fine-grained basalt. With his right eye – what he had come to think of as his ghosting eye – he saw columns of red porphyry and pavonazzetto marble, a great dome held aloft. But with his left eye he saw a different vision entirely: he dreamed of a mountain so high it stretched into heaven. And the stars were set about it, winking gold in the darkness. He saw its shoulders clothed with the rays of a distant sun and the fear in his heart quieted.

In the night sky Mars hung above him, red and shining like a ruby.

And then he was *mezzo del cammin*, thirty-five, midway upon the journey of life, when a grey-haired man appeared at his doorstep. Gallo knew him at once for what he was, a bureaucrat, yes, but a visionary, a fellow Venetian, the author of the *ca me ligo* manifesto: a guide for the future. And the Caigoist carried with him interagency budgets, policy briefs, and firm political commitments. He had his own dreams of the heavens. He took Gallo aside, said to him, "Build us a city of knowledge and we will set it among the stars. Build us a place to house our thinkers, our scientists, the mystics of our brave new world."

"Why now?" he asked, and the other only smiled.

"We lived through death, and now what remains but the search for life?"

Gallo had nothing to say to this. He would think on it. But already the decision had been made in his mind, for what else had he been preparing himself all those days? Why else had he mastered the mystery of lithography and substrate if not for this? A new world?

Mars Station Alpha, *ffut!* What a name! Can you imagine?

No. He would name her the San Marco. He knew she needed a ghost inside her if she was ever truly going to live.

2.

Even from the start, Vitale Gallo knew she would need to be beautiful, she would need to be grand. When the Caigoist had come to him, the engineer had said as much.

"If I build you this place," he had said, "we must ask not only how will we make this, but how will we make this beautiful?" He had always thought that if anything would save them it would be beauty.

And was there any city in the world more beautiful – more impossible – than Venice? "She should have been named *Il Fantasma*," his pappa claimed. After all, didn't she accrete around a corpse herself, the pirated body of the blessed Evangelist? Whatever they said, Venice had never been as serene as she seemed to the outside world. She was beautiful, yes, but she was also strange and disturbing, disorienting, snatched out of history.

An impossible city – now a corpse herself, drowned, abandoned to the sludge and slime that birthed her and cradled her for so long. What better ghost to revivify for that marvellous, impossible project?

And so the station San Marco was to become a place of wonder. She would have her own apses and gleaming cupolas, built from graphene and titanium foams, basalt and iron oxide. Her own *calli* and *sestieri*, her own *rii* – canals – filled with a rich broth of cyanobacteria that would keep them breathing, keep them alive. Gallo built her slantwise and askew as Venice had been, so that as her inhabitants moved from piazza to portego they would feel uneasy, they would feel the echo of Venice.

* * *

He went with them, of course, he had made sure it was necessary. The San Marco held secrets – she had to, surely they understood!

Such a thing could not simply be built and handed over to another! – and as its architect it was necessary for him to mind them.

And so he left his pappa, his only living family, and travelled for six months through the darkness aboard a ship called the *Xantho* with a crew of twelve. Physicists, astronomers, engineers, biologists – dreamers all in their own way, survivors like him, through the hard days of almost-collapse.

He worked and he slept and he dreamed of the sound of water rushing past, dreamed the wake stretching behind him, ripples of gravity and force. He thought he would see stars, of course, but the light of the sun was too blindingly brilliant. As he stared out into the distance, the universe seemed to blossom like an immense white rose. He saw things no other human had seen with the naked eye. He saw, as the poet said, gathered and bound by Love into one volume, all things that are separate and scattered through the universe, *sustanze e accidenti e lor costume quasi conflati insieme,* substance and accident and disposition, as if unified. He tried to write of it to his pappa, who he knew would understand: the Gallos had always been subject to their passions, stubborn and proud.

Then they set down upon the red planet and there were no words at all, nothing he could say, nothing at all to explain it, that feeling of sinking his feet into the soil on an alien world. The softness of dust, his body pressing into a surface that seemed to engulf him. Like her namesake, the San Marco perched along the ancient waterways where millions of years ago a geyser of heat had burst through the crust, spilling out ice and glorious brine.

Yet it too was a site of ancient disaster, its molten core a dynamo gone still, without which its precious gases had been flung into space. Gallo found himself weeping: moisture drained away, recycled, fed back to him as pure as springwater.

That night, they sat with their thighs touching the regolith bricks of Dorsoduro as the *rii* pulsed and plashed around them, and they told each other ghost stories.

First went Protheroe, who spoke of the hilltop near where she had been raised near the town of Tywyn. As the heat of an unbearable August scorched the fields, it had revealed the green shadows of barrows, old trenches dug by forgotten Celts. Some nights as a child she could hear her Bronze Age ancestors, trading salt, slaves, gold and furs, the lyrical whisper of their long-dead voices.

Then next went the biologist, a dark-haired half-Sámi named Vassiliev, who said he had tracked herds of mammoths on the Siberian tundra. Except they weren't mammoths, of course, but African elephants, reconstituted and adapted. Scientists had set them masquerading in the shaggy cloaks of their brethren, like the patrons of some long-lost Pleistocene *carnivale.* He had seen an eerie frightened look in the eyes of one elderly bull, as if he were remembering the savannahs and grasslands his ancestors had known, as if he were seeking signs of the route to his graveyard: the place their bones lay white and gleaming beneath the balsam trees.

That evening the dust rose up like fog, and the sun – a pale disc – set in a haze of glacial blue. Vassiliev came to him, his eyes nearly black in the gloom, his laugh biting, his lips urgent as they sought out Gallo's own. Afterwards, he left again, his body outlined against a palette of ultramarine and cochineal reds, careful to leave no trace of his visit.

In the morning he would analyse samples and tend to the cyanobacteria that flowed through the station's *rii*, tethering them to life. It gave Gallo a peculiar source of joy to see such conscientiousness for what he had made.

There was no need to hide, of course. Others among the crew had laid their affections bare. It was to be expected. But with Vassiliev whatever it was lay shallower than even affection. The fear of contamination obsessed him.

He stared at the green lather that filled the channels. "If this stuff gets out," he said, "who knows what will happen? We think we know but we don't. That's the problem with being the first. You don't know anything, do you?" He brooded over the microgravity, stress responses in low-shear environments – the potential for disaster. "It could live, maybe even out there. What if we've come all this way only to infect this place with our own pathogens?"

But in the bad days Gallo had learned there was always a chance of misfortune, some yawning chasm that might open up beneath you. You could love something and lose it anyway.

When the weather was clear, they would go on hikes together into the foothills of the mountain, its grooves and pits streaked black with a rich saline wash. Vassiliev had a steady, wolfish gait, even in his suit. On Earth he had been a long-distance runner and these climbs, he claimed, gave him the only opportunity to properly stretch his muscles. They traversed up rust-red buttes to find mesas of gypsum that sparkled like broken glass, hunting in vain for fossil life. They never found it.

"We will," Vassiliev would say afterward, supremely confident, "it's only a matter of time."

He could be patient, Gallo saw, and methodical. Sometimes he would draw stark, straight lines in the soil, his own kind of offering.

It was only as he reached the end of his scheduled six months that he began to show signs of frustration.

"I can't stand it," he raged privately. "There is nothing for us here. There never was. Even at Vostok Station, where you'd freeze your balls off in twenty seconds, still you find *something*." His eyes were wide, his skin pale and trembling. "I thought, well, it would be wonderful but instead it is so lonely. They cannot understand how lonely it is. The only thing worse than being haunted is learning even the ghosts are dead. There's no one to talk to."

* * *

Soon after, Vassiliev left. They all did. All except Gallo.

His pappa had sent him a message. Another tragedy: some new virus had reached his retirement community in Oslo, unpredictable but deadly. He waved his hand. "Don't worry, my son," said Tommaso Gallo. "As the poet said, our fate cannot be taken from us. It is a gift."

The next message was worse, his breathing laboured. His liver and kidneys were failing.

They could not speak, of course, not even at the end. The distance was too far, their messages syncopated by the time lag.

"Wherever I go," he murmured, "I will have your shining eyes to guide me. And hers too, *mia stella.*"

There were no further messages. His father fell into a coma from which he was not expected to wake.

But by then, the graphene hull of the San Marco had begun to show signs of stress. To be expected. One could only design speculatively. An engineer's experience was needed, Gallo told them, so of course he would stay to oversee the repairs. There was nothing left for him back on Earth.

* * *

The next biologist was Rojas, who followed the routes Vassiliev had mapped and surveyed them, extended them, made her own fresh trails to the foot of the sulphate mountain.

"Come with me," she said to Gallo. "You've been out there. We'll go together."

She was different to Vassiliev, warmer in every way. She loved to laugh. She told dirty jokes and whenever she caught him lost in thought, the black cloud upon him, she would grin, tell him, "Never shit more than you eat, get me?"

He walked through his grief, tried to feed his soul with wonder.

They picked their way through gleaming deserts of opaline silica and there Rojas told him about her abuela who had combed the Atacama searching for bone shards of Pinochet's disappeared. She grew near-sighted with squinting and yet once, Rojas said, the old woman had happened upon a femur twice as tall as she was, the remnant of some lost lizard that would have eclipsed any known today if it were true. But afterward her abuela had told no one, and wherever that grave lay, it lay there still and undisturbed. She could not bear for them to touch it.

"We laugh, we die. Mostly we vanish," she said with a shrug. "But not all, never everything. There were worlds and worlds that lived before ours. Nothing begins and nothing ends. It will be the same here, you'll see. We'll find it."

Gallo said nothing to that. When he looked out at the cracked landscape he heard Vassiliev's words in his ears and a terrible loneliness came over him.

"You're a strange one." Rojas elbowed him with a laugh when the two of them returned to the station. "The San Marco? It's like naming a place after Pompeii. It seems like a bad sign. Were you cursing us?"

She meant it as a joke but it made him cross himself nonetheless.

3.

Another cycle passed. The dust storms of spring gave way to summer. Bands of lead-white clouds capped the distant volcanos, and the polar caps began to recede. But no brine flowed into the chasma. The waterways were stark and hardpan, barren.

Then it was Rojas packing her things for the long trip home: she went gamely enough, tucking away the picture of her abuela. She had hoped to find traces of tube worms or algae, but she too was leaving empty-handed. The only life she found was the life they had brought with them: microbial contaminants, hitchhikers on their spacesuits.

"Ah well," she said philosophically, "if not me, then another. Treat them kindly, Gallo. No more brooding, get me? It's not good out here."

He had volunteered for another tour, of course. What was there left for him back home? No mother, no father, no sisters or brothers. He was the last of his line, but what even did that matter? Besides, there were fears of another pandemic.

"Don't worry," said Rojas with a wink. "The women of my family are indestructible. It's the men I fear for."

★ ★ ★

The supply ferry arrived and departed, but amongst the new crew no one wanted to tell ghost stories. The third biologist was an Algerian named Hadj. She had little time for Gallo and eyed his beautiful *rii* with a look of distaste.

"The system isn't performing the way it ought to," she said angrily during one of their morning sessions. "These channels are leaking, you didn't see? It's dangerous. We don't know – really – how these organisms will mature in this environment."

She left others to take up the surveying. "If I don't rebalance this nutrient feed, we could be dead before the *Xantho* returns."

It was more than that, though, Gallo could tell. She hated the higgledy-piggledy lines of the San Marco, its rises and falls, its peculiar curves. The city he had loved haunted her.

She went to the officers above him, offered her own solution: advance their plans to construct a second base, this one simpler, streamlined, practical and elegant. Wasn't the graphene hull already showing signs of stress? They knew so much more than they did when the San Marco had first been designed. And the technology was changing so quickly, there were advances that could be incorporated, nanocomposites that would be tougher, more flexible, better suited to the harsh Martian environment.

Hadj was young, a wunderkind, barely thirty years old. She patted Gallo, almost kindly. "Wouldn't you like to go home soon, *jaddi*? Haven't you had enough?"

He volunteered for a surveying mission. Several of the new crew were having trouble with space sickness, muscle atrophy and the readjustment to gravity, so he agreed to go out alone. He was practically a native by now and he knew the area better than anyone.

That afternoon he put on his suit and headed out along the old trails he had charted with Vassiliev. The path was harder than he remembered but his anger spurred him onward.

He reached the first peak. Vassiliev's scratches were still etched in the regolith. Nothing had disturbed them, nor would it. Time moved slowly here. Only wind and sunlight, not the creep of green spreading its tendrils, forcing change upon the world.

Below he saw a swirl of dust kicking up, the last of the spring storms. He forced himself onward. "I just need to get above it," he radioed back. Only static on the line. Never mind.

For two days he climbed. On the third he reached the top of the ridge. Out of breath, he allowed himself to sit. By now the dust was clearing again but he kept his radio off anyway. He found he enjoyed the silence.

In the distance, the San Marco gleamed like a mollusc shell, Egyptian blue stretching to dull madder. Her cupolas were limned with gold. She was beautiful. But with his ghost eye he saw only wreckage. They would take what they could of the San Marco and cannibalise it. Soon dust would fill her exposed skeleton. She would lie like a derelict Roman galley among the sand dunes.

He thought then about his mother, who had loved her city and watched it vanish. And his pappa too, who had watched his own evening star fade, leaving him with a squalling infant. For a time there had been no room for poetry, no room for anything but the coiling weight of love, born of loneliness and need. And then, miraculously, he had begun to whisper the old words – *nel mezzo del cammin di nostra vita*, again and again – during the long stretches of night when sleep was impossible. There was grief, there was always grief, but there was also the child who needed to be fed and no one to do it but Tommaso. That was how you survived, lurching from moment to moment, crisis to crisis, giving what you could, the things you intended and the things you carried with you, unknowing. Praying only for those grey-blue eyes to open, for some glancing light to shine within them. To be seen, to be known for a moment.

He and his pappa had returned to Venice when he was twelve years old. The lagoon was treacherous, but Tommaso Gallo had rented a little boat and taken them out, guiding them through the Rio del Trapolin, his son gazing down through clear, bottle-green water on a makeshift reef of rubble, concrete and wooden pilings that had accreted below them, sheltering oysters, squid and mussels. Now shoals of silvery fish darted through the wreckage while overhead cormorants swooped and divebombed into the waves.

"Haven't you had enough?" Hadj had asked him. Perhaps he had. He didn't know what it meant to be alive without his pappa. But what he had built wasn't enough, it wasn't the bastion against history he had supposed it might be.

He took his samples and prepared to leave.

* * *

The route down was perilous in its own way. He had to go slowly, his muscles burning and his breath short. Another three days back. He thought about remaining where he was. He wanted to lie down and sleep.

But down he went, down to whatever was coming. But when Gallo finally stumbled through the airlock, exhausted and aching, he found Dorsoduro abandoned and the *calli* leading outward sealed.

He tried the radio. "What happened?" For a long while no one answered. Then:

"Stay where you are." It was Hadj. Her voice was desperate.

"What is it?"

"We thought we had taken enough precautions," she said. "On the *Xantho*. We thought...we thought...but we didn't know the virus could lie dormant. Not for so long. Six months."

He saw the shape of a hand through the porthole. She was on the other side of the airlock. He could see her profile, the curve of her lips, her chin.

"You should stay in your suit." A tiny gasp. "Not that it would matter, probably. They won't be able to send another ship for months. Probably it's too late for you."

"Where are the others?"

She laughed a harsh, brittle laugh.

"Sick bay. Albescu is dead, O'Neill too. No one else is answering." He could tell she was frightened. It had been like that with his classmates. The brightest of them could be so very fragile. The peculiarity of their talents meant they had seldom faced challenges that could not be overcome with the mind alone. Some things could not be reasoned with, only endured. His generation, his pappa's, those who had survived the bad years, knew that. It had only ever been luck. The ones like Hadj did not understand the nature of misfortune.

He stayed with her through the night, on the other side of the *calle*. She was feverish. There was a hope for some time it might break. She drifted between bouts of lucidity, sharing her plans for the new station. *If only, when all this is over...*

"I shouldn't say." She coughed badly. "The Caigoists and your design. Pure fancy, heh? Oh, *jaddi*. I thought I was the last. I'm glad you're here. Thought I was going to die alone." Then she was speaking to someone else, someone he couldn't see or hear.

Then quiet. Was she sleeping? Gallo didn't know. He tried again to reach the others but the radio remained stubbornly silent. He was the last.

He was afraid then as he had never been before. This was a place that did not know his name, did not care, had no filth or romance of its own. It wasn't like going to another country. Country was a human invention.

But. What were his choices? The scrubbers might maintain his oxygen levels. There was food enough. Maybe. Six months. Could he do it? He thought he could. He would try.

* * *

He woke to the sound of Vassiliev laughing at him.

"There's nothing out here, Gallo." He pressed his cold lips against the engineer's. "It's only a matter of time now."

The engineer was sweating badly and there was a sharp, cramping pain in his stomach.

"Don't shit more than you eat," said Rojas. They were ganging up on him. He tried to push himself up but his muscles were still aching from the hike.

"Hadj?" he muttered over the radio. No one answered him.

Rojas was grinning now and making a rude gesture. "You're dying, *amigo*," she said. Vassiliev looked away. He had never been one to linger on goodbyes.

"Maybe," grunted Gallo.

"No maybes about it."

"Has anyone said you can be a real cow sometimes?"

She snorted and patted his hand with affection. "Only everyone I've ever known."

He struggled again to stand. Managed to get to his knees before the bile rushed out of him, splattering the inside of his helmet. He gagged, popped the seal, and threw it aside. Wiped the vomit away as best he could.

"She said not to do that," said Vassiliev pointedly. "Keep your suit on."

"Nothing for it," Gallo replied. He felt better breathing the station's air. He pulled himself to the airlock, peered through the porthole. He could make out Hadj's crumpled body on the other side. It looked so much smaller now. Her expression had calmed. Her lips were grey-blue.

He overrode the security measures and opened the door, stumbled through the *sottoportico* and upward along the *calle*. His fingers traced the stark angles of a cross. Santa Croce. He almost laughed. Hadj had been right. Pure fancy, all of it, but why not? Why not?

Her eyes were dark, nearly black, fringed with long delicate lashes. He ran his fingers over the lids lightly, letting them close. "*Nel mezzo del cammin di nostra vita...*" he whispered. There were no other sounds, only his breathing and the rasp of the fluid in the *rio* that ran alongside the corridor. A thick green light shone through, leaking out of the channels he had designed. The *calle* stank of vegetation, a smell so earthy and foreign to the station it took him a moment to recall what it was. When had he last smelled something besides metallic recycled air?

Well. She had been right about that too.

He didn't think. He slammed his fist against the *rio* channel until a starburst glittered in the glass. He did it again and again. It shouldn't have broken, it should have been stronger than that, but it seemed everything was failing him now. He heard the tinkling of shards falling, a rush of thickened green.

"Why did you do it?" Vassiliev asked. "Like she said. Pure fancy."

"Because..." said Gallo. He couldn't finish the thought. He saw in his mind sunlight on the canals. The same colour in pictures of the cathedral, columns of Thessaly green marble. It had always been this way, he thought. Nothing was ever only itself. Everything was twinned and mirrored, everything repeated time and again. A city wrapped around a corpse. *Il Fantasma.* It had to be that way, otherwise, what? Otherwise, nothing. Otherwise, the red planet. A dead planet. Otherwise a place so ancient and unchanged that even the ghosts were dead.

Then he was on his back, staring through the viewport in the roof of the cupola. He had insisted on these, one in every *sesterieri*, so that they might look up, see all of creation arrayed above them. The stars glittering in the Heavens, and Earth among them, brighter than the others, with the moon shining nearby.

"Why?" murmured Rojas this time.

"Isn't this what you wanted? All of you?"

Gallo's eyelids fluttered.

Under his spine lay the hard regolith bricks, bricks he had fashioned from the substance of an alien world. Amazing. Vassiliev was standing over him, and Rojas too. There were no ghosts here, so he had brought his own. The ghosts of men and women, the ghost of his home. If the planet truly was dead, maybe he could bring it life. Who knew what might happen given time, given centuries and centuries?

Now the light of the new day was radiating through them, through him too. He understood now: his body was more than just a body. It was its own little *s'ciopon*. It was carbon and water, it was heat, energy, spirit, substance and accident and disposition, unified. And he felt his desire and will, turning like a wheel, driven by that same power that moved the sun in its circuit, the stars as well, everything spinning, glittering, traced with glory.

Vassiliev had been wrong. They weren't alone on the planet. They weren't ever alone. All they needed they carried with them, wherever they went.

He felt rapturous. "It's out there," he whispered to Rojas and Vassiliev. To his father. To Hadj and the others, to all the dead he carried with him. "I can see it moving."

Then a brackish taste filled his mouth as the foaming green waters rushed in around him.

REMEMBER ME

Ronald Malfi

Despite what you may believe, I'm here, existing, in the middle of the street now, and snared in a whirlwind of dead leaves that claws its way along the sidewalk. There is the boom-cackle of children's laughter far off in the darkness, and a squadron of ghouls and goblins parading up the block beneath the purple-tinged glow of a streetlamp. Jack-o'-lanterns leer from porches. A small child in a pumpkin costume wails as his bag of goodies rips and candy spills to the pavement; another child, this one a bit older, stares in horrorstruck fascination at the man who has opened the front door wearing a grotesque rubber mask, one latex eyeball dribbling down the blackened, crenulated side of his face.

I'm on the hunt before I even know it.

I cross the street and hop the curb, taking it all in. I'm sly, calculating, deliberate. Shadows stretch long across the asphalt and a cold mist creeps out from beyond the trees on the opposite side of the street. A pair of headlights appear, carving speedy passage down the otherwise dark stretch of road. Parents yank their children out of the way and someone shouts to the driver to slow down. A convertible, top down, teenagers rowdy and boisterous over the growl of the old car's engine. The driver wears a hockey mask and thrusts a rubber machete over his head in some semblance of vindication, while his passengers – costumed teenagers just like the driver – whoop and holler into the night.

There is the scent of popcorn in the air, the tangy-sweet aroma of sugar mingling with a whiff of someone's barbecue at work. It's not the strains of hunger that these aromas stir inside me, but rather a growing nostalgia for a time now gone. An empty longing. Glow-in-the-dark vampire fangs chomp at the air close to my face;

I actually wince and draw my head back, which is silly, and this silliness brings a smile to my lips. The rubber soles of countless sneakers skid across a shifting terrain of grit and gravel and loose candy in the road.

I'm studying, scrutinising, wondering who it'll be this year. I've developed a sense for it. Young children won't do, because they don't know, and the older ones don't often care any more (if they ever did). Adults remember, but they rarely speak of such things. I'm on the hunt for that slender, unobtrusive passageway that will allow me temporary trespass. Those who not only still remember but also deign to speak of such things…

The hunt.

Kids on bikes whiz by, superhero capes streaming out behind them, plastic dime-store masks tight on their faces. Lights spin to a blur in the bicycles' spokes. I fade into a hedgerow and watch them. They might be the right age, but it's hard to tell, since they zipped by so quickly. Also, those masks.

"Trick or treat!" comes the shrill chorus, and I whirl my head around – or do I? – to see a group of kids huddled as if for warmth beneath a cobweb-sheathed portico, spooky music playing on an invisible speaker, a fog machine dispensing clouds of white vapour into the atmosphere. A woman shambles to the door, face and hair done up like the Bride of Frankenstein's, clutching a plastic cauldron filled with full-size Butterfingers to her breast.

I'm suddenly there, among those costumed children, watching their little paws dart in and out of the cauldron. Their breath comes in eager, greedy gasps, pluming in the cold night air. One brazen entrepreneur makes for a second helping, but is chilled by the Bride of Frankenstein, who intones, heavily accented, "I vant to suck your blood," which is funny because it's a Dracula thing to say, not a Bride of Frankenstein thing. But it does the trick, and the kid retracts his hand and scampers down off the porch in pursuit of his friends.

The woman watches them go for a moment. I lean closer to her and whisper near her ear. I watch as the woman's eyes go large, if just for a moment. There is a distant knowledge skirling behind her eyes. I hold out some hope, but that hope quickly fades as the woman retreats into her house and shuts the door.

At the corner of the next block, a girl dressed in a combo princess-cheerleader get-up is fighting back tears. She's got her midriff on display, and bare legs like those of a prize-winning colt. It's something about a boy who broke her heart. One of her friends – a girl in a sparkly Wonder Woman bustier – tries to comfort her. A third girl – wide-eyed, almost bemused, her face illuminated in the harsh glow of her cellphone – watches as she sucks on a cherry-flavoured Blow Pop.

Are they the right age? They might be. I come up behind them, give it a try. But unlike the woman on the porch, they're too self-involved to even hear me. I don't let this get me down. I hurry past them as the girl's cellphone unleashes a series of sharp, mechanical pings.

Further down the block, a dog barks at my passage. I raise a finger to my lips – *shhhh* – and the dog drops down on its haunches and whines. I reach out to stroke the dog's head, but the beast only spins around and darts across the yard, disappearing around the far side of the house.

A group of boys and girls skip right past me. I open my mouth to whisper, but then stop myself. I'm saving my energy. These children are too young to speak of old ghost stories.

At the end of the block sits one house, dark as midnight, all lights off. No one ventures there, not even to toss rolls of toilet paper in to the trees, or chuck eggs at the front door. Seeing it gives me pause, just as it always does, every year. This is as far as I can go – I cannot leave my street, not just yet – but I don't need to cross the road to know that the man watches from a darkened upstairs window. He remembers, of course, but it's not enough to set me free. It's only just enough to let me linger and meander up and down the street. Just enough to keep me tethered to this world like a prisoner.

I see him, briefly – not from the darkened window of his house, but in what persists of my memories. It's only a momentary glimpse of his face, brief and sudden as a flashbulb explosion. His eyes blaze with a combination of fear and confusion, and then I'm accosted by the smell of burning rubber, hearing the screech of brakes. A dirtier, grittier smell beyond that – a smell that goes deep down. And then I don't see him at all.

You might think it my duty to haunt him, but that isn't how this works. Anyway, who wants to spend eternity making someone else miserable? Making someone else afraid? Not me.

The convertible is parked along this street, the car's teenage occupants having spilled out onto the sidewalk. Hockey Mask smokes through a hole in his mask. There is a girl ballerina and a boy ballerina and some guy in what looks like a zombie cowboy outfit, a fake bullet hole oozing too-red blood at the centre of his forehead.

And I think, *Maybe?*

"What you dummies don't *know*," says Hockey Mask, "is that the veil is thinnest on Halloween night."

"What veil?" asks Girl Ballerina. She's got two puncture marks on her neck, so I guess that makes her a ballerina who's been attacked by a vampire.

"The veil between *worlds*," Hockey Mask explains. He sounds agitated, as though he were speaking to children who should know better. "Between our world and the world of the dead."

"Get the fuck out," says Boy Ballerina.

"Tell 'em," says Zombie Cowboy.

"I just *did*," Hockey Mask says. "Maybe they don't believe in ghosts. Or maybe they just ain't listening."

And I think, *Maybe* you'll *listen*.

I slide up beside him, and whisper into his ear. He goes still. Behind the eyeholes in his hockey mask, I suddenly see the whites of his eyes. Even the smoke from the cigarette appears to momentarily freeze in midair. But it doesn't last long, and before I can even draw away from him, he's blinking like someone awakening from a stupor.

"How 'bout we *show* 'em," says Zombie Cowboy.

Hockey Mask, his eyes now gleaming behind his mask, slowly nods his head. He props the mask up on his nest of black curls, takes one last drag of his smoke before pitching it to the pavement, and then motions for the others to follow him. He's heading into the woods that run along that side of the street.

And I think, *Yes. Maybe.*

A thrill shudders through me. I follow them, able to do so because they're technically still on my street, albeit on the other side of it... although I can't truly say anything is *technical* about any of this. It's all atmosphere and circumstance. It's all feeling and vibe and a sense of *yes* and *no*.

"This is bullshit," says Boy Ballerina.

"Absolute to the utmost," says Girl Ballerina. "I mean, isn't there a party or something happening tonight?"

Zombie Cowboy, he just laughs.

They only need to walk a few paces before they come upon a clearing in the woods. The house here – or what remains of it – looms in the darkness like something once alive. Moonlight drips down its charred, blackened hide. Where the windows once were are now only ragged portholes; where the front door once stood now stands a gaping black chasm that tunnels down to nowhere. It's so black and ruinous, if you didn't know it was here, you'd be liable to walk right by without seeing it.

"Creep Factor ten," says Girl Ballerina.

"What happened to this place?" asks Boy Ballerina.

"What's it look like?" says Hockey Mask. "Bad fire."

"Was anybody killed?"

"Let's go inside and I'll tell you."

The ballerinas share a look. Boy Ballerina says, "Inside the *house*?"

"Looks dangerous," Girl Ballerina says.

"It's worse than dangerous," Hockey Mask informs them, rather nebulously. "Let's go."

Before the ballerinas can protest, Hockey Mask is carving his way through the fire-scarred trees toward the old house. Zombie Cowboy pivots and heads in that direction, too, his silver spurs jangling. Another glance shared between them, and then the ballerinas are bringing up the rear. I cannot tell if they are brother and sister or boyfriend and girlfriend, but I sense a closeness between them that doesn't translate to the other two.

The front door of the house is a crooked rectangular portal with nothing but black mist swirling beyond the threshold. "Watch your step," Hockey Mask says, in what strikes me as a rare show of concern, as he steps over a heap of blackened boards, then enters the house.

"This place will come down on our heads," Boy Ballerina says, although this doesn't stop him from following Hockey Mask inside.

Zombie Cowboy extends an arm toward the gaping black doorway. Girl Ballerina looks like she wants to turn and bolt back to the street, and I can't say I blame her, but she doesn't. The pull is too strong. She climbs over the smashed and fire-scarred boards and vanishes into the black. Zombie Cowboy goes last, though as he does, he glances once over his shoulder and pauses, as if hearing some noise just beyond the periphery of his vision. Or perhaps he senses something. But then he enters the house, too.

I'm there with them, gliding through the darkness of this place. Their footfalls creak on the warped and damaged boards. There's a *sssst-sssst* sound followed by a slender finger of light as Hockey Mask's face comes closer toward the glow of his cigarette lighter. "What do you think?" he asks his companions, a devilish glint in his eyes. He's grinning like one of those jack-o'-lanterns I glimpsed earlier on people's porches.

"I think someone should tear this place down," says Girl Ballerina. She's staring up at the sightless chasm that is the ceiling of the house's main foyer…or where the ceiling should have been. It's like staring into a black hole.

"Yeah," Boy Ballerina agrees. "Tear it down."

I sense a subtle shift in the atmosphere of the place. It's Burn Boy. He's come through the passageway tonight, same as I have. Crossed through the thinning veil, if you prefer. I don't see him at first, but then the shape of him materialises in one pitch-black corner at the opposite end of the room. He's enveloped in a clot of grey smoke, and if I look closely at his skin, I can see bright orange embers winking there. I can see his eyes dart about in the darkness, too, like lighted embers themselves; they light on me, hold me in their gaze for a moment, then shift to the quartet of teenagers whom I have followed here on this night.

The teenagers don't see him, of course. Only I can see him, since we are of the same ilk. Just like only he can see me.

"This is Burn Boy's house," says Hockey Mask. "Couple years ago, a fire broke out. No one's really sure what started it – faulty wiring, or maybe even the kid playing with matches. Who really knows?"

"Who really knows," echoes Zombie Cowboy.

"Whatever the case, the kid's parents were out for the night, so he was home alone. Got trapped in the house while it burned around him."

"Can you smell it?" Zombie Cowboy asks. He's taken on a reverent tone for effect. "Can you smell the burn?"

"It's Burn Boy's smoke," Hockey Mask says.

"The whole *house* smells like smoke," Girl Ballerina says. "It's in the wood."

"Is it?" says Hockey Mask. "Is it just the wood?"

The ballerinas are quiet for a moment. From where I linger just behind them, I can see they are thinking things through. I can see Burn Boy smouldering in that darkened corner, too.

"I *can*," says Boy Ballerina. The awe is evident in his voice. "I can smell the smoke."

"It's just the house," insists Girl Ballerina.

"No," says Zombie Cowboy. "It's Burn Boy. That's the smell of his skin frying."

"Sizzle, sizzle, sizzle," says Hockey Mask.

The embers along Burn Boy's flesh grow brighter.

"And if you listen," adds Hockey Mask, "you can hear his screams echo through the house..."

There are no screams, no sizzle, but Burn Boy continues to grow brighter in that dark corner with each passing second.

"There!" Boy Ballerina shouts, startling his companions. He points midway up a charred and crumbling staircase. "Did you see it?"

"See what?" Girl Ballerina asks.

"See what?" Zombie Cowboy asks.

"Smoke!" He's still pointing at the staircase. "I swear, I just saw a wisp of smoke!"

Burn Boy burns even brighter in his corner across the room.

"I remember seeing the flames through the trees," Zombie Cowboy says, and to his credit, not without a vein of reverence in his voice.

Burn Boy's skin flares a bright yellow-orange. A cloud of smoke roils up from his flesh and floats up through the chasm to the second floor of the house. His eyes burn just as fiercely, lighting on me once again, a flash of greedy, giddy excitement there now. And then, in a flash, Burn Boy is on the move.

Freed from his prison by tonight's retelling, Burn Boy races across the room, a streak of fire and smoke in his wake, and charges through the doorway. He's out there among the trees, leaving behind a screen of smoke. Going to wherever Burn Boy has been waiting all year to go.

We all have places we wish to go.

"Boo!" Hockey Mask shouts, and everyone jumps and cries out. Then they're laughing, because this is *Halloween*, and this is *fun*.

"Tell 'em about Johnny," Zombie Cowboy suggests.

"*Riiiiiight*," Hockey Mask says. His grin once again matches those of the jack-o'-lanterns I glimpsed earlier. "Good old Johnny."

Boy Ballerina clears his throat. Asks, "Who's Johnny?"

"Come on," Hockey Mask says, and leads them all out of the house. Back out in the woods now, they don't head back toward the street, but deeper into the trees. I follow, drifting past the front of Burn Boy's house – he'll be back before the night is over – and through the trees right along with them.

"Johnny was in a motorcycle gang in the Fifties," Hockey Mask begins. "They were one of the toughest, meanest gangs in town. My grandparents remember when they used to ride up and down Main Street, smashing shop windows and shit like that. Johnny was like the second-in-command, or whatever you call it when you're in a motorcycle gang. He was just as tough and mean as all the others, but then he fell in love with the gang leader's girlfriend."

"*Awwww*," says Zombie Cowboy, and it's suddenly clear they've rehearsed this little routine. "True love, you know?"

"Gag," says Boy Ballerina.

Girl Ballerina slugs him in the forearm. Boyfriend and girlfriend, I decide.

The trees grow sparse as a larger clearing appears on the other side. The quartet continue in that direction, but I do not. I can't go that far; it's too far from my street. I'm still tethered. So I linger behind, watching. Listening.

"When the gang leader found out," Hockey Mask continues, pausing along the precipice at the edge of the clearing where a rocky valley lies below, "they all jumped Johnny one night. Beat him up bad."

"You don't fuck around with a fellow gang banger's girlfriend," Zombie Cowboy adds.

"They weren't gang *bangers*, they were gang *members*," Hockey Mask reiterates, clearly miffed that Zombie Cowboy has perhaps gone too far off-script. "Anyway," he goes on, "they looped a chain around one ankle and tied the other end to the back of the gang leader's motorcycle. They dragged Johnny up and down that rocky field, shredding his body to ribbons. They only stopped when Johnny's leg came off. But by then, he was already dead."

"Fuck," says Boy Ballerina. He looks like he might be ill.

"Bullshit," says Girl Ballerina. "That didn't happen."

"Like hell it didn't," says Hockey Mask. "And to this day, on Halloween night, you can hear Johnny's cries on the wind. And later tonight, you'll hear the single thump of his motorcycle boot coming up your walkway toward your house."

"How does a guy with one leg walk up a walkway?" Girl Ballerina asks.

"He's a ghost, dummy," says Hockey Mask. "Ghosts can do whatever."

"What about the girlfriend? What happened to her?"

"What do you mean?"

"Well, she was fooling around behind the gang leader's back, too. They must've done something to her, same way they killed Johnny."

Hockey Mask appears to consider this, as if for the first time. Finally, he says, "Uh, they killed her, too."

"Did they? How?"

"Same way. Dragged her behind the motorcycle."

"Her leg come off, too?" Boy Ballerina asks.

"Yes," says Hockey Mask, and with confidence.

"She thump one-legged up to your house at night, too?" Girl Ballerina asks. She's taunting Hockey Mask now. She doesn't believe a word of it.

"Yeah," Hockey Mask says. I can tell he's making a mental note to add this to the story for next year. "Yeah, she's been heard thumping along, too, on Halloween night. All over town."

"You're full of shit," Girl Ballerina tells him, although she's staring down the embankment and at the dark swathe of land below. Maybe something down there has attracted her attention after all.

The story of Johnny is fiction, which is why there is no remnant of Johnny lingering about down there. However, something *has* happened down there in the distant past, because I can see the place in the land where it's smudgy and lit with a faint, ethereal glow. It's what remains when too much time has passed, and you and your tragedy are no longer remembered: a dull pulse of light that only the dead can see. A grave-marker of sorts. A memo to the cosmos.

Death for the dead.

"Let's get out of here," Boy Ballerina says. "My stepdad's got a bottle of Wild Turkey in the garage."

They're excited by the prospect, so they trudge back through the trees toward the road. I follow, rushing up beside Hockey Mask, whispering words into his ear that he cannot hear, yet I am hopeful – panicked and hopeful – that he might catch on to some glimmer of what I'm desperate to impart to him.

Remember me? Remember me?

When they reach the car parked in the street, Hockey Mask has already got another cigarette poking between his lips, and he's chasing the tip around with his plastic lighter. Girl Ballerina is checking her phone now, looking bored. Boy Ballerina is watching a trio of slutty vampires as they slink up the sidewalk, paying him no mind. Zombie Cowboy has maybe caught something from my whispers – something on the wind, perhaps, the way a wolf may catch the faint scent of blood – because he's looking around, a touch of confusion in his eyes. It's similar to the way he'd glanced over his shoulder before entering Burn Boy's house. Maybe that's just wishful thinking on my part, but I've also come to learn that some people are more attuned to the other side of things than others. Despite all his energetic storytelling this evening, perhaps Hockey Mask was the wrong target. The wrong ear in which to whisper.

I float from Hockey Mask to Zombie Cowboy. *Please please please please,* I whisper-shout into Zombie Cowboy's ear, though there is no sound to accompany it. *Remember me! Remember me! Remember—*

And then something vague and distant becomes more focused in his eyes. I see it, like the widening of an aperture. It takes on substance. Clarity.

"You know," Zombie Cowboy says, "a kid was killed on this street a few years ago."

"Cut the bullshit already," Girl Ballerina says.

"Yeah," says Boy Ballerina. "Let's go drink."

"It's not bullshit," says Zombie Cowboy. "I remember when it happened. You remember that, Jake?"

Hockey Mask – Jake – stares at his friend…but then he's starting to nod his head, too. He's remembering.

"Some kid from the neighbourhood got hit by a car on this street," Zombie Cowboy says.

"For real?" Girl Ballerina asks. She's apt to believe this story because it's a *true* story.

I know it is.

"Yeah," Zombie Cowboy says, and he even looks a little queasy. "The kid died. Far as I know, they never even found the guy who hit him."

"That's awful," says Boy Ballerina.

"If it's even true," says Girl Ballerina, although her face – her eyes – betray her. She *believes.*

"Oh, it's true," says Hockey Mask. "I remember people walking down this street with candles after it happened. I was young, but I remember seeing that."

"Yeah," Zombie Cowboy says. "It's true, all right."

I look down at my hands and find they are beginning to glow with a dull white radiance.

Once again, I'm seeing the pale white face of the driver and those impossibly wide eyes behind the glare of a windshield, just before the suddenness of the impact. Just before the stink of burning rubber tyres, the squeal of brakes. Just before a cloak of darkness wraps me up.

"Was he drunk?" Boy Ballerina asks.

Zombie Cowboy says, "No, man, he was just a kid."

"No, I mean the driver."

"Oh, right. I guess no one will ever know."

Hockey Mask says, "I'll bet you a hundred bucks that whoever that dude is, he's being haunted by that kid's ghost tonight..."

And just like that, I've been co-opted into Hockey Mask's repertoire of ghost stories.

The haunting part, of course, is not true. It would be possible – particularly now, as I watch my hands grow brighter and feel myself fill up with power, much as Burn Boy had done before me – but my time to wander far in this realm will be achingly brief, if it happens at all, and I do not wish to waste it tormenting someone who is already tormented. As I feel my feet lift off the pavement, I know there is something more important for me to do tonight. Something I have been aching to do all year.

"What's that?" Girl Ballerina says, turning her head slightly in my direction. Perhaps she's heard me rise off the pavement and float past the trees, one of my feet snagging in a low-hanging branch. The branch comes loose, shudders, and unleashes a cascade of dead leaves all around her. She can't see *me*, of course, and it would take great concentration for me to even reach out and touch her (and even then she might not feel it), but she can suddenly sense my presence. They all can; they're all peering up at the place where I've ascended through the trees. Trying to see if there's something there.

"They say that on this night," Hockey Mask continues, his voice more reverent now, "the veil is thinnest, allowing the dead to cross over..."

Only if they're remembered, I tell him, although I know it's no use. He can't hear me, can't see me. And anyway, I'm moving far beyond them now, carving passage through the trees, until I come out above a grid of dark, lamplit streets. A few costumed older kids still ring doorbells, shout at one another, laugh with their friends as they huddle upon street corners. At the end of the street, I see the wide-eyed man's house, dark and shuttered against this night, and I wonder if he's remembering me, too, and remembering the stink of burning tyres and the squeal of his brakes. I bet that he is.

At one point, I see Burn Boy. He's racing down the block, trailing a contrail of smoke, his skin on fire. No one else can see him, but a few people pause as he races by, smelling the invisible smoke roiling through the air. Burn Boy laughs each time someone makes a face at his passage, smelling his acrid stink, and every time someone says to their friend, *Did you smell that? Smelled like smoke,* he burns brighter and laughs louder.

Go, Burn Boy, go, I shout to him, but he can't hear me either. Anyway, he's too busy doing his thing to listen. *Go, Burn Boy, go,* I repeat nonetheless.

I ghost farther through the town, above it, sailing over a wash of headlights downtown, and then straight out to the black ribbon of highway. The world is cleaner here, or maybe that's just the part of the world I inhabit. The part that surrounds me as I make my way through it. I have been re-energised by the telling of my tale, but I can already feel the power waning. It won't last all night, but if I'm lucky, it'll last long enough.

Had I remained on my street, I might have heard Hockey Mask tell his friends the rest of my tale: how the boy's mother, so distraught by the death of her son, drove out to the Leeds Bridge one night, climbed the railing, and cast herself into the icy waters. How they were buried together, mother and child, in Leeds Cemetery up on the hill that overlooks the town.

Maybe he's telling it right now.

Maybe I'm given strength by his memory of my tale. Maybe I get even a little strength from the wide-eyed man who never forgets, hiding silently in his dark, shuttered house. Like I've mentioned, there is nothing truly *technical* about any of this. Just *yes* and *no*; just *here* and *not here.*

Maybe…

And then I see her below, shimmering with a dull white light along the span of the Leeds River Bridge. She's peering down into that black, moonlit water, preparing to jump, just as she's jumped every year since my death. I go to her, and when she sees me, the anguish flees her face, filling it instead with joy. Or whatever passes for joy in these intangible, temporary facsimiles of bodies.

Don't jump, I tell her, just as I always do, and even though she cannot hear me, only see me, she obeys.

We cannot touch one another – there are so many rules – but somehow we still do: I glide into her and she glides into me. I feel the warmth of her spirit centre, and I hope she can feel mine, too. She speaks to me, and although I do not hear her words, I sense their meaning and intent, the way you'd feel someone's heartbeat by placing a hand to their chest, knowing they're alive.

My strength is already fading, and so is the night. But we remain together for what time we have left, the conclusion of my tale, mother and child, all but finished, yet at the same time, never truly finished. Sometime in the future, our tale will be forgotten, and we will no longer be here to do this – will be just a glowing spot on a landscape, death for the dead – but for now, this is what we have, and who we are.

The boy who remains…

Remember me?

WITCH'S CLUTCH

Simon Strantzas

Rusty Cleft had to be seeing things. Until that moment, he'd almost convinced himself the Witch's Clutch wasn't real, and yet there one was, planted in the background of a newspaper advertisement for a small hotel pub, invisible to anyone who didn't know what they were looking at.

But Cleft knew exactly what it was. And what it meant.

The hotel was in Caledon. It would take less than three hours to get there. All he needed was a ride. By the time Siobhan returned his call he already had his meagre duffel packed. She resisted at first, citing her existing weekend plans, but being a graduate student meant she'd have to make sacrifices, and Cleft wasn't above reminding her of them if it led to a real Witch's Clutch.

Once Siobhan arrived, Cleft folded himself into her tiny Kia. Even with the seat pushed back, his knees brushed uncomfortably against the dashboard. She fumed for the entirety of the trip, not speaking at all, but Cleft hardly noticed. Everything was secondary to his discovery. It would change both his reputation and career. No longer would he be called a copper-curled stick insect by his undergraduates. No longer would he be dismissed for the awkward way he dressed, or mocked by his peers for his views. The Witch's Clutch would rewrite everything, prove he had something to offer.

The town of Caledon was smaller than he expected, tucked within tall woods and autumnal colours. There seemed to be only one road leading in, as though there were nothing more to see beyond its furthest border. Cleft watched the worn-down houses pass by his window with increasing excitement.

By the time they arrived at the hotel pub, The Bull & Goose, Cleft could hardly keep still. The hybrid was so close, as was his imminent success. He imagined himself being honoured before a room full of his peers, his pockmarked face beaming down at them with satisfaction. Their applause was still ringing in his ears when he stepped out of the car, barely giving Siobhan time enough to put it into Park.

"Are you excited?" he asked, looking up at the unpainted and splintered sign hanging above the pub's door. When he glanced over, though, he found her silently thumbing through her phone. He wasn't surprised: being silent was something Siobhan was good at. She still hadn't told him she had requested a new advisor, nor that her request was already granted. In only a couple of weeks she'd be gone. He wondered if it ever occurred to her that he might discover her betrayal before she left. He also wondered if she even cared.

The photograph from the newspaper clearly showed the pub's exterior, so it didn't take Cleft long to estimate the spot from which it was taken. Siobhan followed close behind him, eyes still on her phone, as he searched the area for the Witch's Clutch. She didn't look up until she collided with him, not expecting such a sudden stop.

"I don't understand," he muttered.

There, in the fresh loose dirt at his feet, was a shallow hole. Whatever had been there had been removed.

Siobhan readjusted the sunglasses seated atop her head.

"You seriously telling me we drove here for nothing?"

Cleft had to force himself to speak.

"It was here. Someone took it." He pointed at the footprint pressed into the damp soil. Large enough for an adult woman or small man. "They must have known what it was."

"How? I don't even know what it is."

"The Mi'kmaq called it a *ste'gmiui ge'luswa'latl*, or *spirits' embrace*. The plant – well, hybrid, really – has a lot of myth and folklore surrounding it. But no one has actually found one."

"And you think some other sociologist just happened to stumble over it before you? Isn't that a little too convenient?"

Cleft looked down at the hole again. She was right. What were the odds? Unless…

"What if it wasn't a researcher?" he said, tamping down his renewing excitement. "We know the Witch's Clutch has connections with the New World. What if we've stumbled upon some vestigial pagan religion? What if one of these cults knew exactly what it was when they saw it?"

Cleft's mind started spinning. It seemed impossible, yet was there a more probable explanation?

"Why don't you go check us in at the hotel," he said. "I'm going to look around some more."

"I thought you needed me here. Isn't that why you had me drive?"

"I won't be long," he said. "I'll call when I need you to come get me."

She studied him for a moment and Cleft half-wondered if she was about to insist on staying. Instead she snorted.

"I guess I'll keep my phone on."

"Thanks," he said, under his breath, as she retreated through the underbrush. The faint rustle of plants and branches followed her. By the time they finished their song, Siobhan had loaded both her and Cleft's bags onto her shoulder.

Cleft adjusted his glasses – the yellow lenses the colour of his skin – and watched until she was safely inside the hotel, then turned his attention back to the underbrush where the Witch's Clutch had once been. He searched for any sign of ritualistic activity from those who might have found it first. A tree with rope burns, perhaps; or a cluster of stones laid with intent and purpose. What he discovered, though, were only more footprints. They proved him right, though – a cell of worshippers had to be nearby. And he had to find them. In his Moleskine he noted the various prints, their different sizes and shapes, as well as the prints of the herd animals that were intermingled with them. These looked to be made by sheep. Possibly a large goat. The meandering tracks led deeper into the thick underbrush beneath the overgrown maples, ashes, and pines. He hurriedly followed them, his head stuffed with more fantasies of his academic coming out.

Cleft walked for hours, his attention so focused on the footprints ahead of him that he failed to notice how dim the daylight had grown. Only when he looked up did he realise he had no idea where he was or how to get back. There had been no roads, no telephone wires. Not much of anything to suggest a location from which Siobhan might pick him up. No, that wasn't true. There was, amongst the thickest boughs and trunks, the flicker of artificial light off in the near-distance. It was a beacon hidden by leaves. Perhaps if he followed it he'd find his way back to the Bull & Goose.

But that would also mean giving up his pursuit of whomever had taken the Witch's Clutch. If he abandoned the trail he might never be able to pick it up again. He might lose the hybrid for good. Cleft stood in deep green underbrush and stared at the light glowing brighter in the distance, and wavered.

Then he remembered that welcoming applause.

★ ★ ★

When Cleft finally travelled far enough to see where the tracks ended he was surprised. There was a small rundown house ahead of him, squeezed between a pair of ancient birch trees. Its peeling white exterior gave the impression it was abandoned – none of the wooden slats of its siding ran parallel to the ground. The trees that flanked it only worsened the house's appearance, buckling its walls as though the trunks had tried and failed to crush the place but were gathering strength to try again. Yet the moment the breeze quieted he heard soft giggling from the rear of the dwelling. Cleft's heart skipped.

He had done it. He had found them.

It was all he could do to keep from running. Cleft followed the tracks past the trees and along the side of the house. He dragged his fingers along the wood siding in hopes it would slow him down. He wanted to savour the upcoming moment – his discovery of a heretofore unknown religious sect.

What he found instead was far more mundane and confusing.

The yard was made of a hard dirt that supported only patches of grass and clover. Along its edges stood a row of trees in a circle, thick woods that had been carved out for the homestead. At the foot of these trees were various sized pens, some holding livestock, others empty. In the middle of the yard sat an older woman on a tree stump. She was near his age, her grey hair streaked with fading chestnut and tied in a loose bun atop her head. In her lap she held a young girl less than ten years old, who waved a small stick in the air as though it were a wand. The child wore a white dress and tights that made her look like a porcelain statuette. In front of them a woman in her late twenties sat cross-legged, denim shorts cut high enough to expose her thick pocked legs. The three smiled and laughed with one another. Cleft immediately felt the embarrassing heat of intrusion. He tried to back away.

But it was too late. The child spotted him.

And she screamed.

"I'm sorry!" he offered in a rush, frantically waving his hands. The younger woman leapt up and snatched the child to her bosom as though to shield her. The older woman's eyes were similarly alight as she bolted to her feet, brandishing a pair of shears that had appeared in her hand.

"Who are you?" the older woman demanded. It took a moment for Cleft to remember that answer.

"I'm from Marsden College," he stammered. "I was doing some research and…and…I thought you might be…" He realised what he was about to accuse this family of. Instead, he fumbled his Moleskine from his pocket and unfolded the newspaper clipping he kept between its pages. "Have any of you seen this plant before? I'm trying to find the people who dug it up. I followed their tracks here."

The older woman glanced at the photo.

"No," she said.

Some of his hope slipped away. He folded the clipping and returned it to his notebook.

"Is there maybe anyone else who could have taken it? Anyone else who lives in the area?"

She shook her head. More of his hope fled. He couldn't accept what was happening. His plea, almost in defiance, to no one in particular: "But I saw a light in the woods. Just a little ways back…"

The old woman's face changed. Softened.

"Forgive us, we weren't expecting anyone today," she said, lowering her shears. "There have been others. In the woods, I mean. We sometimes see them. I think they have a farm nearby."

Cleft flipped through the pages of his Moleskine, his other hand digging out the small pencil from his jacket's front pocket. "Can you tell me where to find them?"

"We've only seen them at a distance," she said. Then, to the younger woman: "Have you spoken to them?"

"I don't speak to people I don't know," she said. Then looked at Cleft.

The older woman smiled.

"Sorry we can't be more help."

And that was it. A dead end. Crushing disappointment. Cleft lowered the Moleskine. He'd followed the wrong tracks and had lost his chance – at recovering the Witch's Clutch; at finding those who had it. Around him grew longer shadows, the sun fell closer to the horizon. The trees, the bushes, the footprints began their fade into the encroaching dark. There was nothing left to do but go back.

"Are you okay?" The woman touched his arm.

"I'm fine," he muttered.

He had to call Siobhan. Let her know where to find him. She'd be angry he stole her weekend, but he didn't care – she'd be gone soon anyway. Off to a mentor who could do more for her. He probably would have done the same in her place. But when he took his phone from his pocket to dial her number he discovered it had no signal. He resisted the sudden urge to hurl it into the woods.

Instead, he sighed. Collected himself. Then slid the phone back into his pocket.

"May I borrow your telephone?" he asked, adjusting his glasses. "It's getting darker and my assistant needs directions to pick me up."

"Sorry. We don't have one," the older woman said.

"But what if there's an emergency?"

Both her and the younger's brows furrowed as though confused. The animals in the surrounding pens huffed and snorted. It would be dusk soon. How was he going to get back to the Bull & Goose?

The child seemed to read his mind. She appeared beside the older woman, tugging her sleeve.

"Is he coming inside?" she asked. Her smile was wide and toothy.

Cleft blanched. That was not what he wanted. But it was true he had no way of getting back.

The women must have realised the same. Why else did they seem so uncomfortable? He wanted to say something but was conflicted.

The old woman spared him the suffering.

"Of course he is," she replied, her eyes fixed on his. "We wouldn't want him to get lost again."

The inside of the house was as cramped as Siobhan's Kia. He had to duck when passing through the door frame, and continued ducking as the top of his head narrowly brushed each joist in succession. The odour that greeted him was as vague as it was sweet and comforting. Like linseed and lemon. Like leather and a burning pine log. For a moment he forgot his disappointment and closed his eyes, inhaled deeply.

"I appreciate the help," he said as the old woman directed him to a beaded couch. He sank into it immediately upon sitting, the fabric scratchy as hay. The younger woman sat across from him on a small love seat, hoisting the child into her lap. An awkward silence followed.

"My name's Rusty Cleft," he eventually said.

"Is that so?"

He shifted awkwardly. The beads pushed into his spine.

"My name is Atrai," the older woman said. "And this is Lasha. The young one is—"

"I'm Cleo!" the girl shouted.

"You certainly are," he smiled.

Cleft surveyed the house. He noted the wrinkled curtains, the slanted windowsills. Everything appeared askew; it made him uneasy. "So," he said, "you three live here? In the middle of nowhere?"

"It's not nowhere," Cleo giggled. "And not just us."

"No?"

She rolled her eyes like marbles.

"Daddy lives here, too."

"He's travelling," Atrai informed him. Then, to Cleo: "But he'll be home soon, won't he?" The child nodded excitedly. "When he does I wonder if you'll even recognise him. It's been so long."

"I will! I will recognise him!"

Atrai smiled. Then to Cleft once again: "He's been gone a long time. And she's still so young."

"I understand."

"I thought you might."

"Or maybe he's never coming home," Lasha said before Atrai could hush her. "Maybe he doesn't want to."

Cleft felt the temperature drop. He shifted again in his seat.

"Maybe I should leave."

Atrai shook her head, brushed away his concerns.

"Oh, it's much too late," she said.

And she was right. He bent to look through a small dirty window at the starless night. Siobhan would never find him even were he to call. He wondered if she was concerned. He suspected his absence had escaped her notice.

"You must be hungry. We'll make you something," Atrai said.

"I couldn't ask you to do that."

"Nonsense. It will make you feel better."

Atrai stood. Lasha and Cleo followed. As she turned toward the kitchen, Cleo dashed to Cleft and handed him her stick. She smiled, then scrambled after Atrai. Only Lasha remained. She hesitated, as though about to say something, then silently followed, leaving Cleft alone.

Immediately his thoughts spiralled toward the Witch's Clutch and those who took it. They were out there, somewhere in the dark, while he sat with these three strange women. He tried calling Siobhan again but the calls would not go through. Everything was collapsing around him. Marsden College and his future never felt so far away. Nor as unreachable.

A rich and meaty smell distracted him; caused such stomach growling he worried the women had overheard it. He stared at the kitchen door, listening for their voices.

Without warning, the door swung open, startling him. Atrai emerged, large black stone bowl precariously balanced. Its contents steamed, the vapour twisting around her head, and close behind her were the younger Lasha and the child. One carried a thick loaf of bread, the other a set of mismatched utensils.

"Any luck getting a hold of your friend?" Atrai asked, beckoning him to a table and setting down the stone bowl in front of him. Cleft watched the oil congeal on the surface of the broth in rings around the floating vegetables.

"Not yet," he said, his head swimming from hunger.

"Let's hope she calls soon. The air feels ripe for a storm."

"It always storms when Father's coming back," the child said before Lasha yanked her arm to quiet her. Young Cleo yelped. Cleft did not like the sound.

"Please—" he started to say before being hushed.

"Your broth is getting cold," Lasha said, dropping half a bread loaf to the side of the bowl. "Eat while there's still time."

Cleft looked at Cleo, who was frowning and rubbing her arm, then at Atrai, smiling and unalarmed. Cleft felt he should say something but was distracted by the meal they'd prepared. He wiped his mouth. Then did so again before tearing a piece of bread and dipping it into the broth. As soon as he tasted the morsel his hands were moving spoonfuls over his tongue as fast as he could swallow them. The meal was salted and warm and expanded in his stomach, soaking up his discomfort and worries. Numbing and soporific satiety flowed through his body, and he was powerless to prevent himself from putting the bowl to his mouth and slurping down the dregs. His only regret was there wasn't more to savour.

Across from him, the three women watched.

He leaned back in his chair. Exhaled a greasy heat. Atrai carefully collected the empty bowl and handed it to Lasha. The younger woman took it wordlessly and carried it into the kitchen. Cleo, on the couch, swung her small white legs slowly. Hypnotically. Everything felt strange, as though time were being drawn out. But it was a good feeling, and one he did not wish to disrupt. Instead, he allowed himself to sink further into his chair. Sink until its arms reached out and embraced him.

Cleft blinked and suddenly Lasha was back, seated beside Cleo. When had she returned? She placed her hand on the girl's legs before speaking. Those legs stopped swinging.

"Why did you come?" she asked. All three women appeared at once larger and less substantial. Light flickered like fire across their faces.

"Information," he mumbled. "Research."

"Research?"

He murmured, then leaned to the side and struggled to pull the Moleskine from his pocket. It was more slippery than expected. Perhaps his fingers had grown too large.

"Have you seen this?" he asked as he fumbled through the pages. When he found the clipping of the Witch's Clutch he showed it to them.

"You've asked us this before."

"I have? Did I tell you what it was?" The women glanced at one another. Cleft couldn't recall if he even knew. The words eventually came to him, as though rising through molasses.

"It's an…an anomaly. Plants – nightshade, mandrake, and jimsonweed – entangled, fused with one another in…I guess in a ring. The Witch's Clutch appears in so many cultures, going far back. Far, far back." There was something else he wanted to say about it but the thought slipped free. He knew it was close, but he couldn't find it. "The name's kind of a botanical joke: the three weeds happen to also have wiccan importance. You know, like witches and warlocks. And the circle…" Cleft wondered why it was suddenly so dark, then realised his eyes were closed. He opened them and discovered he had been somehow transported back to the beaded couch. The three faces hovered over him as their hands gently laid him down.

He had more to say but couldn't. His mouth was dry. Gummy. Not that he minded. He didn't mind much of anything. Those faces floating above him slipped in and out of his vision, confusing themselves with one another, blending and shifting and overlapping.

The women muttered in a slow monotone and their words twisted in wrong directions. He felt the pressure build in his head. Cleft squeezed his eyes shut and opened them to find the child, sat astride him, kneading and stretching his face. Her head turned as she spoke to the others. Yet they didn't look how he remembered. Their faces were plastic as he weightlessly lifted into the air. The walls trembled and hummed, lulling him. It took effort but he smiled at the child, then closed his eyes a moment to rest. He opened them later, well after dark.

And in the midst of a violent storm.

Rain pelted the sides of the small house with fury; bright flashes illuminated the sky. Cleft's heart pounded as he leapt from the couch, disoriented. Everything looked twisted in the dark. And worse than that whenever lightning struck.

But that wasn't what woke him. Something thrashed in his chest – not looking for escape, but instead to grab hold of everything and pull it in. A sucking insatiable need. He clutched himself tighter but it did no good. The hunger could not be quelled.

The sound of pounding continued. He realised it hadn't been his heart. It was the door. The door that led into the house. It was too small to fit through, and yet it sounded tremendous. Was there someone there?

Cleft heard voices behind him. Around him. He glanced back but saw no one. He stood alone, facing the door as it throbbed with pressure. Hinges creaked and buckled. The pounding intensified as though a pair of giant fists were splintering the wooden frame. The storm hurled itself against the entrance, demanding to be let in. And the need inside of Cleft welcomed it, told him to open the door. It begged and it pleaded. Cleft took an unsure step forward.

And then the frame exploded. The door swung so hard on its hinges Cleft felt the crack. But all he knew was someone was standing in the doorway.

Or, rather, someone wasn't.

Because there was no one. No matter how it felt, no matter what he imagined in the corner of his eye, there was no one. Just a deluge of rain and howling wind. There was no one stepping into the house as furniture blew aside. There was no one growing larger as the sky flashed bright then black. There was no one reaching out for him as the storm threw Cleft back over his heels, drove him into the ground.

There was no one towering over him as everything went dark.

No. Worse than dark.

Went to nothing.

★ ★ ★

Nothing but the floral smell of tea brewing. Cleft's eyes opened and saw daylight across the low ceiling. Sitting up made his head swim, and standing took a great effort, but he eventually found his balance. He wiped his face and brushed off the leaves and dust that had collected on him at some point while he slept. All that remained of the night before was a carousel of images that didn't make sense.

He sat again on the couch, held his head in his hands. What made him agree to stay in such a strange house?

Cleft lowered his hands.

He had to get out.

Siobhan was not going to rescue him. She was at the Bull & Goose somewhere outside the woods, no doubt still asleep. Even if she weren't, he couldn't get hold of her – his cellular phone had turned black overnight and stayed that way. He felt anxious, abandoned, but pushed the feelings aside.

He heard a chair move behind the kitchen door. Before he knew why, he was stumbling toward the sound.

The three women – the older, the younger, the child – sat among clutter, holding one another's hands at a small table, eyes closed. Cleft's entrance awakened them, however, and their stares turned toward him. Only Cleo had an expression he could read. It was disappointment.

"Did we wake you?" Atrai asked, releasing the hands of the other two as she stood. Lasha put hers in her lap. Cleo, on the edge of the chair, spoke disappointedly into her chest.

"I thought he was Daddy," she said.

Atrai hushed her. "He'll be here soon."

In the daylight, things felt even stranger. Something was off, but Cleft could not explain what or why. Only that nothing felt as it should. Nothing looked as it should, either.

"Are you okay?" Atrai asked him.

"Of course," he said. "I'm just surprised I didn't hear you cleaning up."

Their look, queer. Unsettled. Lasha's eyes narrowed.

"What do you mean?"

"The storm last night. I opened the door. The wind, it…it turning everything over. But I don't see any sign of it now."

An expression flitted across Atrai's face. Lasha did not acknowledge it. Instead, she shrugged.

"There was nothing wrong with the house this morning."

Did he dream it?

Cleft looked at the women but his mind raced with how he'd misjudged the situation. What happened with the house and the storm didn't matter. Or he ought to pretend it didn't.

He fixed a smile to his face. Everything was okay. Normal.

"I should be on my way now that it's day," he said. "My assistant is expecting me."

"You were able to get hold of her?" Atrai asked.

"Oh, yes," he lied. "Thank you for letting me stay the night."

"It was no trouble," Atrai said.

Cleft gathered his things as quickly as he could while the women silently watched him. Something was about to happen. He needed to escape before it did.

"Where is he going?" Cleo asked. Lasha pulled her close. Embraced her. Stroked her hair.

"It's time for him to leave."

"No!" Cleo shouted, pulling herself free. She ran to Cleft and wrapped her arms around him. "You can't leave! You can't!"

Cleft didn't know what to do. The door was so close. He was almost out.

"Cleo—" he began.

Then he saw it.

And instantly he knew it was already too late. He wasn't going anywhere.

"What is that?" he sputtered, unable to express his confusion and disbelief.

"What do you mean?"

He pointed, unable to speak. By the door from the kitchen hung what looked to be a wreath. But it wasn't.

"The Witch's Clutch."

The two women looked back. Then at one another. Cleo squeezed tighter yet Cleft was too numb to feel it.

"That's a strangleweed," Atrai said. "To feed to the animals."

"No, it's a Witch's Clutch. It's… Oh, God," he said, crumpling over his knees. "You took it. It's you I've been looking for this whole time."

There was no religion. No discovery of an unknown sect. No paper. No book. There was only three women collecting plants for their farm. He'd been chasing nothing, and that's what he had. Nothing. In an instant he saw himself back on that imagined awards stage, but there were no longer any applauding peers in the audience. The theatre was empty.

"I'm sorry," Atrai said, placing her hand on his as she looked at the others. "We didn't know."

"But… I showed you the clipping…"

Lasha reached out for his other hand. "We would have told you had we realised. We were distracted."

"Distracted? By what?"

"Daddy," Cleo said, placing her hands on his chest. "We want Daddy home so badly."

"We do our best with the plants and livestock while he's gone, but it's *his* garden," Atrai said. "He's the only one who knows how to keep it going."

"Would you like to see it? The garden?" Lasha asked.

Immediately Cleo's face lit up. "Yes! You need to see it! It will help."

Atrai replied, "It's the least we could do."

But Cleft barely looked up. His life was in ruins.

"I really should go."

"Come, let us show you," Atrai said. "And afterward you can take the Witch's Clutch and be on your way."

"You need to see it!" Cleo repeated.

The women all stood and each took the hand of another – oldest, younger, child – and when Cleo extended hers to Cleft he did not resist. Her tiny hand burned like an ember in his massive palm, but he didn't let go. Instead, he allowed her to pull him up from the chair.

The four left in procession; Cleft, the last link, stooping to move through the tiny door frame. Outside he realised how cramped he'd been; he stretched his limbs and looked up at the trees swaying above, all moving in the same continuous direction. As though circling.

Atrai led the train across the trodden dirt that surrounded the small home and toward the sound of livestock. Cleo's hand flexed and pulsed within Cleft's like a tiny bird; he did not squeeze tighter for fear of crushing it. He saw no more evidence of a thunderstorm than there had been inside – no mud or downed branches or faint odour of rain. Nor was there a cloud in the sky. Everything was bright and clear and slightly unreal. As though the moment wasn't one he was experiencing but instead one he was watching be experienced. A spectator at far remove.

Why hadn't he left? Was the Witch's Clutch and what it might bring really worth staying for?

When they reached the rear of the house, Cleft saw the tree-encircled yard once again, its edges lined with small pens. The animals, however, were silent – he heard only snuffling in the woods and the scrabbling of hooves and claws on the hard dry dirt. The ground had become littered with tracks overnight, and all appeared to be pointing toward the area the women were ushering Cleft toward. As though the animals had been gathered in a circle for an audience. Or, no, not a circle. A spiral. A spiral that wrapped around and around the garden, drawing in tighter and tighter toward its eye. Cleft pulled back, hoping to get a better look at the myriad of hoofprints – some the size of his own feet – but the women were unwilling to slow until they reached the centre of the whorl.

"What is this?" Cleft asked.

"This is Father's garden," Atrai said, releasing her sister's hand and stepping in front of him. Standing a bit too close. "You want to remember it, don't you?"

Cleft swallowed.

"Where is he?"

"He'll be here. Soon."

"Yes, but where is he?"

Atrai smiled, put her hand on his chest, then began to slowly pace around him, dragging her fingers lightly across his flesh. His skin prickled.

"What...what are you doing?"

"We tend the garden every day," Lasha said, releasing her other sister's hand and placing hers on Cleft's face, slowly grazing it with her fingers as she followed a step behind Atrai. "We tend it for Father. You can smell it, can't you?"

Cleft could smell it. At once the smell of manure and hay, but also something more, something musky and pungent. Something that made his thoughts swim.

"What's happening to me?" he whispered, his mouth dry as cotton. He felt a tug, as if Cleo were trying to release his hand, but his fingers wouldn't open. When he looked down he discovered why.

What he expected to find was Cleo's hand clamped on his, fingers interlaced and locked tight. Instead he saw a knot of dark green tendrils twisted around his hand like vines. He didn't understand why; only that he needed to be free. He yanked his hand away in panic but only managed to lift Cleo from the ground. Her limbs flailed lifelessly.

The tendrils that looped over his hand thickened as he watched, his thoughts swimming further away. The tiny leaves that sprouted grew quickly, curling in on themselves. Little pink buds the size of buttons sprung up along his arms. He felt Cleo's hand coming apart in his own like a crushed flower. He gripped tighter to keep from losing her but her hand had already gone.

Circles and spirals and circles. Spinning around and around him. Like a pinwheel. The world constricting upon him, then spreading wide in pulses.

Cleft couldn't think. He looked down into Cleo's face but it too was coming apart. Pale skin sliding away, green stalks unfurling. The white cotton of her tights tore as twigs pushed themselves out. Her eyes collapsed.

There was no air left in his lungs to scream. Atrai and Lasha continued to encircle him, droning underbreath. No matter how he struggled he could not turn his head to follow them. Each time they reappeared they were changed. Tendrils extended, bright petals turned colours, small berries grew in clusters, elaborate flowers lifted from thorny stalks and stretched outward. With each revolution the vines around him tightened. The circles drew closer to constrict. To strangle. Like the slip of a noose.

Cleft's mouth. Wide. Silent.

Frantically he clawed at the weeds interweaving around his body. The green from Atrai fused with the green from Lasha fused with the green from Cleo. The end of one disguising the beginning of the other. An ouroboros of serrated leaves and browning stalks. Their looping vines climbed his body, squeezing his limbs until they were numb, choking his throat until the blood slowed and a darkness full of stars enveloped his vision. The strangling weeds grew thicker and tighter as he succumbed to them.

But no, that wasn't quite right.

He didn't succumb.

Beneath the muddy numbness he felt something else. Some secret only just revealing itself. Some primal connection to a current within the earth. One into which he was tapping. Into which he was rooting. As his mortal body weakened he felt that underthing slide into him. Undo that which had been locked away. A caged animal breaking free.

It happened in his legs first. Bone reshaped, seams split. Leather came apart and cotton tore. His feet touched the ground, remade. Stronger, tougher. He clomped down in an overload of sensations. Then the transformation took his body. An overwhelming feeling of warmth as the world embraced him. The secret world. And he realised in his final fleeting moments that the Witch's Clutch was not what he believed. The hybrid wasn't strange; it was the only thing that was right. The joining of the disparate into the whole. Every single thing a piece of the one thing. The everything.

His clothes shredded. He snuffled. Made a sound like a bleat. And felt for the first time in forever that he was part of something.

In the embrace of his daughters, he finally belonged.

CAMP NEVER

J.S. Breukelaar

1. Sister

Our mother slows past the ruins of the trailer. Mouth breathing against the front seat passenger window, Gabby can't look. It's stuffy inside the car, and I'm sleepy from the long drive from the city, but I can't *not* look. Someone has stepped onto the mountain road, holding a long stick. The lengthening shadows trick it into Bertha Kimmel, swinging her swan head cane like it is a performance instead of a punishment. Like she has a choice.

But it's not her.

It's just Jarryd, the campground manager's son, dragging a branch off the road to let us pass.

"Nice to be back," Mama says, cracking a window to talk to Jarryd. "Terrible about the Kimmels, though."

Jarryd nods under his hunting cap worn backwards. "I tried to save her," he says, chinning at where, in the grudging light, the burned-out lot looks to be still smoking.

We had been away when it happened. It was the year Dad left us, we had to stay in the city. But we heard about it from another camper, Janice-from-the-mountain. How Mr. Kimmel set fire to the trailer while his family slept inside. They finally caught up with him somewhere around San Antonio, we heard, but that didn't bring them back.

Mama had been obsessed with Bertha Kimmel. We all were. Sitting cross-legged beside the campfire with a child tucked under her arm, all of us transfixed by her Hedy Lamarr accent and her tales of a Winter Witch with the face of an angel and one foot that of a swan. Sometimes. Other times it was Queen of the Dead with a beak for a mouth and an army of undead consorts hellbent on cleansing the world of sin. The dads trying not to stare, the moms taking in her shiny leggings and toenail polish. But she had only to wave the cane and abracadabra! There was Jarryd, to top up her wine or help carry the kids back to the trailer. He cowered a little in her presence, like she scared him (I think she scared us all a little). Like there was something broken in him drawn to what could never be fixed in her.

"We shouldn't have come," Gabby half-moans. "Nothing's the same."

Her face is a heart-shaped reflection against the passenger window. I blow a plume of air against the back seat window, invisible even to myself. I can't remember the last time I've eaten. She rummages noisily around in a bag of chips. She's eleven years old but there are more than five years between us. Whole orders of being maybe.

"Some families are just not meant to be," Mama says to Jarryd.

Our mother is held together by Busch Light, scrunchies and will power. She teaches folklore studies at City College, and she was the one who told Bertha Kimmel about this inexpensive camping ground in the middle of nowhere, after they became friendly through an online Ancestry Group. She got the Kimmels a good deal on the trailer outside of the main area, near our tent. Camp Never, Gabby called it. Because every year at the end of our vacation, manoeuvring the station wagon down the switchback to the highway, our father would say the same thing. *Never again.*

It's weird seeing Mama's worried brown eyes in the rearview instead of Dad's cold pale ones looking right through me.

Jarryd says, "They found the lighter."

"I know," Mama says quietly. "I'm sorry, Jarryd. We'll all miss them."

"That's how they knew it was him," Jarryd says, more quietly this time, pounding on the ground with the branch. "Him, him, him."

Mama takes her foot off the brake. "Say hi to your mother, Jarryd," she says through her teeth.

★ ★ ★

Bertha Kimmel had been a dancer with the city ballet until a fall down the stairs. After that she walked with a cane. Dad had said that the sapphire eyes on the swan head tip were probably paste and that it was just some prop she'd dredged up from wardrobe. But even Dad admired her style, because when Mama asked, he just shrugged and said, "Fake it till you make it, I guess." He had a lot of those sayings.

Bertha invited us to come watch the ballet she choreographed and directed. It was called *The Wild Hunt*, and our mother promised we would one day. But then Dad left us and the Kimmels died in the fire, so we never got there.

One summer evening when I was thirteen, I was heading back to the tent alone. I walked past daisies in tyre planters. There was a rusty playground. I could see me pushing Gabby on the swing when she was little, the two of us normal and happy. But I didn't think it had happened like that. Bertha Kimmel came out of the rest rooms and stood in my path, her pale hair blown across her face. In the halogen light affixed to the outer wall, her features beneath the veil of hair looked monstrous, her lips bulging and misshapen.

"Katerina," she said, swinging the cane. "The name means *pure* – from the Greek *katharos* – you know this?"

I didn't.

"And also derived from the name of the Goddess Hecate, protector of households."

She pushed the veil of her hair aside, and her face returned to normal – the high cheekbones and the slight hook to her nose.

"The most powerful magic once came from the home," she said, "where the heart is. In winter, the Queen visits the households to make sure the work is done, especially the spinning. Clean heart, clean soul, *ja*? The bad ones – she punishes by slitting their bellies and stuffing with rocks and sawdust instead."

She made a slitting motion with her cane, right down my middle. She moved toward me, languidly repositioned herself into a perfect fourth position, her right foot angled behind her left. And then she put her hand on mine. I'd braced to make a quick getaway, not with my back to her, but not quite facing her either. Her hand was cold and a little damp but steely around my fingers, the veins visible through her skin.

"You have great bones," she said.

★ ★ ★

Mama stops the car beside a spreading oak. Gabby jumps out in a cloud of wrappers and crumbs. I move sluggishly, limbs heavy. The forest hangs like an old beanie off the bowed top of the mountain. Young pines and yellow birch trees straggle closer than I remember, new growth budding from limbs blackened by the fire. We help unload and Mama quickly pitches the two-man tent she and Dad used to share. Janice-from-the-mountain – all tattoos and attitude – has come to get her, holding two beers and a plate of uncooked veggie patties, and they both stand looking over at the ruins. Skeins of ash rise and fall in the breeze.

Janice says, "Debris sometimes washes to the surface when it rains."

"After all this time?" Mama sips her beer thoughtfully. "Weird."

They wander off, leaving me and Gabby to pitch our tent. It's not afternoon any more but not dusk yet either. The familiar wintergreen smell has a smoky aftertaste. The long shadows are fading and the blue draining from the sky. Mama is wearing a necklace that belonged to her grandmother – a filigree rectangle with a small oval diamond in the middle as clear as water. The way her dark curls are pulled up in a loose bun makes her look what Dad called 'optimised' – something that he read about in his self-help books and could never be.

"Dear all," his goodbye note read, "I'm sorry."

Gabby didn't cry. She just went into our room and lay on the bed. I stood in the doorway for a while and watched her. Dad's mantras ran through my head – *no pain, no gain, kiddo. Sticks and stones, sport.* But I didn't think any of them would help.

Now, we drag our tent into a flat place between the breaching roots. Screams echo across the ridge from the swimming hole. It's hard not to think about all of the Kimmels perishing in the fire, except Mr. Kimmel.

"Peeper alert," Gabby mutters into her collar.

Jarryd lopes past on his evening rounds and side-eyes Gabby under his hunting cap, cowering a little in that soft and boneless way of his, thirty going on fifty, rarely out of his mother's sight due to some scandal in the showers before our time and passed around as self-renewing whispers every year. Gabby tosses the curls she got from Mama and pokes out her tongue, and in the uncertain dappled light, she looks only half visible, fading in and out. Despite our age difference, I always thought she was twice the person I'd ever be. Popular, pretty, the chosen one. But since Dad's been gone, she's seemed smaller somehow, younger, less sure of herself. Like he took a piece of her with him when he left.

It's the only part of him I really miss.

I looks-could-kill Jarryd until he picks up speed toward the office, glancing back once as he passes the Kimmel place. A scrap of begrimed police tape floats down from a tree. The impossible smell of burned flesh is suddenly strong enough to make me want to gag. The sun drops behind the ridge and the faint stars begin to spin.

I hear Bertha Kimmel's drunken whisper from that night after the campfire tales. I hear other things. Crying. The snick-a-snick of a fire. I don't know if I'm asleep or awake.

"Her children all dead, she cried for a long time in the dark under the ground." The words are in my mouth, don't ask me how. My legs give way. "And then she became a little wicked."

"Who?" Gabby stands over me with dimpled hands on her knees. I've sunk onto a gnarled root.

"The Winter Queen," I say, my mouth and mind disconnected. Which is mine? I don't know any more. "Goddess of Spinning, *ja*? Protector of mothers and children."

"Spinning? Seriously, Kat, it's July." She has Doritos down her T-shirt, vivid grass stains on her knees.

"She wears a veil to cover her beak," I mumble. "A bride's dress..."

"To hunt?"

"To sleep."

Katerina! Wake up.

I can't—

"Wake up!"

It's Mama. She wraps a blanket around me until my teeth stop chattering. Gabby tells her I fainted, and then she bursts out crying. I feel nothing. Mama says maybe it's my period coming. She smells of beer. We eat a silent meal, Gabby refusing to look at me. I don't finish my hot dog, sleep dragging at my eyelids. My sister gets into a onesie with flannel rabbit ears on the hood and comes back for my leftovers with some more potato salad, stuffing food into the hole where her heart used to be.

"Why didn't they clean up better after the fire?" Gabby asks with her mouth full.

"Hard to get trucks up the mountain, I imagine," Mama says. "Expensive too. Probably just waiting for it all to grow over. We'll ask to move tomorrow."

"Can I sleep with you?" Gabby says. "Kat sleeps like the dead."

What Dad used to say.

"Silly bunny." Our mother chugs the last beer from the six pack, and weaves toward her tent. "Wake Kat if you need to go."

"I'm scared, Mama."

"Use the pee-tree, okay? Kat, you're in charge."

* * *

Wake up. Wake up! my father calls, pounding at the door. *You can sleep when you're dead, Kat.*

I sit bolt upright in utter darkness and feel two things. The need to pee, and also the root of the oak tree jutting against my butt. Gabby's sleeping bag is empty. My flashlight beam falls across a Sparkling Grape Chupa Chup stuck to the flannel lining. She must have tried to wake me up and couldn't.

Wake up.

I plunge through the open tent flap, coming head-to-head with a family of rabbits, their fur shimmering in the full moon. They spin their eyes and hop away in slow motion like in a dream. But this isn't a dream because my heart is pounding and my feet feel icy. An invisible boot dribbles a soccer ball along on the bend in the dirt road that slopes down toward the main area. All around the pines stand stock-still. Waiting.

There is no one at the pee-tree.

"Gabby?" I whisper.

I'm supposed to be in charge.

Wake up.

The whisper comes from the silence, everywhere and nowhere. I've taken a few steps toward the dirt road, when a crunching noise from the Kimmels' place makes me freeze.

I slowly turn, like I have a choice. Splintered bones sparkle in the moonlight, no longer hidden beneath the rubble as they are by day. The flute of a finger sprouts from the earth. A glittering flower of baby teeth blooms from a tiny jaw. The delicate curve of a rib.

The crack of a branch up ahead. The backwards hunting cap, the slight stoop of someone not old but soft and out of shape.

Jarryd.

He carries something in his arms, and wow, what a big rabbit. The rabbit's hood has fallen back and dark curls tumble over Jarryd's arm. The flashlight drops from my hand.

"Gabby!" But the sound is just a nightmare croak of condensed breath. Anyway, Mama must be out for the count – all that beer – and we are too far from the rest of the camp for anyone to hear. Jarryd's hunting cap melts into the trees and my sister's floppy ears with it.

Silly bunny.

Adrenaline jolts my legs into a starting-block run, but something has wound around my ankle, rooting me to the spot. I look down and think I might be sick. A skeletal hand with blackened finger bones sprouts from the ash and holds me fast. The grip is so cold it burns. I struggle, stirring up the slag. Something snaps, a flare of pain up my shin. I flop down on my belly, eat dirt.

"Jarryd!"

It comes out a mangled wheeze. But saying his name out loud, that's when I know.

It was him.

Jarryd, the manager's son, who'd set the fire. To free Bertha maybe, or free himself from her spell, or maybe the fire was meant for Mr. Kimmel, and Jarryd tried to save her like he said, but it was too quick. The fire got them all.

They found the lighter.

Because Jarryd stole it. Doused the trailer in gasoline, lit it with a match and whoosh! Dropped the lighter with Kimmel's prints as evidence. The bones tell me, so I know it's true; her children speak through them. Mr. Kimmel and the fragrant smoke rings he hid behind. But he didn't do it – oh, he wanted to in that secret part of him too slow to catch her fall down the stairs – but he couldn't. He didn't have the guts. So Jarryd did it for him.

Bertha's death grip tightens around my ankle.

Why me? My mouth hinges open to the swirling stars. Splintered bone cuts my tongue, and flying debris catches in my hair. Smoke closes my throat. A cold blade of bone slices opens my belly. Bringing my hand to the wound, gore spills through my fingers. On my knees, I fumble my entrails back into the cavity as best I can, stuffing it with ash to soak up the blood. Not your stick and stones, Dad, but ash and bones, because I'll do anything to save my sister.

The world goes black and white, like a filter has slid across my vision. Ahead of me, a gleam of silver flashes a signal against the charred earth. Splayed across the tiny bones, crushing them, I reach for the tip of Bertha's cane. Just the head at first breaching through the cinders, then the begrimed sapphire eyes, and finally the long, pointed beak – pushed up from the ground by an unseen hand. The beak bites. The metal scorches my hand and the smell of my burning flesh pushes me to my feet. Leaning on the cane I take my first shallow breath in this new state, filling my lungs with smoke and tears.

Bertha lets me go.

Jarryd's footprints glimmer into the black woods. My nostrils twitch with the smell of his sweat; my tongue unfurls to catch my sister's sugary drool. I yank an entrail where it flops from my closing stomach cavity, toss it into the scrub. At first it is a slow limp on my twisted ankle, my right foot flopping awkwardly in front of me, but the momentum I gain acts like a drug. Like love. Possessed of a speed and purpose I've never known, jagged as lightning, I slash through the undergrowth with the cane, the monochromatic trunks and vines passing in a silvery blur.

Ahead, half hidden by limbs and branches, is a hunter's shack. In one balletic leap of will I am inside. The walls hang with stuffed animals mouldering from nails and brackets – a rabbit, a raccoon with a chewed ear, a woodchuck leaking sawdust. There are no windows, like one of those black-box rehearsal rooms at school, except that rehearsals are over and this is opening night, dead things my captive audience.

Gabby lies on the dirt floor, her onesie covered in filth. I can hear the river. There is vomit on my sister's chin. Did he slip her the same mickey as Bertha and the kids, so they'd sleep through being burned alive? Jarryd has his back to me, rummaging at a sink – a plastic tub filled with sawdust – and his hunting knife on the draining board. I unleash the long thin blade from Bertha's cane with a sound like a soft kiss.

Jarryd pivots and his lips stretch into a rapture of terror and recognition – a joy you only feel once.

"You?" he says, seeing someone who is not me. Not entirely.

He thinks he knows her. Because he's broken and she, Bertha, is unfixed. He thinks he sees her, come back to him.

But then he sees me, and his expression drops.

His fingers flutter toward his hunting knife, getting ahead of himself. The rage tastes hot and sweet in the back of my throat. I am a goddess now, and a witch, a protector and avenger. In that hairbreadth of time my blade is at his sternum, and then he is foetal on the boards. He wrinkles his brow to try and make sense of the widening slash down his belly, the flop of his guts, watching me dump sawdust into the cavity, and then into his mouth too, so I don't have to see his lips move for the last time, or hear her name on his lips.

Bertha.

My sister lifts easily, but the dope dead-weights her against my chest. My twisted ankle gives and I stumble off balance, fracturing the porous bones of my pelvis. This time I scream with pain. But I don't let my sister go.

By the time I've brought her back to our mother, unharmed except for a gash on her forehead and the nightmares that will plague her for life, I am myself again, at least on the outside. It is under my skin that the blisters ooze, and deep in my heart where the cold embers glow. When we get home, I hide the cane at the top of my closet, forget about it for now.

We never go camping again.

2. Hunter

The summer stretches out for another month before school starts. Gabby says she doesn't remember anything after Jarryd knocked her unconscious. Dad's ghostly gutless sutras all but fade from my memory, except one: *You don't know what you've got till it's gone.*

The bruises on my ankle fade but the cracked pelvis leaves me with a slight limp. The doctor suggests a cane.

"Why not use the one in your closet?" Mama says, keeping her eyes on her laptop. "You won't be able to get anything like that in a medical supply store."

She doesn't say she recognises it. Doesn't mention it ever again.

Janice-from-the-mountain keeps us looped in on the investigation. The police find footprints in the ash. Jarryd's of course, and mine, and a third blurry set: well-formed calcaneus, but with the indents of the right navicular, metatarsals, and proximal phalanx deeper than the left. Possible sign of an injury or limp, according to the report. They're similar to Bertha Kimmel's, except the limp is on the other side. Old man Kimmel is in jail hospice with terminal lung cancer. So, the police say crazy Jarryd did it to himself – slashed his own belly with his hunting knife and tried to stuff himself with sawdust like the woodland creatures he talked to alone in his shed.

I am still skin and bone, and Gabby is starting to get curves. I am still invisible compared to her; a week after school starts, she's invited to more sleepovers and parties than I ever will be. But now I think of it more as a superpower than as sub-optimal. Once I was as scared as my father of what nothing meant. Now I know that nothing is everything.

★ ★ ★

A year goes by. Mama moves us closer to City College and to my new school when I get into the Theatre Arts programme. On Friday afternoons we meet Gabby at the subway for noodles or a movie, just us three. The family we're finally meant to be.

In my senior year, I audition for the part of Titania in *A Midsummer Night's Dream* and land the understudy role. Gabby and

Mama come to watch me fill in for the lead when she gets mono. I don't go to parties. The only dates I go on involve rough fumbles in the projection room between rehearsals. Gabby urges me to socialise more, especially with boys – you can't stay a virgin forever, she reminds me. So when a new guy in class asks me out to a Spider Man festival at the Odeon I say yes. I do it for her.

Gabby lies on the bed, propped up on an elbow like a dark cherub. "Your hair is amazing. Like lightning," she says.

My pride. It turned almost white after that summer – from shock, Mama says. I find products from the drug store to bring out the shimmer. I pose in front of the mirror, twirl Bertha's cane that I got down from the closet, and tell myself is just a cane, after all. My breasts are small, my belly flat and hard, a six-pack ghosting beneath my skin.

"I can see your ribs," Gabby says.

They're not my ribs any more. They ache sometimes, like they've been broken. And I still don't know what they want.

Gabby watches Paco and me leave from the window of our shared bedroom. I can tell right away that he's self-conscious about his weight, like Gabby. He crosses his arms over his chest, stomach sucked in, and he hides behind a patchy stubble like a young bear. Later when we kiss, his hands move down my sternum, my hollow belly, and down to my jutting pelvic bones in a kind of wonder. My hungry tongue meets his tentative one, and I swallow smoke.

I wake with a jolt in the back seat of his car, Paco snoring softly beside me. *Katerina – the name means purity, protector of households.* I check the time – after midnight. I shouldn't have left Mama and Gabby alone so long.

I find my shoes, my phone, let myself out as quietly as I can. The swan head is hot in my hand and I am wobbly as I dial for a ride. My white hair throws dancing reflections across Paco's windshield. The ride comes and somewhere around midtown, a slit opens in my belly and blood begins to seep through my dress. The pain is sharp and cold. Holding the gaping edges of the wound together with both hands, I tell the driver to pull over. He reminds me what neighbourhood we're in, but I am out of the car before it fully stops. My hands at my belly, I watch the tail-light glow change from red to black, in a monochrome world of shuttered stores and stunted trees dipped in silver from the low full moon. Instead of back to Gabby and Mama, the smell of smoke takes me down a back lane, behind a karaoke bar. Some white kids with nice watches and three-hundred-dollar sneakers are kicking the life out of a drag queen, and one of them looks up as I approach. I'm tall for my age, skin and bone. My dress is black with blood. Anger rises in me like a winter storm, obliterating the pain, freezing everything in its path. The others run, all except for the first guy, the one with the biggest watch. He wipes spittle off his lips, trying to work out his next move. The hunter in me leans into the anticipatory beat of his heart: *What now, what now, what now?*

"Now, nothing," I say.

Yackety-yack with the swan's beak across his face. Blood and teeth and tongue. He can't get back to himself, to this moment. He'll never get back. And then I unsheathe the blade with the kiss of death, slash from sternum to pubes, and will him to look down at his own viscera as it spills.

★ ★ ★

The years pass. I drop out of college. I hunt. Gabby starts a computer engineering degree. Mama and Janice-from-Bed-Stuy go hiking every month. Mama marries the City College Programme director. His people are from Seoul, and they honeymoon in Korea, and then Austria where Mama manages to trace Bertha's roots, and eventually her own, back to a tiny town in the Tyrol. She Skypes weekly from this or that village, visiting a contact in Vienna, a day spent in the archives at the Museum of Folklore in Munich. I live for our weekly family chats – never miss a single one, no matter how hard the hunt, how it leaves me feeling flayed, adrenaline draining from my body and starved for sleep. I want to tell my sister and my mother how what I do, I do for them. To keep them safe. But the confession dies on my lips.

Bertha's cane becomes me.

★ ★ ★

I get a job at a dive bar downtown called Jakes's, named after a giant bald eagle cast in fibreglass – made to look like bronze – that sits on the bar. I rent an apartment around the corner where no one can find me. I clean and sheath my blade at the scene of my kills; there are never witnesses. My limp is not so bad you'd notice, and my clothes are a colour out of night. Together, Bertha and I are invisible except to those for whom we are the last thing they'll ever see – me reflected in one dead eye, her in the other.

In punishing the guilty, we protect the innocent – the way Bertha could not protect her own children. She cried for a long time in the dark, but now, through me, she rides again. The Queen of Lore rode in winter. *We* hunt in all seasons. The Queen of Legend punished bad children, but she and I must wait until they've grown up. Till they've had a chance to save themselves and choose not to.

The choice is theirs. Their souls are hers.

And most important, my sister is mine.

⋆ ⋆ ⋆

Gabby finishes her degree and turns up on my doorstep late one September. She looks good. Her crossover dress makes the most of her curves; grown-out highlights in her curls. She wears Mama's necklace. Dad had been sending her money for a while but then his new wife's kid needed braces, and the construction industry being what it is… I offer her the couch.

I still hunt, careful to clean up before coming home. One of the swan's sapphires pops out, and I search for it in the spilled guts of a sinner, but I can't find it before the police arrive. A fractured wrist after a lethal slash, a smashed knee fleeing the scene – my bones are not what they used to be. The city overflows with evil and the gutters run with the blood of the damned. An eye for an eye, Dad, no rest for the wicked. Put that in your pipe and smoke it.

But I wonder sometimes: how much bad blood will it take to fill the hole in your heart, goddess, where your children once were? Will there ever be enough thunder and lightning to put out the fire?

⋆ ⋆ ⋆

One November dawn, I let myself into the apartment to find Gabby sitting in the kitchen drinking coffee. I peer at her through the grainy light, angling my head away so she won't notice a burst blood vessel across my sclera. She's found a job in a software start-up, is looking at rentals. I move stiffly toward the coffee pot. The coffee's hot but that's not why I wince.

"Are you hurt?"

"Don't move out," I say. "We'll find a bigger place together."

I need her here; I like keeping her close. Some nights I scare myself. Some nights Bertha scares me. In return for saving my sister, how many more souls will I have to lay at her feet, and at what cost to my own?

"You look a hundred per cent like shit," Gabby says, sitting back in her chair. "Must have been a hot date."

"They're all hot," I say, my smile lopsided because I've lost another tooth.

A briefcase sits at her feet. Her hair is pulled back in a glossy ponytail. Her nails are unvarnished, softly curved. The only jewellery she wears is Mama's necklace at her throat.

"They never last, though, Kat, do they? What's wrong with them?"

I know, because we are sisters, that she's too kind to say, *What's wrong with you?* But I can't tell her. And I can't tell her about all the hurt and harm out there with only us to stop it. The guy using his step-kids to get under-age dates. The hedge fund guy with a sideline in snuff films. The kiddy-porn guy and the other guy. I don't tell her that the world goes black and white when I hunt, and Bertha's rage freezes everything in its path. How it buries me like an avalanche, until I don't know how to dig myself out, or if I want to. It's so dark in there. So cold. How I wake up some nights shaking so my bones rattle, and how the only thing that gets my blood flowing again is the hunt. I don't tell her about the gash in my belly that no longer quite closes. Or about nights sitting alone in the park, holding the swan's long neck in my hand like a blood-smeared question mark.

I don't tell her that whoever said you can sleep when you're dead doesn't know shit.

Gabby sits straighter on her chair. "Remember that boy you were with for a while in high school? The big guy – Paco? Whatever happened to him?"

I have forgotten his name. What is interesting to me is that she hasn't.

Gabby brings Thai home that night and we light candles and drink wine. We stay up listening to music until late and I miss the call to the hunt. The wound opens in my stomach, and I bandage it in the bathroom. I drink more wine to dull the ache. Wash down an Ambien and wake up on soaked sheets.

Bertha punishes me. Some kid mugs Gabby the next day walking up the subway stairs – steals her wallet and rips Mama's necklace from her throat. I hunt for two nights straight to make up for it, and when I limp home, everything feels broken. I shuffle to the bed on my knees like a penitent, curl up on the floor shivering, spit out another tooth.

She needs me to live and so I kill for her. Together we dance. Together we are optimal. Together, we have become more than a little wicked.

The media calls them ritual killings. The police are searching for information about a sapphire found at the scene of what they call 'a gruesome disembowelling'. I rub dried blood off the swan head. I rub it till its good eye gleams.

But I know now that it's just a matter of time.

3. Queen

I look Paco up. He has a proper beard now. He's single. One evening in December, Gabby stops by Jake's for a meal as she sometimes does, and I shove a flyer in front of her.

"'Scary Christmas Party?'" she reads.

"Jake's does it every year," I say. "What about I take the night off – and we dress up as the Queen of the Wild Hunt and her consort?"

Passing commuters stumble past the window with blue faces from their phone screens.

"Bertha Kimmel's story that used to scare the hell out of us? Why would we do that?" she asks.

"For Mama," I say, and it's kind of the truth. "And for us too. We never got to Bertha's funeral."

Gabby's beautiful eyes darken. "We never got to see her dance."

"This would be our way of honouring her."

"You mean like some kind of a memorial?"

I hesitate. "Why not?"

Gabby pokes at her burger. "Maybe it *would* help put closure on the whole thing."

We manage to dig up a mask from a costume store that's going out of business. It's a horrifying thing with a lolling tongue and tentacle-like pointed horns, but Gabby loves it. Unable to find a traditional *Perchten* costume woven from corn leaves or goat skin, she settles on a bear suit she finds at a Goodwill thrift store. She cuts off the head, and it does the job. For me, we find a bridal gown with a veil. Gabby fashions a crown from a Christmas wreath, and we sew kewpie dolls on it to symbolise the dead children whose bones sprouted from her garden beneath the earth – Queen of the Dead, Goddess of Dualities, Winter Witch, also known as *Perchta*, or Berchta, or in English – Bertha.

The finishing touches are some fake diamond earrings that look a little like icicles.

"Too much?" I ask.

"You're a Queen," Gabby says. "Fake it till you make it."

I wince.

Mama Skypes from the Tyrolean village of Ellmau. These days, she and Ken pretty much travel all the time. Mama found Austrian ancestors of her own, something she always suspected. "I knew there was a connection there," she says, "why I was so drawn to Bertha. She was my people – your people too." We can hear the Christmas parade from the street outside her hotel. Pipe music and boozy singing and brave year-end laughter.

I self-consciously adjust my veil, remember that night long ago at Camp Never, when Bertha told me I had good bones, but for what?

Gabby asks, "The Winter Queen – witch – whatever. Was she married? I mean the bridal gown and all those children and spinning and everything."

But then we lose the connection and Mama freezes on the screen, her mouth stretched and distorted, her nose melting.

"Mama?" Gabby is about to restart the app, when our mother's voice comes back, although her image doesn't regain its integrity.

"...cultures everywhere keen to give a bride a groom," she is saying. "Maybe that's why Queens of the Dead traditionally wore white – Hecate, Holda, Frigg, Marzanna – who knows? She wasn't married, no. With those horny consorts – who needs a husband?"

"Better dead than wed," I say.

And into the night we go, my sister and I. Arm in arm, our merged shadows whirl around us in the lamplight. My sister's horns are curved and lethal. Bertha's cane twitches in my hand like a live thing.

* * *

Untold mojitos later, Gabby's fur suit is sprinkled with pretzel crumbs and Jake the eagle wears the devil mask. I've refused more proposals of marriage than I can count. The ridge between my stomach muscles has begun to pucker and sting and I know it's time. My bones grind. I tongue a new gap between my molars, scan the crowd.

"That suit is seriously funky," I say, because goodbye feels too hard.

Gabby puts her soft hot hands over my cold bony ones. "Not tonight."

Wake up.

Does she know? My face flushes, but it is too late for confessions.

Half the bar is singing 'Silent Night'. The other half starts in with 'Paradise by the Dashboard Light'. My sister is singing both, the slurred choruses all mixed up.

"I'm sorry I didn't wake up that time at camp," I shout above the noise.

"I'm sorry I didn't try very hard," she says, smiling unsteadily.

I stare at her, not understanding. I lean in closer.

"Something woke me up and drew me outside," she says in my ear. "I thought I heard my name, that maybe it was him, you know—"

"Dad?"

"—but when I got a ways to the pee-tree, I froze. I knew I should try and wake you but I was so scared I peed my pants. I started back toward the tent, but then…he grabbed me."

There must have been a rustling, I think, a strangled scream, when Jarryd came out of the dark to take her. I would have slept through it all, if not for…Bertha.

She used Gabby as bait to lure out her killer. She waited for me in the dark, in the ground. But why me?

Katerina. The name means pure.

You needed someone pure to avenge the death of your children, Katerina. I needed a miracle to save my sister. You woke up inside me, but I was never fully asleep. I was always in there somewhere, I want to tell my sister. And now I'm back.

Gabby and I are crying. Holding hands. The room spins. A door opens somewhere. Winter rushes in with a hint of subway steam and unfallen snow. A heavyset guy stands on the threshold, wearing a skeleton suit stretched over his girth and wielding a scythe. He pulls off the hood and grins. I wave and he raises the scythe. Ice glistens on his beard but his smile is warm. Gabby sits up straighter, the fur suit hugging her curves.

"Is that who I think it is?" she says, brushing away tears.

"Paco," I say. "He answered my message straightaway."

"You set this up, you devil?"

"He's been waiting all this time," I gently extricate my hand. "He just didn't know for whom."

"Paco," my sister says, the name sounding right in her mouth.

I pull the veil over my face and slip out the side door. My bridal slippers crunch on broken glass. Bones jut beneath my skin of sin. Deep in the park I find a bench under a white pine and sink down onto it, listening to the muffled swish of a skateboard, smelling weed.

I lift the veil, raise my head to the stars. Beneath the silk of my gown, the wound opens, and I can feel the warm flow. The cane quivers in my hand, the swan head sizzling with heat. Down what street of night does our unending pain take us tonight, my Queen?

The swoosh of the skateboard gets louder, stops, so now I know.

She has brought the hunt to me.

My eyes travel slowly up from a loose-laced sneaker on a skateboard, to dirty jeans and a slender tattooed hand aiming a .22. at my head.

"Wallet. Jewellery."

He looks around sixteen, same age as I was when Bertha found me. "They're fakes," I make the earrings tremble. "Obviously."

"That isn't." He jerks the gun at the silver-tipped cane lying across my knees, a comet tail of vapour off his knuckles. "Obviously."

He holds the gun steady, like he can find his way around a firearm, or at least fake it till he makes it.

"Finish school. Send money to your mother."

"You don't know me," the kid says.

It's suddenly snowing. Not seriously. The flakes vanish as soon as they fall, leaving a kiss of cold on my skin. It's nice to think about snow carpeting the sidewalks and back alleys. Covering up the dirt. My fingers inch toward the cane.

"Wake up." Abracadabra! Unsheathing the blade and standing in one motion.

His jaw goes slack at the black flower of blood blooming at my belly. He back-walks into his skateboard and fires. The bullet enters my heart and I drop back down to the bench, still holding the cane – it has outlived its usefulness. Darkness calls, seeps into the edges of things. The kid runs, his footfalls leaving no sound. The moment holds me in silence like water holds a swan in sleep. Long enough to see my sister running toward me in a bear suit, flakes of snow in her curls, Paco at her back. And then the world roars in. Sirens. Distant thunder. My sister crying my name, arresting my fall. *Kat!*

Wake up.

Because another beckons. And in the downward plummet, toward a platinum-white light, the name comes back to claim me, taking me to where two children wait beneath the earth, and they are mine. I am so glad to see their small, huddled bodies, hear them call my name. *Mother.* My arms open wide as the world to never let them go.

Never again.

BIOGRAPHIES

Nina Allan is a writer and critic. Her novel *The Rift* won the BSFA Award and the Kitschies Red Tentacle, and her novelette *The Art of Space Travel* was a finalist for the Hugo Award. Her essays and reviews have appeared in a wide variety of venues including *The Guardian*, *The Quietus* and *The TLS*. Her most recent novel is *Conquest*, published in May 2023 by Riverrun/Quercus. Nina lives and works on the Isle of Bute, off the west coast of Scotland.

Peter Atkins is the author of the novels *Morningstar*, *Big Thunder* and *Moontown* and the screenplays *Hellraiser II*, *Hellraiser III*, *Hellraiser IV* and *Wishmaster*. His short fiction has appeared in several award-winning anthologies and has been selected eight times for one or more of the various Year's Best books. His newest book is the story collection *All Our Hearts Are Ghosts*. *Rumours of the Marvellous*, his previous collection, was a finalist for the British Fantasy Award. He can be found on Facebook under his own name and on Twitter and Instagram as @limeybastard55.

J.S. Breukelaar is an American-Australian author living in Sydney with her family. Her works include the short story collection *Collision: Stories* and the novels *The Bridge*, *Aletheia*, *American Monster*, and most recently *Vandal: Stories of Damage*, a three-novella collaboration with Kaaron Warren and Aaron Dries. She is a Shirley Jackson Award finalist and a multiple Aurealis and Australian Ditmar Award winner, among others. Her stories, essays and poems have appeared or are forthcoming in numerous publications including *The Dark*, *Black Static*, *Fantasy*, *Tiny Nightmares* and elsewhere, including several Year's Bests. Described by *This is Horror* magazine as a 'killer female author who is smashing boundaries with each word she writes', Breukelaar teaches at LitReactor and at the University of Western Sydney. You can also find her at thelivingsuitcase.com, and everywhere else at @jsbreukelaar.

Simon Clark's novels include *Blood Crazy, Vampyrrhic, Darkness Demands, Stranger, Secrets of the Dead* and the award-winning *The Night of the Triffids*, which was broadcast as a five-part drama series by BBC radio. Weird House Press has recently issued Simon's new collection *Sherlock Holmes: A Casebook of Nightmares and Monsters* and a novel *Sherlock Holmes: Lord of Damnation*. Simon lives in Yorkshire, England, where he can be seen roaming this legend-haunted landscape with a black and white Border Collie by the name of Mylo.

Brian Evenson is the author of a dozen books, most recently the story collection *The Glassy, Burning Floor of Hell* (2021). His penultimate collection *Song for the Unravelling of the World* (2019) won the Shirley Jackson Award and the World Fantasy Award and was a finalist for the Ray Bradbury Prize. Other recent books include *A Collapse of Horses* (2016) and *The Warren* (2016). His novel *Last Days* won the ALA-RUSA award for Best Horror Novel of 2009. His novel *The Open Curtain* was a finalist for an Edgar Award and an International Horror Guild (IHG) Award. His 2003 collection *The Wavering Knife* won the IHG Award. He is the recipient of three O. Henry Prizes, an NEA fellowship and a Guggenheim Award. His work has been translated into more than a dozen languages. He lives in Los Angeles and teaches at CalArts. A new collection *Good Night, Sleep Tight* will be published in 2024.

Mark Gatiss has had a long and varied career as an actor, writer, director and producer. He is best known as a member of the *League of Gentlemen*, and as the co-creator and executive producer of the multi award-winning BBC series *Sherlock*, in which he played Mycroft Holmes. He both wrote for and appeared in the modern revival of *Doctor Who*, and was the writer and executive producer of *An Adventure in Space and Time* for its 50th anniversary celebrations. He also co-created the BBC and Netflix drama *Dracula*, and has written and directed several BBC ghost stories, including *Count Magnus*, *The Mezzotint*, *Martin's Close*, *The Dead Room* and *The Tractate Middoth*. As an actor, screen work includes *Mission Impossible: Dead Reckoning Parts 1 & 2*, *Operation Mincemeat*, *The Father*, *The Favourite*, *Christopher Robin*, *Gunpowder*, *Wolf Hall*, *Coalition* and *Game of Thrones*, and on stage, *Coriolanus* (Donmar Warehouse), *The Boys in the Band* (Park/Vaudeville Theatres), *Three Days in the Country* (National Theatre: Olivier Award for Best Actor in a Supporting Role), the title role in *The Madness of George III* (Nottingham Playhouse), and Jacob Marley in his own adaptation of *A Christmas Carol* (Nottingham Playhouse and Alexandra Palace). He has recently directed Steven Moffat's debut play *The Unfriend* for the Chichester Festival Theatre, which has transferred to the Criterion Theatre in the West End.

Alyssa C. Greene's work has appeared in *Fence*, *Pleiades*, *North American Review* and elsewhere. She also co-hosts *Say Podcast and Die!*, a podcast about the Goosebumps books, queerness, and horror. A graduate of the Clarion Science Fiction and Fantasy Writers' Workshop, she received her MFA from the University of Utah and currently lives in New York City. Find them on Twitter as @ acgreenest and on Instagram as @caffeinemotivated.

Carly Holmes lives and writes in a small village on the banks of the river Teifi in west Wales, UK. Her debut novel *The Scrapbook* was shortlisted for the International Rubery Book Award, and her debut story collection *Figurehead* was published in limited-edition hardback by Tartarus Press and reprinted in paperback by Parthian Books in 2022. Her award-winning stories have appeared in journals and anthologies such as *Ambit*, *The Ghastling*, *Black Static*, *Uncertainties* and *Shadows & Tall Trees*, and have twice appeared in Ellen Datlow's *Best Horror of the Year* series. Carly's second novel *Crow Face, Doll Face* will be published by Honno in October 2023.

Amanda Cecelia Lang is a horror author and aspiring recluse from Denver, Colorado. As a die-hard scary movie nerd, her favourite things are meta-slashers, Eighties nostalgia, and the rise of a fierce final girl. Her stories currently haunt the dark corners of many popular podcasts, magazines, and anthologies, including *NoSleep, Tales to Terrify, Uncharted, Dark Matter, Cast of Wonders* and *Mixtape: 1986*. Her short story collection *The Library of Broken Girls* will debut in the Spring of 2025. You can follow her work at amandacecelialang.com – just don't be surprised if she leaps out at you from the shadows.

Eric LaRocca *(he/they)* is the Bram Stoker Award-nominated and Splatterpunk Award-winning author of the viral sensation *Things Have Gotten Worse Since We Last Spoke*. His other work includes *You've Lost a Lot of Blood, We Can Never Leave This Place, They Were Here Before Us* and *The Trees Grew Because I Bled There*. A lover of luxury fashion and an admirer of European musical theatre, Eric can often be found roaming the streets of his home city, Boston, MA, for inspiration. For more information, please follow @hystericteeth on Twitter/Instagram or visit ericlarocca.com.

Ronald Malfi is the award-winning author of several horror novels and thrillers, including the bestseller *Come with Me*, published by Titan Books in 2021. He is the recipient of two Independent Publisher Book Awards, the Beverly Hills Book Award, the Vincent Preis Horror Award, the Benjamin Franklin Award, and his novel *Floating Staircase* was a finalist for the Bram Stoker Award. He lives with his wife and two daughters in Maryland, and when he's not writing or spending time with his family, he's performing in the rock band VEER.

Dr. Helen Marshall is a Senior Lecturer of Creative Writing at the University of Queensland. She has won the World Fantasy Award, the British Fantasy Award and the Shirley Jackson Award for her two collections of short stories. Her debut novel *The Migration* argued for the need to remain hopeful, even in the worst circumstances, and was one of *The Guardian's* top science fiction books of the year. With her colleagues, Professor Kim Wilkins and Dr. Lisa Bennett, she runs the What If Lab at the University of Queensland, which specialises in creative arts, speculative fiction and imagination-led workshops for researchers from different backgrounds and disciplines.

Lucie McKnight Hardy's stories have featured in a variety of publications, including *Best British Short Stories 2019*, *The Lonely Crowd*, *Uncertainties IV*, *The New Abject*, *Black Static* and as a limited edition chapbook from Nightjar Press. Her debut novel *Water Shall Refuse Them* was published by Dead Ink Books in 2019. Of her second book *Dead Relatives*, *The Guardian* said: 'This short story collection confirms the author's reputation in the field of literary horror.'

Mark Morris (Editor) has written and edited around forty novels, novellas, short story collections and anthologies. His script work includes audio dramas for *Doctor Who*, *Jago & Litefoot* and the *Hammer Chillers* series. Mark's recent work includes the official movie tie-in novelisations of *The Great Wall* and (co-written with Christopher Golden) *The Predator*, the Obsidian Heart trilogy, and the anthologies *New Fears* (winner of the British Fantasy Award for Best Anthology) and *New Fears 2* as editor. He's also written award-winning audio adaptations of the classic 1971 horror movie *Blood on Satan's Claw* and the M.R. James ghost story 'A View from a Hill'.

Reggie Oliver is an actor, director, playwright, illustrator and award-winning author of fiction. Published work includes six plays, three novels, an illustrated children's book *The Hauntings at Tankerton Park* (Zagava, 2016), nine volumes of short stories, including *Mrs. Midnight* (2011 winner of the Children of the Night Award for best work of supernatural fiction), and the biography of the writer Stella Gibbons, *Out of the Woodshed* (Bloomsbury, 1998). His stories have appeared in over one hundred different anthologies and three 'selected' editions of his stories have been published, the latest being *Stages of Fear* (Black Shuck Books, 2020). His ninth volume of tales *A Maze for the Minotaur* was published by Tartarus Press in 2021.

H.V. Patterson lives in Oklahoma, USA, and writes speculative fiction and poetry. She has work published or upcoming in *Etherea Magazine*, *Siren's Call* and Wyldblood Press, and anthologies from

Sliced Up Press, Eerie River, Creature Publishing, and Black Spot Books. Her poem *Mother; Microbes* was recently selected for the inaugural volume of *Brave New Weird* from Tenebrous Press. Though she finds rabbits cute, she's convinced that hares are up to something. She promotes women in horror through Dreadfulesque (@Dreadfulesque on Twitter and Instagram), and you can find her on Twitter @ScaryShelley and on Instagram @hvpattersonwriter.

Sarah Read is the Bram Stoker Award-winning author of *The Bone Weaver's Orchard, Out of Water, Root Rot,* and the forthcoming *The Atropine Tree*. You can find her online at inkwellmonster.wordpress.com.

Angela Slatter is the author of five novels, including the 2021 Queensland Literary Awards Book of the Year finalist *All the Murmuring Bones*, and *The Path of Thorns*, which made the Oprah Daily Top 25 Fantasy Books of 2022. Her debut novel *Vigil* was longlisted for the 2018 Dublin Literary Award. She's also written eleven short story collections, including *The Bitterwood Bible* and *The Tallow-Wife and Other Tales*, and three novellas. She's won a World Fantasy Award, a British Fantasy Award, a Ditmar, two Australian Shadows Awards and seven Aurealis Awards. Her work has been translated into multiple languages. She's collaborated with Mike Mignola on a new series from Dark Horse Comics, *Castle Full of Blackbirds*, set in the Hellboy Universe, and screenwriter Victoria Madden (*The Kettering Incident, The Gloaming*) is making a film of Angela's novelette *Finnegan's Field*. She can be located on the internet at angelaslatter.com, @AngelaSlatter (Twitter) and angelaslatter (Instagram).

Simon Strantzas is the author of *Nothing is Everything* (Undertow Publications, 2018), *Burnt Black Suns* (Hippocampus Press, 2014), *Nightingale Songs* (Dark Regions Press, 2011), *Cold to the Touch* (Tartarus Press, 2009) and *Beneath the Surface* (Humdrumming, 2008), is the editor of *Aickman's Heirs* (Undertow Publications, 2015), *Shadows Edge* (Gray Friar Press, 2013), and was guest editor of *The Year's Best Weird Fiction, Vol. 3* (Undertow Publications, 2016). He is also co-founder and Associate Editor of the irregular non-fiction journal *Thinking Horror*, and columnist for *Weird Horror* magazine. Collectively, he's been a finalist for four Shirley Jackson Awards, two British Fantasy Awards and the World Fantasy Award. His stories have been reprinted in *Best New Horror, The Best Horror of the Year, The Year's Best Weird Fiction* and *The Year's Best Dark Fantasy & Horror*, as well as published in *Nightmare, Cemetery Dance, Postscripts, The Dark* and elsewhere. He lives with his wife in Toronto, Canada.

Stephen Volk is best known for being the evil mind behind BBC TV's notorious – some say legendary – 'Halloween hoax' *Ghostwatch* and for creating the award-winning ITV paranormal drama series *Afterlife* starring Lesley Sharp and Andrew Lincoln. His feature screenplays include *The Awakening* starring Rebecca Hall, Dominic West and Imelda Staunton, William Friedkin's *The Guardian*, and Ken Russell's *Gothic* starring Natasha Richardson as Mary Shelley with Gabriel Byrne as Lord Byron. He was also behind ITV's supernatural thriller *Midwinter of the Spirit* starring Anna Maxwell Martin and David Threlfall. For the stage he wrote *The Chapel of Unrest* starring Jim Broadbent and Reece Shearsmith, and won a BAFTA for Best Short Film for *The Deadness of Dad* starring Rhys Ifans. He is also the author of four short story collections – *Dark Corners, Monsters in the Heart* (which won the British Fantasy Award), *The Parts We Play* and *Lies of Tenderness*. His other books include the acclaimed *Dark Masters Trilogy*, which features Peter Cushing, Alfred Hitchcock and Dennis Wheatley as protagonists, while *Under a Raven's Wing* sees Sherlock Holmes and Poe's detective Dupin investigating bizarre crimes in 1870s Paris. His website is stephenvolk.net.

Ally Wilkes's Stoker Award-nominated first novel *All the White Spaces* was described by Paul Tremblay as 'heady and haunting'. Her second novel *Where the Dead Wait* is slated for publication in late 2023, and (writing as AV Wilkes) her first novella was recently published by Cemetery Gates Media. Ally grew up in a succession of isolated – possibly haunted – country houses and boarding schools, and after studying law at Oxford University, she went on to spend eleven years as a criminal barrister in London. Her short fiction has been published in *Nightmare, Three Crows, Cloisterfox* and others, as well as anthologies such as *FOUND: an anthology of Found Footage Horror.* Ally lives in Greenwich, London, with an anatomical human skeleton. When she isn't reading horror, you can usually find her hanging upside-down (like a bat) on her aerial silks. You can follow Ally on Twitter @UnheimlichManvr or via her website allywilkes.com.